Also by Leslie Lynch

Unholy Bonds

Opal's Jubilee

Christmas Hope (Novella)

Christmas Grace (Novella)

Visit her website at:
www.leslielynch.com

HIJACKED

Leslie Lynch

Copyright

Hijacked
Edited by Pam Berehulke, Bulletproof Editing
Cover art by Marion Sipe, Dreamspring Design
Copyright © 2014 by Leslie Lynch
All Rights Reserved
ISBN-13: 978-1-941728-09-3

Dedication

To all persons who grapple with the aftereffects of violence:
There is hope.
May you find healing and peace.

A portion of the proceeds from this book will go toward the funding of Post Traumatic Stress research and treatment.

Part One

Chapter One

HAIL MARY, full of grace...

Cold air bit at Ben Martin's face as he crouched in the recesses of a poorly lit airplane hangar. He'd gone from hunter to prey a handful of minutes ago, and his mind reeled at the reversal of his fortune. The image of a rabbit quivering beneath a bush flickered through his brain. His imagination filled in the shadowy edges of the picture with Arctic wolves waiting for the doomed bugger to make a fatal dash.

Pray for us sinners...

He shivered, and couldn't say whether the shudder came from the cold or his thoughts. The hunters, so close on his heels that his back tingled, needed nothing but a blaze of harsh light to expose his hiding place.

...now, and at the hour of—

No. This would *not* be the hour of his death.

Ben tried to quell the rapid beat of his heart and quiet the rasp of his breath. He'd ricocheted through two miracles already tonight, two more than he deserved. Unless the Almighty slipped him one more, he wouldn't live to see dawn, less than an hour away. Panic rose, and he squelched it. *Not helping.*

His gaze shifted to a pilot on the far side of the warehouse-like space, readying a Cessna for flight. Ben didn't want to involve a civilian, but he was flat out of options. Other than hoping for a giant hand to reach down and pluck him out of Louisville, Kentucky—which was not likely—this was it. The pilot, poor bastard, was Ben's ticket out of danger.

The wind blew a burst of frigid air into the cavernous room. Ben shivered again, this time from the cold. He lifted his hand to rub his left arm, which throbbed in concert with his pulse, and flattened his lips. Denial had its uses, like glossing over the fact that he'd been shot. Seemed pretty reasonable to him, since he recoiled from the idea with enough horror to make him puke. Didn't matter that the wound was minor, he still got queasy when he thought about it. He'd staunched the bleeding and applied a rudimentary dressing, but the doggone thing had shifted. He tugged it back into place, wincing at the sting of movement.

His heartbeat, a bit slower but now very loud, drummed in his ears, and he shook his head to clear the rhythmic pounding. It obscured sounds he needed to hear, such as another employee showing up. Or the cops. Adrenaline pumped madly, surging into his veins. He shifted his weight, his fingers twitching in readiness.

It was too soon for the adrenaline, but he had no control over it. Ben muttered, "Hurry up," and willed the pilot to move faster. He had no more than fifteen minutes before the drug dog found him, unless his decoy attempt had succeeded. He made a soft, derisive sound. Not much else had gone well over the past couple of hours. No reason to expect he'd fooled the dog.

The memory of Roger Grantree's voice, dispassionate and traitorous, wormed its way into his mind and broke his concentration. *Bastard set me up. Blew my cover.* Rage and an equal measure of stunned disbelief roiled in Ben's gut. He shoved the emotion away even as his stomach clenched at the gall of his partner's betrayal. Granted, they'd only partnered for this operation, but Ben had trusted the guy. *Trusted* him.

Grantree was dirty, had misled Ben and thwarted every step of his investigation. But Ben had figured out the guy's scam, and had gotten close to the truth. Too close. Close enough to hear Roger order his murder over the tinny cell phone speaker. Ben didn't know how far Roger's influence extended, but tonight he'd seen local law enforcement, his own federal agency, and Louisville drug dealers. And they were all looking for him. He swallowed in an attempt to rid his mouth of the coppery tang of fear.

Hangar doors creaked on their rollers as the pilot put every ounce of his weight into the chore of wrestling them open, and Ben forced his attention back to the man. Wiry and slightly built, he was dressed for the weather with a toboggan hat, wool coat, and gloves. The ease and efficiency of his movements gave the impression of youth, but it was hard to tell. His breath puffed out in little white clouds as he hauled back on the tow bar, moving the plane in groaning millimeters until momentum finally got it rolling. Its white wings and fuselage glinted in the dim light of the hangar, then faded into predawn darkness outside.

Ben took advantage of the pilot's preoccupation to dodge between parked planes and cross the expanse of hangar floor. He darted behind a mechanic's chest-high toolbox near the massive doors. Metal rang against concrete when the pilot unhooked the tow bar from the nose wheel, then strode with unswerving purpose— toward the toolbox. Ben ducked his head and held his breath. He did the Zen thing and tried to render himself invisible, to become one with the universe, one with the toolbox. *Whatever.* He tensed his muscles for attack, since he didn't have much confidence in meditation as a form of escape or evasion.

The footsteps stopped on the opposite side of the toolbox. Metal clinked on metal. Then, silence. A bead of sweat trickled down Ben's brow. If the pilot elected to use it, the tow bar—or any tool on top of the cart, for that matter—would double as a painfully effective weapon.

The moment expanded until his nerves were a whisper away from snapping, and...the footsteps moved away, their cadence normal, unhurried. He sank back, let out a quiet breath, and tried to calm the thudding of his heart.

He peeked around the edge of the box. The pilot headed for the far door, his back to Ben. Ben slipped through the pool of light outside the hangar and blended into the shadows cast by the plane, and waited as the guy wrestled the doors again.

A fine tremor started in his hands but he squeezed them hard, pushing away the weakness of fear, pushing past the pain. *Focus.* Focus on the pilot—his ticket to safety.

The rollers at the top of the second door squealed in their tracks, then quieted when the door thumped closed. The pilot walked to the plane, backlit by a single bulb over the doors.

Secure that he couldn't be seen in the shadows, Ben spared a glance toward the street. The expanse of runways and taxiways allowed him to see a quarter of a mile, maybe a bit more. His breath caught. A drug dog with its handler came into view. Even factoring in the airport's perimeter fence and the less-than-direct route to his position, they'd have him made in ten minutes, max.

No time to finesse this.

He pulled his gun, thumbed the safety to verify it was still on, and grasped it left-handed, leaving his uninjured arm free. The pilot opened the cockpit door and leaned in, but didn't enter the plane. Adrenaline flooded Ben as he slipped around the plane, his footfalls masked by gusts of wind. He crowded the smaller man, trapping him between the door and the fuselage.

"Do exactly as I say and you'll be all right." Even to himself his voice sounded guttural. Threatening. Desperate.

The pilot went utterly still. Grateful for the guy's good sense, Ben opened his mouth to issue orders.

But the pilot erupted in a flurry of movement, arms and legs flailing, glaring evidence of an untrained fighter. A couple of blows landed before Ben managed to grab the guy's arms and pin them to his sides. The smaller man twisted in Ben's hold and he almost lost his grip, almost dropped his gun. He let loose an instinctive jab to the guy's jaw, barely remembering to pull the punch at the last second. He needed the guy alert enough to fly.

Stunned by the blow, the pilot looked up at him. His huge, dark eyes were luminous, reflecting light from the bulb over the hangar. A red mark, precursor to a monster bruise, decorated his cheek.

A cheek that was smooth.

A cheek that bore no evidence of ever having grown a beard.

Because the cheek belonged to…a *woman*?

He snatched the knit hat off the pilot's head, and stared at distinctly feminine features under a mop of short hair.

"You're a girl!"

Chapter Two

LANNIS PARKER'S HEART hammered against her breastbone and her breathing stalled. Her hands began to shake, and her fingers went bloodless and cold inside her gloves. Nobody had ever hit her before. Except for one time. Her mind skittered away from the unwelcome memory and she forced herself to think. To try, anyway.

Her senses reeled, overwhelmed by the sheer size of the guy and his menace. Broad shoulders blocked her vision, and his height made her feel diminutive. Powerless. His features were shadowy and indistinct, but there was enough ambient light that his eyes glittered. She'd caught a glimpse of a gun, too, and had bumped her elbow against it as she'd fought him.

Then his words sank in. *Girl!* Girls were powder puffs, lightweights. She'd learned to hold her own in a male-dominated profession, and nobody called her *girl*. Fury—as irrational as it was searing—ignited within her, freeing her from the icy paralysis of fright.

He grabbed her chin and jerked it so the outdoor hangar light shone in her eyes. She closed them against his scrutiny and pressed her lips together, partly in anger, partly to keep them from trembling. She would *not* let him see her terror.

"Open your eyes." He spoke with authority, like he expected immediate, unquestioning obedience.

She scrunched them tighter.

He tightened his grip. "Open. Your. Eyes."

His tone, his urgency, his touch convinced her to let this small battle go. She opened her eyes, stared into his with defiance and as much disdain as she could muster. Which wasn't much. She was scared spitless.

"Do exactly as I say. Cooperate, and you'll be safe."

Safe? She didn't think so. His hot breath brushed her face, and she recoiled. Her head bumped the aluminum skin of the fuselage behind her, creating a hollow echo.

"Fly me out of here. No lights. No radio. Got it?"

He paused, and when she didn't answer, he increased the pressure on her chin. It hurt. Tears stung the back of her eyelids, and she blinked them away. He'd be impervious to negotiation, even if she could find her voice. She knew that as surely as she knew her plane. Maybe she'd find an opportunity to escape once he allowed her to move.

She gave him a reluctant nod. He let go of her chin and slid his hand down her side, patted her torso, her pockets, then her hips. He was…he was searching her. She gasped, her breath coming short and shallow. She would fly him out if she had to, but by God, she wouldn't let him grope her. Lannis slapped at his hands, twisted away, but he still had her cornered, and nothing she did slowed him down. He made an impatient noise at her resistance, but in the space of several seconds he'd felt her up without *feeling* her up, a distinction she recognized through the red haze of fear. That distinction alone kept her from slipping over the edge of panic into hysteria.

Which was a good thing, because when he bundled her into the plane and shoved her across the seat to the far side of the cockpit, she could still think. Her feet tangled on the fuel selector between the seats, and he gave her a moment to free herself. Lannis yanked the other door handle up and tried to dive out. Headfirst, feet first, sideways, it didn't matter. Any way she could escape. But he moved faster than a normal man should be able to, whipping his arm across the cockpit to snag her coat and drag her back. He gripped her wrist and heaved himself into the plane, using her arm as leverage. She pulled away and he jerked her back.

"Damn it, I just need you to cooperate." Frustration sharpened the words. "Fly the damn plane!"

Lannis flinched. She couldn't help it, although she controlled it before it turned into a full-body shudder. A heartbeat passed, then she nodded and shot a sideways glance at him.

He released her and slammed his door. "Let's go, darlin'."

"I'm not your darling." The words popped out before she thought about the wisdom of arguing with an armed man.

He bared his teeth, but if he meant to smile, it held no humor. "Doesn't matter. Get this bird in the air."

She hesitated. He pulled his gun from wherever he'd put it, and pointed it at her. The hairs on her forearms prickled to attention. Lannis dragged her gaze from the small black hole of the gun's barrel and looked at his unrelenting eyes. Her breath snagged in her throat, her vision narrowed, and her ability to think took a nosedive. *Focus. Concentrate. Think, damn it!*

She gulped a breath and reached across the hijacker, brushing against his body as she did, and flipped the electrical master switch on. Tiny bulbs over the instruments glowed, and the plane's rotating beacon came on, its red pulsating light reflecting off the hangar doors.

"Turn it off! Turn the damned light off!" He shoved the gun against her collarbone, and she froze. Her mind shuddered to a halt.

She shifted her gaze in his direction without even twitching any other muscles. "But—"

"Shut up!" His face was taut and his body radiated impatience that bordered on violence. "Pay attention! No lights, no radio. Go!"

Her mouth went dry and she flicked the master off, which got the gun away from her body. Lannis drew a shaky breath and dredged up her memory files of the checklist. She didn't dare ask him for the laminated copy stored in a pocket near his knee. Under normal circumstances, she could run the checklist blindfolded; but the disruption, the changes from routine, threw her.

Master switch on for the start, but turn the rotating beacon off. Don't turn the avionics master on. No navigation lights. Don't shout, "Clear prop." Her fingers were numb and stiff from dread, and she fumbled the switches. What else? She didn't dare make any more mistakes.

Out of habit, she grabbed a headset, needing the familiar action to regain her composure. But he ripped it from her hands, yanked the prongs out of the jacks, and flung it into the back of the plane. It thumped against the top of the rear seat, then rattled as it fell into the baggage compartment.

The gun reappeared. Her breath deserted her, and her hands began to shake. She reached across the yoke to hit the starter, and didn't know whether to shed tears of relief or frustration when the prop caught on the first try. At least the smooth sound of the engine made him stow the gun.

The winds favored the runway that required taxiing to the other end of the airport, so she headed in that direction, hoping someone would notice she was operating without lights. Maybe violation of the Federal Aviation Regulations would attract attention. And help. Unfortunately, the airport resembled a ghost town at the moment.

"Where are you going?" The hijacker shifted his eyes to glance at some police cars parked haphazardly a couple of blocks away. The headlights of one car flicked on and it began moving, its beams illuminating the street that led to the airport entrance. He motioned with the gun. "Take off on this runway. It's closest."

Lannis's mouth dropped open. "I can't! There's a tailwind on that one."

The guy lifted a thumb and clicked something on his gun, the action deliberate, laden with meaning. She didn't know if it was the safety or if he'd cocked it, but even as unfamiliar with guns as she was, the small sound was ominous. Her flare of hope at the sight of the police car fizzled. She reversed direction and approached the runway he designated, then stopped to check the plane's engine operation.

"Just take off!" The gun came up again.

Lannis shoved the throttle forward and skidded the plane onto the runway. Without checking anything. With a tailwind. On a runway with a slight uphill slope. *Oh God...* She hadn't prayed in years, but this seemed a good time to start, though no more words came to mind. The plane was going to take more runway to get airborne and would have a lower rate of climb initially, which made the eighty-foot trees at the departure end look like enormous airplane-snatching monsters, their greedy tentacles swaying and bobbing in the wind.

Desperately, she hoped that no other aircraft were using any of the runways, either taking off or landing. She had no way of knowing without the radio.

She glanced at the engine instruments as the plane accelerated—slowly—and saw the oil temperature was still too cold to register. She'd never heard of an engine failing simply from taking off before it had reached normal operating temperature, but it wasn't good for the internal workings in any case and she'd never even considered doing it.

The takeoff roll ate up several hundred extra feet of runway. Finally the nose lifted, then the main gear came off and the plane began to climb...with excruciating lethargy. Lannis focused on coaxing every scrap of performance possible from the plane. Orvis, her boss, liked to talk about his Alaskan bush flying years, and his voice rolled through her head. *Stick to basics. Just keep flying the plane. Don't give up on it before it gives up on you.*

"Come on, come on, you can do it, that's it." The chant came out in the softest breath as her world diminished to the plane, the air, and the trees. She banked slightly and aimed at the shortest of the trees ahead. The engine roared and time seemed to stop, then the plane hurtled past the crowns of the trees. Leaves brushed the wheels and there was a slight jerk, and they were free. Lannis released a breath and continued to coax a climb from the plane. She'd never, *ever* flown that close to an obstacle, and she was dizzy with relief at clearing it. But they were airborne. And still alive.

"Fly up the river to the north, away from town. Stay low." The guy uttered his instructions with a dispassionate voice.

How could he be so calm? Lannis shot a disbelieving glance at him even as she mentally reviewed the topography, the towers of the area. She knew the airspace and radio frequencies for the traffic flight by rote, so hadn't brought her flight bag today. She pictured it, stuffed with helpful maps as it sat on her living room floor, and ground her teeth in frustration. On top of everything else, she regretted the lack of charts.

In fact, right now she regretted a lot of things, most notably agreeing to Mark's request to fly the traffic flight for him this morning. He'd called a mere five hours ago, half-tanked and on his way to "get lucky, if you know what I mean." His irresponsibility at putting far too little time between alcohol and flying irritated her, never mind that it stirred dormant memories of what she'd been all too familiar with a couple of years ago. Still, she'd considered bailing him out, and putting off her mandated vacation, if only by a two-hour flight.

She had hesitated. If Orvis found out, he'd skin her alive. *That* conversation had been real fun. "Take the time off. You'll burn out," he'd said. He'd chewed on his ubiquitous unlit cigar and glared at her, fists planted on hips so skinny she often wondered what held his pants up, daring her to defy him. "You wanna go the formal route with the FAA, Lannis? I can arrange it."

She believed him. He would, faster than a race start at Churchill Downs. Even though she'd followed his deal to the letter—no more drinking, weekly AA meetings—she'd be out of work without a reference, and fighting to reinstate her hard-won pilot's license if she didn't bow to his arm-twisting. Her face had burned with anger, but she'd backed down.

So when Mark remembered Orvis wouldn't be in until midmorning because of a meeting, she'd agreed. Orvis would never know, and what he didn't know wouldn't hurt him, right?

But now it had hurt her.

She tugged her thoughts back to the terrain. The only tower she really needed to worry about was the monstrosity out northeast of town. Flight instructors called it an artificial mountain, as it rose nearly two thousand feet above the ground. *Ah.* There it was, strobes flashing rhythmically. She made a subtle adjustment in heading so the plane would be well clear of the tower. Good plan, since its summit was almost a thousand feet above them.

Her thoughts churned. If she could somehow turn the radios on without his noticing, she could dial in the code for hijacking. He probably didn't know much about planes, so she could bring the mixture control back far enough to make the engine run rough and set it down in a field once it got light enough. Maybe—

"Where's the manual for the plane?" he said.

Her heart sank. He was savvy enough to ask about the manual. Plus, he seemed smart enough to understand the technical material in it. He was scary, but not unhinged. He was too alert, in control, aware. Desperate, yes, but not crazy. Ruthless, absolutely. But not high. Definitely not stupid. Lannis caught her lower lip between her teeth and tipped her head toward the back. "In one of the pockets behind our seats."

He'd put his gun down. She hadn't seen where, but it wasn't in his left hand anymore. Heart beating faster, she waited until he was twisted, rummaging through the seat pockets, and struck at him with all the strength she had. Her elbow made solid contact with the side of his head, and the plane wobbled.

The next second was a blur, ending with his hand fisted in her hair and a brutal jerk forcing her to face him. Lannis gasped and tried to stop tears forming over the stinging of her scalp. His lethal eyes were only an inch from hers.

"Knock. It. Off. I said you'd be safe if you cooperate. Don't make this harder than it has to be."

She sensed the plane begin to bank and descend, the engine whining at a higher pitch, the airspeed increasing. Her lips went dry and numb. She managed to whisper, "We're going to… Let me fly… Please."

He gave her an angry shake and released her.

Experience took over as she reduced power, rolled the wings level, and pulled out of the dive. Gave it full power and established a climb. She kept her eyes trained on the instruments because she knew she'd panic if she saw how close to the ground they undoubtedly were. An invisible band of terror squeezed her chest.

He reached behind the seat again, and she did the only thing she could.

Flew the plane.

Chapter Three

BEN GRABBED the aircraft manual, then glanced outside and got his bearings as best he could in the pale dawn. Her concentration gave him a moment to rub his aching arm, and he flexed it gingerly. His toes still hurt. They'd curled, right up into his boots, tighter and tighter the closer they got to the trees on takeoff. He hadn't known toes could do that; he'd thought it was just a figure of speech. Now his head hurt, too. He wrestled his fury down a notch or two, until it simmered as irritation instead.

He didn't want to take an innocent's life in his battle to save his own, but he didn't want to die in a plane wreck, either. He had to respect his pilot's ability to adapt and cope, especially after that harrowing takeoff. However, now that they were airborne, he was as much at her mercy as she was his. He had to keep his guard up, keep her from capitalizing on his vulnerability. Keep them both safe.

"Turn south." He bit out the words, his voice tight. The plane banked gently to the right. He flipped through the book, ignoring the sections on emergency procedures and maintenance.

Performance. That was his first priority. Paper rustled as he waded through pages of graphs until he found some that made sense. He held the book up, trying to catch some light from the morning twilight, and squinted to make out the words. The plane would fly about four hours with full fuel, giving it a range of about five hundred miles. It needed around six or seven hundred feet of runway for landing, two football field lengths or so. Less than a quarter of a mile.

Systems were next. The master switch didn't need to be on once the engine was running. That would ensure the radios could not be used. His arm burned as he reached up and turned it off, an action not lost on the pilot. Her eyes widened and her knuckles went white on the yoke. He wiped down the cover of the manual in case he'd left a print and replaced it behind the seat.

He retrieved her backpack from the floor where she'd tossed it before the preflight and dug through it. It was small, meant for light use. Not much in it. A few dog-eared sheets of paper with aeronautical diagrams on them. A couple of aviation magazines. Lip balm with sunscreen. Pens, a pencil. A set of keys, none to vehicles. That would explain why he hadn't heard her drive up this morning. A thin wallet with less than twenty dollars in cash, no credit cards, no checkbook. A Kentucky driver's license, FAA pilot's license, and medical certificate in neat plastic sleeves bound together at one side.

He held them up to the window. There was enough light now that he didn't need to squint. Lannis Renee Parker, age twenty-six. Five feet, seven inches tall, and one hundred thirty pounds. Brown hair, brown eyes, but he already knew that. Thick coffee-colored hair with a hint of curl to it, as a matter of fact, and eyes that reminded him of rich milk chocolate. Commercial pilot and flight instructor certificates with qualifications in single- and multi-engine aircraft.

He frowned and glanced at her. "What does 'instrument airplane' mean?"

She licked her lips. "I can fly inside the clouds, by reference to instruments." She motioned at the side window. "As opposed to looking outside at the ground, like right now."

Ben grunted. The rest was self-explanatory. Ground instructor. Organ donor. Address within half a mile of the airport.

"Do you live with anyone, Lannis?"

"Wh…what?" She frowned, her eyebrows drawing together as she glanced at him.

Impatience edged his words in spite of his efforts to rein it in. "Do you live with family? You married? Have a boyfriend?"

She wiped her hands one at a time on her jeans, and shook her head in the negative.

He noticed her hands trembling, and steeled himself against her distress. "When is this plane supposed to be back?"

She shot him a quick glance and hesitated, then answered reluctantly. "Nine."

"Who's expecting you? When? Do you have other flights today?"

"Ramon," she blurted, a note of triumph in her voice. "The traffic reporter. He's already been to the airport and called the boss to complain that I'm not there!" Her expression brightened with naked hope.

"He's sick," he said. "Who else?"

Lannis's eyes widened. "How do you know that?"

Ben flipped her license holder closed. "There was a message on the answering machine saying the flight was canceled. I erased it before you showed up." A heartbeat passed. He added dryly, "I was expecting Mark."

The color left her face. Without warning, she yanked back on the yoke, snapped it to the right, and stomped on a pedal at her feet. The plane's gyration threw Ben left, into his door, and pain exploded in his arm. His head thumped against the window and the metal frame. He sucked in a breath and willed himself to not pass out. Through a red haze of agony, he grabbed the yoke and overpowered her pressure on the controls, bringing the plane back to a semblance of straight and level.

The pain began to abate with another breath. It took one more before he could speak. "What was that all about?" This time he let irritation tinge his voice. He flexed his arm, winced, and wondered if his bandage had held.

Lannis glared at him and burst out, "You're lying! You're going to k-kill me—" She faltered, and then lifted her chin, a spark of defiance in her eyes. "I don't have to make it easy for you."

He sighed, rubbed his forehead with the heel of his hand, then pinched the bridge of his nose. "Lannis, you will be okay. You can trust me on that. I'll get you back home when it's safe, and provide details to cover for you. It's too risky for you to know more than that."

Confusion played across her features for a moment, and then the fight drained out of her. She abruptly looked as exhausted as Ben felt, and her shoulders sagged. She gave him a stiff nod, and her lower lip began to tremble.

"Okay. Let's try that again. Who will expect you? When?"

"No one." The words wobbled. "Eleven days."

He shot her a sharp glance. Those answers bought him a lot of time, but he wondered why she wouldn't be missed. He gave himself a mental shake. Not his concern, at least for the moment. "What about the plane?"

"Maybe tomorrow afternoon." She shrugged. "The weather system coming in will ground them this afternoon and tomorrow morning, at least. If the reporters are still sick, it may be even the next day."

"Was it full of gas when we took off?"

"Yes." Defeat flattened her voice.

Tension flowed out of Ben's shoulders and he took his first easy breath in hours. He could put lots of distance between himself and the folks who wanted him dead. He'd go to ground, have time to think things through, figure out who he could trust. His plan began to gel, to have a life beyond "get out of Louisville alive."

Three for three, in the miracle department. He glanced at his unwilling pilot, her lips pressed tight in a mutinous line in spite of her capitulation.

Uh, I think I'm gonna need four.

Chapter Four

LOST. Anxiety built in Lannis's gut like towering cumulus clouds on a hot summer day. Familiar landmarks were hours and miles behind her, and the lack of charts or radios left her feeling as naked as if she'd forgotten to put on her jeans. The continuous search for towers and virtually invisible power lines strung between ridges gave her a task to focus on and helped keep terror at bay. Even so, unease ate steadily through her meager store of composure.

Of course, she'd had plenty of time to mull over the hijacker's words, which didn't comfort her as much as he seemed to think they should. *When it was safe.* Safe from whom or what? She certainly didn't feel safe with *him*. He'd said he'd cover for her. What the heck did that mean? He said she should trust him. *Ha.* She didn't trust anybody, so why should she start with a violent criminal?

Lannis held the hijacker responsible for the dread that crept up and down her spine, too. She'd never been lost before and hated it, hated feeling so vulnerable. She could only guess at their location, other than the generality of being in the Appalachians east of Nashville, or even Knoxville. Maybe they'd even gone as far as North Carolina or Virginia. He had finally allowed her to climb to a higher altitude over the mountains, the safety of which eased her mind some. However, they'd been airborne for well over three hours and the fuel gauges would show critically low levels had the electrical system been on, so she broke her silence.

"Um, we need to land soon. We're almost out of fuel."

"Yeah, okay." He'd been actively searching the ground for the last ten or fifteen minutes, but gave no more indication of what he wanted her to do.

Lannis worried at her lip with her teeth, let a few more minutes pass, then tried again. "I don't know where we are. We need to get to an airport soon."

He grunted and she shot an irritated glance at him, annoyance flaring at his lack of an appropriately concerned response.

"How much time left until you run out?" he asked.

She lifted her eyebrows in disbelief. "We land before we run out."

"Just answer the question, Lannis." He returned her glare with another one of those dagger looks.

If nothing else, she'd learned that he had no patience and expected full—and immediate—cooperation. "Maybe another half hour. At the most." Then, unable to contain her anxiety, she blurted, "Do you know where we are? So I can find the nearest airport?" She thought his eyes softened for a fleeting moment, then hardened.

"I'll tell you where to land."

Lannis held his gaze for a heartbeat, then turned her attention back to the plane. In a habit so ingrained she didn't think about it, she conducted a continual evaluation of the terrain for good landing spots in case of emergency. The nearly unconscious process suddenly became much more conscious and much less academic. She hadn't seen any roads in the last two or three valleys they had crossed, much less towns with airports. The sick feeling in her stomach spread to her limbs. She took a deep breath, tried to shake off the sensation, stomped out flickers of panic. Glanced at her captor.

Six feet of solid muscle coupled with that understated air of authority made him seem huge, like Arnold Schwarzenegger in *The Terminator*. He'd taken off his baseball cap some time ago, revealing dark hair, shaggy and overgrown. She already knew those cold eyes were pale blue, like the ice she felt when he turned them on her. He hadn't shaved for at least a day, maybe two, judging by the stubble on his face. His jeans and coat weren't shabby or dirty, but they were scuffed and had a couple of small rips, like he'd fallen or crawled. She guessed him to be just a few years older than herself, in his early thirties.

He whistled tunelessly as he scanned the terrain below. He straightened and pointed, evidently satisfied with what he saw, if she read his expression and body language right. "See that clearing down there? Put it down so it's close to that old barn."

"In a field?" Her voice rose. "You're out of your mind!"

He looked at her, his eyes shuttered. "Can you do it?"

"Yes, but—"

"This is basically a glider with an engine, right?"

"Yes. What does—"

His expression tightened with annoyance. "Are you going to keep arguing with me?"

Her temper flared. "Yes!"

He reached up, turned the ignition off, and pocketed the key. The engine obliged by stopping, although the propeller continued to turn. He leaned back, looked at her, and waited. A muscle in his jaw clenched, the only clue to his emotion.

The muted susurrus of air flowing over the wings replaced the usual drone of the engine.

An eternity later, although it was likely only a second or two, she forced her paralyzed muscles to react. She pulled back on the yoke, established best glide speed, and gained a valuable two hundred feet of altitude in the process.

Her fingers tightened on the yoke. "Bastard!"

He lifted one shoulder in a shrug and said, "We already established that. You have an important job to do. I suggest you get on with it."

Lannis didn't have to think half a second to appreciate the practicality of that statement. Her training kicked in and her focus changed from the man beside her to the critical situation he had created. Again. Anger sent blood rushing to her face, but she shoved the emotion away.

The wind was favoring the direction he wanted to land—thank God for small favors, since that was the only size he seemed inclined to grant at the moment—and the field appeared to be fairly smooth.

She knew how deceptive that could be, though. The clearing was maybe three quarters of a mile long, so there was plenty of space. But without the engine, she didn't have the luxury of a go-around if the first approach didn't look good. He'd cut the power at a low enough altitude that she didn't have time to waste on a restart even if she could talk him into it.

"It'll be safer if you let me have the flaps to slow us down."

"What do you need to get them?"

"The master switch."

"Don't pull something stupid." He flipped the red switch to the ON position.

Lannis immediately put ten degrees of flaps down. She was in good position, turning base a little high even without power, and waited until she had the field made before adding the next ten degrees.

"Scoot your seat all the way back. Snug up your seat belt and shoulder harness," she said. "Open your door and stuff the flight manual in it, above the hinges, to hold it open in case the fuselage buckles. Shut the master off after I get the rest of the flaps down." She popped her door open and shoved some sick sacks in it, then reached down between the seats to turn the fuel supply off.

Still looking good. Lannis silently thanked Orvis for insisting his pilots practice power-off landings from the traffic pattern, and for sending them to grass strips on occasion—good experience that was coming in handy right now. She added the final few degrees of flaps, bringing the plane to the slowest possible speed for touchdown.

"When we land, get out as fast as you can. There's not much of a chance of fire, since we're almost out of fuel anyway," she said, shooting him a quick, baleful glance. "With the electrical system off it shouldn't be an issue." She sent him a withering look. "But since we're out here in the middle of nowhere, we can't risk injury. Any questions?"

The hijacker sat loose-limbed and relaxed, a bored expression on his face, and a spurt of incredulity skirted the periphery of her attention. She wrestled her focus back to the approach. *Pretend it's a runway.* She reached for the throttle out of habit, and cursed under her breath when she remembered it was useless. *Almost there...*

Grass brushed the wheels and Lannis pulled the nose slightly higher, slowing until the wings no longer produced lift. The plane settled, then jerked as the thatch grabbed the gear. She hauled back on the yoke as hard as she could, wrapped her arms around it, captured it with her forearms instead of her weaker hand grip, trying to keep the plane from nosing over and flipping onto its back. At only thirty miles an hour, she thought it would work.

It did. The plane dropped the last few inches onto the ground, decelerated abruptly, and shoved them into their shoulder harnesses. Hard. It stopped rolling and they rocked back in their seats. Her fingers fumbled against his as they unbuckled belts and harnesses, and they scrambled out their respective doors in an anticlimactic coordinated maneuver.

Lannis looked at the hijacker through the open doors of the cockpit with a mixture of giddy relief and anxious concern for the plane. Her first real forced landing! And it had been successful.

Then her mind kicked in. If she could get to the woods, maybe she could lose him, then circle back to the plane later and use the radios to get help. Without considering the consequences, she whirled and took off across the meadow. Her legs were stiff from sitting for so long and threatened to give out with the first few steps, but she pushed herself to ignore the discomfort. His legs had to feel the same, and since she ran almost daily, she felt some confidence in her ability to outrun him, at least with a head start.

As long as he didn't shoot. *Oh God.* The gun. She'd forgotten it. Her gaze irrevocably drawn, she looked back over her shoulder, heart pounding and throat closing in panic.

He was in hot pursuit, no gun in hand, face set in a murderous rage, and gaining. His expression lent her the impetus for a burst of speed but she couldn't keep up the pace for long. His weight struck her off-balance as he tackled her, then twisted so he took the brunt of the fall. He grunted, then took a couple of tight breaths, the air hissing through his teeth.

"Lannis, knock it off! You're not in danger from me." His voice rasped in her ear, the heat of his breath on her cheek in stark contrast to the cold air bathing her face. "Don't try anything again. You will lose. My patience is just about shot. Do *you* have any questions?" He delivered his parody of her landing instructions with a hint of temper.

Lannis shook her head, reeling from the impact and the sensation of having been enveloped by his bulk. His chest worked like a bellows at her back, his steely arms wrapped snug around her rib cage, and his thighs were warm and solid against her legs. She stiffened at the intimacy, but before she had enough time to panic, he disentangled himself and stood, using her hip as a prop to push himself up.

The hijacker caught his breath on a groan, and a grimace flickered across his features. He closed his eyes for a moment, then opened them and extended a hand to help her. Galvanized, she scrambled upright, brushing her hands on her jeans in pointed refusal of his aid. He sent her a sharp glance and dropped his hand.

"Help me put the plane in the barn." He started back toward the plane, which was fortunately—or unfortunately, if she wanted a signal fire—not burning.

She hesitated, wondering when she could chance another escape attempt.

He sighed without turning around. "Lannis, darlin', don't bother. Push me much more and I promise to make your life a lot more miserable than it is now."

Annoyed that he read her mind with such ease, Lannis scowled at the back of his head and trudged behind him to the plane.

It wasn't difficult to push the plane into the run-down, somewhat lopsided barn, although one wing and the nose hung out once they got it positioned inside. Afterward he said, "If you need to pee, go find a bush. But stay where I can see you."

Her face blazed with embarrassment, but now that he'd mentioned it, her bladder demanded immediate attention. Feeling terribly exposed and vulnerable, she hunkered down behind a thicket of honeysuckle vines. She jerked her jeans back up as soon as she could, mostly for modesty, but also because it was flat-out cold. The hijacker stepped out from behind an ancient rusted tractor, tucking his shirt and straightening his belt. He beckoned to her, a peremptory quality to the gesture that mirrored what she'd learned of his character, then disappeared into the barn.

She found him rummaging through the plane, pocketing small items. Lannis peered into the cockpit. There was nothing to secure and no reason to complete the usual end-of-flight ritual, but it felt wrong to leave the plane this way. She leaned in to look for her backpack but didn't see it. Glancing up at him, her gaze flicked past the top of the radio panel. Her eyes widened and her breath stilled as she remembered the ELT switch.

The Emergency Locator Transmitter. A radio with its own battery, intended to provide location information after a crash to aid in search and rescue. The g-forces created by impact triggered the transmitter, although it also had a manual switch for testing its operation during regular maintenance checks. The signal was audible to aircraft passing overhead, provided they were monitoring the emergency frequency. Once the signal was detected, a search would be instigated. It could be traced to this location shortly after that, provided the battery lasted long enough. The switch was usually behind the baggage compartment and not accessible without removing a panel, but this plane was atypical.

Its switch was on the instrument panel.

Lannis's lips went dry. She placed her arm on top of the dash, tried to look casual, and surreptitiously watched her captor, waiting for him to turn away. A moment was all she needed. He glanced at her...and held her gaze. Her heart jumped into her throat as she adopted a nonchalant expression in spite of his already-proven ability to read her mind. She attempted a smile that was weak, at best.

The hijacker's brow furrowed. His eyebrows drew together, stopped just short of colliding, and his gaze sharpened as he stopped gathering supplies to study her. Lannis struggled to maintain eye contact. If she looked away, even blinked, he'd know she was hiding something. She was sure guilt was written all over her face anyway, but she grimly hung on to the idea that if she didn't back down, she might be able to pull this off. Maybe. The moment stretched on forever.

Don't blush. Her cheeks warmed anyway.

He frowned, and crooked a quizzical eyebrow at her. Finally, he broke eye contact, and went back to his preparations. Lannis slid her hand until it was just above the ELT switch. She leaned between the seats, pretending to search for her backpack.

"Let's go. Close it up."

She jumped, and felt her pulse accelerate. "Do you know where my backpack is?"

"Yeah, I've got it. Come on." His voice was sharp with impatience.

"All right, all right. Don't get your boxers in a twist," she muttered, pulling herself up. She bumped her head on the yoke and jerked her hand down from the dash, fumbling the ELT switch into the ON position as she passed it.

At least she hoped she did. She didn't dare look or she'd draw his attention to it, and she had no doubt he'd carry out his promise to make her life miserable. Or worse.

But it was her only chance, her best chance, and maybe her last chance. She'd risk the consequences. She had nothing more to lose.

Chapter Five

BEN COULDN'T BELIEVE his ears. *Get my boxers in a twist?* It was obvious she didn't think he'd heard her, but it certainly wasn't what he expected from her. He coughed to cover a burst of laughter that caught him by surprise and neutralized his impatience. He must be getting punch-drunk, although his evasion of death, for the moment at least, was heady enough to allow a moment of humor.

He motioned for her to come around the plane, and picked up an oil rag he'd taken from the baggage compartment. She held back, eyeing him with suspicion.

The light moment faded. He glared at her. She wasn't the only person having a bad day, and it was far from over. "Get over here."

She inched about a millimeter closer, angling her body so she could turn and bolt. Frustrated, he snagged her coat and pulled her within range. She looked like a doe, wary and vulnerable, and he felt a moment of compassion. But he wasn't out of danger yet, and as long as she could be linked with him, her life was at risk.

"I'm going to blindfold you until—"

She shook her head. "No," she said, and tried to twist out of his grip. She slapped at his hand. "No!" Her voice rose, and a thread of panic laced through it.

"Only until we get—"

She threw her whole body into resisting him, and Ben gave up on reasoning with her. He pushed compassion aside and jerked her around so her back was to him. With as much speed as he could muster, he threw the rag around her head, positioned it over her eyes, and yanked it into a tight knot. His task was made nearly impossible by her struggles, but he finally managed. Then he grabbed her wrists, pulled them to her sides, and enveloped her in a bear hug.

"Lannis. Calm down." His injured arm trembled and stung from trying to restrain her. She began to hyperventilate. He shifted his grip to his good arm and brought his left hand up to cradle her cheek. It was damp.

Tears.

Guilt rolled through his gut.

He changed tactics. "Hush, darlin', shh." He rocked gently and pulled her snug against his body. Keening cries alternated with the sharp sound of her in-breaths as she fought his control and desperately tried to regain her own. Gradually her weeping slowed, then turned into hiccups and sniffles. He continued to hold and comfort her until she went still in his arms, exhausted from the emotional storm.

"Lannis, I'll keep you safe." He softened his cop voice to a lover's murmur. "I can't risk letting you find your way back here, so the blindfold's going to stay on until we're over a ridge. This is for your well-being. I know you don't understand, but you have to trust me on this. If you can't or won't cooperate, I'll tie you and carry you out of here. Your choice."

He'd bet his last dollar that she'd be horrified at further helplessness. Giving her an option that offered her even an illusion of control tipped the scales toward her cooperation, unwilling as it might be. "Do you want to walk or be carried?"

"W-walk."

"Okay," he said, and let loose. He turned and placed her hand on his belt in back. "Hold on. Both hands." When she'd anchored them, he started walking. She stumbled against him, but after a few ungainly steps found a rhythm that matched his. At the edge of the forest he stopped, grasped her shoulders, and turned her around several times. She bit her lip until it was white but didn't resist.

He replaced her hands on his belt and hiked into the trees.

Chapter Six

THE SLIVER OF CONTROL Lannis had clung to fled her. She was mortified that she'd broken down and hated that she'd responded to the hijacker's comfort. Every cell of her body revolted against her dependence on him, not that it did any good. She had no idea where they were or where they were going. She was tired, hungry, and more frightened than she'd ever been.

No, she'd been at least as frightened one other time, but that hadn't lasted a long time. It had seemed like it, but it hadn't. Not like this. This was surreal.

She wobbled, off-balance from holding on to his belt. The climb was difficult, not because it was steep but because she had to rely on his body movements to guide her. He set a brisk pace, pushing her to her physical limits. Emotionally drained, she could do little more than concentrate on putting one foot in front of the other. Conscious thought faded as she retreated into a dazed state.

It seemed to last forever, the climb, then a descent filled with slips and missteps. She bumped into his back several times and felt him brace his body to keep her stable. At long last the terrain moderated, then became level. She heard the sound of a small stream nearby, birds chirping, squirrels chattering alarm at the invasion of their territory. The hijacker repeated the turning exercise, removed her blindfold, and stuffed it into his pocket.

Lannis blinked in the weak daylight and rubbed her eyes. They felt gritty and tired and were probably red. She automatically looked up at the sky. Disappointment slid through her. An overcast cloud layer obscured the sun, rendering it useless as a directional reference. They were in a clearing ringed by ridges, and she didn't know which one they had just come down. He began to walk and she followed, aware that even this small hesitation might set him off. Resentment simmered that he was so sure of her compliance he didn't even look back.

The afternoon dragged on as she trudged behind the hijacker. He favored game trails, if that, and there were no signs of people or civilization anywhere. Moss on the trees indicated that he was taking her northeast, more or less. Deeper into the wilderness or closer to a town? There was no way of knowing, but she kept track of landmarks so she could at least find her way back to the valley nearest the plane.

He stopped at a swift-flowing creek and Lannis washed her face, the icy water refreshing to her swollen eyes. She scrubbed her hands across her cheeks and winced at the pain in her jaw. She'd forgotten about his blow this morning, and gingerly pressed on it with her fingers, trying to assess the damage.

He glanced at her but made no comment. She made a compress of wet leaves and held it to her cheek for a few minutes. The cold water soothed what felt like a doozy of a bruise.

It didn't much matter. Lingering long enough for the compress to make a difference wasn't on his agenda. He stood and made an impatient noise. Disgusted, she threw the leaves down and trailed behind him.

But every so often, she glanced longingly at the clouds and wondered if a jet had picked up her ELT signal yet. That hope, slim as it might be, let her feel just a little bit less alone.

Her thoughts slid to her mom, then to her sister, and a pang of regret stabbed her heart. They wouldn't miss her for a lot longer than it would take Orvis to miss her, and she squirmed at the realization. Shame and something akin to resentment rolled through her. The basis for the estrangement quite rightly landed at Lannis's feet, but though she fervently wished she'd never had cause to initiate it, she didn't know how to end it.

But her family didn't deserve the pain of coping with her disappearance, and she redoubled her resolve to escape.

~

They'd been hiking for hours and Lannis was dragging farther and farther behind. The hijacker glanced back once in a while, but even those glances were getting more infrequent.

Plodding up a slope, it slowly dawned on her that he was quite a ways ahead and he'd just shot a look at her, so it would be a while before he checked again. She was next to a large boulder, with a cut and a little ravine running off of it. *I could...*

The impulse carried her behind the boulder. Her heart pounded in her chest and blood rushed loudly in her ears. She put her gloved hands over her nose and mouth, closed her eyes, and concentrated on slowing and quieting her breaths. She'd make her way down the ravine and disappear into the woods. *Go. Now!*

She opened her eyes, focusing on her escape route and the forest floor. And saw her captor's boots. Her gaze flew upward and met his cold stare. The look in his eyes sent a shiver of dread down her spine. She'd pushed him too far. She whirled to flee, fear spiking her tired muscles with energy.

He grabbed her shoulder and stopped her, then contained her against the rock with his body. "Consequences, Ms. Parker." He snagged her wrists and pulled them above her head, holding them with one hand. Lannis struggled to escape his grip, inhaling the cold scent of his fleece-lined jacket as she did.

He groped in a pocket and pulled out a length of twine he must have brought from the barn, wrapping it around her wrists with angry motions. But though he jerked the knot tight, he had bound her over her gloves, and not so tight as to cut off circulation to her hands. He looped the other end, put his hand through it, and stepped away from her. Without his body for support, she lost her balance, staggering against the boulder to keep from falling. He gave a sharp tug on the thin rope, the message unmistakable. She shoved herself upright and made an awkward attempt to reposition her hat.

He hiked along the faint trail so fast that her lungs burned. Every time she dropped back, he'd jerk the cord, expressing his impatience and fury in absolute silence.

Then she tripped at the same moment he pulled. She soared through the air, unable to draw her arms back to break the fall. She smashed to the ground and air whooshed from her lungs.

Her diaphragm quivered, and Lannis couldn't catch her breath. She gaped and thrashed in a desperate struggle to jump-start her lungs, something she took so for granted that she had no idea how to *make* them function. The hijacker leapt to her side, a spray of small stones and debris peppering her thigh. He knelt at her side, hesitated, then pushed her onto her back. Lowered his face to hers. *He's going to kiss me! What...?* She arched, trying to twist away, but her strength was waning, her vision narrowing. Then his mouth covered hers, one hand under her chin pulling it up, the other pinching her nose shut.

His lips molded to hers and he blew air into her. Warm, moist breath entered her mouth, filling her throat. Inflating her lungs. It was without doubt the most bizarre sensation she'd ever experienced. Lannis froze, realizing his intent. He tasted clean and sharp and male, and she hated that she noticed. He drew back and his breath left her body. She steeled herself to helpless endurance of the intimacy when he leaned down to deliver another life-giving respiration. On the third one, her body decided to join the party and exhaled in a long, wheezing cough.

He backed off and she rolled away from him, coughing and gasping. He reached across her body, freed her hands, then grasped her shoulders and pulled her up, propping her against a fallen tree. Her head lolled back and one leg slid down, the other flopping to the side. He pushed his ball cap back on his head, scratched his forehead, and crouched on his heels in front of her.

"When's the last time you ate?"

Lannis regarded him with foggy confusion.

"Did you have breakfast?"

She wondered why he cared, then gave up trying to understand him and wheezed out an answer. "No."

He removed the gun from his coat pocket, stowed it at the small of his back, then dug deeper in the pocket. He produced a package of peanut M&Ms and dangled them in front of her.

Lannis pushed up on an elbow and grabbed at the packet. "Food!" She ripped the bag open with trembling hands and clumsily tipped the candy-coated nuts into her gloved palm.

He engulfed her hand with his, stopping her from downing several at once. "Slow down, or you'll puke. Don't waste them."

She knew he was right and rationed herself. Even so, her stomach spasmed around the first piece, and she was overcome by a wave of nausea. Somehow he knew what she was feeling and pressed her head down.

"Breathe. In through your nose and out through your mouth."

She did, and the nausea passed almost as abruptly as it had come on. She finished the rest of them slowly, savoring the brief burst of chocolate in each piece. Once she was past the danger of queasiness, he stood and pulled a wicked-looking knife from a sheath at his ankle beneath his jeans—why was she not surprised?—and began cutting boughs. Daylight was beginning to fade, although the overcast skies had never quite let the day feel fully begun.

She wobbled to her feet and looked around for a place to pee. Without looking at her, the hijacker said, "Stay close." Lannis went as far as she thought she could get away with, and had a little more privacy than the first time. On her way back to camp, she picked up some branches he had cut but hadn't yet gathered, and dropped them at his feet.

"Thanks." He didn't break his concentration as he wove branches together to make a small lean-to.

Lannis sat down, as she couldn't see anything else that needed doing. She looked at the sky again. The cloud cover had turned thicker, darker, and the ceiling had dropped. She estimated the precipitation and colder temperatures of the front would catch up to them sometime during the night. The shelter he'd built looked like it would shed most of the rain, and would be downright cozy if they got snow instead.

He stood and said, "Get your shoes off and climb in. I'll be there in a minute. We'll use my coat over our arms and yours over our legs. Keep your hat on to conserve heat."

There really was no alternative, but Lannis's gut twisted at the thought of sleeping with him. Never mind that the context of this sleep was definitely not sexual. Shared body heat was the best option for survival. She knew that, but it didn't change how she felt. His feet crunched on dried leaves as he returned. He put his hand on the small of her back, urging her to the shelter. She resisted and he stopped, facing her.

"We both need sleep, badly. This is the best we'll get for tonight. It's not a big deal." He touched her elbow, and this time she moved. She climbed into the cave of vegetation and removed her boots, then her coat. He followed her in, taking up an enormous amount of space, and shucked his coat. It was dark inside the shelter, and all she could see was his silhouette. He kept his hat on, too, and reached for her, pulling her up next to his body, covering them both with the coats.

She stiffened at the contact. He murmured something—it sounded sort of like a prayer or a benediction—then rested his hand briefly on her head, sliding it down to stroke her cheek.

The tenderness of his gesture belied the turmoil of the day. Events played through her mind in flashes, and she wondered who he was for the thousandth time. Whatever she'd expected, though, it wasn't gentleness. Lannis closed her eyes, suddenly too exhausted to fight him anymore.

"Sleep, darlin'."

In the moment that Lannis slid into blessed oblivion, a sense of security blanketed her. She struggled to stay awake to examine it, but her body prevailed and the thought slipped away as darkness claimed her.

~

Sleep overcame her like a switch flipped off. Her body relaxed in one heartbeat, then melted against his. Ben breathed a sigh of relief. He would sleep soon, and well, but his mind churned with unsettling images.

Snippets of last night's fight floated into his consciousness now that the threat was distant. Terrance "King" LeMasters, the contact he'd developed with excruciating patience over the last four months. Who had baited him with the promise of a meeting with the main man, the drug lord who had a stranglehold on Louisville. Who instead had handed him over to two corrupt Louisville policemen. "Powell" glinting on the only nametag he could see in the sparse lighting of the alley behind the convenience store. Grantree's voice, distorted but recognizable over the other cop's cell phone, ordering Ben's murder.

He still felt the slice of that betrayal, the only one that could rattle him beyond rational thought. Which it had. The gunshot wound that came entirely too close to killing him had sent him into primal survival mode. Now Lannis Parker bore the brunt of the fallout.

Anger surged through him, and he struggled to suppress it. There was nothing he could do about what had happened. The best he could do was to take care of her now, and make sure there was no link between them afterward. No way for either the druggies or the crooked cops to use her, to lean on or harm her in order to get to him.

Thank God he'd grown up in the mountains of Tennessee. It looked different from the air, but he'd recognized enough to choose a familiar area of the wilderness to set the plane down. Another day or so of hiking should put them close to where he wanted to come out. His arm was not infected, although it remained painful and throbbing. If they both managed to avoid getting diarrhea from drinking untreated water, his plan would work fine.

Hours of sifting mentally through his contacts, friends, coworkers, and supervisors had finally netted him one name, one person he could trust, one person who could risk helping him. He'd contact John McNaughten once he got back and begin the process of ferreting out the crooked faction of the Louisville Police Department. And of the DEA. Revulsion rolled through him at the idea that Roger Grantree might not be the only bad apple in his own agency. He found himself doubting his own boss now, an even more unsettling notion.

A yawn caught him by surprise, and he rubbed his tired eyes. He pushed the lingering emotions away and settled in to sleep, enjoying the feel of Lannis's body next to his. The singular juxtaposition of firm and soft that was the essence of female. The curve of her slender waist as it flared into her hip. Vulnerability countered by strength. Her warmth against his belly, thighs, and chest.

Yeah, he'd take the unwitting comfort she provided. Slightly cheered, he rearranged his head on the branches.

Things could be worse.

~

The Tennessee Wing of the Civil Air Patrol notified CAP Colonel Hank Murphy of the ELT signal at six p.m. He muted the national news he'd been watching on TV to take the information. Not much to go on, he thought. No planes reported missing or overdue. Area airports already checked by telephone. And of course, weather that would hamper an airborne search was moving in.

On the bright side, the call came in while people were still awake. That was quite unusual, actually. Two in the morning was much more common. If an aircrew was available, they could potentially get an hour or so of search time in before weather grounded them.

He went to the computer and logged on to check fleet availability. His eyes scanned the list and he sighed with resigned disappointment. The closest plane was in the shop for its 100-hour inspection, so it was torn apart and unusable. And the next closest plane was already useless, with low clouds, poor visibility, and a dangerously low freezing level pinning it in place as the cold front moved through. Ground teams, less effective in mountainous terrain but immediately deployable, were his only option. He picked up his roster and dialed.

"Hello, Major Deane? We've got a plane to find..."

Chapter Seven

LANNIS CAME AWAKE in stages, dreaming of an ocean, drifting on gentle waves in a tropical paradise, warmth radiating from a sandy beach. The water rippled under her and—

Yesterday's events bullied their way into her mind, awareness crashing over her like a rogue wave. She stiffened and her eyes popped open. Her right arm and leg were draped with shameless abandon over the hijacker's torso and thighs in a sleepy bid for his body heat, and she had plastered herself to his side. Before she could react, he jiggled her shoulder and rasped in a sleep-roughened voice, "Rise and shine, sleepyhead. Time's a-wastin'." He extricated himself from her limbs, grabbed his coat, and clambered out of the lean-to.

Lannis jerked away from him, bumping her head on the branches overhead. Snow sifted down through their shelter, glittering in the few rays of light that filtered through the weave. She groped for her shoes, found and fumbled them on, then shoved her arms into her coat and stuffed her fingers into chilled gloves. Cold air nipped at her face.

Scrambling out, she squinted against the diffuse light that penetrated a layered cloud cover. A couple of inches of snow had fallen, and the forest looked magical. Wisps of mist added to the beauty of the scene. They also added to the lack of directional clues. Lannis hoped he knew where in blazes he was going, and taking her, as well. The hijacker—what was his name?—was ready to hike. After all, there wasn't a breakfast buffet in sight. The thought caused her stomach to growl. Audibly.

"Hey, do you have any more candy, or a granola bar or anything?" She hated to acknowledge him at all, especially after having slept all over him.

"Nope. I emptied the vending machine, and that's the only one I had left."

"What's your name?" The question popped out without permission, and Lannis snapped her mouth shut, wishing it had remained unasked. Nevertheless, she looked him straight in the eye.

He held her gaze, and said, "Call me Jack."

Incredulous, she stared for a moment longer, then laughed. "You're joking, right? I'm supposed to call you Jack, as in 'Hi, Jack' or"—she gave a little wave with her gloved hand, fingers wiggling—"'hijack.' And I'm supposed to do that with a straight face?"

Jack actually colored a little, then laughed, and the smile transformed him. Lannis caught her breath. When he wasn't fierce and threatening, he was good-looking, even handsome in a sort of uncivilized way. He took his hat off and brushed his hand through his hair. He grinned. "Yeah, darlin', you won't forget it."

Lannis pushed aside an unwelcome fascination with his mouth, and said, "Well, I'm not your darlin', and I know Jack's not your real name. I'm just tired of thinking of you as 'hey, you.'"

His grin disappeared and he said evenly, "I figured you'd already named me something far worse and didn't need any more ideas to expound on that theme." He turned away. "Take care of yourself. It's time to go."

Lannis felt her face heat, and looked at her feet, embarrassed. She had. The name she had chosen was one she had rarely uttered out loud. Glancing through her lashes, she saw he had gone back to ignoring her. She went to find a bush.

~

At Louisville Air, Mark joined the rest of the instructors lazing around the classroom, telling stories and laughing at each other's obvious exaggerations. The clouds trailing the cold front had hung on longer than forecast, and the weather was unsuitable for student flight. After a day and a half of cancellations, it looked like this afternoon's traffic flight might be able to get up, barely, so Jeff left to preflight the plane.

Ten minutes later he walked back in. "Where's 438? It's not in the hangar, and I can't find it out on the ramp."

There was a mild stir as pilots traded blank looks. Mark felt a prickle at the back of his neck, and the hairs on his forearms stood up. He'd traded with Lannis Parker yesterday morning, but she hadn't recorded the flight on his time card like they'd agreed. He hadn't given it much thought at the time, although he'd called Bob at the radio station and casually verified that the flight had been canceled. Lannis had mentioned something about taking a few vacation days, visiting her aunt in Tennessee, and hadn't been at work since.

"Who flew it last, Jeff?" he asked, dreading the answer.

Jeff flipped the clipboard open. "Lannis, Wednesday afternoon. I can't be absolutely sure, but I had a night student Wednesday and I'm pretty sure the plane was in the hangar when I left."

"Go ask Orvis. Maybe the owners went someplace with it," Mark said. The conditions of the leaseback allowed them to use the plane when they wanted. Maybe they'd done so and Orvis had forgotten to mention it, since the weather had been too bad to fly the traffic anyway.

Then another possibility struck him, almost too strange to consider, but still... Lannis wouldn't use the plane without authorization, would she? He knew her pretty well, as well as anyone did, and couldn't imagine her doing something that rash. *Naw.* He'd never met anyone quite as focused, as politely controlled, as her. She wouldn't do anything to jeopardize her license, and airplane theft would definitely do that. He dismissed the thought and followed Jeff into Orvis's glassed-in office.

"Orvis, do you know where 438 is?" Jeff repeated the story, and Mark added the bit about the radio station cancellation Thursday. Never hurt to cover his tracks—and Lannis's, for that matter.

Orvis frowned, and shook his head. "No, the owner didn't take it. It should be in the hangar if Lannis put it away like she was supposed to. You say it's not anywhere?" he said, as if asking again would magically make it appear.

"No, I looked in the hangar and out on the ramp," Jeff said. "I don't see it."

Orvis pushed himself up from the desk with sudden urgency and began to bark orders. "Jeff, call the station and cancel today's flight. Tell them it's weather, or a mechanical problem, but save them a wasted trip. Mark, get the rest of the pilots and we'll run a search of the airport. If it doesn't turn up, I'll call the police."

Mark took a deep breath and started to ask about Lannis's vacation plans, but Orvis interrupted him, his color deepening to a blotchy red. "Get with it, boy! Don't dillydally around! Let's get to the bottom of this."

Mark flushed, snapped his mouth shut, and left the office, his back rigid. *Fine.* He didn't have to stand for Orvis's rudeness. If Orvis didn't want his help, it wasn't Mark's problem.

Lannis didn't fly the morning flight he'd pawned off on her. The plane went missing for some other reason, one that couldn't be traced to him. Not his problem, not his fault. *No, siree.*

He went to the classroom and organized the instructors for a ramp search, which turned up nothing. When the cops showed up to take the report, Mark faded into the corner of the room, doing his best to remain as unremarkable as possible. When the cops split up to take everyone's statements, he drew the guy named Powell—the more intimidating of the two.

But he made it through the brief interview without sweating, without stuttering. Mark breathed a sigh of relief, and headed out the door to go home. He glanced back and caught a glimpse of Orvis, hair standing on end from running his hands through it, sitting down with the cops. The guy looked uncharacteristically frazzled, and he wondered if he should go back and tell them he'd traded with Lannis yesterday, but he rejected the notion as soon as it formed. He wasn't involved, especially since Orvis had blown him off.

Nope. He had no sympathy for his boss—and no idea why he couldn't shake the sense that Lannis was somehow involved.

~

It was the first time Powell had taken a report of a stolen plane. The interviews went quickly as no one knew anything. The plane could have gone missing anywhere in a forty-eight-hour time frame. Everyone involved with the flight school and charter business was accounted for, except for a lone vacationing instructor.

He privately wondered about a possible connection with the undercover cop who'd evaded them, the first night that the plane could have disappeared. He gave a slight shake of his head when he saw the question mirrored in Neal's eyes. They'd discuss that twist when they were in the car. He flipped his notepad shut. "We'll talk to the folks in the tower, see if they have any record of it taking off, and put out a bulletin for airports within—what did you say?—a four-hundred-mile radius, make it five hundred in case of tailwinds. We'll notify the FBI, since the chance it crossed state lines is pretty high."

Orvis Larson shook his head, clearly distressed at the magnitude of the problem. "Yeah, it could be anywhere. A private strip, or they could have refueled and gone across the country."

"Or already across the Mexican border, if they stayed low and were lucky," Neal added. "That is, if it was stolen for drug running."

Larson's shoulders drooped as he stood to see them out.

Powell and Neal settled into their patrol unit and looked at each other.

"Do you think Martin's a pilot? The K-9 unit was headed in the general direction of Bowman that night," Neal said. "They lost his trail on the street before they got that far. Shanahan said he circled around and backtracked, maybe hitched a ride."

Powell grunted. "Dunno. Trying to run a check on him at this point would raise red flags with the DEA. Grantree's too spooked right now; we can't contact him till this blows over."

Silence.

"Why would he take *that* plane, if he was a pilot? There were easier ones to get to out on the ramp." Neal's logic was irrefutable.

More silence.

Neal faced forward and started the cruiser.

Powell tapped a finger on his notepad. "Maybe the pilot that went on vacation is a factor here. She was the last one to fly it." He flipped the page to find Ms. Parker's address. "Why don't we go pay her a visit, to at least confirm what her boss said."

Chapter Eight

BEN SET A SLOWER PACE for the day but, even so, had to stop frequently for Lannis. Her uncomplaining struggle to keep up was a godsend, and he wished he could transform his gratitude into a tangible offering of food. *Yeah, right. Me, Tarzan...* He shook his head at the absurd thought, although she elicited protective instincts that surprised him.

His arm throbbed. The wound wasn't infected yet, but he needed to change the makeshift dressing soon. Another instinct surfaced. Like an injured animal, he balked at Lannis discovering this weakness. He'd been able to rinse most of the blood from his sleeve in the airport restroom, so as long as he didn't take off his shirt, he'd keep that little piece of information to himself. She wouldn't hesitate to aggravate his injury in a bid to escape. She had already done so once.

He'd best remember that her feisty character was a double-edged sword.

At dusk, Ben led Lannis around the edge of a large field toward a barn. It was the most evidence of civilization he'd seen since they'd landed the day before. The field had been worked in years past, although it lay fallow now. The barn was in good condition, compared to the one where they'd abandoned the plane. They'd have a roof over their heads tonight, but he'd trade it for food. Lannis would probably agree.

She trudged slowly behind him. He hadn't let her drop back at all, not keen on a repeat of yesterday's episode. As a result, they hadn't made much progress in the way of distance, but it was good enough. The barn tonight, and then into town tomorrow. A motel, a hot meal, and a phone. That sounded more than fine to him. Downright decadent, even.

Glancing back, he frowned. Lannis's bruise had blossomed into brilliant purples and greens and showed no signs of fading. Maybe he needed to keep her under wraps for a few more days until it did. It was pretty noticeable and he wanted, needed, to blend in once they got to town.

He ducked in the doorway. It felt a good ten degrees warmer inside the barn, out of the biting wind. Ben grabbed a bale of hay and cut the twine holding it together with his knife, broke it apart, and strew it on the packed dirt floor. Lannis glanced at what he was doing, then looked away and clenched her fists.

"Um," she said.

"Get your stuff off, Lannis."

"Could I sleep over there?" There was a note of pleading in her voice. She pointed at another pile of loose straw.

"No." He didn't even look where she was pointing. "You'll sleep here, next to me, so I know exactly where you are."

She looked briefly angry, but let the coat slide off her shoulders, wincing as she did. She dropped to the dirt floor to pull off her shoes, setting them next to the makeshift bed. Ben grabbed them and tied the laces together, then stood and tossed them over a beam about two feet above his head.

She wasn't going to like the next part one little bit, but he was far more fatigued than he let on. He needed to sleep without worrying about her whereabouts or intentions.

"Your shirt and jeans, too." He held out his hand.

Her head snapped up. "No."

"Yes," he said. "I won't make it easy for you to sneak out while I'm asleep."

She licked her lips and opened her mouth, then closed it, like she was scrambling for a negotiating position.

"The other option is for me to tie you. Believe me, Lannis, it's painful after an hour or so. Your choice."

She shook her head, slowly at first, then faster. "No." She swallowed hard. "I...I promise I won't run." Her gaze shifted left, then back to Ben.

A tell. "We both know you're lying. I wish I could trust you, but I can't." He scrubbed his face with one hand, then held out the other. "I need sleep. Just hand over your clothes. Or you can choose the rope." His tone alternated between steely and cajoling, but remained implacable. He figured it was too much to ask, but he hoped she'd trust him enough. Enough that she'd cooperate instead of fight. A night restrained meant aching joints for her and no rest for either of them.

Twin spots of color flared on her cheeks. She whirled away and stood rigid, hands fisted at her side.

Trembling belied her emotions as she struggled to contain them, and Ben could nearly read her despair at her powerlessness. He didn't blame her, but he was going to prevail here.

She began jerking her shirt buttons loose. Relieved, he released the breath he'd been holding.

She shrugged out of her wool shirt and flung it at him. It fluttered to the ground, and he sent a pointed look at her T-shirt. Her lips flattened, but she yanked the tee over her head and threw it, too, then began working on her jeans. He bent, picked up the shirts and folded them, then stashed them under his side of the straw pile. She stripped the jeans down her legs, refusing to look at him, and pitched them at his head. Hard.

Ben snagged the jeans out of the air before they made contact. His fingers curled into the fabric, and he held them a moment longer than necessary. The fibers were still warm from her body. He didn't let himself think about that, and twisted, grabbing feed sacks he'd scavenged to lay over the clothes.

Discomfort and anger radiated from her in waves. Her faded sports bra and high-cut athletic underwear were far from seductive, but revealed the effects of a highly active life. Gently defined arm muscles. Toned, flat belly. Strong shoulders. He'd expected that, but the winter clothing had camouflaged curves, as well. Feminine curves he couldn't help appreciating. It wasn't the time, place, or situation to enjoy as much as he'd like, though. Ben squashed his response.

"Come to bed," he said.

She shook her head, and defied him in angry silence. Goose bumps popped up on her arms and legs even as she rubbed them in a losing attempt to stay warm.

Irritation pricked at Ben and he stalked across the dirt floor. She lifted her chin, thrust it at him, dared him. Dared him to take one more step, dared him to come closer, dared him to touch her. He halted, taken aback at the fury in her eyes. He folded his arms across his chest, mostly to keep his hands from the temptation of forbidden goods. Even though these weren't quite the circumstances that the rules were made for, he would not abuse his position of authority— or his own values—in order to take sexual advantage of her. Too bad she couldn't appreciate that. He wished he could start over with her, meet her on equal terms.

She stood on the tips of her toes and leaned close, nose to nose. Unfortunately, that brought the soft swell of her breasts within inches of his folded arms. Ben sucked in his breath, his gut. Tried to suck in his chest without stepping backward.

She shook her fist in his face. "*I hate you!* I hate what you've done to me, what you're doing! I wish...I wish—" She narrowed her eyes and clamped her lips together.

It wasn't difficult to read her intent. She'd love to see him six feet under. Well, so much for a do-over, no matter how many aspects of her character he appreciated.

He dug deep and found a mild voice. "It's cold. We're both tired." He raised an eyebrow. "I understand what you're saying. But think about the choices you've made in the last couple of days. At the very least, they've made your life more miserable than it had to be. At most, your decisions have saved you—along with me." He hesitated, then added, "Make no mistake. I'm grateful for that. I'm just pointing out that you hold more power in this situation than you give yourself credit for." He stepped to the side and gestured toward the bed he'd made.

She stiffened, then swept past him, as regal as a queen dressed in satin and lace. She dropped onto the feed sacks with unconscious grace and turned her back on him. He covered them both with the coats and lay next to her, careful to keep the contact minimal.

Her breath caught on a silent sob, and she shuddered. Ben smothered his urge to reach out to comfort her. She wouldn't welcome it. A few minutes later, her muscles went lax and her breathing deepened, then slowed.

Frustration coursed through him. He tried to bring to mind a comforting psalm, or a fortifying verse from one of Paul's letters, but drew a blank. Maybe a quiet conversation with the Almighty...but he heard only wind howling around the barn. *Trust in the Lord.* Well, hell, that was great in theory, but in practice, sometimes it sucked. Like now. Exhaustion amplified his sense of being a rat in a maze.

He huffed out a sigh, forced his muscles to relax. Put his predicament in a box in his brain and sealed it. Let his guard down. And finally, slept.

~

Officer Neal knocked on Lannis Parker's door, not really expecting a response. The house was quiet and dark, even though it was dinnertime. He leaned to the side and peered in the front window through a crack in the drapes. The streetlight illuminated part of the front room, which was devoid of furniture. There was, however, a flight bag lying partially open near a closet. A headset poked out of the bag, along with what was probably a logbook, and a ragged, well-used chart stuffed carelessly behind it.

Powell reached past him and tried the door. Locked. They went around the house, but no other drapes were open enough to see much, and the back door was locked as well. No tracks led through the remnants of snow that had fallen two days ago. The house gave every appearance of having been secured and left unoccupied for several days.

Neal glanced at his partner, and raised an eyebrow.

"We'll keep an eye on her house and talk to her when she gets back." Powell paused, his expression grim. "If she knows anything about Martin, she's a complication we'll have to"—he adjusted his gun belt—"neutralize."

Chapter Nine

A LOUD *CRACK* catapulted Lannis from sleep, and she jolted upward. In the nanosecond it took for her to identify the noise as a gunshot, its echo faded. Her heart thudded heavily in her chest, hesitated, then settled into a frantic pace. Straw, still warm beneath her, crackled as she twisted to look at the bright doorway. Dust motes floated peacefully in rays of sunshine that illuminated the dim interior of the barn.

Disappointment slammed into her. She was not home, waking from a monster nightmare. She was in a barn somewhere in the Appalachian Mountains.

And she was alone. *Alone! He* wasn't in the barn! Shoving disappointment aside, she scrambled on hands and knees to dig her clothing out from under the gunnysacks that had been their bed. She cursed under her breath as the sleeves of her shirt twisted and tangled in her haste to thrust her arms into them. She grabbed her coat, intent on muscling a bale of straw under the beam where Jack had thrown her shoes. It would give her just enough height that she'd be able to reach them.

But the spot where they'd hung last night was vacant. No shoes tied together, dangling from the rough wood. Turning, she groped the pile of straw in a desperate search for them. It was still very cold, and even with wool socks she wouldn't get far without protection for her feet.

A shadow flickered across the floor, plunging the barn into gloom. She glanced up. Jack's broad shoulders blocked the sun as he leaned against the door frame, holding her shoes in one hand.

"Looking for these?"

Lannis's heart plummeted. Adrenaline already flowing through her veins spiked as she realized her intent to escape was obvious. Again. She nodded warily, and searched his face for clues to his mood. His voice had been bland, but she knew that was not a reliable barometer of his temper. The sun was behind him, he wore his ball cap low over his eyes, and thick stubble on his face camouflaged his expression. She'd have to assume he was angry. Her muscles, now on an adrenaline overload, tensed in preparation to flee his wrath.

He extended the shoes toward her and pushed himself away from the door. "Breakfast will be ready in a bit."

She made no move to reach for them, wrapping her arms around her torso instead. He dropped them on the dirt floor, then bent down to pick up his coat from the rumpled straw bed. "Hot tea and cooked meat. Can't beat it after a couple of hungry days."

Lannis's stomach emitted a low, long growl. He laughed, the sound far more lighthearted than the situation deserved. She squirmed inwardly at his amusement. Her body's unconscious response countered her resolve to resist him, even if he'd just provided what they both needed. Food. Her belly rumbled again. He left the barn, whistling, and she brushed bits of dirt and straw off her socks before shoving her feet into her shoes.

The swift flash of his even white teeth, combined with the fading strains of his whistling, led her to deduce that Jack wasn't harboring a grudge. She doubted he would drop his guard because of it, but he might. The thought brought a grim smile to her face.

Patchy sunshine drew her outside, and Lannis felt a small surge of hope in the face of improving weather.

He'd built a campfire. Nothing was as effective at lifting spirits as the crackle of burning wood, the scent of its smoke, the primal promise of heat and safety. Lannis's smile softened and turned genuine.

Jack knelt on one knee, skinning a small animal, maybe a rabbit or squirrel. Lannis was too hungry to be squeamish, but even so, she didn't look too closely. His ease in wielding the knife made his experience apparent. The gunshot that had woken her suddenly made sense. A can of water sat over the fire, small bubbles beginning to rise in a simmer.

She wandered to the stream and crouched on the bank to wash. The shock of the cold water on her face stole her breath for a moment, but took off at least one layer of grime. She rinsed her mouth and touched her jaw, testing. The bruise on her chin wasn't as sore as it had been, nor were her ribs.

Wiping her hands on her jeans, she stood, then sighed. The lure of food was stronger than the instinct to escape. She trudged back to the fire. Jack dipped a jar of the hot liquid and offered it to her in silence. It smelled like lemon, and she sipped. A track of heat warmed her insides, and Lannis sank onto a nearby log and turned her face to the sun. Some minutes passed as she let her muscles relax.

After another sip, she cleared her throat. "What's in this? It's good. Kind of lemony."

"Mint leaves of some sort, maybe lemon balm. We're lucky to find some this early in the season, especially as cold as it's been." Jack rotated the meat, judged it done, and pulled it from the spit he'd fashioned. He made the sign of the cross, bowed his head, and closed his eyes for a moment, then cut a leg off the unidentifiable animal and handed it to Lannis.

My hijacker is Catholic? Maybe he was Mafia. Didn't they come from Sicily, or Italy? His coloring might fit, with that black hair. The incredulous thought faded as the distinctive odors of wood fire and roasting meat wafted on the breeze, making her weak with hunger and anticipation.

"Not too fast," he said.

She nodded, unsure of her ability to keep from gorging on it. She bit into the leg quarter, catching a drip of meaty juice on her chin with a finger. Chewing sent her digestive system into overdrive and nausea rose, threatening to send the bite right back up. Jack was there in an instant, pushing her head between her knees, and she breathed noisily, battling the urge to gag. When the nausea finally passed she nodded her head, and the pressure from his hand disappeared. She sat up, took a deep breath, finished chewing, and swallowed.

It tasted better than any food she'd ever had in her life. Warily she took another bite and, when nothing untoward happened, tore into it, licking her fingers to get every little drip. Even so, he rationed their Spartan meal to make it last a half hour.

Lannis picked up a bone and inspected it for any missed scraps, gnawed fruitlessly on its knobby tip...and heard the drone of a plane in the distance. She stiffened, trying to gauge its distance and altitude. Its sound had the singular quality of a small single-engine plane, and now that she could see the sun and had directional cues, was proceeding from north to south.

Had the ELT worked? Hope sparked. She wanted to leap up and wave her arms, to call it closer, though the plane was too far away for the effort to bear fruit. Instead, she willed herself to remain motionless, lest Jack recognize that rescue was just over the horizon.

Chapter Ten

BEN SAW THE sudden tension in Lannis's posture, then heard an airplane. It wasn't close, but he didn't want to take the chance anyone might spot the smoke from the fire. He cast her a warning glare as he extinguished it and abandoned his plan of using the barn for a base for a day or two. Too risky. Grantree had a long reach, and had too many resources at his disposal.

"Let's go," he said. She didn't obey immediately, but looked at the sky with a hopeful expression. Ben took a step toward her. She jumped to her feet and faced him, looking suddenly uncertain.

"Um…if they fly over us, we can get some help."

He barked a humorless laugh. "Not a chance, darlin'. We don't need any help. Come on." He shot her a look promising retribution if she defied him. Lannis eyed his weapons and the twine as he gathered his small stash of supplies with quick and efficient motions. The light in her eyes faded, replaced by disappointment, a flash of fear, then angry submission.

Ben grabbed the backpack and slipped into the woods. She followed, stomping her feet in protest, but at least she was cooperating. His good mood from breakfast evaporated.

Overhead, the airplane in the distance changed course. Flew southbound, a little closer than before. Then northbound. Closer.

A search pattern. Desperation, unnerving in its familiarity, settled in Ben's gut. Naked hope was written on Lannis's face as the plane inexorably drew nearer, but he had no intention of letting anyone find them. At one point the plane got close enough for him to get a look at it, and he pulled her behind a cedar, thankful that they both wore dun-colored coats. Tough to spot, especially from the air. He peered around the cover of branches and saw a military-type logo and the letters CAP on the underside of the wing of the low-flying plane. Civil Air Patrol.

He didn't know much about them except that they were somehow associated with the Air Force and looked for crashed airplanes. The chances of another airplane having gone down in this area were beyond slim. He'd known their plane would be found, of course. Eventually. But not this soon.

Abruptly he stilled and focused his attention on Lannis. She gazed up through the trees with a longing expression, and he narrowed his eyes in suspicion.

There was no reason for their plane to have been traced here. He'd made her fly below the capabilities of radar, and with the electrical system turned off, there was no way for the plane's radios to transmit any kind of position information. Even though it had probably been reported missing by now, there would be no reason for anyone to look *here*.

If it flies over us, we can get some help. Most planes were going from point A to point B and would not fly back and forth across their course. Until just this moment it had not been evident it was Civil Air Patrol. Yet she'd known, known from the first there was a high likelihood it was a search plane, looking for the plane they'd flown.

Looking for them.

"Lannis." He didn't soften his voice or his anger. Startled, she looked at him and stumbled, off-balance from her sudden change of focus. "What did you do to call in the Civil Air Patrol?"

Guilt flooded her face, and she made a hasty—and unsuccessful—attempt to put on an innocent expression.

"N-nothing."

"Not buyin' it." He loomed over her. "What did you do?"

She backed away, her face paling. "I didn't do anything. Maybe they're p-practicing." Her voice shook, and the words sounded forced.

"Yeah, right, and I'm the Easter Bunny. What did you do?" he snarled, and backed her into a sycamore.

Lannis turned to flee. He grabbed her arm and forced her to face him, incensed that she hadn't figured out that running from him wasn't a good plan. He clamped his hands in a viselike grip on the side of her head, and she grasped at his forearms for balance.

Ben lowered his face until he was nose to nose with her. "Talk."

Lannis squirmed as his hands tightened, creating pressure on the sensitive areas of her ears and jaw. "Ow, stop. You're hurting me."

He knew that, but he also knew it wouldn't last, wouldn't even bruise. Just achieve some cooperation. He added another pound or two of pressure.

She gasped. "All right, all right. I turned on the ELT."

"What's the ELT? What does it do?" He wanted to howl his frustration, but corralled his emotions and deliberately loosened his grip.

She blinked against a sheen of tears that appeared in her eyes. "It's a radio signal, on its own b-battery. It provides location information when a plane crashes. I...flipped the switch when I was looking for my backpack."

Ben flashed back to the moment that she had looked at him through the cockpit with that weak, and now obviously guilty, smile. No wonder. "How long will it last before it wears down and dies?"

Defeat thickened her voice. "Two days, max. It's probably dead by now."

"But it worked well enough to get them this far." His fury deflated.

She nodded, and lost the battle against her tears. Twin tracks of liquid misery trickled down her cheeks. Ben released her, feeling her betrayal like a knife to his gut, and knowing he had no right to direct his wrath at her. She swayed as she rubbed her ears and temples, then swiped at her face with gloved hands.

Ben swore under his breath and weighed his options. The most pressing item on his agenda was to avoid the attention of authorities, *any* authorities. Civil Air Patrol spearheaded the attention of a host of authorities.

Less important, but critical in his decision-making, was his arm. It was healing without infection, a determination he'd made that morning before Lannis awakened. He'd cleaned the wound, replaced the jerry-rigged bandage of now-dried, bloodstained paper towels with a relatively clean rag he'd taken from the plane.

He wanted to get into town and call John. Put an end to this mess. Thanks to Lannis's gutsy move, that was now out of the question. Plan B—actually plan D or E by now—constituted heading into deep woods, and into deep hiding.

He didn't like it, but he could live with it.

Too bad Lannis had to come along, but until he could guarantee her safety in Louisville, it was still the best alternative.

~

Sheriff Sonny Dole's county straddled Tennessee's Great Smoky Mountain National Park, where plane crashes were more common than aircraft hidden like Easter eggs in the backcountry. The Civil Air Patrol ground crew flanked him at the entrance to an ancient barn, looking at a single-engine Cessna, N63438 emblazoned on its fuselage. Late-afternoon shadows plunged the makeshift hangar into darkness, requiring the use of powerful flashlights to adequately inspect the plane.

It appeared to be undamaged, its key perched conveniently on the pilot's seat, like it was waiting to be rolled out for use again. Tracks in the grass fit with the aircrew's assessment that it had been landed intentionally and pushed into the barn. There was no evidence of the pilot at the scene and no obvious trail led out of the clearing.

Sheriff Dole whistled. "Good work on the spotter's part. Not much visible from the air." He snagged a stalk of last year's grass and tugged it free. "You say the emergency signal—what did you call it?"

"The ELT, sir," the ground team commander answered. "Emergency Locator Transponder."

"Yeah, the ELT. It was reported midafternoon on Thursday?" He scratched his head, trying to put the facts in a cohesive timeline.

"Yes. We had ground teams out that evening, plus all day yesterday, but we didn't get a good hit on the location until this morning."

"This plane was reported missing and presumed stolen late yesterday from Louisville, Kentucky. Guess this is where it ended up." Sheriff Dole chewed on the dried grass.

"But the ELT was reported before that," said one of the cadets in the ground crew. "That doesn't make sense."

"Yeah, I know," said the sheriff. "It's possible it was stolen before it was missed. I'll check with Louisville about the timing." He tossed the stalk on the ground. "We'll get a fingerprint team in here tomorrow. It was probably used to transport drugs, or maybe positioned here to use for hauling marijuana out later in the growing season. We'll bring in the drug dog from Knoxville. Cover all the bases."

Sheriff Dole pulled out yellow crime scene tape, although there wasn't much need for it, and began to string it across the wide opening. He spoke over his shoulder as he tied off one end. "Kentucky can coordinate the retrieval in a few days. If the timing fits, it looks like you folks can call off your search."

Chapter Eleven

Dismay flooded Lannis. They'd been approaching more populated areas, as evidenced by the barn they'd stayed in last night, but Jack was leading her deeper into the wilderness. A pervasive sense of demoralization settled over her, sapping her already stretched emotional reserves.

They'd been hiking for hours, and the spurt of energy she'd gotten from breakfast dwindled and disappeared well before the sun reached its zenith. It was now midafternoon, she wasn't thinking clearly anymore, and she was tired. So very tired.

What had he said at the very beginning? The part about having nothing to lose was easy to recall—that was branded into her psyche—but wasn't there something else? Something about trusting him, that it had to be this way? Why?

Scrambling up a small rise after him, she tripped and fell heavily to her knees, catching herself with her hands. Her head drooped and tears dripped off the tip of her nose into the dirt.

Jack's booted feet appeared in front of her, and his strong hands grasped her arms, lifted her, then shifted to pick her up. Too drained to resist, she buried her face in his shoulder. He carried her a few steps and sat on a rock outcropping.

"I just want to go home," she said, her words muffled in his coat. "Please. I'm begging."

"Not yet." His voice was gentle, and regretful. "I don't blame you for everything you've done, but both our lives depend on staying out of sight for now. You'll have to hang in there for another few days."

Lannis felt confused, almost as if she should apologize for turning on the ELT and inviting the attention of the Civil Air Patrol. Mostly she just felt exhausted.

"Sleep." It came out slurred.

"Hmmm?"

"Sleep," she said more clearly. "I need to sleep."

"Okay, darlin'." He leaned back, settled himself against the hill. She welcomed the slide into unconsciousness.

~

Lannis woke in a drowsy haze, becoming aware in slow degrees of the steady rise and fall of Jack's chest under her cheek. Shadows covered the ground where sunlight had been. The air was chilly in the shade where they slept, and she'd burrowed under his coat for warmth. She flexed her arms, and nuzzled into his heat. Her left hand bumped something hard at the small of his back. Lazily, she explored its contours, then realized what she was feeling.

His gun. Startled, she willed herself to remain relaxed against him. Her hand was wrapped neatly around his gun *and she could get it*…if she didn't wake him in the process.

One of his arms was thrown possessively around her, but their legs were not intertwined. His other arm was flung out, palm up in the dry leaves. His breathing was regular and deep, the same way her ex-husband used to breathe when he was dead to the world. Cautiously, she raised her eyes to his face and saw her captor for the first time in the vulnerable state of sleep. Stubble giving way to a short, thickening beard, he looked peaceful and exhausted at the same time. His usual intimidating expression was gone, replaced by tranquility, complete with laugh lines that made him look years younger.

Lannis steeled herself against an undesired shift toward seeing him as a human being—even criminals could have a sense of humor, she told herself—and began to withdraw the gun from his belt, a millimeter at a time. Her breath hitched and she forced herself to mimic his slow, peaceful respirations. Anxiety shot through her, making her fingers tremble, and she stopped. Visualizing herself as a blanket tossed over his body, she released the tension in each muscle, one by one. Then, lightly grasping the butt of the gun with her fingertips, she began to tease it from the small of his back.

It took excruciating minutes to accomplish, and when the gun was free, she stopped. Calculated her next move. A light film of sweat formed on her forehead and immediately evaporated in the cold air. A shiver tried to take hold, but she suppressed it.

One chance. No room for failure. Gathering her courage, she scrubbed her face, hard, back and forth on his chest, and pulled the gun from beneath him, hoping he'd interpret the sensation as her, and nothing else. She slid the weapon behind her back and pushed at his chest with her other hand as she sat up.

Jack woke with her first move. He blinked the sleep out of his eyes and waited for her to disengage before shrugging his coat into place.

Lannis's mouth went dry.

He stretched, and leaned forward to rub his face. "Feel better?" he asked. He yawned, then glanced at her with a smile.

"Um, yeah," she said, heart hammering in her chest. Space. She needed a little more space or he'd relieve her of the gun before she had a chance to take advantage of it. She left the gun on the ground behind her and rubbed her eyes, then turned, snatching it to her belly as she scrambled to her feet. "Gotta find a bush."

She took several steps, then turned and pointed the gun at him, holding it with both hands. That helped control the shaking some. A little, anyway. Besides, that's what they always did on TV. She swallowed twice before she managed to squeak, "Jack. Put your hands where I can see them and don't try anything, or I'll use this."

Chapter Twelve

BEN GLANCED UP. His smile dissolved in disbelief. A lightning bolt of comprehension sliced through him. *My gun!* Her stance was ridiculous, but rather than amusement, he felt the sober chill of fear. She obviously didn't know how to handle a weapon, which multiplied the volatility of the situation. He could see the red dot indicating the safety was still on, but she just might be able to fumble it off before he got to her. Since he always kept a round chambered...

Cold sweat beaded on his brow. Every instinct screamed at him to attack, and every muscle tensed in readiness. Never mind the utterly suicidal nature of the urge—an urge rooted in the reality of his razor-thin escape from death by gunshot mere days ago. He shoved the memory aside even as his pulse kicked into triple-time.

He held out his hands, palms up, attempting to appear as nonthreatening as possible. "Okay, darlin', your call," he said, and waited. Her uncertainty made him jumpy, and he ruthlessly squelched his reaction. Otherwise they'd feed on each other's unease and the incident would spin out of control. Not that it was in control now. At all.

"Um..." Lannis backed away two more steps, then stopped. "Your knife. Toss it over here. Underhand." She pointed the gun at the ground between them, then brought it back up. Aimed it at his chest.

Sweat trickled down his temples. "Okay." Ben kept his tone conversational and let one hand creep toward the knife. He nodded at the gun. "It doesn't look like you know about firearms. You wanna talk about—"

"No." Lannis adjusted her grip on the gun, and the tremor of her hands transmitted to the barrel. "I may not know anything, but I bet I can figure out enough."

Ben froze. "You're right, Lannis." He flicked a glance at her. "Absolutely right. Do you want me to get the knife out? I'm not moving unless it's okay with you."

She nodded once, the movement jerky, and her tongue darted out to lick her lips. He slid the knife out in slow motion and tossed it gently into the grass. If she stooped to pick it up, he could rush her, kick the gun out of her hands. She sidled over and toed the knife away, then kicked it far out of his reach. She snatched it up, keeping the gun trained on him the whole time. He bit back a curse.

Let her go. He could catch up to her during the night. Regain his weapon. Regain control.

She hesitated, and he wondered if she dared get close enough to him to tie him up. If so, he could take her down without hurting either of them.

Then she pointed the gun at his feet. "Your shoes. Give me your shoes. Underhand."

His mind flashed to last night in the barn. Smart girl. He had to give her credit for effectiveness without bloodshed. She waved the gun at him again.

"Okay, okay," he muttered, and sat. He removed and tossed them to her as softly as he had the knife. This was going to slow him down, but he'd still prevail.

She swallowed, her nervousness feeding his. "Your socks, too."

Ben complied, clenching his jaw in frustration. Finished, he looked up at her and lifted an eyebrow. Silence surrounded them as he wriggled his toes in the cool air.

Lannis stuffed the socks in the shoes, and after a moment of one-handed fumbling, abandoned trying to tie them together. "Don't come after me. I might be sitting behind a tree waiting for you to show up." Her voice wavered, undermining her bravado. "So I can shoot you."

Ben willed his muscles to relax. They both knew she was bluffing, but he'd gain nothing by pointing that out. In fact, the sooner she took off, the quicker he'd be able to track and catch her. She glared at him, and still pointing the gun at him, backed into the woods. He heard her break into a run.

As soon as she disappeared, he scavenged leaves and bark, and dragged lengths of twine from the backpack. *Nice of her to have left me that.* He packed leaves around his feet and tied bark over the leafy cushion with bitter efficiency. In less than twenty minutes he was prepared.

He plunged into the forest after her.

Ben focused his anger on the task at hand. Tracking Lannis. Not that it was difficult. She'd left a path a blind man could waltz down. His makeshift footwear was adequate in spite of the blisters that were already forming, and he was making good time. Near dusk he heard her thrashing her way through brush and deadfall.

He'd already figured out that she was headed back to last night's barn and, with a mental review of the terrain, set off at an angle that would bring him out in front of her. In relative silence he went around a small hill, passed her, and found good concealment in the shadows of a thicket. She clambered up the hill, holding the gun in one hand and his shoes in the other, looking at the ground— probably trying not to trip—and panting from exertion. He had to admire her physical condition. She'd made it farther than he expected.

He waited until she was mere feet away, then stepped in front of her and smacked the gun from her hand. Her head snapped up. Shock, recognition, and fear flickered in her eyes. He snatched his shoes from her other hand, as he'd watched her stuff the knife in them along with his socks. She was breathing hard enough that she wouldn't be running far now. Even so, he eyed her with caution as he leaned over and retrieved the gun. A quick glance satisfied him that the safety was still on, and he replaced it in his belt at the small of his back.

Defeated and with perhaps a hint of relief in her expression, she reverted to sullenness. She sank down on a rock to catch her breath, and glanced at his feet. Her eyes widened at his footwear, and guilt flashed across her face.

Ben salvaged the twine, brushed leaves from between his toes, and eased his socks on. He grimaced at the tender areas, gingerly pulled on his shoes, and said, "Let's go." He nudged her, sending her in front of him this time. She glanced back at him, frequently. With wary eyes. And managed to keep a brisk pace in spite of her weariness.

He looked for a good campsite as they hiked, and found one before long, with a stream and a rocky overhang. He probed the corners with a stick to make sure no critters had claimed it first. "Why don't you get some dry wood for a fire, and I'll see what I can find for food," he said. As close to dark as it was, she wouldn't stray far. Yet he didn't trust her to *not* attempt another escape if the opportunity presented itself.

He wasn't going to let that happen. With a spurt of irritation, mostly at himself, he vowed she wasn't going to get within a yard of his gun again. Being relieved of his own weapon and having it aimed at him rankled. *You'd think I was a flaming rookie.* The only saving grace was that none of his peers would ever know.

~

Lannis returned with another load of deadwood and a bundle of mint. Jack sat motionless at the edge of a quiet pool of water, a bit upstream from the overhang. He'd separated the twine into strands, then tied them together to make a line, which swayed gently in the light current. She put down her burden in silence and sat, chin on knees, arms wrapped around them.

She reached down and twirled her shoelace with one finger, counting the days. One night in the shelter of branches that he'd made, and last night in the barn. That meant that this was Saturday, and she had eight days of vacation left. Snorting, she grabbed a piece of grass and began chewing on it. Some vacation! Actually, it had been more exciting than anything she could have possibly planned, but even so, she would have preferred mind-numbing boredom to this. Glancing up, she saw Jack watching her, one eyebrow raised in silent question. She felt a blush warm her face, and looked away.

"When do I get to go home?" she asked in a low voice.

His voice was a soft rumble. "Probably midweek."

"You're not just stringing me along, are you? I mean, how do I know that you're telling me the truth?" She looked up and caught his gaze, kept it this time.

"You'll just have to trust me." He studied her for another long moment. "I know you've got no basis for that, but it's the best I can do for now."

He looked at the fishing pole and frowned. "I guess we'll go vegetarian tonight. Sorry." He pulled the tin can he'd used that morning out of Lannis's backpack. It had gotten smashed during the day, so he bent it back to a semblance of its original shape, and tossed it to her. "I'll get a fire going while you get water. While you're at it, see if you can find any nuts the squirrels missed over the winter. I saw some walnut trees over there," he said, pointing toward the creek. He nudged a broadleaf plant that Lannis had known only as a weed with his boot. "If you see any more of these, bring them. They're edible."

By the time they finished a supper of boiled nuts and greens, it was full dark. The dying fire popped, its dance of light and shadows hypnotic. Lannis instinctively shrank from the utter blackness outside the circle of firelight, and leaned closer to the meager heat.

The flickering red glow illuminated the sharp planes of Jack's face from below. His eyes glittered beneath his cap, and reminded her of the first morning at the hangar. Otherwise they were fathomless shadows.

He'd had ample reason and opportunity to exact retribution for her escape attempt today, yet he'd done nothing but see to their needs. Her heart had nearly stopped when he'd caught and disarmed her, but he hadn't harmed her. For an outlaw, he exhibited an odd mix of ethics and empathy.

Fair or not, he still scared the starch out of her. She shivered again, and it had nothing to do with the temperature.

Chapter Thirteen

"CAN YOU FLY it out?"

Orvis glanced at Sheriff Dole, then looked at the mountains, contemplating the terrain. "Yeah. It'll be dicey." He walked toward the plane, which he'd thoroughly preflighted while Dole's deputy flattened the grass of the clearing with the ATV. A runway it was not, but Orvis had done the best he could to sway the odds toward him.

This was Sheriff Dole's third trip into the valley in three days, and the man looked tired. He'd spent yesterday on the investigation. The sheriff's office had taken fingerprints, which would take time to process. Knoxville's drug dog had been brought in and alerted, but it was a mild alert, as if the scent was old. A thorough search had turned up nothing more interesting than gum wrappers. The Air Force had suspended its role in solving the mystery of the pilot's whereabouts, as two more days of searches by the Civil Air Patrol and local ground crews had netted no leads.

"It vexes me to say it, but whoever dropped it in here did a good job. It's in as good condition as if it were still sitting on the ramp." He resisted the impulse to pace the field one more time, to recheck the takeoff distance. He'd already determined that it was sufficient. Barely.

"You sure you don't want us to put more fuel in it?" Sheriff Dole nodded toward the five-gallon cans of avgas they'd hauled in.

Orvis gave the man a wry grin. "No. I've got enough to get out and over to Pigeon Forge. Beyond that, it would just add weight, and being light is the only saving grace going for me." He mentally reviewed his plan. Short field takeoff procedure, hold a fairly tight radius turn, and spiral around the bowl of the valley to gain altitude. Doable, but only because the terrain rose gradually in the direction of the takeoff.

Light winds favored his route and kept unpredictable turbulence to a minimum. It was still chilly, a factor that improved performance of the aircraft. Both those advantages would disappear as the sun warmed the air.

A glance at the eastern ridge verified that the sun would break the horizon soon. He grimaced. *Better sooner than later.*

He walked to the plane, nodded to the sheriff, and strapped himself in. Moments later he lifted off, knowing the takeoff and ensuing climb looked deceptively easy to the small group standing watch near the ATVs. Orvis flew graceful arcs until he was well clear of the ridges, then banked the plane and turned northwest for the twenty-mile flight.

~

Jack stopped at the crest of a ridge and Lannis bumped into him, then rocked back a step. Wisps of white smoke lifted lazily from the chimney of a log cabin in the valley below them. Hunger had slowed her reflexes and dulled her thinking, but her heart began a slow thud at the sign of civilization. The lone building stood at the end of a dirt track, and a battered red pickup truck with homemade rails attached to its modified flatbed sat out front. A couple of long-eared hound dogs lounged on the porch. Out back, a plot of previously tilled soil lay fallow, awaiting spring planting.

Lannis's spirits lifted, bubbling up from some well of reserves she hadn't known existed. She and Jack had spent several days of relative calm, the product of a cautious truce and the cooperation necessary for survival. However, beyond securing the bare necessities in food and shelter, he hadn't appeared to have much of a plan, other than staying away from civilization and keeping her lost, both of which he accomplished with admirable success. She chafed at her dependence on him, but her energy level couldn't support another attempt at escape.

She'd broached the subject of going home a few times, and had been met with maddening platitudes. "Trust me," he'd said. "Be patient."

This was it, though. She knew it. *Home! I get to go home!*

Jack turned to face her and hesitated. His expression was uncharacteristically unguarded. Regret colored his features and softened his eyes. Stunned, she backed up another step. *He's not going to…* Betrayal shot through her heart like a spear. *He lied. He lied to me!*

She sucked in a quick breath and let loose a banshee scream.

~

Lannis's shriek pierced Ben's eardrums, and he winced even as he leapt and slapped his hand over her mouth.

"Stop it! Would it be too much for you to just trust me?" They were close to where he wanted to come out, but he didn't want to do it here, where they would be obvious. He wanted to get down the mountain, where they could have emerged from any number of trails and a variety of directions. The words had been on the tip of his tongue, but her scream derailed his explanation. "Can you listen to me?"

She bit him.

"Ow!" He snatched his hand back, but replaced it—more carefully—when she inhaled for another shriek. He yanked the same rag that had served as a blindfold out of his pocket, stuffed it in her mouth, then tied it behind her head. She didn't make it easy, thrashing and using her teeth. But he prevailed, and the only result of her struggle was to wedge the gag deeper between her teeth. She tried to shimmy out of his grip, and sliced her knee up between his legs. He deflected it with a quick, instinctive twist of his hips. Breathing hard, he grabbed her shoulders and shoved her against a tree.

"Decision time. Go in front of me and keep your hands where I can see them, or get tied up again."

Her eyes flashed, and she cursed him from beneath the gag. The individual words were a mumble, but her meaning was crystal clear. She raised a fist as if to slug him.

He gave a humorless laugh. "I should've known. You always pick the hard way, don't you?" He pulled the twine from his pocket and snagged her hands, binding them with ruthless efficiency, and wondering if she would notice that he'd purposely given her enough slack to allow for both balance and comfort. He stepped back, anger hardening his heart. She brought her bound hands up and clawed at the gag, then yanked at the twine.

Suddenly aware that her efforts were unsuccessful and destined to continue that way, her rage faded to despair. She sank to her knees and rocked back on her heels, head bowed. She blinked her eyes several times, and squeezed her eyelids shut. A moment later, she lifted a heavy gaze to him. A sheen of tears shimmering in those bottomless chocolate-brown eyes almost fooled him into feeling pity for her. Then he realized they were tears of anger, not distress.

"If—*if*—you behave for the next sixty minutes, I'll untie your hands." He used his cop voice, grim and implacable. Raising an eyebrow, he waited for her response. She searched his eyes for a moment, then nodded her defeat.

He grasped her arms and pulled her to her feet. With a pointed look at his watch, he directed her along the crest of the ridge, and pushed her ahead of him. She rubbed her tears away with the back of her hands, and stumbled forward.

~

Exactly sixty minutes later, after following his instructions with excruciating care—some of which Lannis suspected had been given for the sole purpose of demonstrating her level of compliance—Jack stopped her. Without fanfare he untied her hands, muttering under his breath at the stubborn knots, which her yanking had compressed into pebbles of fiber. For a moment she thought he'd use his knife on them, but one strand loosened and he worked it free. Finally he pulled the bindings loose and stuffed the twine into his pocket. He grasped her chin and made her look at him.

"No more funny stuff, or this goes right back on."

Lannis nodded against his grip, and rubbed her wrists. It was more out of reflex than need, because he'd tied them over the top of her gloves, so her skin was not abraded. After a searching look, he dropped his hand. She resisted the urge to untie the gag and rip it from her mouth, knowing that he would do exactly as he said.

"That way," he said, and pointed.

She went ahead of him, taking care to keep her hands in his view.

They descended the ridge to follow the dirt road, its rutted track feeling like an interstate highway after days of hiking rough terrain. Eventually it connected with another road, this one paved. They had walked on the unimproved road, but paralleled the paved one by about thirty feet. Vehicles roared past infrequently, their engines seeming overly loud after days of silence in the forest.

Lannis forced herself to ignore the proximity of the cars and followed Jack's curt instructions to the letter. After the last few days, she'd begun to think he wasn't as harsh as he'd been at the start, but her short-lived attempt to defy him had disabused her of that notion. His stony insistence on her total compliance was both terrifying and familiar. Her rebellion had drained her, physically and emotionally. She retreated to a place of numb, robotic functioning, thinking no further than how to carry out Jack's next instruction.

Chapter Fourteen

BEN TUGGED ON Lannis's coat, stopping her. She turned and stood dutifully. He untied the gag, stuffed the soggy cloth back in his pocket, and wiped his hand on his jeans. A smear of dirt marred her cheek. He lifted a hand to wipe it away. She grimaced, but didn't flinch or resist as he rubbed it clean with his thumb. Her skin was soft, and a wave of regret at her involvement in his situation rolled through him.

He glanced across the road at a Forest Service trailhead, then back at her, taking in her uncharacteristic apathy. "We're going to head into town. Follow my lead, and don't speak unless I tell you to." He paused a heartbeat, waiting for a reaction, and when she offered none, he continued. "You won't get away with anything, so don't try. As unhappy as you are now, it'll be much worse if you try to cross me at this point. Understood?"

Still no response. He tipped her head up with a finger beneath her chin until she had to meet his gaze. "Do you understand?" He saw a spark of misery flicker, then fade to dullness. She gave him a nearly imperceptible nod and he dropped his hand, hating what he was doing to her. With any luck, her part would be over in twenty-four hours, forty-eight at the most.

When he got the rest of the mess sorted out—and he deemed it safe—he'd seek her out to try to make reparations for circumstances that had hogtied him nearly as much as they had her. He turned her toward the road in the now dwindling light.

"Let's go, darlin'." His voice was quiet.

~

Bewilderment settled over Lannis like a soft cloak. Jack's anger, cold and contained and cruel, had dominated his attitude since she'd bucked his control, but something that looked a lot like sadness flitted across his face just now. Mental snapshots of him flashed through her mind, snippets of his sheltering, feeding, caring for her over the last several days. *So, which one is he?* Too weary to sort through the puzzle, she simply did as he said and dragged herself down the incline and across the ditch to the road.

She needed sleep. Or a drink. Like maybe a fifth of tequila, or a bottle of wine. Or two. The thoughts popped into her mind, and she couldn't say they were unwelcome. Yearning slammed into her for the numbing relief booze could deliver. She'd reached her limit, couldn't go on. In direct contradiction to her thoughts, her feet kept putting themselves one in front of the other.

Night fell, and she walked. Jack pulled her off the road every time a car approached. Lannis began to anticipate stolen moments of respite as she crouched next to him in the shadows. She closed her eyes against the glare of headlights to retain her night vision, and once she thought they'd slept for a while, or maybe only she had. He'd never made her hike after dark, and she lost her sense of time, although the moon tracked its silent path across the sky. The night stretched on until it seemed there'd never been anything but darkness.

Her legs trembled and hunger gnawed through her spine. Jack's hand fell on her shoulder, but instead of pulling her into the trees, he stepped out into the roadway and waved down what turned out to be a rattletrap pickup. Lannis was so tired she hadn't heard it coming. Brake lights glowed and the driver, a man with a shock of unruly white hair under a University of Tennessee Volunteers ball cap, leaned over and rolled down the window.

"You folks got trouble?" Concern and a healthy touch of caution colored his voice.

"Hey, thanks for stopping. I need a ride to town, to get my wife to a doctor. We were camping up the Wild Turkey Holler trailhead and she fell." Jack gestured vaguely at the road behind them. "Bumped her head, and hasn't been acting quite right. Would you mind?"

The driver waved them in. "Sure, no problem. Glad I can help." He looked at Lannis with open curiosity, and she was suddenly aware of the sorry state of her clothing and filthy hair. She felt a furious blush heat her face. She threw a dagger glance at Jack, who took her elbow and helped her into the truck. Sliding onto the seat next to her, he draped a possessive arm around her. Stiffening, she opened her mouth, and received an immediate warning squeeze to her left shoulder. Jack leaned in front of her and extended his right hand to the Good Samaritan for an introductory handshake.

"Greg and Linda Johnson. Appreciate your help, sir." The warning pressure on Lannis's shoulder continued. She snapped her mouth shut and turned to look at him. The smile on his face did not reach the ice in his eyes. She faced forward, fists clenched.

Handshake accomplished, he sat back.

"Pleased to meet you. You kin to any of the Johnsons around here? I'm Bud Johnson, out of Ralph's line," the old man replied, curiosity brightening his features.

"No, sir, my relatives are all out of the Vermont area."

Bud nodded, then squinted at Jack and said, "How come you folks don't have a vehicle? Or gear?" His eyes narrowed and his look turned suspicious.

"My friend dropped us off here yesterday. Linda and I have always wanted to hike the Appalachian Trail, but we don't have time to do it all at once, so we like to pick up a piece of it here and there." Jack scratched his nose and glanced at Lannis with an expression that combined distress and affection. "He was going to pick us up Friday at the other end. We left our gear at the campsite. I'll go back and get it once I'm sure Linda's okay."

Lannis shook her head. He sounded convincing, even to her, and not one bit of it was true. It was such a good story that anything she said to contradict him could be attributed to a head injury. Glancing at Bud, she saw that he bought it hook, line, and sinker. She dropped her head back and closed her eyes. Jack's arm urged her closer, inviting her to rest her head on his shoulder. She resisted for a moment, then gave up and leaned on him, sliding into an exhausted, restless doze. Unable to drift into a deep sleep, she remained dimly aware of the steady rumble of male voices talking about sports, the gentle rocking of the truck on the road, and Jack's solid warmth.

What felt like only minutes later, he shook her awake. "Here we are, darlin'. Come on, Linda. Wake up. Let's get on into the hospital."

Linda? She sat up, bewildered. *Who's Linda?* Hospital?

It all clicked into place as Jack helped her out of the truck with syrupy-sweet concern, thanking Bud again for his "kind assistance." He pointed her up the walkway to the emergency entrance of a small hospital. Bud watched for a moment, apparently to make sure she would be able to get into the building on her own two feet, then roared off. A cloud of black smoke indicating a badly maintained, oil-burning engine hovered in the lights. She wrinkled her nose at the smell, then gasped as Jack swiftly changed direction and led her away from the hospital.

"Hey!"

He hustled her around the side of the building before she was fully awake.

"What are you doing? Where are you taking me?" Her voice rose as she pulled away from him. "I want to go home! You said I could go home!"

"Hush, darlin'." His voice was a soft murmur. "Soon. I promise." He reestablished his grip on her, and started down the sidewalk. Streetlights created oases of artificial light and leached the normal color from their skin. Jack loomed as a ghostly shadow next to her. The sudden and abstract return to civilization threw Lannis off-balance.

They came to a main street, and Jack guided her to an alley behind several small motels. At the third motel he grunted in satisfaction and led her around front. He procured a room, rattled off another set of phony names, and pulled a wad of bills from the pocket of his jeans, all the while keeping a weather eye on her. She blinked in the bright light of the lobby, hanging back, ashamed of her unkempt state. Smiling, he thanked the owner, saying something about "the worst camping trip ever," and how "a shower would be so welcome for his sweet wife," or some such bullshit. He led Lannis toward a room on the end of the one-story Mom-and-Pop motel, turned the key, and held the door open for her.

~

Hot shower. Ben's skin crawled with filth, as did his scalp, and if he'd had enough energy, his fingers would itch in anticipation of the pleasure of getting clean. *Long, hot shower.* He planned to use an entire bar of those little motel soaps on himself. He'd be a gentleman, though, and let Lannis go first.

And food. Hot food. Real food. His mouth watered in anticipation. Caught up in his fantasy, he didn't notice Lannis's hesitation, at least not immediately. Eager to get settled, he made an impatient, abrupt gesture, then looked, really looked at her.

Her exhaustion had vanished. She stilled, barely breathing, and stood ramrod stiff. Her eyes were unfocused, the pupils dilated, and waves of intense distress radiated from her. She shook her head, hard, then lifted one hand and fisted it defensively. Her other hand clutched the front of her coat. She stepped back and shook her head again.

Ben frowned. What in blazes was going on with her? He crooked an eyebrow and extended his hand. She glanced at it, then back at him, and retreated another step.

"No." Her voice was low, guttural. "*No.*"

She's going to bolt. He didn't understand why. Or rather, why at this particular moment. He sensed her gathering her muscles to flee, and in the split second before she could, he closed the gap between them. Wrapped his arms around her. Contained her with the care he'd give a fragile egg. He knew she'd fight him if she felt restrained. He rubbed her back and, after a moment, rested his chin on her head. She was rigid with what he could only assume was…fear? Why here? Why now? They'd both been through far worse over the past week, and she'd never reacted like this. He followed his instincts, murmuring soft sounds of wordless comfort. Eventually the tension in her muscles diminished by small degrees.

"You okay? Come on darlin', come on in." He turned and propelled her toward the door. She resisted for a moment, then moved slowly, with obvious reluctance. "You'll feel better after a shower." They entered the austere room and he closed the door. The click of the latch echoed loudly. Lannis flinched, her entire body jerking at the noise. Her face went one shade paler, emphasizing the dark circles under her eyes and giving her a haunted air.

Ben's bewilderment deepened.

Chapter Fifteen

LANNIS STRUGGLED for composure and scrunched her eyes shut. She took a shaky breath, then faced the room. One bed. Queen-sized. A small television with rabbit ears, the set bolted to the chipped pressed-wood dresser. A little bubble of hysteria fizzed in her belly and she almost laughed. She hadn't seen rabbit ears for years. No cable, then. As if it mattered. A telephone.

A telephone!

Jack had had the same thought about the phone, because he was unplugging it, then stowed the cord in her backpack. He shot an appraising glance at her, but didn't voice the questions in his eyes. He tipped his head toward the bathroom and said, "Go on, you'll feel a hundred percent better when you're cleaned up."

Woodenly she moved past him and peered into the cramped, utilitarian room. No window. That's what he'd been looking for when he'd taken her down the alley behind all the other motels.

"I can't stand putting these clothes back on." The thought popped into her head and she spoke without thinking.

Grimacing, he nodded agreement. "Yeah, I know. I'll run out to Wal-Mart and get us some clothes after we eat. I'm going to order a pizza while you're in the shower. What kind do you like?" She pressed a hand to her empty belly, and he laughed.

"Anything except spicy sausage and anchovies."

"Sounds good. It should be here when you get out." He shooed her toward the bathroom with a wave of his hand. "Take your time." He sounded envious.

The lure of clean towels, thin as they were, and warm, soapy water overrode Lannis's antipathy toward the situation. She took a deep breath, stepped into the bathroom, and closed the door firmly. It didn't have a lock. She snorted in disgust. It stuck at one point and she had to push hard to engage the latch. That was the most security she could manage against Jack. However, she was out of his sight for the first time in six days—except for the ill-fated escape attempt—and she'd make the most of the precious moments of privacy. She stripped her clothes off and piled them on the toilet tank. Though they were unbearably filthy, she couldn't stomach the thought of picking them off the floor to put them back on.

She turned the spigot on and didn't even wait for it to heat all the way. Tepid water sluiced over her, rinsing away a week's worth of grime and a week's worth of strain. A shuddering exhale surprised her, and a sob burbled up. A torrent of emotion caught her off guard, and she buried her face in her hands, accepting the comfort of the water on her skin as she gave in to tears.

Lannis wept, muffling the sounds and trying desperately to rein in her tears. She did *not* want Jack to notice, to investigate, to ask questions. Nor did she want to acknowledge the vulnerability that had triggered the crying jag. It took her several minutes, but she battled the tears into submission, then grabbed the soap. She lathered and scrubbed and rinsed every square inch of her body. Then did it again.

On her third cycle, her skin as red as her eyes and as raw as her emotions, Jack rapped on the door. Lannis jumped, and swiped angrily at her eyes. She couldn't erase the evidence, but she'd try.

"You okay in there, Lannis?"

"Yeah." Her voice cracked, and she cleared her throat. "I'm almost done." She thrust her face under the cascade of steamy water again, and thought she'd never take hot water, showers, and soap for granted again. Ever. It felt so good that it was hard to tear herself away from it.

However, her weeping had unleashed a yearning for booze that magnified into an ache, a craving that was physical, nearly doubling her over. She could definitely tear herself away from the shower for a drink. Anything alcoholic to blot out the anxiety boiling up inside her.

And the memories. Memories from four years ago, memories once safely buried, memories exhuming themselves in spite of her best efforts to keep them locked away. Yeah, she needed a drink. Or six. Preferably six. At least six.

Wonder what Jack would say if I told him I need to go to an AA meeting? Somehow she didn't think that would fit into his plans. Her lips trembled. Lannis pressed them together in a battle to contain the flood of emotion. But the tears won.

~

Ben paid for the pizza, put the box on the dresser, and knocked on the bathroom door again. "Lannis, are you all right in there?" He heard a muffled sound he couldn't quite identify. He put his ear to the door. "Lannis?" The muffled sound was more distinct now, and recognizable. She was crying, and trying to keep him from hearing.

Aw, shit. He hung his head. He'd rather face corrupt cops and guns than a crying woman, but since the cause of this woman's tears lay at his feet, he girded himself to do the right thing. "You want to talk, Lannis?"

"No." Her voice was thick with emotion, but the word was clipped.

"It's almost over. With any luck, you'll be home this time tomorrow, or Thursday for sure. Trust me. Please." He ran a hand through his hair in frustration. "Someday I'll explain it all to you, but for now it's too dangerous for you to know more."

Lannis hiccupped. A moment passed in relative silence. "Right." She didn't sound convinced.

Ben supposed he didn't blame her. "Pizza's still hot. If you're not too waterlogged, you'll feel better after you eat." The faucet squeaked and the flow of water stopped.

The distinctive aromas of yeast, cheese, and Italian spices made his salivary glands churn into overdrive, and he went out to grab a slice while he waited for Lannis to get out of the bathroom.

The anticipated pleasure of the first bite faded as Ben thought about the mess he'd dragged her into. Inadvertently, to be sure. Nevertheless, it weighed on him.

How was he going to keep her safe after she went home?

Chapter Sixteen

THE BATHROOM DOOR finally squealed open. Ben glanced up from the television. He'd been watching a local station out of Knoxville, looking for any mention of the plane, crooked Louisville police, turncoat DEA agents, or drug kingpins. He was heartened to see he wasn't in the news. As earth-shattering as the events had been for him, though, they probably didn't command enough clout to hit the airwaves this far away.

Lannis emerged, running a hand through her hair, fluffing it in a distinctively feminine move. She wore her flannel shirt—buttoned—and carried the T-shirt she'd worn for a week. A towel wrapped around her waist and tucked into itself served as a skirt. Her eyes were red and puffy, and she pointedly refused to make eye contact.

She tossed the shirt on the other chair and took a piece of still-warm pizza. Bringing it to her nose, she closed her eyes and inhaled before taking a bite. Her fingers trembled as she ate. After the second slice she slowed, and put one hand on her belly. She sat on the edge of the bed, tugging at the towel to keep her legs covered.

Ben unfolded himself from the plastic chair and turned the TV off. "Hey, Lannis." He stretched and glanced at her. She wasn't going to like this one bit, but it would be best to get it over with. "My turn." She looked at him quizzically. He gestured toward the steamy room behind her, and saw the moment understanding dawned. She didn't move a muscle, but somehow shrank into herself. Since he was between her and the door, there was no place for her to run. She didn't look like she was up to fighting, but he couldn't take anything for granted where she was concerned. "I have to restrain you." He kept his voice neutral.

She shook her head, her expression turning trapped.

A note of cajoling laced his words. "There's no other way."

"I...I won't run." Her gaze shifted left, then back to his. "I promise."

Ben sighed. There was her tell again. He shook his head regretfully. "Just for a few minutes." He slipped his belt off and motioned for her to come close.

Of course she defied him, and he grabbed the bedspread at the same time he reached for her. Before she had a chance to realize what he was doing, he billowed the coverlet around her, wrapped her and neatly tucked her arms in, securing them in the folds.

"Hey," she said, but he didn't pause. He drew his belt snug around her bundled form, just above her elbows. She tried to kick him in the shins, but the bulk of the bedspread deadened the force of the blow. Tipping her onto the bed, he reached across it for her backpack and pulled the phone cord out. Struggling furiously now, Lannis made difficult work of it for him, and Ben had to use his body to contain her legs. Three loops later, he had her knees tied and stood, breathing hard. She glared up at him, both livid with anger and desperate with fear.

"I won't be long. I won't gag you if you stay quiet, but I'll be back out here before you draw a second breath if you scream." He dropped the rag on top of the dresser, next to the television where she could see it. "Your choice. You have total control over that." He waited for a moment and, when she remained silent, headed for the bathroom, leaving the door open.

~

Lannis wriggled, testing his knots, and tried to work her hands loose from the bedspread's folds. She realized quickly that she couldn't free herself and muttered a curse under her breath. She'd thought she was cried out, but tears welled in her eyes again.

She heard clothes rustling, the soft hiss of his zipper, his shoes as they thumped on the bathroom floor. He started the shower, and the pipes clanked as the water heated.

He was naked, and only a wall separated him from her. She tried to tell herself Jack wouldn't hurt her, not that way, not with his body. He'd had plenty of opportunity, but hadn't. She chided herself, saying that getting naked was required for taking a shower. That she'd been naked and vulnerable a few minutes ago and he'd not threatened her.

Her breath came quicker, shorter, and suddenly there wasn't enough oxygen, enough air.

The memories she'd stuffed back into their dark hole crawled out again. They crept, and once they breached her defenses, they seethed and swelled with unleashed power. They dragged her greedily into their sinister gloom, filled her lungs with malevolent destruction, suffocated her. Terror flared, then flamed. She panicked. Hyperventilated. She closed her eyes and made a desperate attempt to control her response.

Breathe! Slower. Deeper. Can't scream. *He'll gag me…won't…won't survive that.* Breathe. Nothing else mattered. Nothing.

Nothing.

She opened her eyes to prove that her demons were inside her, not flesh and blood ghouls—they weren't—and blocked out everything but the blank, dead TV screen. And sought a mindless state, an alternate reality.

~

Ben pulled his grungy jeans on and grimaced at the stiff, dirt-encrusted fabric, then shrugged into his shirt and stepped out of the bathroom. Lannis lay quietly on the bed where he had left her. *Well, there's a first.* For a change she didn't fight. He'd truly expected to find her on the floor after struggling hard enough to require another shower.

"Okay, darlin', let me get you undone," he said. She didn't respond, which didn't surprise him much. He figured she'd be plenty mad at him and the silent treatment was fairly appropriate. *Okay, more than appropriate.* Guilt tapped at him, and irritated, Ben wondered what other options he had. The only ones he could come up with guaranteed death—his, or hers, or both.

He sat, and his weight on the mattress rolled Lannis slightly toward him. He reached behind her to undo the knots. Glancing down at her face, his motions stilled as he realized that her silent calm could better be described as a trance. Her eyes were wide and unfocused, pupils dilated. Her face was pale, her breathing shallow and rushed, her skin warm and dry. His own mouth going suddenly dry, he shook her shoulder.

"Lannis."

No flicker of eyes or eyelids. No change in breathing. No indication that she even recognized his presence. Alarmed, he tried to come up with a medical reason that she'd be awake but nonresponsive. He hadn't hurt her. Had he? His mind replayed the struggle of restraining her. *No.* He hadn't struck her; her head wasn't injured. A small frisson of relief unfurled that he wasn't responsible for this…this trance. Something caused it, though, and he started with the most obvious. She couldn't be epileptic and still be able to get a medical certificate to fly airplanes. Or diabetic. This almost looked like shock, except her skin would be cool and clammy if it were shock.

He continued to undo her bonds, and call her name as he began sorting through his experiences for an explanation. Lots of what she had done was logical for someone who had been kidnapped, although her persistence and fiery spirit in resisting and attempting to escape had been more intense than he'd expected. But persistence and that fiery spirit were characteristic of her responses, even in defeat.

Until this moment.

"Lannis, darlin'." Still no response. The way she looked right through him was downright spooky.

What had changed to bring on this complete withdrawal from her surroundings? He'd restrained her before and she'd been unhappy about it, but she'd handled it.

Her response to the motel room formed in his mind's eye. That hadn't made any sense, but he hadn't thought about it much at the time, attributing it to accumulation of stress and fatigue.

Then the crying jag in the shower. She hadn't lost control that thoroughly before the motel room, either. She'd expressed many emotions throughout her ordeal. Anger, a whole range of it, from silent jaw clenching to volcanic eruptions. Fear, of course, and some bouts of tears when he'd blindfolded her or when exhaustion got the best of her, but she'd managed to get past them and go on. She'd had subdued moments of struggle to compose herself, but never anything like this.

This looked like a total disconnect of her mind from reality. The image of one of his buddies from the Army popped into his head. Don Porter had undergone treatment for post-traumatic stress disorder after being pinned down without help in a particularly vicious gun battle in Afghanistan.

Post-traumatic stress? Triggered by the motel room in particular? Stunned, he finished untying and unbuckling her limp, unresisting body. Ben left the bedspread loosely cocooned around her.

A light sweat beaded on his brow as he wondered if she'd made an irrevocable leap off the deep end. *Lord, I could use some help here...* He stroked her arm and murmured reassurances, and kept calling her name. He'd heard once that hearing was the last sense to go with anesthesia, and the first to return during recovery. Between that and touch, maybe he could keep her grounded, bring her back.

If not, he'd call 911, his own situation be damned. Several minutes passed. Her breathing deepened and evened out, and her color began to return. At long last, she blinked and focused groggy eyes on his face. A bit of the tension flowed from his muscles.

"You're out of the shower," she mumbled. "Sleep. I gotta sleep."

"Lannis, darlin', are you okay?" He brushed a lock of hair away from her forehead.

Twin furrows appeared on her forehead. She looked confused. "Yeah. Why?" She squinted at him.

"No reason. You were just kind of out of it." He rubbed her shoulders. "You want to sleep for a while, or eat?"

Her eyes drifted closed. She took a deep, shuddering breath, and fell asleep the same way she had the first night, melting into the bed with the exhale. Ben sighed. He stood and opened the box of pizza, then took a piece and bit into it. For all his anticipation, it tasted like the cardboard it came in, but he chewed and swallowed anyway. Between bites, he reloaded his gun and stashed it under his pillow.

When he'd eaten enough to chase the shakes away, he stripped his filthy clothes off and pulled the bedspread off Lannis. She made a tiny sound of protest but slept on while he worked the sheet out from under her legs, covered her, then tucked it deep under the mattress on her side of the bed. He crawled in on top of the sheet next to her, and pulled the spread up over them both. She snuggled into her pillow and shoved her hips back, into his belly. He bit back a groan. Awake or asleep, she didn't make it easy for him.

He fell asleep in the middle of the thought.

Chapter Seventeen

Ben snapped awake, instantly alert, every muscle tense but motionless, ready to fight. He didn't know if it was sound or movement that woke him, but the sense of threat that accompanied it was real. He palmed his gun in silence but didn't take the safety off. Yet. It would make too much noise.

Or maybe it was the silence that woke him. The hairs on his forearms rose. He didn't hear Lannis's soft, regular breathing. Her body heat radiated through the sheet, and a detached part of his brain noted that she wasn't overly warm, wasn't feverish. He slid his free hand to her thigh and felt tiny quivers in her muscles.

Suddenly she exhaled, a husky mewling sound, and moved restlessly. She elbowed his hand away, then thrashed, tangling her feet in the bedcovers. Raspy, keening moans convinced him quickly that she still slept, that it was her that had wakened him. *A nightmare.* Ben leaned up on one arm and gently touched her cheek. "Lannis." She jerked awake with a gasp and twisted violently away from his touch, jolting the entire bed with the force of her movement.

"Lannis, darlin', you're having a bad dream." Ben kept his voice calm, his tone comforting. "You're safe. Wake up." He switched the lamp on. She stared at him wild-eyed, without recognition for a long moment. Then relief flooded her face as she transitioned from the dream's web.

"Uh…"

He could almost see her scramble to rebuild her defenses. She retreated into wariness. "Why don't you get up and wash your face?" He stood and put some space between them.

She untangled her feet, re-tucked the towel around her waist, threw the covers back and padded to the sink. She sighed, the sound weary and sadder than anything he'd heard from her. The faucet squeaked as she turned the hot water on and saturated a washcloth in steaming water. She buried her face in the cloth and stood immobile, then did it again.

Head bowed, she folded and refolded the washrag in a not very well-camouflaged bid to avoid him. Finally she turned toward Ben, glanced at him, then at the floor. Dark shadows made the skin below her eyes look bruised. Her hands fisted, and Ben didn't think she knew she was doing it. She looked exhausted. Haunted. Vulnerable. But she lifted her chin, and after a brief hesitation, took a deep breath and straightened her back.

Compassion rose in him, and this time he didn't fight it.

~

Lannis hadn't had a nightmare for nearly a year. It was one more straw on the back of a camel staggering under an impossible load. Jack pinned her with his stare, a brooding expression on his face. He looked like he wanted to talk, and she wasn't about to accommodate him. She brushed past him, climbed into bed, and pulled the bedspread over her head. She turned her back to him, and waited in tense silence. Lingering scents of yeast crust and tomato sauce made her mouth water, and her stomach clenched. She ignored the pizza. Tried to.

Jack stayed motionless for several seconds, but then he moved with the catlike, near-silent grace she'd become attuned to. The mattress creaked as he sat on the bed behind her, leaned against the headboard, and rested a hand lightly on her head. His palm warmed her scalp. She sensed his strength. And his restraint.

What an odd quality for a hijacker, a kidnapper, a criminal. Mentally she shook her head, trying to clear her thoughts. She was so tired she felt drunk. Off-balance, sluggish, uncoordinated, and unfocused, but without the numbness that was her reward when she drank. She needed a drink. Badly.

Afraid of another nightmare, she lay still, apprehension keeping her tense, but she couldn't maintain that level of vigilance for long. Exhaustion claimed her against her will. Blessedly, her sleep was dreamless this time.

~

Lannis woke to the sounds of water running at the sink. Jack was up. She could hear him working soap into a lather, washing, rinsing. She blinked sleep-bleary eyes, getting her bearings. For once, he was not between her and the door. It was just feet away from her, and he was across the room from it, his back to her. Her pulse kicked up. If she could get up, muffle the sound of the chain being removed, muffle the sound of the door being opened, she could get out. Get away.

She forced herself to remain relaxed, her breathing slow and deep. Let him assume she was still asleep. Muscles demanded to be stretched, but she resisted the urge.

The opportunity was only spare moments long. Lannis slithered from the bed, hoping the mattress wouldn't squeak this time, hoping he wouldn't look in the mirror, hoping he wouldn't turn, and scuttled barefooted to the door. She left the towel in the bed; she didn't have enough hands to deal with it. Escape trumped modesty.

She used her body to contain the sound of the chain and unhooked it, setting the links vertically so they wouldn't swing against the frame of the door. Then she unlocked the door. It made the softest *snick* and she winced. Her palm was slippery with the sweat of fear, so she grasped the knob tightly and began to pull the door open. Her heart was hammering so loudly she was sure he could hear it.

Out of nowhere, Jack's hand slapped the door above her head and slammed it shut with enough force to break her grip on the knob. A yelp of surprise escaped her before Lannis could prevent it. He twisted her arm behind her back, threw the dead bolt, replaced the chain, then frog-marched her to the sink. Her gaze flew to meet his in the mirror.

Jack's cheeks were flushed, his eyes sparking with fury. His grip tightened. "Look at yourself, Lannis." His words were clipped and his voice barely controlled.

Unable to defy him, she looked. He was dressed in his jeans, shirt on but unbuttoned, droplets of water on his face and in his beard. Her shirt rode up, threatening to expose vulnerable female flesh. She'd been willing to run that risk a moment ago, but no longer. She grabbed at the tail of the shirt with her free hand and tugged it down. The difference in their sizes, a difference she'd understood from the beginning, was graphically demonstrated in their images. A full head taller, half again as broad in the shoulders, he dwarfed her.

Her lower lip began to tremble.

"Why do you make everything so hard? I made a promise. I'll keep it." Frustration roughened his voice. "Look at me!"

Holding on to defiance like a lifeline, she lifted her chin and met his eyes in the mirror.

His mouth was set in a line of unyielding determination. "Have I harmed you? Other than the bruise when I thought you were a guy?" He didn't wait for a response. "No! I've taken care of you, and anything that's happened has either been an accident or a product of your resistance and lack of trust. *What triggered the nightmare?* Answer me!"

His question stole the breath from her lungs. *No!* She didn't want to think about it, didn't want to let it have more power than it already did. Saying the words would make it *real*—and she couldn't deal with that.

Feeling like a worm trapped on a hook, hysteria began to build in her gut. Lannis found a reservoir of anger she didn't know she had, and pushed the panic aside. She latched on to rage in a desperate bid to deflect his attention. "I hate you!" Her anger finally erupted, bringing a flush to her cheeks. "You kidnapped me, and you've controlled every move I've made for the last week. I can't even pee without your permission! You don't think I should have a nightmare over that?"

He laughed, but there was no humor in it. "Not buying it, Lannis. I know all that, but that's not what's gone on with you over the last few hours. Why did the motel set you off?"

Stricken, she realized that he'd put more of the pieces together than she'd given him credit for. She opened her mouth, then closed it, with the absurd thought that she looked like a fish now, instead of the bait.

He shook her again. "The truth, Lannis. Don't try to make something up."

She closed her eyes against his scrutiny. He wouldn't back down—she'd learned that much about him—and he'd maneuvered her into a corner. She couldn't think of an alternative other than what he wanted. What he demanded. The truth.

Her defenses shattered. Tears escaped in spite of her efforts to contain them, and she struggled to swallow over the enormous lump that formed in her throat. "I...I...was...r-r-raped." Her voice dropped to a whisper on the last word. The only thing holding her upright was Jack's grip.

Raw and razor sharp, pain ripped through her belly, leaving her emotions exposed and naked. Lannis crumpled, shame stealing her strength.

Chapter Eighteen

BEN FELT LIKE he'd taken a sledgehammer to the gut. He knew the statistics, and had no use for men who forced themselves on women. He'd never knowingly encountered a victim, though. Lannis tried to pull away from him, tried to curl in on herself. Ben refused to let her withdraw. He pulled her fists around his back, and she drew him close with her own tension. He wondered if she'd ever talked to anyone about it.

"You don't have to face it by yourself anymore." He half carried her to the plastic chair and sat, pulling her onto his lap. "Hush, darlin'." He snagged the bedspread and tugged it over her. She buried her face in his shoulder and wept. Gulping sobs shook her whole body.

Gradually her crying subsided, and she melted against him, probably out of exhaustion rather than trust, but that was okay. Touch, capable of providing comfort at the most fundamental level, also carried the potential to re-traumatize her. Even though touch was crucial in giving him a chance to breach her defenses, he wouldn't, couldn't let it hurt her.

"Have you ever told anyone, Lannis?" He purposely kept his voice low. Neutral.

A negative shake of her head was his answer. So she hadn't reported it, which was more common than not. He ruthlessly tamped down a spurt of rage. Kentucky didn't have a statute of limitations on felonies. She could still file charges, but without corroborating evidence of some sort... "How long ago did it happen?"

"Almost four years ago. July," she mumbled.

Ben worked his handkerchief free and gave it to her. She blew her nose, trying to wrap her arms around herself afterward. He snagged them and pulled them around his body instead, pulled her back to his chest.

"Tell me what happened." It was a command, the words steel beneath velvet. When she shook her head, he said, "Yes. You need to understand that you're not alone anymore, and someone else needs to hear your story for that to happen." Regret laced his words. "I'm here, I care, and I've caused you more distress than you deserve. Not letting it out at this point, well, it'll fester, cause more pain in the long run. Let me help you carry the burden." He waited. Lannis was still for so long he began to wonder if she'd fallen asleep, except for her breathing. Shallow, nearly silent, as though she was attempting to vanish, trying to render her very self invisible.

Then she took a shaky breath.

"He was a transient pilot—from somewhere else, overnighting in Louisville. I said I'd go out for a drink with him after I was done working." She started out slowly, with long pauses between sentences, but the words began to tumble out. "We stopped at his motel afterward. I didn't have any reason to not trust him. I mean, he wasn't a jerk or anything, and he hadn't tried to hit on me, but even so, I asked him to not close the door when we went in his room.

"He said okay, and went over to hang up some clothes or something, and I started looking at his charts. He was from New York, and I'd never seen charts for that area. I was looking at the airspace around the Statue of Liberty, and didn't notice…"

She hesitated. "He got over by the door and closed it and locked it and put the chain on, and I knew… I knew he was going to rape me."

Her body shook with an involuntary shudder and her voice went flat. "He beat me up. He was very careful to just hit me where my clothes would cover me, but I didn't notice that at the time. I don't remember any of the blows landing. I didn't know if he was going to hit my face or my body, or if he was going to use his fist or his foot, and I couldn't defend myself against him. He knew some kind of martial art, karate or kickboxing, or something. After that I didn't fight him. I just let him do what he wanted. And he…"

She trailed off. Shame filled her voice and she hunched her shoulders as she mumbled into Ben's chest. "He wanted to do lots of things, some I'd never even heard of before." She paused, the next words whispered. "Some that I didn't know were possible."

She stopped, unconsciously gripping Ben's back.

"Anyway, he got tired of using me after a couple of hours, and I threw up on the bed while he was in the bathroom. Then I got dressed and walked home."

She went silent. Ben thought about all the things she didn't say, and mentally cursed the type of man who could do that to a woman. "What happened afterward?"

"I went to work the next day and tried to pretend that it didn't happen." She rubbed her face on his shirt.

He could understand denial and shame, even though she had nothing to be ashamed of. "Since then? How has your life been?"

She shrugged. "I started drinking a lot, and sleeping around, and then Rudy—he was one of the guys I drank with—we got married, but…" Her voice trailed off again.

"You're not married now, Lannis. So, you divorced? That's not so unusual, especially when there's trauma in someone's history."

"Yeah, well. Uh. One night I got drunk and hit him, I think several times, but I'm kind of foggy on my part. He hit me once in self-defense, or maybe as a reflex, then got in his car and didn't come back that night. When I got home from work the next day, he'd moved out. I haven't seen him since."

She was quiet, but Ben sensed there was more.

"I got really drunk that night and showed up at work the next day—well, not even hungover. Still stinking drunk. Orvis, my boss, had me in the office before anybody else figured it out, and read me the riot act. He kicked me out and made me go to AA, and still holds it over my head, in case I ever think I can get away with it again.

"So now I live alone. I don't date. I don't drink. I just work. I'm supposed to be on vacation this week. Orvis forced me to take the time off. He threatened to go to the FAA and get my license yanked if I didn't. He thinks I'll burn out."

Ben laughed softly. "Sounds like Orvis is a good friend."

Lannis snapped her gaze up to his for the first time since she'd begun talking, and narrowed her red, swollen eyes.

"Yeah, I mean it." He touched her cheek. "Without him, you'd have self-destructed by now, wouldn't you?"

Surprise flared in her eyes, then she nodded. "I guess so."

"It sounds like you were well on your way. Have you considered going to a support group or anything?" Ben continued to lazily stroke her back.

"No." The answer was instantaneous, and as if she knew he was going to ask why not, she continued. "I'm—I was—too ashamed. If I talk about it, then it was…real." Her voice cracked.

"Lannis, you don't have anything to be ashamed of. You were the victim of a violent crime. A felony. How big was he?" Ben had a good idea, but wanted her to say it.

"Around six three or six four, two twenty."

"Muscular, not fat, right? Since he was into martial arts."

"Um, yeah." She nodded.

"He left how many bruises?" Ben asked, knowing full well that she'd carried those painful reminders with her for a week or more.

"Around twenty," she said without pause. Ben winced, both from the image that flashed into his mind and his own experience of how that felt. And he'd never had that many at one time. She had to have endured considerable suffering in silence.

"Okay, a guy who has eight or nine inches and ninety pounds on you, is trained in martial arts and isn't afraid to injure you, decides you're his mark. You didn't *let* him do anything. You just happened to be in his line of sight and couldn't get out of the way. There's no shame in that."

She shifted uncomfortably. "But…"

"But what, Lannis?"

"But I…participated in my own rape. I was stupid. Naive. I walked into the room on my own. I wasn't coerced or forced. I didn't scream, not at first, anyway. I didn't even fight. I didn't do *anything* to stop it. For a long time I wasn't even sure what happened was rape." Guilt choked her voice.

He hooked his fingers under her chin, and used gentle pressure to push past her resistance, lifting her face. "Open your eyes, Lannis."

She shook her head, eyelids clamped together tightly, lips trembling.

"Yes. Now."

Resigned, she opened them and met his gaze.

"You didn't deserve what happened. No matter what. Walking into the room of your own volition did not even *imply* consent to sex. The beating was meant to coerce, to force compliance. He outclassed you big-time size-wise. Besides, he was trained. You were not." Ben raised his eyebrows. "Then there's the adrenaline response. Fight, flee, or freeze. No one can predict what they'll do. There's no way of knowing if screaming or fighting would have changed the outcome anyway, and either response might have resulted in your death. You survived a terrible attack that you were in no way prepared for and that you in no way deserved."

Lannis stared at him, eyes wide, lips parted in unconscious, fragile hope. Ben figured she'd have to hear these things over and over before she began to believe them, but she sure needed to hear them for the first time now, since she'd had years to solidify her erroneous convictions.

He stroked her cheek and watched as her eyelids grew heavy, then drooped and closed. "Go to sleep, darlin'," he murmured. "You've had a rough morning."

Chapter Nineteen

Ben HELD HER for nearly an hour. His legs went stiff and his back developed a crick, but he bore it with quiet stoicism. The minutes ticked by, and he weighed Lannis's need for recuperative sleep against his mounting sense that it was past time to contact John. The attention of the Civil Air Patrol, and consequently law enforcement, had made it too risky until now, but his Judas of a partner in Louisville had plenty of opportunity to concoct a better cover-up as the days passed.

Meanwhile, she lay melted against him, boneless, fists finally relaxed, and clasping him in unconscious acceptance of the comfort of his body. At a very basic level she was beginning to trust him, whether she knew it or not. When she woke up, he would probably be right back to square one, but at least there was a chink in her armor.

When she woke, he'd encourage her to talk to someone—a counselor, or a crisis line at the very least, or maybe a priest or pastor. She was strong, a survivor, and had the potential of living a vital, engaged life, as opposed to the emotional desert she inhabited now. She didn't see it yet, but with help she could overcome her past, not exist as its prisoner.

Muscles in his thigh began to cramp and he shifted, stifling a groan. "Lannis." He rubbed her back briskly. "Time to get going. Rise and shine." Groggy, she pushed herself up, away from his chest. The moment she realized she'd been sleeping on his partially bare torso, she blushed furiously and snatched the bedspread around her. His mouth quirked up and he stifled a grin at her hair, bed-head spiky. He flicked a finger at the worst of it. "Go comb your hair and we'll get some hot food." The leftover pizza looked as unappetizing as it smelled, and since she hadn't eaten any of it, Ben mentally put feeding her at the top of his list—after they lost the homeless look.

She scrambled to her feet and fled to the bathroom. He heard the shower start, run for a moment, then stop. After another moment, she emerged, running her hands through her now-tamed locks and dressed in jeans as dirty as his. He held out his hand to her, a silent declaration of support. She glanced at it, stuck her nose up, and leaned past him to grab her coat.

Ben snorted. "Aw, come on, Lannis. You just shared something with me that you've told no other human being." He snagged her elbow, pulled her close, and looped his arms around her. If he thought she'd accept his embrace, he was wrong. She stood rigid inside the circle of his arms, drawing into herself and creating a distance in spite of his proximity.

But she's not pushing me away. He kissed the top of her head, the damp hair cool against his lips, and she stiffened. He sighed, then released her. "Okay, then. Let's go get some clean clothes at Wal-Mart."

~

Lannis blinked in the bright sun, and tried yet again to formulate a plan to get away from Jack. Her mind was boggy with fatigue and the emotional drain of the past few hours, though, and she changed her focus to trying to figure out *where* they were.

The town wasn't big, but there were a lot of stores along a highway that doubled as its main street. They walked past tourist shops and businesses that catered to vacationers, almost like a disjointed theme park without much of a theme. They passed a few intrepid tourists on the sidewalks, but Jack steered her clear of them with that implacable pressure on her elbow or the small of her back, and she couldn't dredge up the energy to defy him.

It was about a mile and a half to the Wal-Mart, a stroll in the park after the past week. Flat. Paved. Sidewalks, even. Finally the name of a store specializing in stoneware clicked in Lannis's mind. Pigeon Forge Pottery. Pigeon Forge, Tennessee. East of Knoxville, if she remembered correctly. Her knowledge of Tennessee geography was pretty limited.

Not that it mattered. Really, nothing had changed. Jack still held the upper hand, and she knew him well enough to be certain that he'd thwart any effort she made to buck his control.

Still, when they got to Wal-Mart she considered making a scene, finding a security guard, or just opening her mouth at the cash register and hoping the cashier would actually do something. However, Jack draped his arm around her shoulder as they entered the store, his message unmistakable. He'd anticipated exactly that response from her. He smiled and nodded a good morning to the greeter and took a cart with his free hand. He steered it to the clothing section, and leaned down in what undoubtedly appeared to be a lover's whispered intimacy.

His voice hard and totally at odds with his actions, he murmured into her hair, "Don't blow it now, Lannis." His breath heated and tickled her ear. "You'll be home by evening if things go the way I hope. Otherwise, you'll be home tomorrow. Either way, you're almost there." Then in a normal tone of voice he said, "Pick out what you need, sweetheart."

She grabbed a pair of jeans in her size and turned toward the dressing room.

He stopped her. "No. I want to get out of here ASAP."

She shrugged, tossed the jeans in the cart, then added a T-shirt, sports bra, underwear, and socks. When he'd done the same, she turned away from the checkout area. His iron grip on her arm halted her. "Where do you think you're going?"

"I want a toothbrush. I'm tired of using twigs or my fingers." Head up, she waited. When he released her, she strode to the toiletries section and grabbed a toothbrush. And toothpaste. The rest she could live without for another day, but this would be another little bit of heaven, another blessing she'd taken for granted. He apparently reconsidered the necessity of a toothbrush, because he tossed one in the cart, too, along with shaving cream and a razor.

Jack herded her through the shortest checkout lane. He kept one hand on her in warning, grabbed a handful of candy bars and a phone card, and paid in cash. They were out of the store a scant ten minutes after entering it. Jack led her back to the main street, and absentmindedly handed her a candy bar while they walked. She ripped into it, her mouth watering before she even got all the paper off. It was king-sized, so it took four big bites to demolish it, and she'd just crammed the last of it in when he stopped at a pay phone. He rummaged through the plastic sacks for the phone card, then punched in several series of numbers. He pulled her flush against him, looking over her head at passersby as he listened to the rings.

"Hey." Jack's voice was clipped, curt. "Is your line secure?"

Lannis could hear a male voice on the line, but couldn't make out words. *Secure?* From what? A wiretap? Who asked questions like that, or more importantly, had to think that way?

"Yeah, I'm calling from a pay phone with a prepaid card." A police car turned onto the street and drove slowly toward them. Jack turned casually into the kiosk, his grip tightening and forcing Lannis to turn with him. "I need your help." Lannis looked with longing at the police car as it passed. Trapped between Jack and the phone booth, she could feel tension radiating from him and knew she faced retribution if she tried to attract attention. She jerked her focus back to him when he spoke again.

"Well, they got it wrong on both counts. It's some other folks that went bad, and I'll lay bets that it's my partner who's putting out the word that I turned, right?" Jack's voice was tight with barely restrained rage, rage deeper than any she'd elicited from him. Sarcasm dripped off the word *partner*.

He took a deep breath, and when he spoke again his voice was neutral. "I need an airline ticket from Knoxville to Louisville for one Lannis Parker. Today." Jack spelled Lannis's name, then added her address. "Plus some receipts in case anyone checks on her whereabouts. Start with Thursday." He turned to Lannis. "Did you have any plans for your vacation?"

She shook her head in the negative, eyes wide. Documentation? Receipts? And he remembered her address from reading it off of her license *last week*.

Who is he, and who does he work for?

He tried again. "Did you mention anything to anybody about what you might do?"

"Uh…well, yeah, I told Mark that I might go see my aunt in Tennessee, but I wasn't going to do it," she said.

"Why not? What were you going to do instead?"

"Nothing." She bristled.

"Don't you have any friends to spend time with?"

"I told you. I work, I don't do anything else, and what's it to you anyway?"

"You really did let him win, didn't you, Lannis?" Jack said. "You, darlin', are in dire need of a friend." He pinned her with a rakish smile and said, "And when this is over, you're going to get one. Me."

Lannis blinked. That was definitely a threat, not a comforting promise. "I don't want a friend," she muttered.

Jack ignored her. "Where does your aunt live? What's her name?"

She tried to pull away from him. "No, don't bring her into this."

"Lannis, your life is at stake." He sighed. "Your aunt is not in danger."

"You can't know that!" Lannis began to struggle.

Jack said into the phone, "Hold on," and dropped the receiver. It dangled on its coiled metal cord and bounced against her thigh. "Lannis, stop it. We'll contact her and tell her you need her to say yes, you came and visited for a few days if anyone ever asks—and no one will, most likely." Jack had finally gotten a good grip on her arms and pulled her into his embrace again.

"You promise?" Her voice shook.

"Yeah, darlin', I promise," he said.

Lannis heard conviction in his voice, saw it reflected in his eyes. Recognized the same quality she'd seen and sensed in him since the moment she'd first encountered him. *No matter what, he does what he says he'll do.* Her shoulders sagged as she accepted she'd have to trust him. Again.

She recited Aunt Edie's address and phone number in a resigned tone. Jack picked up the phone and relayed the information.

"Oh, and I'll need some cash. Maybe a grand." He went silent for a moment, listening. "Yeah, one more thing. A Cessna 172, tail number N63438. I need to know if it was reported missing, maybe stolen from Bowman Field in Louisville sometime between Thursday and Saturday."

Mention of the plane sparked Lannis's attention and she looked at him, unspoken questions dancing on the tip of her tongue.

"Pigeon Forge. Don't bother looking for me. I'll find you." Jack straightened, rolled his shoulders as if a weight had been lifted from them. His voice warmed with genuine gratitude as he said, "Thanks, buddy," and hung up.

Lannis wondered anew at his situation, his identity. She'd winced at the venom in his voice when he mentioned his "partner." A grand! A thousand dollars, just like it was a twenty-dollar bill. Everything he'd asked for, his buddy agreed to provide without question.

Jack had told her that she had to trust him, her life depended on that trust, that her life was in danger just by being associated with him.

But he could be on either side of the law and all that could be true. Organized crime syndicates could come up with receipts and documentation just as easily as one of the alphabet soup spy-type organizations. She flashed back to his habit of grace before meals, complete with a sign of the cross, and wondered about a Mafia or Mob connection again.

On the other hand, if he really was a criminal, would he have listened to her this morning with such compassion? Her head was beginning to swim with conflicting thoughts. She didn't notice that they'd walked down the street and he'd guided her into yet another motel until he held the door to the lobby open for her. She questioned him with her eyes, but he simply requested a room under another set of names. After he completed the transaction, he took the key and ushered her to the room. This time she didn't hesitate at entering, and didn't flinch when the door closed.

"What's this all about?" she asked.

Dropping the bags on the bed, he shrugged out of his coat. "I just wanted a place to change clothes."

Dumbfounded, she stared at him. "Why didn't we just change at a—" Before she finished the question, she realized why not. Separate restrooms. He couldn't control her if she was in the ladies' room. She could talk to someone, or leave a note.

"Oh." Apparently it was worth fifty or sixty bucks to him to be in control of her when she changed clothes, even if he planned to put her on a plane in a few hours.

She didn't know whether to laugh or cry. Or scream. She sat heavily on the bed, tired to death of being under his thumb. Jack tossed the plastic sack with her new clothes to her, and she automatically caught it. She got up and went into the bathroom to change, not surprised to see that there was no window in this one either. The clean clothes, taken for granted until today, felt heavenly. She wadded up her dirty ones and wondered if she wanted to keep them. Probably not. Every time she wore them she'd think of this ordeal.

When she came out of the bathroom, she saw he'd changed already. Of course. He couldn't go into the bathroom and leave her unattended, unless he tied her up again. She couldn't suppress a shudder. In silent retaliation, Lannis took malicious satisfaction in the fact that his bladder was going to nearly burst unless he took her into the bathroom with him. *Ugh*. She shoved that image out of her mind. Quickly. She got her new toothbrush and toothpaste out, and brushed her teeth for nearly five minutes.

"If you want to take a nap, you can. We'll hang out here for a while, until our ride gets here." He set the shaving cream and razor next to her toothbrush on the counter.

Lannis dropped her stuff on the floor and lay down on the bed. She closed her eyes, the lids still raw from tears, and exhaustion swept over her. She surrendered to sleep, not sure whether it was a blessing or a curse, not knowing if rest or nightmares would fill it, but too tired to fight.

Chapter Twenty

A TOUCH ON LANNIS'S SHOULDER—which she intuitively recognized as belonging to Jack—roused her and she rolled over, groaning. However long he'd let her sleep, it wasn't long enough. She stumbled to the sink and washed her face, then went into the bathroom and closed the door.

When she came out, she looked at him and a shock of awareness slapped her awake. Her jaw dropped, and she snapped it shut as soon as she realized it. He'd shaved while she slept. The short dark beard had made him look dangerous, even deadly, but clean-shaven, he was lethal in a much more civilized way. Focused, sharp, alert, missing nothing—and handsome, if she was willing to admit it to herself. Squashing her uninvited appreciation of his even features and the strong planes of his face, she gathered her clothes and stuffed them into one of the Wal-Mart plastic bags.

"Lannis, when you get back home, try a support group or maybe talk to a counselor about the rape. At least call the crisis line and talk to somebody. It doesn't have to be face-to-face, but you deserve to heal." Jack's voice was almost tender.

His words laid her bare to his inspection, his judgment. His pity. Lannis wanted to curse him for bringing it up, but her throat went tight and her mouth dry. She grabbed the open front of her flannel shirt and drew the edges together in a convulsive movement. She sensed him looking at her and refused to meet his eyes.

"It happened; you can't change that. It's part of your history, whether you like it or not. You don't have to let it be the single event that defines your entire life."

She busied herself with the sack, refolding dirty clothes she didn't even want. Hiding the trembling of her fingers in fabric. Wishing she had the strength to rip them apart since she couldn't rip him apart. Out of the corner of her eye, she saw him shrug.

"Just keep it in mind. You're only alone if you choose to be."

He opened the door, and she let her breath out before scuttling past him into the cool air of the morning. A sense of reprieve allowed her to take in her next breath.

Lannis ducked her head and focused on the sidewalk. In silence, Jack directed her back toward the Wal-Mart at the other end of Main Street, but this time they walked slowly. The strip of motels in their wake, they pretended to window shop, or at least Jack did. She watched him survey groups of tourists as they strolled. He even used the reflection of the plate glass windows to search covertly. At least she was pretty sure he held no affection for the froufrou antiques displayed in one of them.

Then the hair on her neck prickled. A shiver from a sense of being watched skittered down her spine. She sidled closer to Jack and grabbed his hand. He raised an eyebrow in silent question, a moment of astonishment quickly controlled.

"Somebody's following us, or watching us, or...something," she whispered. A flicker of his eyelids acknowledged her statement but other than that, he didn't change expression. It was evident to Lannis that his muscles were tight with heightened tension, but to anyone else he still appeared relaxed. He reversed direction as though they'd decided to go back to a store they'd already passed. She could see him scanning the area, his eyes moving constantly.

"There." She pointed with her eyes, fear in her voice. "The guy in the gray jacket. You see him? Sunglasses, a dark blue cap? Over there, kind of behind the hot dog stand."

Jack grinned and relaxed. "That's my buddy." Taking a circuitous route, he worked his way over to the man, pulling Lannis, who hung back. He ordered hot dogs for the two of them, then wandered near his buddy. "Looks clear from my side."

The guy answered in a low voice. "From here, too. I've been here for fifteen minutes and haven't seen anything unusual." Leaning past Jack, he said, "Hi. You must be Lannis. It's a pleasure to meet you." She nodded stiffly, but didn't reply. "What's the deal?" he asked Jack, nodding toward her.

"She was in the wrong place at the wrong time. She saved my life, flew me out of Louisville. Had to lie low with me until I could get a cover that'll keep her safe. There were a couple of complications that made it stretch out longer than I wanted." Jack wolfed down his hot dog, and wiped his hands with a napkin. "I owe her big-time."

Lannis stared at him, open-mouthed. Those few sentences both revealed more than she'd known and concealed most of what had happened over the last week.

Jack nodded at her untouched hot dog. "If you're not going to eat that, I can help you out." She handed it to him, too unsettled to eat and annoyed that she was giving away the first real meal she'd had the chance to eat in days.

"Well, you have a plane to catch." Jack's friend unfolded himself from the fence he'd been leaning against and pointed toward a parking lot down the street.

Jack tossed their plastic bags and her backpack into the back of the nondescript tan pickup when they got there, and herded her into the center of the bench seat. She fastened her seat belt, concentrating on it much longer than necessary. The men dwarfed her on either side and she tensed, trying to shrink enough that she wouldn't touch their thighs or arms.

Jack glanced at her and casually draped his arm around her. He smiled and squeezed her shoulder, in silent acknowledgment of her discomfort.

"What time's her flight?"

"Three fifteen."

Lannis glanced at her watch. Two and a half hours from now.

Jack looked more relaxed than he had since she'd known him, except for the afternoon she'd gotten his gun, when he'd been asleep. "It's almost over, darlin'." She shot him a dagger look. He threw his head back and laughed.

"Do you want a report on the plane now or later?" The driver watched the exchange with a sharp gaze, his eyes curious.

"Now." Ben sobered, and pulled Lannis closer to him. She sat stiffly in his embrace.

"It was reported missing Friday afternoon. Thursday morning, before the tower opened, one of the controllers heard a plane take off while he was climbing the stairs to the cab. He said that's not unusual. I'm assuming that was you guys, but that conclusion's not in the police reports.

"In a separate development not tied to the theft, at least initially, an emergency signal was reported in the Appalachians Thursday afternoon, east of Knoxville. The Civil Air Patrol started a search late Thursday and located the plane on Saturday.

"Turns out it was the same one that was reported stolen in Louisville on Friday. It had been abandoned, partially hidden. A drug dog showed a response on the pilot side but when they tore it apart it was clean. They dusted it for prints and all the employees at Louisville Air were fingerprinted for comparison—except for a pilot, Lannis Parker, who's on vacation. Which, coincidentally, began Thursday. The investigating officers stopped by her residence and verified she was gone. No one knew where she was, but she'd mentioned visiting an aunt in Tennessee. She's not a suspect, just a loose end. The owner of the fixed base operation flew the plane out on Monday. That's it."

A chill shuddered through Lannis. *Orvis.*

Jack's arm tightened around her shoulder as his friend continued. "The report was filed by the same two officers who mopped up a shooting, nonfatal, Wednesday night. A drug deal gone bad, two guys who tried to do each other in." He looked directly at Jack. "That was at a convenience store four blocks from Bowman Airport. They called in the K-9 unit because one of the dealers got away but the trail ended at a street and they called it off. The guy apparently caught a ride. No buses or taxis out that time of morning, nobody reported anything out of the ordinary."

"What was the name of the second officer?" Jack's voice was cold.

"Powell is the senior officer, Neal's the junior one."

Silence reigned for several moments. Jack absently kneaded Lannis's shoulder. She was rigid with shock, and barely registered the caress.

"Okay, Lannis, this is what to expect when you get home. Probably nothing until you get back to work, but when you do, you'll be sent to the police department for fingerprints. No big deal. Your prints are supposed to be in the plane. *If* you are questioned, you went to see your aunt." He looked at his buddy. "Do you have the receipts?"

The guy nodded.

"Just maintain your usual, uh, aloofness, and it won't be a problem." Jack hesitated, then appeared to come to a decision. "We know that some of the officers who can't be trusted are Powell and Neal. Grantree, although he's working as a liaison in Narcotics and it's not likely that you'd cross paths with him. There are more, but we don't know who. Yet. Your cover will hold, as long as you stay cool and stick to the story. Questions?"

She shook her head; she was too numb to think of any. Slight tremors began in her hands. Jack pulled her closer and kissed the top of her head.

"You'll be okay," he murmured.

Hating herself for it, she burrowed into his neck, gaining comfort in his strength. After a moment she took a deep breath, pushed away, and sat up. She stared forward, too distressed to focus on the passing scenery. Jack's friend dug in his inner jacket pocket and handed Lannis an envelope filled with receipts. She took it and leafed through the contents with growing astonishment.

"How did you get all these together in such a short time?" She looked straight at him for the first time. His expression reminded her of Jack. Hard. Intelligent. Shuttered. Like Jack, not forthcoming with answers.

He shrugged and glanced in the rearview mirror, his gaze lingering for a moment, searching the reflections of vehicles behind them. With a jolt, Lannis realized he was looking for a tail. She swiveled and looked out the back window. No one followed as he entered the interstate without signaling. She turned around and read the signs with cautiously growing hope. They were headed toward Knoxville. Several miles later she began seeing signs for the airport, and clenched her fists in anticipation.

Indeed, the guy turned into the airport at Knoxville, and took the ramp into the short-term lot. He parked, and Jack got out, pausing for a moment to stretch. Lannis unhooked her seat belt and vaulted out of the truck cab as if it were on fire. Jack leaned past her and pulled his gun from his waistband, his knife from his boot, and stuck them in the glove box. His buddy tossed him the keys and he locked it, then locked the truck and sent the keys back in a quick airborne arc. He retrieved her backpack from the truck bed, opened it, and removed the twine. Her breath caught and she looked at him, suddenly wary. His mouth quirked up in a half smile, and he dropped the thin rope back in the truck bed. He handed the backpack to her. She scowled and snatched it—from a full arm's length away.

The other guy walked around the truck and handed her an airline ticket, along with another envelope. She reached for them with caution usually reserved for handling poisonous snakes barehanded, then scanned the ticket and stepped away from the two men.

"There's cash for a taxi when you get to Louisville, plus some extra, to cover expenses while you were gone."

She stuffed the envelope in a coat pocket along with her gloves and focused on the ticket. Knoxville to Louisville, on a commuter flight. Momentarily stumped on the date, she frowned while she backed up to last Thursday, added seven, and looked down again, confirming that the date on the ticket was indeed today's date. Departing at three fifteen, just like Jack's friend had said.

She blurted, "You really are going to let me go home." Her gaze found Jack's. Searched his eyes.

He nodded. "Like I said all along. You just couldn't bring yourself to trust me." He put his hand on her shoulder in what he probably thought was a companionable gesture and turned toward the terminal. "Let's get you on the plane."

She pulled away. "I can get on by myself."

Jack's expression didn't change, but his eyes went hard and Lannis could tell that he wasn't going to allow her to board without his escort. Not willing to test him, she dropped the subject and checked the contents of her backpack. Everything was still in it. She stuck her arms through the straps and shrugged it onto her shoulders.

In silent defiance she set off toward the terminal building, knowing both of the men would be on her heels. Within two strides, they flanked her. She consoled herself with the thought that they wouldn't be allowed to accompany her past the security checkpoint. Cheered at the notion, she bypassed the ticket counter for the security gate since she didn't have baggage to check.

At the checkpoint, however, both men stayed with her. Uneasy, she looked at Jack. She handed her ticket and ID to be checked and received the nod to proceed. Jack's friend flipped out a leather-bound badge and spoke quietly to the security attendant. Lannis craned her neck in an effort to see his badge, but he purposely kept it at an angle that prevented her from seeing any details, tipping it even farther away from her when she leaned in.

The woman nodded and directed them to a line separate from the rest of the passengers. Both of the men went over and Jack's buddy pulled his gun out. *I should have guessed*, Lannis thought wryly, *he'd be carrying a gun, too.* They joked their way through their security check in easy camaraderie. Then it dawned on her. Jack was unarmed now, too. She took malicious satisfaction in that fact, and a smile twitched at her lips.

~

Ben glanced at Lannis as John explained their way through security. She flashed him a brilliant smile from her place in line. There was a hint of vengeance in her expression, but even so, he was jolted by her smile. It was her first since he'd known her, and it transformed her, even though it was at his expense. He grinned back, earning a scowl as her face flushed and she stuck her nose up in the air. He chuckled.

John stopped what he was doing and gave Ben a thoughtful, measured look. Ben crossed his arms over his chest and returned it with a gaze that said *the subject is off-limits.* John let it go, but Ben knew he'd get the third degree in private. He turned and caught up with Lannis on the other side of the checkpoint.

Only a few minutes remained before boarding. They walked down the concourse to the gate, and Ben spoke in a low voice to Lannis. "Don't contact the police when you get home. I can't guarantee your safety if you do, only that you will die if the wrong ones get a hold of you, if they think you have anything at all to do with me. Remember, you went to see your aunt. Do you understand?"

She nodded once, the movement brief and stilted.

"Lannis, I can't protect you any longer." He stopped, and turned her to face him. "Please trust me on this. *Please.*" He searched her eyes, and after a moment, stepped away. He'd done the best he could. He prayed she'd listen to him, but knew she'd cut off her nose before admitting she heeded his words. His hands felt empty at his sides and he clenched them against the barren sensation. He glanced at the gate. Boarding had begun.

He stepped back, touched the brim of his cap, and said, "Thank you. God be with you."

Lannis stared at him, her expression unreadable. She glanced at John, turned, and walked toward the gate. Her pace picked up and she flashed a swift look over her shoulder as if to verify they were indeed releasing her. She handed her ticket to the gate agent and he stuck it under the scanner. It didn't take the first time, and she jittered toward the door while he repeated the process. When the agent finally waved her onto the plane, she turned her back on Ben in a gesture of rejection as absolute as the Titanic's final descent into the icy depths. She walked down the Jetway, her spine rigid, her steps clipped and quick.

Some of the lightness he'd felt at John's unhesitating support evaporated. He caught himself hoping she'd turn so he could see those expressive brown eyes one more time.

But he only got the back of her coffee-colored hair.

Chapter Twenty-One

LANNIS DIDN'T RELEASE the tension in her muscles until the turboprop pushed back from the gate. She didn't really relax until the plane was on the runway, and she wouldn't describe it as loose-limbed. Not even close. More like a slightly lower level of military alert. Orange instead of red. Takeoff, usually a moment of exhilaration for her, lost its visceral thrill as she gave way to her swirling thoughts. She pressed her face against the oval window and watched the earth fall away.

From the beginning he'd asked her to trust him, said he wasn't going to hurt her. That she'd go home when it was safe.

Jack *hadn't* hurt her. Well, much. Anger flared for a moment as she remembered how badly he'd scared her and controlled every move she made. Then a quiet inner voice said, *I'm going home.* She had to admit, at least in this, he was truthful.

The other guy pretty much confirmed what little Jack had disclosed, and he'd had a badge that appeared to be legitimate, at least to TSA. There was no way they could have gotten through security if they weren't in law enforcement. She didn't think they would have had the guts to attempt it if they were criminals, even if they were involved in something as sophisticated as organized crime.

Shivering, she skipped to a detail in the report about N63438. It sounded like Orvis flew it out. And he got it out without hurting himself. Lannis felt a rush of gratitude and relief for him, glad to hear he'd done it safely. In her concern for making a safe emergency landing, she hadn't considered the challenge of getting the plane out. She couldn't even thank him for teaching her how to get it into the valley undamaged without blowing her cover.

My cover.

Sagging into her seat, she realized she'd decided to follow Jack's advice. When had she come to that decision? Had she succumbed to Stockholm Syndrome, where victims ended up identifying with their captors? No, she didn't think so.

She believed him. Every single thing he said, he'd followed through on. If nothing else, she'd learned that with him, what he said was what she got. Suddenly tired, she leaned her head against the cool Plexiglas window and closed her eyes.

~

Silent by mutual understanding until they got to the truck, John slammed the door a bit harder than necessary and glared at Ben. "Time for the rest of the story. Why didn't you call me from Louisville that first night? Those rips in your coat sleeve look sort of like bullet holes." His tone was tight and a bit sarcastic, but Ben heard the underlying concern. "Are you injured? And what's up with Ms. Lannis Parker?"

Ben made a dismissive gesture. "Powell shot me at the convenience store." He dug a bill out of his pocket to pay for parking and tossed it at John. "He and Neal, along with at least a few more cops, are in on the drug ring that Roger Grantree and I had been trying to bust. Roger's in on it, too. He set me up." Ben blew out an angry breath. "The cops were going to feed me to the fish in the Ohio River after they murdered me.

"I couldn't think of anyone I could trust." Ben glanced at John. "Sorry. The only thing I could think about was getting out of town. Way out. When she showed up for a flight that had been canceled—I knew that, she didn't—I commandeered the plane. Couldn't do it legally because I didn't have my ID." He slanted another look at John. They both knew it was a death wish to carry police ID while undercover. "By the way, I thought she was a guy. At least, a guy was supposed to show up. They apparently traded duty."

John pulled onto the highway. "How's your arm? You're not favoring it too much, so I'd guess it's healing okay."

"Yeah, the bullet went clear through. It's healing without infection." Ben shrugged. "Like I said, I was lucky."

John raised his eyebrows. "You're avoiding the other question. Ms. Parker? She had a nasty bruise that looked to be about a week old."

Ben regarded him steadily. "I've told you everything you need to know."

After a moment of silence, John let it go. He turned the conversation to the problem of Grantree, crooked cops, and how they would expose and take down the cartel.

~

The Louisville terminal was landlocked to pedestrians, at least as far as Lannis knew. She'd gotten all the way to the front doors before it dawned on her that there was no way to cross the interstate without a car. Did taxis have a minimum fare? She couldn't afford one to take her all the way home, but maybe she had enough to get her across the expressway to the neighborhood surrounding the airport. She could walk from there. Standiford Field was only a few miles from her house. But how to get to the fairgrounds and convention center she could see, a quarter of a mile and sixteen lanes of traffic away? Her brain felt muddled with emotion and fatigue, and this obstacle seemed insurmountable, even though her rational mind knew it was a simple problem.

Then she remembered the envelope of cash. Digging it out of her pocket, she flipped it open and stopped, stunned. She counted it once, twice, and then again. There were nine one-hundred dollar bills, and five twenties. One thousand dollars. All of what Jack had asked his friend to bring him. Almost guiltily she looked around to see if anyone noticed her windfall, but people ebbed and flowed around her in oblivious self-concern.

She shook her head. She understood even less about Jack, but she could afford the taxi now. She took out one of the twenties, stowed the rest in an inner zipped compartment of her backpack, and went outside to hail a cab.

Several hours later, Lannis stepped out her back door and lowered herself to the step of the porch. The concrete was cold under her butt, but a faint sense of claustrophobia sent her outside in spite of the chill. The transition from the mountains to civilization and now home had left her off-balance.

She'd dragged the receipts out of her backpack and dropped them on the kitchen table, then stuffed the money under her mattress until she could get to the bank. Other than hanging up her coat, she had nothing to unpack. She was essentially at the same point she'd been a week ago. Except that she only had four more days to kill instead of eleven.

She'd even walked to the convenience store for a frozen burrito. Curious, she'd walked around back to see if there were any signs of the shooting Jack claimed he'd been involved in. She saw a couple of nondescript dark stains in the gravel that may or may not have been blood. A piece of shredded yellow crime scene tape caught in the hinge of the dumpster fluttered in the light breeze. Chilled, she hadn't looked any closer, and hurried home instead.

She made a halfhearted effort to come up with a plan for tomorrow but kept getting sidetracked with memories of the past week.

Groceries. She still needed groceries. That was what she'd do. Then clean her already-clean house. After that, she'd only have three days to kill.

Hours later, Lannis punched her pillow. Hard. Getting angry about not being able to fall asleep was counterproductive and she knew it, but her frustration mounted. She had insomnia because Jack *wasn't* there. She'd come to tolerate, then accept, and then, against her better judgment, derive comfort from his presence next to her at night.

She felt more alone, and lonely, than she had since Rudy left. The craving for a drink, for the oblivion alcohol promised, expanded inside her until she considered getting up and going to the liquor store. She grabbed her watch and pushed the button to light up the time. Ten till three.

Too late. This time, anyway. She dropped her watch on the bedside stand she'd bought at a garage sale and resigned herself to a sleepless night. Then, in spite of her prediction, fell asleep in the quiet hour before dawn, legs tangled in the sheets.

~

One day down, three to go. Lannis wiped her forehead with her sleeve and rinsed the rag she was using to wash her kitchen floor. When the phone rang, she plopped the rag into the sink, welcoming the break. "Hello?"

"Lannis, this is Orvis."

Her breathing hitched, and her thoughts scattered. *The plane! The valley, the police...* She reined them in and scrambled to match her reactions to what he'd expect if she were unaware of last week's events.

"Uh, hi, Orvis. What's up?" He didn't seem to notice her slight hesitation and she eased her breath out in cautious silence.

"I have a favor to ask. I know your vacation was my idea, but almost all the pilots are out with the flu. Would you fly a charter for me tomorrow? If you don't have anything else planned, that is?"

She didn't hesitate. "Sure, no problem. When and where?"

"Eight, Champaign-Urbana." Orvis sounded relieved. "Thanks, Lannis. I owe you one."

"Is it a drop-off, or wait for the passengers?"

"Wait, and return early evening."

"Will do. I'll come in early to get it ready." She replaced the receiver, her spirits lifting. He'd acted totally normal. Nor had he made mention of the stolen plane, or fingerprints.

Best of all, she could go back to work! She'd been dreading the weekend. Sleeping late, shopping for food, then scrubbing the bathroom and kitchen had kept her occupied today, but she didn't have anything to fill up those other three days—or more important, the endless, temptation-filled evenings.

The craving for a drink was wearing her down.

The structure of her work and its absolute requirement of sobriety placed ironclad constraints on her desires. That made it easier to abstain. Lack of structure terrified her.

It didn't matter that the constraints were external. The bottom line was she could adhere to those limits, and if she were able to develop internal constraints someday, that would be a bonus. Now, for tonight, she *had* to stay away from the liquor store.

Cheered, she grabbed her rag and applied herself to finishing the kitchen floor.

~

Lannis glanced up from the computer when Orvis came into the office the next morning. He looked tired, older than he had the last time she'd seen him, and a rush of compassion overrode any lingering resentment at her forced time off. She finished copying weather information onto her flight planning form.

"Hi, Orvis. How many passengers do I have?" She'd looked at the whiteboard schedule when she arrived. She got to fly the retractable gear Cessna, which cheered her even more, but the number of passengers hadn't been listed.

"Three. Again, thanks." He set down a stack of files he'd taken home. "Oh, by the way, 63438 was stolen last week—we got it back—but you need to stop at the police substation and get fingerprinted. They're trying to weed out any prints that don't belong to us. The sooner you can do that, the better." He shuffled through yesterday's leftover invoices on the counter, then looked at her.

She stared at him, mouth agape. She hoped she looked convincing, especially since she knew the police would not find Jack's fingerprints anywhere in the plane. "Really? That's…weird."

"Yeah, it is. You were the last one to fly it. Wednesday's traffic flight." Orvis studied her for a moment. "Did you notice anything unusual?"

"Um, no. I put it in the hangar, and Jeff was up with a night student when I left, so I figured he'd close the office when he was done." Lannis delivered the statement without qualm, since it was true.

"Okay. I just don't want to leave any bases uncovered. If you need to borrow my car to go to the police station, you can."

"Uh, thanks. I'll see. The bus might work fine." She turned her attention back to her flight planning. She began working a basic weight and balance, which she would recompute if the passengers' weights were appreciably different from her estimate. Casually she said, "Oh, Orvis? If you're still short for the weekend, I can work." She held her breath, hoping he'd take the bait.

Orvis grunted, then nodded. Lannis hid a smile and went back to her calculations.

The weekend held a full slate of students whose instructors were sick, so Lannis fell back into her routine like it was a pair of well-loved blue jeans. She was at her desk, reading an industry newsletter, when Mark dragged himself back to work Monday, still pale from his bout with the virus.

"Hi, Mark. Feeling better?"

"Yeah. You're lucky you didn't get it." He sat, groaned, and grabbed his head. "Hey, you hear about 438?" A spark of curiosity enlivened his expression.

"Yeah, Orvis told me. I have to go down to the police department today and get fingerprinted. I guess everybody else already did."

"So, what happened last week, when you switched with me for the morning flight?" He narrowed his eyes.

"Bob called, said Ramon was sick, and canceled the flight." She flipped a page in the magazine. "So I went home." She paused, leaned closer to examine a chart. Almost as an afterthought, she added, "I went to visit my aunt in Memphis, and caught the early bus since the flight was scrubbed."

His eyes glazed over halfway through her explanation. Laying his head down on the desk, he mumbled, "Tell my student to preflight the plane, and then wake me up." A moment later, his soft snores competed with the air traffic control radio in the office.

Lannis breathed a silent sigh of relief. Mark's eyes had been sharp, his question pointed, but he bought her story. That was all that mattered. The tension in her shoulders eased.

When she went to the police substation later that day, no one asked any questions at all. They told her to write her statement after the fingerprinting, but that was it. She glanced up while she wrote, sneaking surreptitious looks at nametags, but none said Powell or Neal.

Over the next few days, Lannis quietly traded traffic shifts until her schedule included no early-morning flights. Memories of her week with Jack began to fade until, surreal as the events had seemed at the time, they took on a dreamlike quality.

Her life returned to normal.

Predictable.

Bleak.

And lonely.

Part
Two

Chapter Twenty-Two

LIGHTNING FLASHED, and a clap of thunder followed on its heels. Huge raindrops began splattering on the concrete ramp.

Lannis had pushed the limits of safety too far, and she knew it. There was no excuse for racing a thunderstorm. She had no right to put her student's life or Orvis's property at risk. She cursed herself silently as she wrestled the tie-down chain through its metal loop under the plane's wing. Her student yanked on his side and she lost her grip. Resigned to getting drenched, she waved him into the office. No sense in his getting his dress slacks and button-down shirt wet. Her wash-and-wear polo shirt had been soaked with sweat by midmorning. Rain wouldn't hurt it.

She regained her hold on the chain and efficiently secured it, then moved to the tail tie-down. Wind buffeted the plane, blowing her hair in a wild dance. She rolled her neck and shoulders, trying to ease the tension that wound tighter and tighter as the days passed. A gust blew her clipboard over, and she grabbed for it. The deluge pounded trees and pavement about two blocks away, and the distinctive scent of newly cut grass mingled with the ozone smell of lightning washed over her. *Here it comes.* Lannis quit stalling and sprinted for the building. Evasion as a coping mechanism had its advantages, but she had no choice at the moment.

The rain caught her, or maybe she'd let it catch her. She flinched as the warm drops pelted her shoulders and hair, and ran down her legs. The wind fought her as she dragged the door open, then capriciously battled her as she tried to pull it closed. In a fickle twist, it turned again and slammed the door, nearly catching her fingers. Lannis shook the water from her hair, stomped her feet on the rug, then ducked her head and made for the restroom, using the guise of getting dried off as an excuse to be alone.

She just hoped the other instructors didn't notice her growing compulsion to avoid contact with anyone outside the strict format of a flight lesson. Their black mutterings at the loss of the afternoon's income would deflect attention from her, but as much as she tried to blend in and act normal, her usual reserve had evolved into full-blown reclusion. It was most obvious when they'd all been chased inside by the storms, and she wouldn't put it past Mark or Jeff to make a comment.

The anniversary of her rape marched inexorably closer, the date burned into her brain in spite of her efforts to expunge it. It irritated her that the date mattered. She wanted to forget the reasons for its significance, wanted to ignore the anniversary, wanted all the memories to go away and leave her alone. But it was as impossible now as it had been then.

She attempted to keep the memories at bay by keeping busy at work. Real busy. And by running after work—six miles, sometimes seven, even eight on occasion, up from her usual three. The idea was to exhaust herself so she'd fall into bed at night too tired to think or remember. Or feel. In that regard, it was working.

She mopped her face with a paper towel, and glanced in the mirror. No wonder the guys picked on her. Shadowy circles beneath her eyes made her look haggard.

She could thank the nightmares for that. They had made a resurgence, striking when she was weakest—in the vulnerable state of unconsciousness, and in the isolated dark of night. Desperation and exhaustion combined to blur the edges of the constraints she lived with at work. Thoughts of buying, oh, maybe some wine coolers or hard lemonade popped into her mind at random moments. Their relative alcohol content was low. Or beer. She hated beer, so that would keep her from drinking too much and getting out of control, right? Surely she could handle that, and then she'd be able to sleep without dreaming. Maybe.

She should go to an AA meeting, or call Althea, although she didn't think either option was worth much. All she ever did when she went to a meeting was sit there, as aloof and withdrawn as she was anywhere else. The last time she'd gone had been well over a year ago.

Even though she knew that the idea of a sponsor was a good one, she'd never put any effort into developing anything other than a superficial *I'm doing this because the rules say I have to* relationship with Althea. In fact, she'd never called Althea before, and felt uncomfortable doing it now. Besides, there was no guarantee Althea was still on the wagon. It wasn't a given for anyone.

So she was back to plan A.

Work. Run. Try not to think about booze. Or the rape.

~

A fast-moving cold front blasted through a few days later, bringing vicious but brief storms during the night. Dawn was brilliant with sunshine and clear skies, a glorious morning with visibility better than twenty miles, quite a change from the usual four miles in haze.

Lannis shuffled her lesson plans to take advantage of the blustery winds in the wake of the front, giving her students the opportunity to experience less than optimal conditions with an instructor sitting next to them. She walked back into the lobby after her first flight of the day, and Orvis stepped out of his office. He waited until she was done with her student, then beckoned her with his chin.

"I got a pop-up charter. I'd like you to take it. Knoxville. Back this afternoon. Two passengers. They're already here, waiting out by the picnic table. Take the 210. I've already rescheduled your students to other instructors."

Surprised and pleased at the rare opportunity to fly a cross-country flight, Lannis said, "Okay. It'll take me about ten minutes to file the flight plan and preflight the plane." She'd checked weather for the region when she arrived for work in the morning, so only needed a quick update from Flight Service. Her spirits lifted. The Cessna 210 had a retractable gear, along with more complex radios and systems than the training aircraft she flew most often. *Playtime.* "I'll go let them know."

She stepped out the front door and saw two men in suits seated at the picnic table. One of them looked familiar, but they were both facing away from her, so she wasn't quite sure. The sun-dappled shade, light and shadows dancing in the breeze, made it hard to see details of their features.

A prickle of unease shimmered across her skin, making it suddenly ultrasensitive. Lannis hesitated. She met a lot of people in her business, and many of them were repeats. While there was the occasional unpleasant personality to deal with, she didn't go out of her way to avoid them, so the unexpected reaction unsettled her. There was no logical reason for her to feel this way. She shook off the sensation and resumed walking.

As she came around the edge of the bench, she said, "Hi. I'm Lannis Parker, and I'll be your pilot today." Their faces came into view and she broke off her introduction, stunned speechless.

Jack! One of them was Jack! His dark hair was shorter, trimmed neatly, and the suit he wore conferred an air of sophistication quite out of character from her experience with him. Her heart thudded in her chest and instinctively she stepped back, then glanced at the other man. She'd never seen him before. Her gaze snapped back to Jack and she stared, thunderstruck. He gathered his sprawled limbs, stood with that familiar cat-like, indolent grace, and extended his hand in an unhurried show of courtesy.

Chapter Twenty-Three

BEN HAD GUESSED there would be a good chance of encountering Lannis when his boss approved the charter flight this morning. In fact, he'd hoped to see her. That she'd pilot the flight was beyond what he'd expected, and gave new meaning to the word *ironic.*

She probably didn't appreciate the irony.

He moved with slow, deliberate movements designed to allay any sense of threat she might feel. *Might feel? Think again, genius.* "Hello, Ms. Parker. My name is Ben Martin, and this is my partner, Mike Ross." He smiled, trying to infuse as much warmth as he could into his voice, his eyes, and his expression, and extended his hand. Waited for her to take it.

She didn't. Her deer-in-the-headlights look gave way to a mix of confusion and distrust. She backed up another step. Her tongue darted out to moisten her lips. She narrowed her eyes and regarded him as if he were a tarantula, or even better, a rabid skunk. As far as chance encounters went, this one was going nowhere fast.

"I—uh, excuse me." She wheeled and fled into the building.

"What was that all about?" Mike looked baffled.

Ben shrugged. "Remember in April, when this all started, and I disappeared for a week?"

Mike nodded.

"Yeah, well, she was the pilot of the plane I, uh, commandeered to get out of Louisville. So she's kind of touchy around me."

Mike rolled his eyes. "'Kind of touchy' is an understatement, man. No wonder. So, are we going to end up driving to Knoxville? That'll push the meeting so late that we won't be able to get everything accomplished today. I sure hate leaving Maggie with the kids overnight. It's usually not a problem, but…"

Ben sighed. "I'll go see if there's another pilot. I'd rather not drive, either."

As soon as he opened the door, he heard raised voices but couldn't make out the words. A man and a woman were arguing, that much was clear. One of the words from the female voice sounded like *no.* Staccato. Repeated. Interrupted and overruled by the deeper male voice.

He stopped at the main desk in the lobby and joined the receptionist in unabashed ogling of the spectacle in the glass-windowed office behind her. A scrawny gray-haired man stood nose to nose with Lannis and vibrated with barely contained emotion. His face was blotchy and mottled in various shades of crimson. Her face was a deep rosy pink. They were both yelling, and neither took a breath to listen to the other. Lannis slammed the flat of her hand on his desk, making a penholder and a coffee cup wobble. Droplets of coffee splashed out, landing on what appeared to be invoices.

Ben winced. This had to be her boss. He hoped she didn't provoke him further by spilling his coffee all over the paperwork. The man waved his cigar at her, punctuating his remarks by poking holes in the air with it. Ben stood back and crossed his arms. *Well, nothing's going to happen until their tiff is over.* He'd have to wait it out.

~

"No, Orvis. *No.* I'm *not* going to take him. The one guy, Ben Martin. I won't."

"Well, why not, Lannis? Give me one good reason!" Orvis was nearly purple with fury.

Lannis slammed her mouth shut and ground her teeth. There was no justification she could give Orvis. Not without telling him what had happened in April. That *she'd* taken N63438. That she'd lied to him. That she'd withheld information.

"I don't have anyone else today. You have to take the flight. *Both* passengers."

Lannis crossed her arms, her motions abrupt and angry. "I don't care. No. N. O."

Orvis threw his cigar on the desk and erupted. "Have you started drinking again? You've been acting weird lately, and I don't get it."

Stung, Lannis shook her head. *No.* She'd sure spent a lot of time thinking about it, but she hadn't done it. And she thought she'd been acting normal, or at least normal enough, even though she didn't feel that way.

"You've stopped flying any of the morning traffic flights—did you think I wouldn't notice? You won't schedule night students unless someone else is here. You're working yourself to the bone. You have bags under your eyes. You're losing weight you can't afford to lose. And now this! If you'd give me a valid reason, I wouldn't make you take the flight. *But you can't!* Drinking's the only explanation that makes sense. So help me God, I'll have your license jerked so fast…" A look of pain flashed over his face before he controlled it, and became inscrutable.

Lannis felt the blood drain from her face. She stood rigid, hands clamped into tense fists, feeling as though she were about to fly apart and had to hold her molecules together. "No, Orvis. No, sir. I have not been drinking." She forced the words through numb lips.

"Can you give me a valid reason to not accept this assignment?" Orvis picked up his cigar and toyed with it.

She shook her head in silence.

"This is a business. I won't throw away a paying customer on a whim."

"Yes, sir." Rebellion boiled to the surface. "Then I'm filing IFR." Instrument flight rules, used primarily for flight within clouds, took a bit more time both on the ground and in the air, as each plane was individually tracked and controlled in a complex system. On clear days, for flights like this, it was more expedient to file VFR, visual flight rules, leaving each pilot to navigate to their destination on their own.

Orvis rolled his eyes and threw his hands to the ceiling. "For crying out loud! It's severe clear out there!"

"Yeah, I know, but by God, I'm going to be on radar and talking to a controller every minute of this flight if I have to take it, and you can't make me do otherwise. Pilot in command, you know." He couldn't override her authority as to how the flight would be conducted, and he knew it as well as she did. She'd already made too much of a scene, and wondered if she'd done serious damage to her standing in Orvis's eyes. Which was worse? That, or flying Ben Martin, alias Jack—and facing the memories his presence resurrected?

"Whatever. Get out of here." He rubbed his forehead, waved his cigar at her, and sat down heavily. Shaking his head in frustration, he pulled out his handkerchief and blotted coffee off his papers.

~

Ben stepped out of Lannis's way as she stormed out of the office. She focused her fury on him and glared, a deep-six look if he'd ever seen one, and said in clipped tones, "The plane will be ready for you in ten minutes. You gentlemen may want to use the restroom now. It will be about a two-hour, maybe two-and-a-half-hour flight."

Her sarcastic emphasis on the word "gentlemen" was not lost on Ben, nor was the fact that her arm had nearly been twisted off to force her to comply with her boss. *Orvis, that's his name.* Ben had a good idea of the leverage used. She was not having a good day, which seemed to be the norm for her when Ben was involved. He felt a spurt of empathy.

She shoved past him to get to what must be the flight planning area. He nodded at her back and, whistling tunelessly, went to fetch Mike.

After the recommended pit stop, he and Mike walked across the ramp to the plane, and Ben nearly burst out laughing at the energy Lannis was expending on the preflight. Her footfalls echoed as she stomped around the plane, and he could hear her muttering from twenty steps away. She checked something on top of the wings, hauling herself up with enough power to launch herself clear across them. When she saw them coming she stopped muttering, but looked no less murderous.

Mike said in a low voice, "Are you sure this is safe?"

Not taking his eyes off her, Ben nodded. "Yeah. She's got a hell of a survival instinct. Superior, actually."

They reached the plane, but she hopped down and put herself between them and the doors before they could board. Guarding the plane. Granting access only at her authorization.

"Your weapons." Ice crystallized on her words, and she stuck her hand out in a brusque challenge. In obvious afterthought, she added, "Please." It was just as obvious she didn't mean the courtesy.

They both stepped back.

Ben said, "Uh-uh. No way."

And from Mike, at the same time, "No, ma'am, I don't think so."

"Yeah, well, if you want to fly with me, you will not be armed." Lannis arched a brow at Ben and crossed her arms.

He tamped down the frustration she always ignited in him, bared his teeth in what might pass for a smile, and said, "As law enforcement officers we are permitted to carry our service weapons on board aircraft. In addition, regulations do not allow us to relinquish our weapons. However, if it makes you more comfortable, *ma'am*, I'll give you my ammunition for safekeeping during the flight. Would that be acceptable?"

Her bravado slipped a bit. She hesitated, then nodded, the motion jerky. Clearly, she had expected that they would choose to not fly rather than surrender their weapons to her. Ben removed his gun from its holster, expelled the ammo and handed it to her, holding her gaze the entire time. She flinched when he pulled his gun out, a frisson of fear skittering across her features, quickly controlled.

He rotated the gun, keeping it pointed at the ground, and showed her the empty chamber. She tore her gaze from his long enough to glance at it.

"Mike, your ammo." Ben knew that his partner would balk at Lannis's demand, but would comply with a direct order from him, albeit reluctantly. "Now." After a slight pause, he heard the other gun being emptied. Lannis accepted the magazine and glanced down to check the chamber.

Looking up at Ben, she added sweetly, "Your knife?" The steel in her eyes belied the sugar in her voice. Still holding her gaze, he leaned down, removed it from its scabbard on his ankle, and gave it to her, handle first.

"Mr. Ross?"

Mike shook his head and said, "I'm not carrying anything other than my service weapon today, ma'am."

Lannis lifted her chin and sent them individual dagger looks. "Mr. Martin, have a seat in the back. Mr. Ross, you may sit in front, unless you'd both prefer to sit in the back."

Ben stifled a smile at her attempts to control the situation. Control him. He'd forgotten how energized she made him feel, how much he relished the verbal sparring in spite of the aggravation.

Mike spoke up. "Ms. Parker, if you don't mind, I was up all night with my kids. I'd just as soon be able to stretch out in the back and sleep, if it's all the same to you."

She flushed, then sent him a quick nod. They boarded, and she took the opportunity to stash the ammunition and knife in a storage pocket of the cockpit. On the pilot's side.

"You'll need the shoulder harness on for takeoff and landing, as well as the headset, in case of emergency." She shot a scathing look at Ben, and he remembered her instructions for the forced landing, which he figured was her intent. "Keep your lap belt on for the whole flight, loosely at least, in case we hit unexpected turbulence. The headset reduces fatigue caused by the engine noise, but using it during cruise is up to you."

She stopped her briefing and looked at Ben with an inscrutable expression, as if she'd just remembered something.

"May I see your ID, please?"

He smiled. "Absolutely." He fished his badge out of his inner jacket pocket. "Mike, you might want to show yours, too." Lannis took the items proffered and studied Ben's intensely, then compared it with Mike's.

"Your driver's license, Mr. Martin?"

Ben laughed, pulled out his wallet, and handed over his driver's license, library card, credit card, and medical insurance card. His grocery store discount card didn't have his name on it, nor did his frequent-buyer coffee card, so he didn't give them to her. Scratching his head, he couldn't think of anything else he had with him that would verify his identity.

She inspected them in silence, then suddenly looked at him, her eyes narrowing. "Benjamin *Jackson* Martin?"

He nodded. "The first rule of covert ops. Use a cover that's close enough to reality that you won't forget when you're under duress." He added helpfully, "Like you visiting your aunt."

Mike looked confused, then rolled his eyes. He stretched his legs out, leaned back, and tried to find a comfortable way to sleep with the headset on.

Lannis slowly handed the cards back to Ben, gave him a searching look, then busied herself with the plane.

He belted in and made himself as inconspicuous as he could while she flipped switches and ran checklists, conducting tests of the engine and systems. It was clear her voice was familiar to the controllers, as they engaged in light banter with her. He was glad to see that. He'd seen her at her most vulnerable and it was reassuring to see her at her best, to see her comfortable and...confident.

He noted dark circles under her eyes, and frowned. Her voice didn't sound nasal, so it probably wasn't from allergies, the Ohio Valley crud that was so common here. Was it lack of sleep? Or exhaustion? Maybe she'd been sick.

He heard the controller tell her to expect a four-minute delay for traffic spacing. She acknowledged the instruction, sat motionless except for a tiny muscle tic in her jaw, and ignored her passengers beyond the necessary safety briefings.

Ignored Ben.

She broke her silence on the takeoff roll. "It's not nearly as interesting when it's done the right way, is it, *Jack*?" Her voice was tight.

In fact, the takeoff was smooth, comfortable, and unremarkable, a feat in itself given the unpredictable wind gusts. As soon as they leveled off, Mike removed his headset and settled back without opening his eyes. Lannis stayed busy, or at least maintained that appearance for half an hour. Finally it was clear there was nothing more she could do to stonewall Ben. Silence reigned for several minutes, except for the drone of the engine and Mike's snores in the back.

"How've you been since April?" Ben asked. He thought for a moment that she was going to refuse to answer.

"Just peachy keen." She bit out the words.

"Hey, Lannis, how's about you skip past the hostile part, and we just have a conversation?"

"Why?" Her eyes sparked at him. "I don't know why it matters to you anyway."

"Aw, come on." Ben figured they'd go round and round for hours, if not days, if he didn't cut to the important stuff now. "You matter to me, and you know it. I'm glad you didn't contact the police when you got back. We busted eleven guys on the police force. Way more than we'd thought. So you ran a huge risk of putting yourself right in the middle of all that. Did you have any problems at all? With your story?"

"Um…no. Yeah, it worked. Everybody bought it," she said slowly.

"Good. How about the other stuff? A support group or a counselor?"

She shook her head. "No."

"I still think it could help you, darlin'." Ben didn't bother hiding his disappointment.

She shook her head again. "I'm fine."

"You look really tired. Have you been sick?"

She flushed. "No." She snagged her bottom lip between her teeth and worried at it, and her fingers tightened on the yoke, the knuckles turning white.

Ben read her body language and didn't believe her, but air traffic control interrupted before he could press the issue. Whether she wanted to talk to him about it or not, something was wrong.

After she got off the radio she turned, looked directly at him, and said, "Please. Just drop it. Leave me alone." Her voice trembled on the last word.

He gave a half shrug and nodded. He couldn't force her and there was no use pushing her. He had firsthand knowledge of her propensity to push back. This wasn't the time or place, in any case.

He rode in silence for the remainder of the flight.

Chapter Twenty-Four

LANNIS RETURNED the ammunition to her two passengers before securing the plane. Jack—*no, Ben*—invited her to come with them for lunch.

"No, thanks."

"You sure?"

"Yup. I sure am."

"Suit yourself." He turned to go with Mike. "We should be back in about four hours, maybe four and a half."

Taken aback at the ease with which he accepted her rejection, she stopped tying down the plane and stared at him as they walked away.

After they left she checked the weather, preflighted the plane, and filed the flight plan for the return. That took a whole fifteen minutes, so she went in search of food. Standard pilot fare, otherwise known as vending machines filled with stale, unimaginative cuisine, was all that was available. Lunch with the men would definitely have been better than this, except she wouldn't have been able to stand the tension. Either way, her stomach wasn't too happy with the idea of food.

Her thoughts went back to Jack's ID. It seemed legitimate, and looked exactly like Mike Ross's. DEA. Drug Enforcement Agency. Could she trust his documentation? It looked official and everything matched, but then she thought about the receipts his buddy had provided on short notice in Pigeon Forge. Plus, he'd certainly used a bunch of different names there.

Unsettled, Lannis paced from the pilot lounge to the weather center, past the front counter to the vending machines. Normally she'd sit and watch the planes while she waited, but Jack's...Ben's...appearance today had rattled her to the core.

She'd already been shocked, furious, and terrified today, and the feelings had opened a Pandora's box. Memories surged back, no longer surreal or dreamlike, and the accompanying emotions rolled through her in waves. She still cringed over losing her temper, something that hadn't happened since the last night she'd seen Rudy. Well, not counting the week with Jack. Ben. Whoever. She huffed a breath out with enough force to momentarily blow her bangs upward. She couldn't afford to let her emotions get the better of her again.

She needed physical exertion. Something to take the edge off her nerves. Something other than a drink, which she was beginning to crave with frightening intensity. She went outside to walk, maybe even jog between the long rows of hangars despite the heat.

By the time Ben and Mike were due back, Lannis had rechecked the weather three times and preflighted the plane again. Hot and sweaty, she stood in the restroom and cooled her face and neck with a dripping paper towel. The cold water trickled down her forearms, and between her breasts. Droplets collected on her elbows, dripping on the tile floor. Her anxiety had abated, thanks to exercise and sheer emotional exhaustion. She was relieved it was time to fly, and welcomed the focus that kept all the rest at bay.

When the men arrived, both wordlessly unloaded their guns, handed her the ammo, and showed her the empty chambers. Just as silently, she accepted the bullets, along with Ben's knife, and stowed them in the front pocket again. The heat of the day was at its peak, so both men removed their jackets and laid them in the back. Lannis showed them how to adjust the vents for air circulation once they were airborne. As before, Mike went to sleep as soon as he could.

Only a few more hours. Then this day would be over, and she could draw an unrestricted breath of air. She reminded herself she'd done it before, could do it again...and believed herself.

Almost.

~

Ben sensed Lannis's moodiness, not that it was difficult, and watched her out of the corner of his eye. The air was bumpier at altitude this time, and when a chart slipped off her lap, he reached down and handed it back to her.

"Thanks." She avoided his eyes.

"You're welcome." He paused, then added, "I've never really thanked you for what you did for me in April. I know it was against your will, but even so, you saved my life, and I do owe you for that."

She swiveled and looked at him, eyes wide and unguarded.

He raised an eyebrow. "I mean it." He extended his right hand. "Thank you, Lannis."

Her eyes betrayed her conflict, the struggle between her desire to keep an icy distance from him and acknowledgment of his genuine sentiment. She hesitated, then shook his hand, a brief, businesslike pump, withdrawing hers as soon as politely possible.

Ben smiled inwardly at her wariness, even as her small concession hinted at a chink in her well-constructed defensive walls. He changed the subject, asking her about their position, charts, radio exchanges…anything he could think of that was neutral and nonthreatening.

It struck him with a jolt that this was the first normal conversation they'd ever had. Her initial replies were stilted, but after a bit she loosened up. Once she began to relax, she became subtly animated, revealing passion for her work, though her natural reserve still held sway.

She fascinated him with her hedgehog defenses, complex personality, and quick, intelligent mind. He'd be lying to himself if he denied that she attracted him physically, too. He was all too aware that the situation that had initially brought them together was finally over. It was going to hit the media this week. Ethically, he was free to pursue a relationship with her, if she was willing—which she'd made clear she was not.

Suddenly he wanted to know if it was him, specifically, that she had no interest in, or men in general, given her experiences. Whatever the answer was, he'd have to tease it out of her. She wouldn't give it to him easily.

He made the decision without hesitating. His first priority was to prevent her from building her walls again, although she needed enough space to feel safe. It was going to be a fine line to walk, but he already relished the challenge.

~

After landing, Lannis wrote the numbers from the Hobbs meter and the tachometer on the plane's clipboard and handed it to Ben, with instructions to give it to the receptionist for billing. Mike stretched and she watched the two men amble to the office.

She glanced at her watch and saw that the line crew had left for the day. Grumbling but resigned, she refueled and serviced the plane, wrestling the temperamental, bulky fuel truck across the ramp. She sighed in relief when she was done, her arms aching from pulling the heavy hose and reaching high above her head to wipe the wings clean of bugs. Now all she had left was five minutes of paperwork and she could go home.

This had been a bear of a day. She felt drained and numb, but still had an undercurrent of unfocused anxiety that made her feel off-balance and jittery at the same time. She walked into the office and stopped short.

Jack…no, Ben was leaning against the counter, relaxed, tapping his fingers absently.

He should have been out of here ten minutes ago! While she hadn't purposely dragged out the refueling, it had taken her quite a bit more time than was required to settle an account.

He smiled, laugh lines crinkling around his eyes. "Ms. Parker, could I buy you dinner?"

Lannis shot a quick look at Orvis in his glassed office, swallowed, and, careful to not offend a customer in front of her boss, said, "No, thank you, Mr. Martin." She made her voice sound professional and distant, but not rude.

Disappointment flickered across his features, but he didn't look surprised. "Well, I appreciate the excellent flight, and enjoyed your company. Thank you." He left and Lannis, realizing she'd been holding her breath, released a long sigh of relief.

She finished her paperwork, then cautiously scanned the parking lot before she left the building. The last thing she needed was another confrontation with Ja—Ben. Especially today. She didn't see him, and set out for home. Head down, the rhythm of her steps lulled her. Bits and pieces of her time in the mountains with him surfaced. Embarrassment heated her face as she recalled the night in the motel, followed quickly by awareness of her unreasonable response to seeing him today.

Frustration settled on her shoulders like an unwelcome hair shirt.

Lannis dragged her gaze from the sidewalk…and discovered she wasn't home, but in front of the liquor store. She slowed, her commitment to stay sober wavering. The compulsion to numb her emotions was as overwhelming as the emotions themselves.

Her hesitation was only momentary. Lannis crumbled under the weight of discomfiting images, caving to the promise of oblivion. She detoured into the store. Dug crumpled bills out of her pocket. Closed her mind to the consequences.

And grabbed a bottle of her old friend Jose.

Chapter Twenty-Five

SHE WAS LATE.

Ben paced the lobby of Louisville Air. His bid to approach Lannis on her own turf had just lurched down an alley he hadn't foreseen.

From what he gathered, this was a first. Lannis was never late to work, never called in sick. Her failure to show up, or even call, was uncharacteristic to say the least. When he combined that with her stress level yesterday and obvious signs of fatigue, a niggling concern for her welfare sprouted in his gut.

He cursed silently, then strode to Orvis's office and pushed the door open. "Mr. Larson, I'm concerned about Lannis Parker."

Orvis narrowed his eyes. "She didn't want to fly you yesterday. Why was that? Why would you be concerned about her?"

Ben made a wry face. "We met some time ago under less than optimal conditions. She told me about her brief, uh, drinking problem, and your ultimatum. I'm not her favorite person, I'll admit, but I care deeply about her, just as you do," he said. "I'm canceling work this morning, and going to check on her. If there's anything you need to be aware of—" He met Orvis's gaze squarely, held it, and paused for a long moment. Hoped the man would read between the lines. "I'll let you know."

Orvis appraised Ben for an equally long moment, then flipped his Rolodex open and wrote Lannis's address on a scrap of paper. He handed it to Ben. "Okay, son. If she's hurt, let me know. Otherwise"—Orvis sent Ben a silent message with *his* eyes—"I'll give her twenty-four hours to get her act together. But this is her last chance. You understand?"

Ben nodded and pocketed the piece of paper.

Even unfamiliar with the neighborhood, Ben found her house in about six minutes. Hard rock music blared inside, the bass turned up so loud the walls seemed to throb. She couldn't hear the phone or the doorbell with that much noise. He decided not to bang on the door, figuring she probably couldn't hear that, either. He pulled out a credit card to jimmy the lock. As an afterthought, he tried the door.

The knob turned easily. He glowered at her lax security and walked in.

"Lannis," he called over the music. He called again, louder, his voice sharp with insistence and authority. His cop voice. "Lannis!" There was no answer, no movement. Dread building in his gut, he followed the sound to its source.

The door to her bedroom was open, and he recognized the clothes she'd worn yesterday dropped haphazardly on the floor. Waves of nauseating fumes met him—alcohol, both from the bottle and metabolized by her lungs. She lay on her belly, one arm hanging off the bed, sheets tangled around her legs. A fifth of Jose Quervo Gold lay on its side just below her dangling fingertips. There was about a half cup of liquid still in it. A spill of undetermined size puddled under the bed. A trash can was positioned close to her head and, if he interpreted the odors correctly, had been the recipient of at least one offering usually presented to the porcelain gods.

His heart clenched. As thin as she was, she could have drunk enough to induce alcohol poisoning, requiring hospitalization in an ICU. If she'd done it fast enough, she could be past the point of recovery. At least puking would have gotten some of it out of her system. He hoped it was enough.

Wrinkling his nose, he stepped over her shoes, then reached down and touched her cheek. Her skin was warm, and her eyelids fluttered at his feather-light touch. Relief flooded him, followed rapidly by fury. If she was that responsive, she hadn't reached the stage of poisoning. She was just drunk on her butt. She didn't know it yet, but she was going to get a dose of friendship, Ben-style. And she wasn't going to like it. Lips thinning, he seized the back of the tank top that apparently doubled as pajamas.

He jerked her out of bed, and pulled her upward. She woke up enough to recognize her precarious position, and squeaked. Arms windmilling in uncoordinated arcs, she tried to grab anything solid, but netted mostly air. By sheer luck, she snagged the pillow, but couldn't maintain her grip and dropped it. Ben set her on her feet, and she blinked up at him with bloodshot eyes.

Confusion filled her eyes, and she furrowed her brow. Then recognition sparked in her gaze. Her forehead smoothed, her lips tipped up in a smile that Ben couldn't see any reason for, and she fluttered her eyelashes in what could only be interpreted as flirtation.

Before he realized what she was up to, she slipped her arms around his waist, nuzzling his chest with her lips and nipping at the buttons on his shirt. Catlike, she rubbed against him, her breasts warm through the cotton of his shirt.

He tried to grasp her arms to extricate himself, but in the way of the truly inebriated, she managed to evade him, leaving him with the sense that he'd been captured by an octopus.

Worse, his body knew exactly how to respond to hers—and did so. With alacrity.

"Ben, mmm, you feel so good..." Her brow wrinkled in renewed bafflement, glancing around her bedroom. She tipped her head back and looked at him. "Why're you here?"

Gathering his wits, Ben took advantage of her momentarily still arms, and thrust her away from him. "We'll talk later." Heat rose up his neck. Grasping her shoulders, he turned her. "Right now you're going to take a shower." He guided her as she wobbled obediently to the bathroom. He opened the shower door, shoved her in, still dressed in the tank top and boxer shorts adorned with tiny multicolored biplanes—*where in the world did she find those?*—and turned the water on full blast, full cold.

Her shriek banished any lingering concern that she'd done serious damage with her binge. The opaque plastic door bowed with her efforts to open it, rattling with her blows. Grimly, he held the door closed. She was still so addled that she couldn't figure out how to turn the hot water on, which meant he'd have to stand guard to keep her from burning herself. He waited till she stopped beating the door, then opened it, tossed in a washcloth, and pointed at the soap.

"Get busy," he ordered curtly. Mouth open in outrage, water dripping off her nose, she looked like a bedraggled waif, except her clothes were now molded to her body like a second skin. The cold water had the predictable effect on her nipples. She looked just as enticing as she'd felt scant moments ago.

He slammed the door. He did *not* need this right now. In spite of what Lannis thought, neither did she. After few moments of silence, she picked up the soap and threw it at the shower door.

"The quicker you wash up, the quicker you can get out. *No hot water.* Not negotiable," he snapped.

More silence. Then he heard her scrabbling in the shower to pick up the soap. Her blurred shape moved as she began to rub it on her arms.

He glowered at the opaque plastic, aware that cold water would cure his altogether inappropriate response to her—and angry that she'd elicited it.

Chapter Twenty-Six

LANNIS DROPPED THE SOAP several times, but finally managed to scrub enough of her reddened, chilled skin to satisfy Ben. She hoped. Shivering, she wished she could shed her soaked clothes, but that was the last thing she'd do in front of *him*. Still perplexed but becoming more rational moment by frigid moment, she realized he'd found her after last night's binge. Shame flowed through her belly to the tips of her fingers, only to be eclipsed by a flash of anger.

It was all his fault! He'd hijacked her plane! He'd kidnapped her! Then he came back! *Why won't he leave me alone?*

She stilled, no longer trying to escape the icy shower as the implication of the sun's position suddenly wormed its way into her awareness.

She was late for work. She was drunk. Orvis would fire her. She had not a shred of doubt on that subject. Plus he'd report her to the FAA. *I'll lose my license!* A sob strangled her and she grabbed her midsection as she slid down the wall, barely noticing as the knobs of her spine bumped their way against the hard tile. Lannis curled around her emptiness and rested her head on her knees.

The door ripped open and the stream of water stopped. A towel dropped on her head, and the door clicked shut. She clutched the towel and buried her face in it.

"Get dressed. You have work to do." His tone was unbending.

As usual. She fought her way to her feet and wrapped the towel around herself, then stumbled out of the shower, straining—and failing—to find a wisp of dignity. He'd seen her in little more than a towel enough times that she wasn't sure exactly why she was trying to cling to modesty, but right now she didn't have much else.

She hazarded a quick glance at him but couldn't hold the contact. "I'm not sure what you mean, because I've just lost my job." Her voice hitched on another sob, which she controlled with brutal willpower, throat muscles working convulsively. "You don't have to babysit me."

"Look at me." His voice was hard, commanding.

She looked at his shoes, his shoulder, at the frame of the door beyond his right ear.

He didn't bother hiding his irritation and impatience. "I'm not leaving the bathroom until you look at me."

She struggled, shifted her gaze, and met his. Ben's arctic eyes bored into hers, searching. She didn't know if she had an answer to his silent question. A slight tremor began in her back as he scrutinized her, but she managed to maintain eye contact, barely.

He seemed to find what he was looking for. "I'll be in the kitchen if you need anything." He left her alone, closing the door behind him.

The tremor graduated to shaking and she sank down on the toilet, sitting on clothes he'd brought in for her. What had she done? Ruined her life. Everything she'd worked so hard for. She'd thrown it all away. She buried her face in her hands and gave in to tears.

"Three minutes, Lannis." Ben spoke sharply from the other side of the door. "Or you'll be heading out as you are."

She jumped. Remembered Ben *always* did what he said he'd do. Still crying, she shed her drenched sleepwear and dried off, grabbed her clothes, now damp and wrinkled, and pulled them on. She brushed her teeth hurriedly and finger-combed her hair.

As she started out the door, she caught a glimpse of herself in the mirror and slowed, seeing herself as Ben probably did. Gaunt. Pale. Dark circles under puffy, red-rimmed eyes. And drunk. In the morning. *What a loser.*

A memory of the dream she'd had just before she woke up popped into her mind. It had been Ben, warm and solid…and safe. She'd held him, filling her arms and her senses with his strength, with his scent, and had buried her face in his chest. He'd made her feel desirable. Sensuous.

Why she would dream of him, and why he would elicit that sort of a response from her was a mystery.

Except… In the dream, he'd been dressed in the same clothes as he was now. In the dream, his eyes had been coldly furious. Not so different from when she'd woken up in the shower.

Her heart plummeted. *Dear God, was that real?* Lannis closed her eyes and bowed her head. It was real. It had to have been. Tears dripped off the tip of her nose. How was she going to face him now?

Impulsively, she opened the medicine cabinet. Aspirin. She had a whole bottle. *After I take them, nobody will have to see what a failure I am, ever again.* But it wasn't there. Confused, she moved aside the items in the cabinet. The bottle of pain relief pills was gone, as well as her leftover cold pills, antacids, and razor. The cabinet held only an old bottle of nail polish that was nearly dried up, some Q-tips, Band-Aids, and nail clippers.

Suddenly furious, she slammed the medicine cabinet, wrenched the bathroom door open, and staggered to the kitchen, bracing herself with her palms on the walls of the short hallway.

"You think you're pretty hot stuff, don't you?" She used a very unladylike word. "Where's my aspirin? Give it back."

Ben trapped her with his eyes. "What do you need it for, Lannis?" His tone was conversational.

Too late she realized his voice was deceptively calm. "Because...because...well, um." Her voice faded as she realized he knew exactly what she'd considered doing, and to answer his question was to admit it.

"Why do you need it, Lannis?" This time he leaned forward, paralyzing her with his steely gaze.

"I, uh, have a headache."

"No dice, Lannis. *Tell me the truth*. Because you're going to start facing life instead of holding it at arm's length or trying to numb out the pain. You just found yourself a friend for the journey." He bared his teeth in what might pass for a smile, but she knew better. "Me."

Her gut clenched.

"Now, *the truth*, Lannis. Why did you need the aspirin?"

Lannis licked her dry lips, and whispered, "Because I was going to take them."

"All of them?"

"Y-yes." She could barely get the word out.

"What, darlin'? I couldn't hear you." Ben held one hand to his ear as if to amplify her words.

A flush heated her neck and spread to her cheeks. She mumbled, "I was going to take the whole bottle."

"Okay, I heard it that time. I don't think it would've been wise for me to leave you an opportunity to do that, do you?" He didn't wait for her to respond. "Have you ever had thoughts of suicide before?"

"No!" Lannis brought her gaze up to meet his, shocked at the implication.

"Truth?" His eyes pinned her in place.

"Yes! I mean, truth! No, I've never thought about it or tried it."

"Then why now?" His eyes bored into hers.

Lannis opened her mouth, then realized she had no good response. She broke eye contact and stared at the floor. "I was ashamed," she mumbled. "Didn't want you to see me as the failure I am."

"Self-pity doesn't become you."

She snapped her head up, ready to fling another angry salvo at him, but the words died on her tongue. His expression dared her to defy him...but she couldn't. "You're right." Her shoulders sagged. Her temper deflated.

"Good job. 'The truth shall set you free.' You need to remember that." He pulled the plastic lid off the ancient can of coffee he'd dug out from the back of her cupboard. "Now, like I said, you have work to do. Change the sheets on your bed, put the tequila bottle in the garbage out back, clean up the mess in your room, and wash out the trash can. When you're done, we'll talk about the next step." He turned back to the coffee.

Lannis wheeled and marched from the room, trying to project an aura of dignity. The effect was ruined when she bumped into the corner of the table, making it screech across the floor, then caught her shoulder on the door frame hard enough to leave a bruise.

As she stumbled down the hallway, she remembered what he'd said about being her friend. She made a rude noise. The nightmares that had plagued her sleep were nothing compared to what her life had just become. A daytime nightmare.

Because now she had a *friend.*

Chapter Twenty-Seven

LANNIS TENDED TO THE BEDROOM and gagged through the task of scrubbing her trash can. Then Ben made her clean up the bathroom. By that time her head *was* beginning to hurt, but she didn't dare ask for anything from him. She could hear him working in the kitchen, and the aromas of toast and eggs began drifting down the hall, along with coffee.

She wrung out her wet sleepwear, hung it on the shower rod, and surveyed the bathroom. There was nothing left to do.

Except face him.

Cleaning the trash can had been preferable to that. Her options were exhausted. Knowing Ben the way she did, Lannis steeled herself to go into the kitchen.

He stood at the stove looking very domestic and nonthreatening. *Hah.* She knew better. He waved a spatula at the table, already set for two.

"Sit. Eat."

She sat, took a small helping of scrambled eggs and half a piece of toast. It smelled good, but she couldn't bring herself to eat more than a couple of bites of either. At close quarters, the aroma of the coffee set her stomach to roiling, so she set the cup down without a taste. She got up, and started to take her plate to the sink.

"Sit down. You need to eat more than that."

"I can't," she said. "It's making me sick." She wavered, halfway across the kitchen.

"So wait a few minutes for your stomach to settle. You *will* eat at least one whole egg and one whole slice of toast."

So much for the idea of him looking nonthreatening. She sank back down at the table and began moving food around the plate with her fork. Well aware that she wasn't going to be able to fool him, she tried tiny bites, and after a concerted effort managed to choke down what he required. By that time, he'd served himself four times as much as she had, and was nearly done. She went to the sink and began washing the dishes.

"We're leaving as soon as you're done, so if there's anything else you need to do before we go, tell me now."

"Ben, I, uh, don't want to go anywhere. I mean, thanks for, well, whatever…" Lannis was sobering up, fast, but couldn't make sense of his assertion that they were going to leave, nor could she figure out exactly what she might be thanking him for.

"Tough. Today's goal is for you to start getting your life back on track. We begin now." His pale blue eyes dared her to defy him.

Anger flared and she took the bait. "You're awfully high-handed, aren't you? Who asked you for advice? My life is none of your business!"

"Yes, it is, Lannis." His voice was quiet. "You saved *my* life four months ago. I owe you. You're throwing yours away, and for no good reason. I'd like the opportunity to help you change that. After today, if you never want to see me again, that's fine. I'll honor your decision. But for today, I will do everything in my power to be your friend, someone who has your best interests at heart."

Seeing the steel in his eyes, she realized he was not likely to back down, as if that concept was even in his vocabulary. The words began to sink in. *Her best interests. Everything in his power.* Her heart plummeted as she remembered Orvis. "My job. I have to—"

"You've been called in sick for today."

She stared at him, stupefied.

"Let's go."

She stood frozen, uncertain.

"All bets are off if you don't come with me now. Your job, your future, your life are in your hands. You've messed up royally and there are consequences. Big ones, either way. You don't have to come. *It's your choice.* However, if you do, you'll have a lot more options than if you decide to stay home." He softened his voice. "You have *everything* to lose."

Stricken, she said, "I've already lost everything."

He extended his hand. "Let's go."

The moment stretched out as she weighed the stark contrast of the alternatives he'd presented. He had never lied to her about anything on this level. Nor could she ignore her bone-deep conviction that he truly meant her no harm. Trusting him was likely the best way out of the dilemma she'd created.

Maybe the only way.

Taking his hand would step beyond simple trust to something else—a deeper meaning Lannis didn't want to examine, a vulnerability she wasn't willing to feel. So she ignored it, crossed her arms, and pushed past him.

Ben stopped her before she got to the door, and she looked up at him. He'd thinned his lips, and a muscle jumped in his jaw. Voice tight, he said, "Your keys, Lannis. You forgot to lock up last night."

Chapter Twenty-Eight

"WHERE ARE YOU taking me?" The low, throaty rumble of his restored Mustang's engine thrummed through her gut. Lannis felt herded and out of control. Anxiety ballooned into fear and she turned to Ben, putting a hand on his forearm. "Please, where are you taking me?"

He shifted gears, and the car accelerated with barely restrained power. "You'll see." Then he relented. "Nothing bad's going to happen."

She removed her hand from his arm and faced forward, struggling with her emotions.

"You have kids, Lannis?"

"What?" She stared at him goggle-eyed.

"I was just wondering if you had kids with Rudy, or if you'd ever been pregnant."

"Uh, no. Although I don't know why it matters." *Especially to you.*

"It'll make more sense later today." He paused. "It's a blessing you didn't bring an innocent child into that marriage."

Was he rubbing her face in her failure? She glanced at him, but he didn't seem to be gloating. Rather, he looked deep in thought.

He pulled into a parking lot in one of the rougher areas of downtown, parked, and said, "Get out." The lot was peppered with small groups of homeless men and a few women. Lannis hunkered down in her seat and shook her head. Ben got out and walked away, however, and staying with him seemed safer. She scrambled to catch up. Wary of the men, she paid little attention to Ben's destination. When a screen door slammed behind her, she jumped and looked around. They were in a large commercial-type kitchen where half a dozen people worked with cheerful efficiency.

Ben was talking to a woman, who seemed to be in charge. "— and she wants to help out today. Serving." The woman peered at Lannis and smiled, waving her in.

"Here you go, then, miss, and thank you!" She handed Lannis an apron, plastic gloves, and a baseball cap. "It's either a cap or a hairnet, and not many choose the hairnet." She punctuated her statement with bell-toned laughter.

Befuddled, Lannis put them on, and was urged gently to the front of the kitchen. The homeless were lining up outside and it finally struck her. A soup kitchen. He'd brought her to work in a soup kitchen. She started to turn around, to object, and was startled to find him at her ear.

"Think hard about this, Lannis. This is where you risk ending up if you don't knock off the drinking. You're not far from it, depending on what Orvis knows and what he decides to do. *Think hard.*" His voice was flat and she shivered, chilled by his words.

One of the volunteers opened the doors, and Lannis spent the next hour dishing up mashed potatoes and gravy. Her stomach rebelled at the odors, and her head pounded.

Once, Ben came up and whispered, "Smile." She tried, but it was wobbly, especially with the image he'd placed in her mind's eye.

He was right. She scraped by from paycheck to paycheck, with only one or two hundred dollars in reserve, although right now she had a cushion left from the thousand he'd given her in April. She had family, but she'd broken off contact with them several years ago, and in any case, they wouldn't take her in if she was drinking. Lannis began to feel as if there were a suffocating, thick pad of wool over her nose and mouth.

Finally the line ended, and the supervisor said, "Have a plate yourself now, miss." Other volunteers had already helped themselves and sat among the people they'd just served.

Lannis murmured, "No, thanks, I'm not hungry." At the same time, Ben said with enthusiasm, "Great, you'd enjoy some lunch, wouldn't you, Lannis?" He pushed a plate into her hands, filled it, and directed her out to sit with the rest. He said in a low voice, "Sit down and eat something. And *smile.*"

Several of the clients scooted over to make room for her. Trapped, she smiled weakly and sat. She toyed with her food, bringing one or two bites to her mouth. Unable to swallow, she put her fork down and tried to appear interested in the conversations around her. At long last, the interminable meal was over, and she returned her plate to the kitchen.

"Thanks, honey. We can use your help anytime you feel like it." The woman waved as Ben led the way to the car.

A few blocks later it became clear he wasn't taking her home, but toward a different section of downtown. Lannis clamped her lips together. It didn't matter whether she liked his plan or not. When it came down to that, it didn't much matter if she knew the destination ahead of time. He'd said nothing bad was going to happen, but that didn't rule out something hard. She steeled herself.

He pulled into one of the hospital parking garages, took a ticket, slapped it on the dash, and parked. With a slight sigh, she got out. After taking two different elevators and following a number of corridors in a bewildering maze, they came to a nondescript office.

Ben pushed the door open and grinned. "Hi, Gladys. I'm ready to go again. This is Lannis Parker, a friend of mine. She wants to volunteer in one of the nurseries. Lannis, this is Gladys Philpot. She's the coordinator of volunteers at the children's hospital."

The plump woman with merry eyes came around her desk and enveloped him in a bear hug. "It's been too long, Ben! I'm glad to have you back." She grasped both of Lannis's hands in hers and said, "It's always a pleasure to meet one of Ben's friends. We're glad to have you on board."

Lannis cringed at the contact and presumed familiarity, and shot a sideways look at Ben. Volunteer? Nursery? What was he up to now? Now sober, her head throbbed from everything he was rubbing her face in today. Otherwise, she'd let him know exactly what she thought—which was that he was arrogant, insufferable, and entirely too bossy about her life.

Gladys rummaged through papers on the desk, and was discussing schedules with Ben. She nodded and said, "Sure, I can set it up for you both to come in on the same day, at the same time."

Lannis narrowed her eyes at him.

He shrugged and looked at her. "It'll save you bus fare and time if we carpool. No biggie." Then he said to Gladys, "Lannis would like to get started today."

"You'll stay with her?" At Ben's nod, she said, "It's not usual, but since we've got the background check underway, I'll make an exception." Gladys beamed at her. "I'll call ahead, if you'd like to show her the way."

Ben took Lannis's elbow as they walked down the hallway to yet another bank of elevators. He punched the button and glanced at her.

She glared back. "I don't know what you're up to. I don't want to spend time here every week. How can you make a commitment like that for me? You didn't even ask!"

He nudged her into the elevator. "I figured with all your trust and control issues, babies would be the least threatening."

Her lips tightened even as the truth of his words prodded at her defenses.

He ignored her look. "You need to break out of your stifling, self-centered, *lonely* cocoon. Volunteering will help you get some perspective and balance. Try this for a month or six weeks. If you find something else that fits better, you can move on. Meanwhile, this is a good first step."

Stung by his words, Lannis ducked her head. He put his hand on her shoulder and gave her a squeeze. He probably meant to encourage her, but she felt even more trapped.

A nurse met her at the door of the neonatal ICU and showed her how to scrub and gown up. When she entered the nursery, the incubators and array of equipment overwhelmed her. Intimidated, she said, "I don't know, maybe this is a mistake."

The nurse smiled. "You'll get used to it; don't let it scare you. The babies are what are important."

Lannis looked past the wires, tubes, beeping monitors, and finally saw the tiny patients. Her heart melted. The nurse directed her to a rocking chair, deftly wrapped a baby from a tiny bassinette rather than an incubator, and handed the wriggling bundle to Lannis.

"The wires are to the heart monitor, and the plastic tube taped to her cheeks is oxygen. Make sure it stays positioned under her nose. Here's a bottle. If you need help, I'll be right over here." She moved to an incubator a few steps away.

Almost afraid to rock, Lannis stroked the infant's cheek. The baby turned toward her finger, yawned, and stretched. Its eyes fluttered open, then locked onto hers with an intensity that was almost comical. A smile teased the corners of Lannis's lips, and then a full-fledged grin broke her face. "Aren't you a sweetheart? What's your name, hmmm?"

"Her name is Alisha. Her parents live in Owensboro. They can only get here on weekends, so it helps out a lot when volunteers can give her the attention we don't have time for," the nurse said.

Lannis's heart melted at the baby's utter helplessness. Ben Martin had been insufferably heavy-handed today, but this moment was a gift.

A pang of sadness rippled through her.

Once, she'd wanted children. Now, she'd messed up so badly she didn't deserve them. But in this nursery, she could glimpse that bit of heaven.

She began rocking.

Chapter Twenty-Nine

Ben watched from the corridor, through the nursery's large observation windows. His breath caught at Lannis's smile. She was pretty even when she was somber, and the flashes of passion he'd witnessed in her fury added life to her controlled features. Yet he felt he was seeing the real Lannis for the first time. Her face was radiant, open, and…happy. Her transformation staggered him.

Her feisty spirit had attracted him from the beginning, and the fact that she was athletic and good-looking didn't hurt. The sense of responsibility for his part in her struggles weighed heavy on his shoulders and he wanted—no, *needed*—to make restitution.

However, she was bent on sabotaging her life. This morning, when he'd found her drunk, he'd decided to ignore his desire for her, to be a friend, but nothing more. He didn't need to tie himself down with someone who carried that much baggage. Now, seeing her face, his conviction wavered. The potential she displayed, even as she tried to conceal it, both from herself and everyone else, was remarkable.

Given time to heal, to work through her garbage, to make peace with her past… Maybe. He could afford to wait and see what she'd do with her chance at a new beginning.

When she came out of the nursery, she spied him leaning against the wall and adopted her habitual scowl. Her eyes widened as she realized he'd watched her through the window, and a blush crept across her cheeks. Ben watched the emotions play across her face, and saw when civility trumped petulance. The ghost of a smile softened her expression.

"Thanks." Her blush faded. "I don't remember the last time I held a baby. I'd forgotten what they're like."

He smiled, and draped his arm around her shoulders. "I figured as much, darlin'." For once she didn't resist his touch.

He took her to a Mexican restaurant for supper. Ben was relentless at making her eat this time, although it took forever for her to chew and swallow each bite, and his patience began to fray. She was tense and distracted. Their conversation revolved around how much she was or was not eating at any given moment, and finally she erupted.

"Stop it, Ben! I'm not anorexic. I'll eat. I'm just too worried right now." She looked desperate. "You work for the DEA, right? What do you do? How did you get into it?"

Surprised, Ben let her change the subject. She'd stepped outside of her carefully constructed walls again. "Yeah, I do. I did a lot of work in the Army that naturally led into law enforcement. I signed on with the DEA because I want to make a difference." He hesitated, and decided to be as open as he'd forced her to be. "My older brother had a drug problem, and even with everything we tried, it killed him."

Lannis stared at him, eyes wide.

Having her full attention didn't make the words come any easier. "It doesn't take a shrink to put those pieces together. I'm under no illusions about saving people. Everybody has to make their own choices, but I'm trying to tip the scales in favor of kids by taking out the dealers, especially the bigger players." He took a sip of water and swallowed the sudden lump in his throat that came when he talked about Danny. "I was working undercover when we met."

He cleared his throat. "After I sent you home, we busted a major ring in Louisville that included the folks you'd expect, plus a bunch of crooked cops, which is pretty unusual. The story's going to hit the media in the next day or so. You knew a lot of this in April. I just didn't want anything to link you to me until it was all over."

She finally spoke, her voice soft and full of compassion. "I'm sorry about your brother."

He nodded acknowledgment and felt a band of sadness tighten his chest. He glanced away, and scrubbed a hand over his face. "Are you about done?" He cleared his throat. "We have one more stop."

She nodded and pushed her plate away, relief written on her face at the reprieve from eating.

Ten minutes later, Ben pulled into the parking lot of the church where her AA meetings were held.

"No." Her jaw tightened, and a muscle jumped below her ear. She shook her head. "No. I don't want to go."

Ben put his hand on hers and tightened his grip when she tried to pull away. "Lannis, after last night, this is the one place you need to be. Stop fooling yourself. You have a major problem. You need to face it, and you need to deal with the part of your life you try to numb with alcohol. It's going to take hard work, and this is the first step." He paused and looked at her. She held herself under rigid control, but the paleness of her face revealed her apprehension.

"Tonight's an open meeting. I'll come in with you, if you'd like." He hadn't been able to push Danny through those doors, but he'd carry Lannis if that was what it took.

Quickly, she shook her head, eyes downcast. Her movements jerky, she opened the door and got out.

"I'll be waiting here for you when you're done."

She hesitated, then squared her shoulders and walked toward the door.

~

Ben turned his radio down when Lannis came out of the church just over an hour later, talking and laughing with a middle-aged woman, a handful of AA literature clutched in one hand.

He released a quiet sigh of relief. He'd pushed her hard today. As difficult as it had been for her, he hoped his tactics had resulted in positive steps on her part.

She leaned down to his open window. "Ben, this is Althea. She's my sponsor. Althea, this is Ben. He's…my, uh, friend."

He stuck his hand out and shook Althea's, concealing his pleasure. Lannis had called him her friend. Never mind that she probably just couldn't come up with a better word to describe their relationship. Still, it made him inordinately satisfied. "Glad to meet you, Althea."

"Likewise, Ben." Althea peered in the window at him with a smile. "You might consider Al-Anon, to recognize and guard against enabling behaviors."

Lannis snorted. "He is so far from *enabling* it's not funny." She shot a glare at Ben, then glanced back at her sponsor. "He's not a warm and cuddly sort of friend."

Althea raised her eyebrows and eyed Ben with a shrewdly assessing look, then turned to Lannis. "I'll see you next week, and like we discussed, it'll be helpful if you check in with me daily for a while."

Lannis waved to Althea and got in the car. She tore off a piece of scratch paper, wrote Althea's name and number on it, and put it in the console between the seats. Ben lifted his eyebrows in mild surprise and whistled tunelessly. Apparently Lannis was willing, of her own volition, to include him in the accountability equation.

He pulled up to her house and parked. "Do you mind if I come in for a few minutes, Lannis? We need to talk about a couple of things."

She hesitated for a moment. "Okay." Her lips quirked in a wry smile. "The house *isn't* a mess."

Ben laughed. "How was the meeting?" He held the screen while she unlocked the door.

She shrugged. "It was all right. I never feel comfortable, but I was glad Althea was there. She was pretty harsh about being my sponsor again, though, questioning my sincerity." She tossed her backpack on her flight bag, went into the kitchen, and pulled a box of tea bags out of the cupboard. "The coffee at AA sucks. Hope you like tea." She dropped two bags into mugs, filled the teapot, and put it on the stove. "So, what did you want to talk about?" She turned and faced him.

"Your drinking. Your job. What you're going to do." Ben regarded her steadily. "The rape."

She flinched but didn't turn away.

"You need to deal with it so it doesn't control your life."

She cleared her throat. "As far as I know, I don't have a job anymore. I suppose I'll have to start looking for something else." Her voice wavered and she struggled to control the trembling of her lips. She took a deep breath, then forged on.

"As for the rest, you're right, which you already know." She slanted him an inscrutable look. "If I don't control the drinking, I'll end up on the streets, so yeah, I'm going to stick with AA." She turned and checked the teapot. "At least I think I've gotten through the first step for the first time. 'Admitted that we were powerless against alcohol.' You rubbed my nose in it enough this morning, made it pretty hard to ignore."

She sighed. "So now it's on to step two. Then three. 'Believe in a Power greater than ourselves,' and 'Turn our will and lives over to God as we understand him.' Which is going to be a problem, because when I prayed for God to help me when I was being raped, he didn't stop it, and it happened anyway. I can't turn my life over to something or someone I don't understand, trust, or believe in anymore." Her voice held an edge of bitterness, along with incongruous yearning.

Ben let her comment slide. Everyone had to find their own way to that answer, and he had faith that she would. It would take time. "How about a rape support group? Or counseling? It's part and parcel of the drinking, but it's its own separate issue. And I would be irresponsible if I let this morning's overdose thoughts slip by without addressing the issue."

The teapot made a preliminary squeal and she pulled it off the burner, poured the hot water, and handed him a mug. "This morning was a fluke. I've never thought of it before, and I won't ever again." She lifted her gaze to him and let him read the candor in them.

"You still need to talk to a qualified person about it."

She sat opposite him and toyed with her tea bag. "You know, I'm pretty overwhelmed here. I can only do so much. I'll do AA. I'll go back to the nursery and hold babies once a week. I don't want to do therapy. I told you that in April. I also have a job to worry about." She made an impatient motion. "Don't push too hard. That's what..." Her voice trailed off.

"What? Finish the sentence." Ben was quiet but firm.

She hesitated again, then whispered, "That's what set off the drinking yesterday. If it had just been seeing you again, I could have handled it. But..." She took a deep breath and focused on her tea. "You showed back up on the worst day of the year for me. The anniversary of the rape."

Shocked, Ben leaned back in his chair. It creaked.

"It's always a hard time for me. It was just...too much."

Ben found his voice and said gently, "If you hadn't felt so alone, maybe you could've made it without the alcohol." He scooted the chair closer and put his arm around her tense, hunched shoulders. "You're not alone anymore." He tugged her into his embrace, offering comfort and hoping she'd accept it. She resisted for a heartbeat, then sagged against him.

"I'm so tired," she mumbled into his shirt.

He stroked her back and murmured, "It's okay, darlin'. We all need to be propped up once in a while."

He held her for a few minutes, then disengaged himself and looked at her. "Orvis hasn't fired you yet. If you're straight with him I think he'll keep you on, as long as you stay accountable with AA."

Lannis looked stunned, then cautiously hopeful. "You're serious? Really?" She snagged her lower lip with her teeth.

Ben nodded. "He thinks a lot of you and will only fire you if you force him. He's willing to give you another chance, but you have to really work the program this time, not just fill in boxes because someone is making you. Do you understand?"

Her face crumpled in relief. "Thank you." It was heartfelt and genuine. She reached across the table and placed her hand on top of his.

Ben smiled. "Will you let me be your friend through this, Lannis?"

She glanced at their hands, then at him, and nodded. She offered a tremulous smile. "If every day we ever spend together is as intense as the ones we've had already, I don't know if I can survive them."

Ben threw his head back and laughed. "Me neither, darlin', me neither." He kissed the top of her head, and pulled out a business card. "Here's my cell phone number. Call anytime—and I mean *anytime*—if you need me. If you won't go to a support group or a counselor, at least start writing in a journal, or a diary. My mom and sister did after Danny died. They said it helped."

"What did you do?" Curiosity sparked her features. "How did you handle it?"

"I spent lots of energy at the gym beating up punching bags, and put in extra time at the shooting range."

She muttered something unintelligible under her breath.

"What?"

"I said hitting sounds like more fun than writing." She shot him a sour look.

He had a sudden image of her angry preflight and the corner of his mouth quirked up. "Yeah, I can see you in boxing gloves. How 'bout I teach you some self-defense moves? I'll take you to my gym after the hospital next week if you want."

Her expression brightened.

He started toward the front door, then stopped and turned. "Get a good night's sleep so you can be on time for work tomorrow. And lock your door tonight."

Lannis turned pink and groaned. She put her elbows on the table and dropped her head into her hands. He walked back, patted her shoulder, and brushed the hair away from her forehead.

"One day at a time, one step at a time." He tugged her to her feet. "Now lock the door after me."

"Ben...thanks for...well, everything."

Surprised, he gave her a quick hug—and allowed himself a moment's delight as her body pressed against his, enjoying her enticing softness, challenging firmness, and the way her head fit perfectly on his shoulder.

Then he reminded himself she was off-limits for that particular pleasure—which underscored a critical quality they shared.

Pointing his finger at her isolation left him with three fingers pointed back at him. He might be able to take satisfaction in being better adjusted, but he was just as lonely.

That insight was just too damn demoralizing to ponder.

Chapter Thirty

"ORVIS, I NEED to talk to you." Lannis shoved her hands into her pockets, giving her damp palms a place to hide.

Surprised by her voice, Orvis glanced up as he juggled a pile of papers, a mug of coffee, and keys to his office. It was early, and she knew he hadn't expected to see any of the pilots yet.

"Yeah, I figured." His voice was gruff, and her unease ratcheted higher. He unlocked the door and ushered her in. He put down the files and sat, indicating for Lannis to do the same.

She lowered herself and balanced on the front two inches of the chair. Taking a deep breath, she plunged in. "I apologize for not coming to work yesterday. I…um, I got drunk."

Once started, the words tumbled out. "I'm going back to AA, and I'm serious about it this time. And Ben—Ben Martin, from the other day—he spent yesterday, uh, motivating me to make some real changes."

Ben had told her she hadn't been fired, but throwing herself at Orvis's mercy highlighted both her failure and her vulnerability. She couldn't stop her hands from twisting in her lap. "Orvis, I know I don't deserve it, but will you give me another chance? Please. I'm sorry I let you down."

Orvis leaned back in his chair. "Looks like Martin got through to you." He gave a short nod. "Good."

Shame brought the heat of a blush to her face, but Lannis forced herself to maintain eye contact.

He regarded her in silence for long moments, then seemed to come to a decision. "It goes against my grain, not following through like I said I would." He grimaced. "I'll give you one more chance, and it's the last one."

Relief flooded her, making her dizzy, and she almost missed his next words.

"I want a weekly report from you. Face-to-face, five minutes. The first time you fail to have a report, or I find out you've lied, you're out the door, and not only does it kick your backside, it locks behind you. No discussion." He punctuated his words with his cigar. "You're on probation. Miss work because you've been drinking, you're fired. Show up with alcohol on your breath, I turn you in to the FAA *and* call the cops."

Lannis nodded her agreement. It was a fairer offer than she deserved. Orvis chomped on his unlit cigar and shook his head in disgust. Exasperation deepened the creases in his face. Her heart sank. Was he rethinking his decision already?

"I want you to get some counseling."

The blood left Lannis's head, exacerbating the dizziness of a moment ago. She steadied herself with a hand on the arm of the chair.

"I don't know what drives you to self-destruction, and maybe you don't either, but you owe it to yourself to figure it out and fix it. Those are the terms." His expression hardened. "Take it or leave it."

She sucked in a strangled breath. She'd refused Ben's advice on that issue, but now she had no choice. Accept counseling and keep her pilot's license? Or walk away from her life's passion because she was stubborn? Her mouth went dry. "Um, does it matter exactly what kind of counseling? I mean, like where, or who?"

"No, as long as it's with a professional."

"All right." Her voice was low, resigned. She caught his gaze. "Orvis...thank you. I won't let you down again."

~

Lannis walked an extra half mile to the grocery store after work and bought a cheap spiral notebook. Once home, she opened a can of soup, dumped it in her dented aluminum pan, and put it on the stove. She eyed her phone. She'd avoided this call for at least an hour. *Stop being a sissy.*

She dialed Ben's number before she lost her courage, and had a sudden memory of junior high school, when she'd had a crush on Ronnie Henderson. Heat flooded her face at the association. She didn't have a crush on Ben, but the sense of being all gangly elbows and knees, uncoordinated and inexperienced and insecure, rang too close to true for comfort.

His voice crackled in her ear. "Martin." The word was abrupt. Detached. Cold.

"Ben." Her confidence teetered. "This is Lannis."

"Hey." A warmer note entered his voice. "How're you doing?"

Hope sparked. She mumbled, "Okay, thanks. You?" Lannis toyed with the phone cord, twisting her forefinger into the coils.

"Fine. I still have about an hour of paperwork. How'd it go with Orvis?" As usual, he cut right to the most crucial subject.

Thankful he'd given the conversation some direction, she said, "He put me on probation. One of his conditions is that I get counseling. I guess whether it's too much for me right now, or not, doesn't matter," she said dryly. "So, do you know how, or who, or…" Her appetite died. She turned the stove off, vaguely nauseated at the aroma of the soup.

"Did you try the Rape Crisis Line?" He didn't wait for a response and didn't seem to expect one. "Their number's in the front section of the phone book, you know, where community resources are listed. They answer twenty-four hours a day. I'm pretty sure their counseling services are free, or at least income-based."

Anxiety closed her throat. Her silence stretched out. She finally found her voice, but it sounded small, even to her. "Okay."

"I'll check back with you after work, see how it went."

She found the number—that part was easy—but couldn't compose a coherent request for what she needed. Her fingers had gone bloodless and numb, and she kept hitting the wrong buttons. Disgusted with her inability to make the call, and ashamed to have to admit it to Ben, she paced the rooms of her small house searching for a measure of the confidence she felt as a pilot.

She could go for a run.

No.

No, she couldn't. The thought formed itself. She knew without analyzing it that she'd end up at the liquor store if she walked out the door right now.

She was stuck in her skin, which crawled with anxiety, and afraid to leave her house. Worse, pride had her trussed like a chicken. She was too humiliated to call Ben…but she could call Althea.

Her fingers trembled and she almost dropped the phone. This time she succeeded. Althea listened with calm acceptance and coached her through some deep breathing exercises, reminded her that desire by itself was not failure. She was able to find a tiny center of stillness, a kernel of serenity to get through the moment, and simple acknowledgment of the craving stole some of its power.

She didn't even wait after disconnecting from Althea. She dialed again.

"Ben, I can't do it by myself." She hesitated. "This is hard."

"I can come over, if you want." His voice held no trace of judgment.

"Yeah, that'll help," she said before she had a chance to change her mind.

She allowed herself the release of being outside, but only as far as the porch, where she planted herself. A while later the low rumble of Ben's car from two blocks away announced his arrival. She flipped her notebook closed, and stuck her pen in the wire spiral. She'd filled three pages while she waited, and noted with surprise that the knife edge of her anxiety had dulled—not enough that she was calm, but enough that the jitters in her belly were now mere flutters.

He pulled in next to the curb and shut down the engine. A wave of awareness washed over her in the sudden quiet. He came up the walk and Lannis stood, then surprised them both by wrapping her arms around him. She buried her face in his shirt and felt him start. After a ghost of a pause, he leaned his cheek on her head and held her. They stood quietly until Lannis sighed, dropped her arms, and stepped back.

"Let's put this devil to bed, darlin'." He took her hand. "What do you need from me?"

"Just being here helps a lot."

"How about a dry run first? I'll play the person on the other end."

Her eyes widened. She made the same suggestion with flight students before they made their first radio transmissions.

Ben squeezed her shoulder in silent encouragement when she finally picked up the phone and dialed. She faltered once on the words "I was raped," but after all the preparation the call was almost anticlimactic.

In the end, she had an appointment for her next day off.

Chapter Thirty-One

LANNIS HUFFED OUT a breath in frustration. While she was glad Ben had made good on his offer to bring her to his gym, she wasn't used to having to work this hard to master a new skill. Her arm tingled all the way to the shoulder from the blow she'd just delivered to the oversized punching bag, but the result was a barely discernible sway.

"Throw your weight into it, Lannis." Ben grabbed her hips, his touch impersonal in spite of its placement. "Since you don't have upper body mass like a guy, you've gotta use what you do have." He rotated her hips as she threw the punch. "Yeah, that's right. Do it again."

Hitting didn't come naturally to Lannis, even after several weeks of gym time. She concentrated hard and slugged the bag, incorporating the motion he'd shown her. This time she felt the power. It was *fun*. She smothered a grin.

"Remember to aim at the far side of the target, not the surface." He demonstrated with a solid *thunk* that rattled the bag's supporting chain. Sweat dripped off his face and down his neck.

She sneaked a look at him, admiring the fit of his half-drenched T-shirt, the muscles that bunched and relaxed as he taught her how to hit. With effort, Lannis pushed his tempting looks from her mind. Refocusing on technique, she threw another punch. Her reward was the same rattle he'd produced. A quiet glow of accomplishment bloomed in her chest.

"How's the counseling going?"

His question took a bit of the shine off the glow, and she shrugged. "Betsy's great, but the subject matter's tough."

He grunted.

Lannis lifted her lips in a self-mocking smile. "She laughed at me when I said I didn't want to be there, and that I wanted to be done ASAP. She's easy to be with, but she digs hard and deep."

"Nothing worthwhile comes easy." He grinned, tousling her hair. "Speaking of not coming easy, lose the gloves. Let's work on self-defense. Chokes or bear hugs?"

The glow faded. "Bear hugs." She hated chokes—especially when he made her close her eyes, stay in a neutral stance, and not react until she felt his hands on her throat. That little exercise pushed her past her ability to stay in the here and now, and sent her into a primal, unreasoning spiral of blind terror. Even so, Ben forced her to do it on occasion, saying she had to train past the panic.

He seemed to intuitively understand the cost of self-defense training to her psyche, and gave her a lot of latitude in setting the pace of training. It required that he invade her space, and he did exactly that with implacable resolve, making her practice the moves he'd taught her, letting her—no, *making* her—hit him until she did it with instinctive explosions that rocked him on his heels.

She tried to camouflage her nervousness under a layer of studied indifference, which was difficult as the familiar tingle of adrenaline skittered across her shoulder blades into her limbs.

"Lannis. Stay with me. This is just training."

She started, realizing her vision had narrowed and her anxiety had begun to morph into panic. She sucked in a deep breath and shook the tension out of the tips of her fingers.

"Okay. I'm ready." The determination in her voice was belied by her involuntary flinch when he stepped close and enveloped her in viselike embrace. She dropped her weight, shoved his hips away, and lifted her knee for a simulated groin kick—he didn't let her follow through on those—then shoved one arm up to connect with his nose, curled her hand around the back of his neck, and yanked him down for a knee to the solar plexus.

He grunted, countering just enough to keep her blows from connecting with full force. "Yup, that'd work. If I wasn't expecting it, you'd have me flat on the ground curled around my nuts. It'd give you enough time to get away." He grabbed their towels and tossed one to her. "A lot better than those girly slaps you dealt me in April. Wanna grab some supper on the way home?"

Puffing from exertion, Lannis nodded. She recognized Ben's gift of a reprieve from additional practice, and tension drained from her muscles. "Sure." He never let her skip the self-defense, but it was almost worth facing it to get the chance to beat the living daylights out of the bag once a week. Almost.

~

Lannis settled into her new routine, making inroads on all fronts except one.

"Althea, I can't get around the next two steps. I'm having trouble with the concept of a God who I can trust, or is loving, or cares. He didn't stop it when…when something bad happened to me and I prayed for help. I'm really trying, but I don't know what to do with this part of the program." Lannis made a face at her Styrofoam cup of coffee, then dumped the dregs in the trash and picked at the cup's rim. They stood off to the side of the room as people mingled after the meeting.

"Well, the program says 'God as we understand him,' or a higher power." Althea tapped a manicured fingernail on one of the brochures that explained Alcoholics Anonymous. "You can use AA as the higher power, or whatever works for you, but you might consider expanding your concept of God. In the Christian tradition, it's clear God gives human beings free will. We're not puppets God manipulates when someone prays. Each one of us makes choices— and God won't step in to change our minds. Unfortunately, someone made a choice that hurt you badly. That doesn't mean God turned his back on you. I believe God wept at your suffering, just as he weeps at the atrocities that we humans inflict on others, often innocents.

"You survived whatever happened, and are growing in ways you wouldn't have had the capacity for otherwise. So I don't see a God who abandoned you, but rather a God who's provided mercy and grace in abundance for your healing."

Althea searched Lannis's eyes, and Lannis squirmed under her scrutiny.

"I know this is a push for you, but forgiveness—your forgiving the person who harmed you—will free up a tremendous amount of your energy for recovery," Althea said. "Keep in mind that forgiving doesn't condone what happened, but lets you stop hauling it around like a ball and chain. You might want to give it some thought."

Forgive the man who'd raped her? Lannis reeled at the notion. *She has to be kidding!*

Then Althea added softly, "It will open up a pathway for you to begin to forgive yourself, as well."

Lannis's breath left her as if she'd just taken one of Ben's demo blows to her gut. She forced her lungs to draw in a shaky breath. Her vision wavered, then settled. *Forgive myself? There's too much I've screwed up, and what's done is done.*

Althea didn't let up. "Who in your life, right now, do you trust?"

Lannis exhaled noisily, and said, "Um, well, you. Ben. Betsy. Orvis, I suppose."

"Give me a reason, for each person, why you trust them."

The answers came easily. "You, because you're really straight with me, don't let me get away with anything, and you listen to what I *don't* say. Betsy, because she's held my confidences. Plus nothing I say shocks her. Ben, he does what he says he'll do, so what you see is what you get. No guesswork there. You've gotta trust that. Orvis…well I've just known him a long time and know his character. He's a good man. Why?"

"Because these people are God's hands and arms and voice to you. Each one of us loves you in a different way and is helping you in your journey. I'm just trying to get you to recognize God in your life, perhaps in a different light than you've perceived him before."

Althea smiled at Lannis, then gave her a spontaneous hug. "Keep on keeping on. You're going to be okay."

Lannis tossed the mangled cup in the trash and made a face. Her sponsor might be right; only time would tell.

All she could deal with was the present, and it held plenty of challenge.

She wished she had as much confidence in her ability to prevail as Althea did.

Chapter Thirty-Two

I'VE GOT THE BEST office in the world. Lannis glanced out her window as her student performed the airspeed exercise she'd given him. Poison ivy's brilliant crimson heralded the onset of autumn and provided an exclamation of color two thousand feet below. Sycamore trees had turned gold, highlighting the tracks of streams and creeks previously veiled beneath thick summer foliage. Vivid blue skies and a succession of trees turning luminous yellows and glowing shades of orange against the backdrop of tranquil green fields made for spectacular views from altitude. When the brightest yellow foliage dropped, often all at once, her imagination saw the leaves as little piles of sunshine on the ground.

Even gray days were wonderful. Instead of simulation, she could take her instrument flight students into the clouds to get some actual experience. Simulation could only go so far. Thunderstorms were infrequent and temperatures still high enough that icing wasn't a consideration, eliminating the two biggest threats to safety of flight within clouds. Plus, it was fun.

Fun. That particular quality had weaseled its way back into her life over the last couple of months, and she hadn't noticed how much it enlivened her days until now. She realized with a tiny start that she was no longer lonely. Thanks to Althea and AA, she wasn't as terrified of finding herself at the mercy of her cravings.

Alisha, the baby she'd cuddled for weeks at the hospital, had gone home with her parents a few days ago. Lannis had cried that night, and had been shocked at the depth of her emotion. She was glad for Alisha and her family, but hadn't realized the strength of the bond she'd formed with the infant. More important, she discovered the tears didn't destroy her, that she didn't need to drink to numb the feelings.

She had lists, courtesy of Betsy's prodding and encouragement. Lannis initially thought they were pointless, but now she relied on them. She had a list of things she could do when she felt anxious or afraid. Another list spelled out things she'd done to survive—some that still worked, plus new strategies. Lannis made a mental note to recopy the list of new beliefs that replaced warped ones she'd developed as a result of the rape. *That* paper was soft and worn through at its creases.

Though an occasional nightmare disrupted her sleep, even they had softened. Her daily runs were back down to three miles, and she felt healthy rather than haunted.

Then there was Ben. He made her laugh when she thought her ability to laugh had died forever.

She had to admit her life was the best it had been for years.

~

Lannis waved to Ramon as he walked toward his car in the waning light, then turned her attention to the plane. With uncomplimentary thoughts aimed at the morning crew, she reached under the seats and dug around, gathering the pile of candy bar wrappers and empty soft drink containers she'd found during the preflight. One bottle had rolled into the baggage compartment, and she leaned in, finally snagging it with her fingertips. She slithered out, balanced most of the trash in the crook of her left arm, and bumped the door closed with her hip, then muttered a mild curse when it didn't latch. Giving up on it for the moment, she stepped over the gear and glanced at the windshield. Good—only a few bugs to clean today.

Something hard slammed into her back, smashing her against the fuselage. Unprepared and not braced, her head bounced off the cowling. Plastic soda bottles flew out of her grip and clattered on the ramp, then rolled under the plane. The breeze snatched the candy wrappers, swirling them before letting them plummet to the ground. They skipped across the asphalt and out of view.

Not funny, Ben. You've taken "training" too far. She went rigid with anger, and started to whip around to tell him off.

A big hand grabbed the nape of her neck and squeezed. Slammed her face into the rivets of the cowling. Prevented her from turning. The rivets, small as they were, created painful pressure points against the bones of her temple and cheek.

"What's his name, bitch?"

The cold voice that growled in her ear was not Ben's. Her blood turned to ice.

"The guy you were with at the hospital the other day."

Adrenaline flooded her system, ratcheted her pulse rate upward even as she felt it energize the muscles in her arms and legs. Time slowed as she had the fleeting thought, *Of course it isn't Ben. He's never been this rough.* A terrible sense of clarity settled over her, unanticipated calm in its wake. She realized how alone she was. This guy could kill her. As if she'd spoken her dread out loud, he smacked her head, hard. She staggered, suspended and supported by his hand on her neck.

"His name! Now!" he yelled.

Horrified, she heard herself say, "B…Ben. His name is Ben." *Oh, God, I can't tell him Ben's real name.* He punched her in the back, over her kidneys. A starburst of pain exploded and stole her breath. Her knees buckled and she sagged against the plane.

"Ben who?" The pressure on her neck increased. Her vision began to blur around the edges.

Lannis scrambled for a second name that wasn't real, something that would satisfy him. "J…Jackson. Ben Jackson."

"BJ." He sounded satisfied and disgusted at the same time. And angry. "Where does he live?" He shook her.

She felt like a rag doll. "I don't know. I've never been to his house." The words came out in little gasping breaths.

He hit her again, let loose of her neck, and she crumpled to her knees. "I don't believe you. Where's he live?"

"I don't know, oh God, that's the truth, please, oh please, stop." She couldn't stem the babbling, and she hated the note of pleading in her voice.

A plane taxied out from another hangar area and turned toward them. She sensed the guy's distraction and had a wild hope he'd bolt. He didn't. Without thinking, she drove an elbow up and back, aiming for his groin. It connected. He grunted, the sound sliding into a moan. She scrambled to her feet, intending to run, but he sent her to the ground beneath the plane with another blow.

Lannis brought her arms up to protect her head as she fell. She registered her impact with the asphalt, but felt nothing. He stepped over her body and drew a booted foot back. The setting sun glinted on his metal chain link belt, a jeweled crown dangling from its end. Grasping his intention, she curled into a fetal position to protect her midsection. He kicked her gut, sending her skidding across the pavement. Pain exploded and drove the breath from her lungs. She blindly grabbed at her belly.

He stepped on her head and ground it into the asphalt with his foot. "Listen up, bitch. You tell Mr. Ben Jackson that he can expect a bullet, real soon. You understand?"

She found enough air to answer. "Yes…I understand." Her voice was thin, reedy. "I'll tell him."

He lifted his foot and she heard his uneven gait as he limped away.

Red-hot shards of pain sliced through every part of her torso and made it hard to think. She smelled the acrid sweat of her fear and tasted the coppery tang of blood. Her tongue found the source of the blood, a split in her lip, then retreated from the sting of the cut. One eye was swelling shut, and the other eyelid was too heavy to lift, but she managed to open it, just a slit. In disbelief, she watched the plane taxi past without slowing. Her gut spasmed and she vomited. Mucus clung to her cheek. She couldn't find the energy to lift her hand, to wipe her face clean.

Oh, God, I need help. With a Herculean effort, Lannis rolled to her knees and grabbed the strut of the plane. Her arms trembled as she dragged herself up. She swallowed the urge to throw up again, and battled her way to the door. Her fingers were cold and fumbled at the smooth metal, but she managed to swing it open over her head, and clawed her way in. She collapsed with her upper body on the floor of the cockpit, her face on the rough carpet next to the fuel selector valve.

Don't quit now. Almost...almost there. Her wrist was as heavy as if a sandbag were attached to it, and she struggled to get her hand up the fourteen inches or so to the base of the control panel. She groped, then settled on the distinctive rocker shape of the master electrical switch. It took another draining effort to force the switch into the ON position. Carefully, she slid her hand two inches to the right and found the avionics master switch with now-trembling fingers. This one should have been easier to flip into the ON position, but her strength was waning and she was afraid she'd lose her grip. Still, she managed to do it.

The last frequencies she'd tuned in were Bowman ground control and the universal emergency frequency. Either one would work. Her arm flopped to the floor and she was tempted to rest, just for a little while. *No...* She forced herself to grab the microphone and depress the button on the mike, which was a bit easier than flipping the switches. She licked her lips and winced, then said, "Mayday, mayday. Please...help. Ramp...on the ramp. Louisville Air." She knew the last words were slurred and hoped they were understandable. Her thumb gave up on the switch before she could repeat the transmission. The mike dropped on the carpet by her face and she gave in to the urge to rest.

Above her, the radio crackled to life. "Say again, aircraft in distress. Understand on the *ramp* at Louisville Air?" Moments later footsteps pounded across the ramp toward the plane. Gentle hands grasped at her shoulders, tugged her out of the plane, and laid her flat on the asphalt.

She managed to get her eye open for a moment. A security guard hovered over her, his gaze sharp as he catalogued her injuries. Another face floated into her visual field. She recognized him as one of the controllers. His face went pale. He reached over the security guard to grab the mike. He keyed it and said, "It's Lannis Parker. She's hurt bad. Call an ambulance. I don't know what happened, but it looks like she got beat up."

Lannis floated in and out of consciousness, awakening enough to jerk when an EMT tried to start an IV. She tried to tell him she was cold. Bone-deep cold. The IV fluid was cold, too, and her teeth began to chatter. But he kept doing things like taking her blood pressure, and putting an oxygen mask on her face. She tried to bat it away, but there were too many people, too many hands, and someone intercepted her, tucked her hand next to her side. Finally— *finally*—someone wrapped a warm blanket over her, and she was lifted into an ambulance.

So many voices. Urgent-sounding phrases that held no meaning for her. A policeman asking questions. She tried to answer him, but her responses were apparently unintelligible, and he quit talking to her, his voice blending into the rumble of words floating past. The doors of the ambulance slammed, and then it was just the EMT. She started to drift off again in a haze of pain. Something important niggled at her brain.

Ben. *Ben's in danger.*

She got her eye open, and desperate to communicate her urgency, rolled her head to look at the EMT. She tried to lift her hand, but it was trapped under the blanket. "Ben Martin... Matter...life and death. Have to...*have to*...talk to him." The mask muffled her words. She twisted her head, trying to rub it away from her face. She recited Ben's cell phone number, then kept saying it, like a mantra.

The EMT said, "Got it," scribbled the number on his clipboard and repeated it. He checked her blood pressure as he spoke, then turned up the volume on the IV. "We'll call him for you but you need to stay calm," he said. "You've lost a lot of blood and you're in shock."

She whispered, "Promise?"

"Yes," he said. He leaned close and looked her in the eye. "Yes, I'll call him. Now, you concentrate on staying in the land of the living. Deal?"

Lannis nodded, satisfied this time, and closed her eyes.

Chapter Thirty-Three

HOSPITAL. A white tile ceiling and more faces moving in and out of her field of vision. The EMTs pushed Lannis on a rolling cart, and spoke quickly, calmly. They maneuvered her into a room, stopped, then several people gathered around her and she was up, then down, moved to another bed. She shrieked and nearly passed out at the bump of the landing and a roll to the side while something slid out from under her. They rolled her back and a doctor prodded her belly and she screamed again. Tears, warm against her frigid skin, dripped down her face and pooled in her ears. Then she felt the familiar and terrifying sensation of intoxication. Floating, the beginnings of lethargy and apathy. Her emotions ebbed, and blessed relief from the pain flowed.

Lannis panicked and began to struggle.

"No! No drugs! Stop!" She tried to scream but it came out as breathless gasps.

"Lannis, what's wrong?" A concerned face appeared. "We're giving you some morphine for the pain," the woman said.

She whispered, "Scared...get addicted to...whatever. No narcotics...please. No drugs...please."

The nurse's eyes widened briefly in surprise. "You won't get addicted at this point, and your body needs pain relief. I'll let them know for afterward, though."

Fuzzily, Lannis thought, afterward? After what? *I need to talk to Ben before...whatever is afterward.* She mumbled Ben's name, and the nurse leaned down to hear.

"He's in the waiting room. You'll see him after your surgery," she said.

Lannis shook her head and earned a wave of dizziness, closely followed by nausea and fresh pain. She moaned, gripped the side rail, and forced out, "Not afterward... Now. Talk to him *now*." The nurse started to say something, but Lannis interrupted, stared directly at her. "No...surgery...'til I talk...Ben. ...refuse...won't consent." Her lips trembled, but she held the gaze of the nurse. "Mean it. No...more...treatment...talk...Ben, first." Finally realizing how serious Lannis was, the nurse nodded once and straightened.

"Okay, I'll go get him, but you have only a couple of minutes before you go upstairs." Lannis closed her eyes, exhausted by the exchange.

It seemed only a moment passed before Ben touched her shoulder, his face close to hers. "Lannis? I'm here."

"Ben." She was momentarily disoriented and couldn't remember what had been so important to tell him. Then it rushed back, and she clutched at his arm. "He said...you... He...expect bullet...soon. Told him...Ben Jackson." The bed she was on began moving, and Ben walked alongside. "Called you BJ... Wanted...where...you live, but..."

"It's all right, Lannis. I understand." Ben squeezed her shoulder, then leaned down and kissed her temple. "Did you get a look at him?"

Lannis shook her head slightly. "'Bout your height. Baggy pants...chain belt...crown, sparkly, hanging off of it... Sorry."

Ben said, "Nothing to be sorry about, Lannis. I have a good idea who it was. I'll take care of it," he said. The elevator dinged and the doors opened. "I'll be here when you get out of surgery, darlin'." They rolled her into the elevator, and he dropped her hand.

"Ben," she whispered, "...be safe."

~

Ben pulled out his cell phone as the elevator doors swished shut and punched the buttons with more vigor than necessary. It only rang once, and Mike answered with the single-syllable shorthand they used with each other, his voice conveying as much tension as Ben felt.

"They've taken her for emergency surgery." He turned and leaned against the wall. "Internal bleeding. She didn't see who did it, but he left a message with her." Ben scrubbed a hand over his face. "Called me BJ, mentioned a bullet he figured I deserve. The only folks who know me as 'BJ' are the ones involved in the ring from last April, and the only one not in jail is Terrance LeMasters. Goes by the street name 'King.' She described the belt he always wears. We've got probable cause. Send someone to pick him up."

"His belt?" Doubt dusted the words.

"He had a diamond crown custom made. He wears it on his belt, one of those chain jobs, like a charm that a woman might wear on a bracelet, but bigger. I always thought it was cheesy. Looked like something a kid would get from a cheap hamburger promo meal."

Mike was silent for a moment, then said, "Isn't he the two-bit dealer who turned state's evidence?"

"Yeah, that's right. The one who sold out the cops in return for immunity."

"I'll get on it. Maggie's on her way to wait with you. I'll be over as soon as I get LeMasters rounded up."

"Thanks, buddy." Ben pocketed the cell phone.

The memory of the encounter with Officer Powell flickered through his mind. The flashes from the barrel of the man's gun. Ben's reflexive move that sent LeMasters into the line of fire. The hot sting of the bullet that found Ben's arm, his blood running warm from the wound.

LeMasters had recovered, and the plea bargain had made him a free man. The bastard didn't know it yet, but he'd just lost his get-out-of-jail-free card.

His jaw tight with tension, Ben stalked off to find coffee.

Chapter Thirty-Four

BEN GLANCED AT ORVIS. He hadn't seen the man since July, and tonight he looked old and drained. Ben figured he didn't look much better. He felt years older than he had a few hours ago. They sat in the waiting room on the surgical floor while the nurses got Lannis settled in her room.

Ben was silent and focused—now, anyway. He cringed inwardly. He'd fallen apart once Mike arrived. Consumed with guilt at his failure to keep Lannis safe, he'd been too distraught to be calmed by Mike's consoling words or Maggie's comforting touches. He still didn't believe them when they said it wasn't his fault, but nonetheless, he was grateful for their support. They'd gone home to their children just moments ago.

Orvis cleared his throat. "Well, young man, your name keeps showing up in her weekly reports. She's been doing real well, and working hard on her problems. Thank you for being persistent."

Surprised, Ben said, "Yeah, she is working hard. And she understands that you're a good friend to her."

Orvis made a harrumphing sound, and reddened. "I called her mom earlier, and she'll be here"—he paused to glance at his watch—"in about an hour, maybe two. I hope she's stopped to check with the hospital since Lannis got out of surgery. I'd hate for her to worry unnecessarily." He rubbed his eyes and missed Ben's astonished expression.

"Her mom? Where's she driving from?" Ben asked, controlling his face. He wracked his brain but couldn't remember Lannis ever mentioning family. *And why haven't I ever asked?* A spurt of disgust set him to clenching his jaw.

"A small town northeast of Columbus, Ohio. I think it's about a four- or five-hour drive." Orvis yawned.

Ben found a neutral tone. "Orvis, I'd be glad to take care of her mother once she gets here. I can put her up at Lannis's place, or a motel if she'd rather." He hesitated, then added, "If you don't mind my saying so, you look whipped."

Orvis grimaced. "It's been a long day, and I don't handle worrying about Lannis very well. I'd appreciate that, Ben. Thank you."

Ben nodded, then stood as the nurses finally left Lannis's room. One of them beckoned the men, indicating they could go in now.

The door squeaked as Ben opened it. Lannis looked small and vulnerable in the hospital bed. Her color was a little better, though, and a little of his tension eased. Without a word, she lifted her arms, reached for him, and crumbled.

He gathered her gently into his arms and held her. "Hush now, darlin'," he murmured. "It's over. You're safe."

"I'm so scared, Ben," she mumbled into the crook of his neck. "The narcotics...I don't want to get addicted, and they won't let me *not* have them. And that guy, he means to kill you and I'm afraid for you..."

"Shh. One step at a time. We're here to help you through this." Careful not to mention LeMasters's name, he added, "He's already been picked up. He's not going to hurt me, or you, anymore." He stroked her face.

Lannis melted into Ben's embrace and took a deep, shuddering breath. After a moment, he motioned with his head toward the door. "You've got another visitor. Let me get you a washcloth while you reassure Orvis that you're going to survive."

She gave a little jerk of surprise and quickly swiped at her face, wincing when she bumped her bruised eye. A shaky smile lit her face as her boss stepped to the bed and took her hand.

"I'm glad you're okay," Orvis said. His voice caught and he looked away, swallowing as he composed himself. Returning his gaze to Lannis, he cleared his throat, and said, "You're just too hard on an old buzzard like me. You work on getting well, and don't worry about your job. It'll be there when you get back on your feet." He squeezed her hand. "Oh, your momma is going to be here in an hour or so. Ben's going to get her settled once she's had a chance to see you. I'll stop in tomorrow afternoon, see how you're doing."

At the mention of her mother, Lannis's face went pale. Her gaze flicked to Ben as a blush tinged her cheeks. He stood behind Orvis and sent her a sharp-eyed glare. She made a belated attempt to school her features into blandness. Ben smoothed his expression as Orvis turned to leave.

The door closed softly behind Orvis, and just as quietly, Ben said, "Your mother?"

Lannis shrank, and mumbled, "I'm really tired now. You should probably leave."

Ben didn't bother to conceal his edginess. "No dice. I'll take some of the blame here, because I never asked you about your family, and for the life of me, I don't know why not, but why haven't you told me about them? Your mom only lives four or five hours away. You could easily have gone home in April, instead of hanging around here, or going to Memphis." In contrast to his words and tone, he dabbed her face, being careful of the abrasions and bruises.

Lannis sighed. "I quit calling or going home after the rape. I was ashamed, and didn't want them to know." Resigned, she relaxed at his ministrations. "I felt like I had a neon sign flashing over me: *Rape victim! Rape victim!*" She made a weak motion, waving vaguely at the air above her head. "I started drinking, and then Rudy and I got married. It was...spontaneous. Justice of the peace down at the courthouse, nothing more than an excuse to have a big party and get drunk. I didn't invite Mom or Lynnie. I didn't tell them about the divorce until close to a year after it was final." She frowned. "Come to think of it, they never even met Rudy." She closed her eyes and turned away from him. "There's too much water under the bridge to fix all that I've ruined."

Ben's heart turned over at the pain in her voice. He tugged on her chin and said, "Look at me."

Her eyelids fluttered open. She looked fragile and unspeakably sad.

"This is your chance to repair those very important relationships." He searched her eyes. "You've mentioned your mom, and a sister. How about your dad? Anyone else?"

She shook her head. "Dad died about eight years ago. Heart attack. It was a total surprise. Mom's a nurse. Lynnie is two years younger than me, and married to Rich. They have a one-year-old daughter, Carly, who I've never seen because I haven't been home."

"No more secrets?" Ben stroked her hair.

Lannis shook her head. "No."

"Okay," he said. "You rest, and when she gets here, I'll wake you."

Lannis nodded, then said, "Don't leave without saying good-bye. Please?" Anxiety laced her voice.

Ben squeezed her hand. "Don't worry. I won't abandon you. Go to sleep, darlin'."

Chapter Thirty-Five

Nearly two hours later, an anxious, attractive woman who bore a striking resemblance to Lannis pushed the door open and appraised the equipment around Lannis's bed with a quick, practiced eye. Ben stood, stretched, and extended his hand.

"Mrs.—" he began, then stopped and said sheepishly, "I guess I don't know your last name. I'm Ben Martin, a friend of Lannis's. She's doing well. Stable. They repaired a torn blood vessel in her abdomen. Other than some bruises and scrapes, that's the extent of her injuries. I hope you had time to get an update while you were on the road."

"Parker. Millie Parker. I didn't take the time to stop, and I was so upset I forgot my cell phone. I needed to be with her." She struggled to keep her emotions reined in, so like Lannis that Ben nearly smiled.

"It's okay to cry, Mrs. Parker," he said. "She's your daughter, not one of your patients."

She burst into tears. "I was so worried when her boss called. At first I thought she'd been in a plane crash. Most people don't survive those. When he told me she'd been beaten…" She drew in a shaky breath. "Well, it tears your heart out when it's your child"—she smiled, her lips trembling—"even if she is twenty-six years old." She fumbled for a tissue and dabbed at her eyes, blew her nose, marshaling her emotions with the same efficiency she'd used to assess Lannis's condition.

"I told her I'd wake her when you got here. Later, I'll take you to her house and get you settled…unless you had other plans? Like someone else you know here?" Ben asked. He was discovering just how much he didn't know about Lannis.

Mrs. Parker shook her head. "I hadn't thought that far ahead. Staying at her place would be a godsend. Thank you."

Ben went to the bed, gently shook Lannis's shoulder, and said quietly, "Lannis, darlin', your mom's here."

She rolled toward him, then stilled abruptly, her hands going to the bandage on her belly. She inhaled sharply, remained motionless, and opened her eyes. "Ben?" She looked confused for a moment until his words sank in, then stared at him with wide eyes, silently imploring him for something.

He leaned closer and murmured, "Do you want me to stay?" She nodded, her anxious glance flicking past his shoulders. "Okay, for moral support, but this conversation is yours." He added, "No details, just that you're sorry you've shut her out and you'd like to change that—but only if that's what you really want." He gave her a piercing look and she swallowed, then nodded. He stepped back, pulled a chair up for Mrs. Parker, and went to the window on the other side of the bed.

"Mom?" Lannis said.

"Oh, baby, I was so worried about you." Millie crossed the room and bent to give Lannis a careful hug. They clung to each other for several minutes, rocking gently. Ben couldn't tell who crumbled first, but before long sniffles and murmurs filled the room.

He leaned against the windowsill, confident they'd work out the estrangement.

~

It was after two in the morning when Ben finally got downtown to the police department. Millie was ensconced in Lannis's house, and Lannis had fallen into a deep sleep. He hoped they wouldn't wake her for a few hours. He was still too wired to settle down, and he had business with Terrance LeMasters anyway. A pointed *conversation* with LeMasters would probably do wonders for his mental outlook. His lips parted in a humorless smile at the prospect.

He approached the desk, flipped out his badge, and requested LeMasters be brought to the small interrogation room adjacent to the cell block. Ben rotated his shoulders in an effort to relieve the stress and fatigue of the evening, and rubbed his neck.

Ten minutes later, the jailer escorted LeMasters into the drab room. The prisoner's dreadlocks were flat on one side, his clothes were wrinkled, and he shrugged the officer's hand off his arm with annoyance as he yawned. Ben felt a surge of rage. The punk had slept in comfort—well, relative comfort; Metro Corrections provided metal bunks, not hotel beds—while Lannis fought for her life. *Careful...* He stuffed his anger into a quiet corner of his mind. He couldn't afford to make any mistakes.

LeMasters lost his attitude momentarily when he saw Ben, eyes widening so the whites completely encircled dark irises. He turned back toward the cell block, an edge of panic evident in his movements, but smacked into his solidly built escort. The officer muttered something and shoved, pushing LeMasters off-balance. He steered him into the room, then withdrew, closing the door behind himself with a final-sounding *thunk*. LeMasters regained his equilibrium and eyed Ben warily. His gaze flicked up to the video camera mounted in the corner of the room. No red light blinked to indicate active taping. He glanced at the tape recorder on the table. No red light there, either. He puffed his chest out and crossed his arms.

"What d'you want, man? This better be good. You got nothin' on me."

"I got your message," Ben said, baring his teeth. "You want to collect on your threat? Here I am." He held his arms wide. "Have at it. Or am I too big to beat up? You prefer women? Ones a lot smaller than you? You prefer ambushing them from behind? Come on," he taunted. "You're just a stupid, penny-ante low-life. Powell's whore. A loser."

LeMasters surged toward Ben, raising fisted hands. "I ain't his whore. He's the loser. He's the one in prison, man, not me." His face twisted and he said, "You messed up my life, asshole. You were supposed to die last April. That was the plan. I don't care if your girlfriend dies. She can't identify me, and you're just guessing. That's the beauty of it. Right in the middle of town, all that open space and nobody around to see. You can't pin it on me, and when I get out you'd better watch your back. She didn't tell me enough, Mr. Ben Jackson"—LeMasters sneered at Ben—"but I'm gonna get you when you least expect it. You're so cocky—you don't have no witness an' you ain't taping, so what's said in here don't matter, 'cause I'll deny everything."

Ben raised his eyebrows. "If you're such a hotshot, why're you in jail?" He unbuttoned his shirt pocket, reached in, and pulled out a small tape recorder. Clicked it into the OFF position. Looked at the loser. "This should put you away for some time. Aggravated assault for starters, accessory to attempted murder... The DA will renege on the plea bargain. You had to stay clean for that to stick."

Terrance's jaw went slack. He swallowed once, twice, then found his voice. "That's entrapment, man. Besides, I didn't say I did it. You ain't gonna get away with this."

With a feral smile, Ben said, "It's legal. And you said enough." He brandished the recorder. "When you meet up with your friends in prison, I suppose your life will get pretty miserable. Whaddya think?"

LeMasters's dark face went a shade lighter.

Ben rapped on the door to summon the jailer. "I suppose that's better justice than I can hope for here. It's certainly going to have to take the place of what I *want* to do to you."

The door opened and he said, "He can go back to bed now." He pocketed the tape and left, whistling.

Ben started to go home, but found himself driving back to the hospital. Terrance LeMasters had called Lannis Ben's girlfriend. The truth of his words had been a sucker punch to Ben's gut. He'd barely controlled his response in front of the man, but the reality caught him by surprise. Lannis had quietly become much more than someone to whom he owed restitution. He felt protective of her. More so than he would have expected.

His relationship with her had been complex from the first moment, and defied easy classification. Captor. Protector. Confidante. Friend. Mentor. She would certainly add "slave driver." He smiled briefly. At one point he'd wanted to add boyfriend to the list—he couldn't deny his attraction to her—but had backed off in the face of her drinking binge. The last thing he needed was to get drawn into a sick relationship. That was the last thing she needed, too. He'd watched, cautiously and from the stance of neutral but compassionate friendship, to see if she actually made the changes necessary for recovery, and healing. She had, in spades.

This evening had proven he didn't know nearly enough about her, although he knew about her strength, resiliency, and will to survive, along with sharp intelligence and an equally sharp sense of humor. She had more layers than an onion, and in spite of her attempts to open up, was still as prickly as a hedgehog. She intrigued him and challenged him.

He gradually reached a conclusion that shook him to the soles of his feet. He felt something more profound for Lannis than he'd experienced for any woman, even Deb, his ex-wife.

His place tonight... Aftershocks of awareness rumbled through his gut. With sudden and blinding clarity, he knew his place, the place he needed to be. At Lannis's bedside, providing support and comfort in one of the most difficult times of her life. Ben wasn't sure whether it was resignation or exhilaration that shimmied along his nerve endings. Either way, he accepted the certainty of his mission tonight.

His smile turned grim. He might think he knew where he was going with this, but Lannis would almost certainly hold a differing opinion. Nothing new there.

Ben turned into the dimly lit hospital parking garage.

And hoped he wasn't making a colossal mistake.

Chapter Thirty-Six

RAISED VOICES. Millie Parker frowned. That was not what she'd expected as the elevator doors slid open on Lannis's floor. This was a hospital, and people needed their rest. If this were *her* unit... Then she recognized the voices. One was Lannis's, tight and high and thin. The other, Ben's, growling and low and vibrating with frustration. Her heart leapt to her throat and she hurried down the hallway. She stopped at the door of Lannis's room.

Ben leaned over the bed, nose to nose with her daughter. His hands bracketed Lannis and were fisted in the sheets on each side of her shoulders. He wore the same clothes he'd had on last night and his face was rugged with fatigue and the shadow of an untended day-old beard. He looked worse than death warmed over.

He looked dangerous.

Lannis, however, didn't seem intimidated. She was white-faced and rigid, her hands fisted as well, and taking rapid, shallow breaths. Between words, her lips snapped tight and she shook her head *no*. Repeatedly. Giving back, sentiment for sentiment if not volume for volume, as good as he gave her.

"—ain't gonna happen in the space of a few days." Ben's face flushed as he nearly shouted the words.

Millie gasped. Ben's head came up and his eyes glittered at her. He pushed himself away from the bed. She noted that even in his anger, he took care to avoid jarring Lannis. He muttered something about stubbornness being a great quality for a mule, but that would mean Lannis was an—well, another word for mule.

"Maybe *you* can get through to her, Mrs. Parker. I've had it with her macho I-can-handle-anything act. I'm going to get some breakfast." Stubble-faced and red-eyed, he brushed past her and stomped down the hall.

Millie's heart slowed, returning to its normal rate. He'd frightened her, but she could now see that Lannis's best interests lurked beneath his ire. Millie raised her eyebrows. "What was that all about?"

Lannis shifted in the bed. Winced. "I don't want to take narcotics for the pain, and he thinks I should. Take them, I mean. He's the most bull-headed person I've ever met in my life."

"Hmm... Takes one to know one," Millie murmured. Rather than give in to her curiosity about Lannis's aversion to the very drugs that could ease the pain evident in her body language, Millie decided to offer an alternative. "I've seen acupuncture used with some success in one of the Columbus hospitals. I'm sure there's someone proficient at it here in Louisville." She put her hand on Lannis's forehead. "You do need some pain relief. See how tight you are? You can't take a deep breath, and you have to, in order to make sure you don't get pneumonia, or a collapsed lung. Would you consider one dose of the meds while I try to arrange something else?"

Lannis closed her eyes, and Millie could almost see the warring desires flicker across her daughter's features. After a moment Lannis reluctantly nodded her head, the motion jerky and abbreviated, then reached for the control to the automated pain medication dispenser hooked to her IV. She took a breath. Depressed the plunger. The lines in her face eased almost immediately.

Millie patted her hand, then went out to the nurses' station and returned with a phone book.

Forty-five minutes and half a dozen phone calls later, an experienced acupuncturist was on his way. Lannis dozed fitfully after pushing herself to her limits through a respiratory treatment. Millie straightened the room, and had just sat down to relax when Ben returned, carrying two cups of coffee. Smiling, she softly thanked him.

He whispered, "Did you get her to take something? She looks a lot more comfortable."

Millie nodded. "Yes, I talked her into one more dose to hold her while I called around and got an acupuncturist. It's been successful for some people, so I thought it would be worth a try." She took a sip of coffee, then looked him in the eye. "Why is she so adamant in refusing narcotics?"

Ben's gaze, underscored by dark circles beneath his eyes, was equally direct. "I am not at liberty to discuss that with you, Mrs. Parker. I'm sorry."

"I don't snoop, but I couldn't help noticing some Alcoholics Anonymous materials on her bedside table."

"These are questions you need to ask Lannis."

Abruptly, she changed the subject, her expression softening. "You look exhausted. Obviously, you didn't get home last night. I'm here for the day, so if you'd like to get some rest, go on home. I'll call if there's the slightest need." Anticipating his refusal, she put her hand on his arm. "I promise."

Ben hesitated, then capitulated. "Okay." He put his coffee down and stood. Stretched. He walked over to Lannis, stroked her forehead, and kissed her gently on the top of her head. He murmured, "Will you be sure to tell her I said good-bye? I don't like to leave without letting her know."

"Of course."

He straightened, sent a tight smile at Millie, and strode out of the room.

She hoped he'd stay awake long enough to drive home.

~

Given the choice between the mysterious action of painful-looking needles or the seduction of drugs... Lannis wasn't sure how acupuncture worked, or how effective it might be, but she knew which option she wanted. To her surprise—and relief—the procedure was simple and painless. Maybe its pain was inconsequential when compared to the post-op pain. In any case, it worked.

However, that success did not exempt Lannis from her mother's single-minded attention afterward. Millie settled in at her bedside with a look Lannis recognized from her childhood. She observed her mom through lowered eyelashes and the thought flickered though her mind, *I come by it honestly.* Bull terrier. Or pit bull. Whatever the metaphor, her mom wouldn't let go of a question until she was one hundred percent satisfied with the answers she'd been given. And she looked to be on the warpath for answers.

Lannis steeled herself, trying to remember some of the concepts and techniques she'd worked so hard to learn from AA and Betsy. Most important was that she didn't have to be in control of everything. In this case, she had no control over what her mom had on her mind. One day at a time. Right now, one minute at a time. No more running away from discomfort or difficulties or pain. For a fleeting moment she wished Ben were here, but he would have removed himself from this conversation anyway.

Resigned, she looked at her mom and said, "We might as well get on with it. Shoot." She smiled, knowing it was wobbly. "What do you want to know?"

Smile crinkles appeared at the corners of Millie's eyes, then smoothed as her expression grew somber. "You know I love you, and nothing will ever change that. I don't know what precipitated our rift, and I'm not going to pry, but there are some things I need to understand. Why won't you take the drugs that will help you?" Puzzlement sounded in her voice.

Lannis closed her eyes briefly. Honesty. The hallmark of everything she'd been working on. She took a deep breath and pushed her pride away, buried it, tamped the ground solid over the top of it. She looked at Millie. Forced the words out, a flush of shame warming her cheeks. "Mom, I have a drinking problem. I'm an alcoholic." She'd said the words weekly for the last several months, but not to someone who meant so much to her.

"You're too young to be an alcoholic!" Millie's face reflected her shock.

"I didn't progress to the DT stage, but drinking got the better of me." A sense of freedom flooded Lannis, and she abruptly recognized the weight of the secret's burden. "I'm ashamed, but I've jeopardized my job and my livelihood by being too drunk to work. Twice. That scares me to death. You know how much being a pilot means to me."

Her voice grew stronger as she spoke. "I'm terrified I'll get addicted to the drugs here, even though everyone says it won't happen over the space of a few days, and that I need them. If I'm at risk for alcohol, what's the difference for drugs? So I made the decision to avoid the risk." Lannis tapped her own chest with a forefinger. "My choice." She opened her hand, held it palm up. "I know there are consequences. Thank you for going to bat for me, for finding the acupuncture guy. I know you and Ben don't agree, but it's the decision that's right for me."

Millie looked stunned. In spite of her promise not to pry, a strangled "How did this come about?" found its way out of her mouth. Stricken, she put her fingers to her lips.

"Some...bad things happened." Lannis pressed her own trembling lips together so she wouldn't say more than she intended. After a moment she continued. "I made poor choices in response, and then I made mistakes. I was ashamed of those choices, and still am, but made it even worse by cutting off contact with you and Lynette." Tears filled her eyes. "I'm sorry. P-please forgive me?"

Millie's answer was a hug.

Lannis hadn't been touched this much in years. She'd perfected the art of distance and withdrawal. She'd allowed no one, *no one*, close enough to hug her. Her walls were tumbling down in the face of Ben's persistence, Althea's insistence on accountability, Betsy's gentle encouragement, and Orvis's high standards. She didn't have the energy to keep her mom at arm's length anymore.

Sighing, she sank into her mother's embrace and relaxed her neck and jaw muscles for the first time in four years.

~

Officer Dennis Mayfield came to Lannis's room that afternoon to take her statement. She regarded him warily and wondered if she could trust him.

He looked surprised, and said, "Yes, of course."

She realized she'd spoken her thought out loud, and flushed, feeling the heat from her chest to the roots of her hair. "I'm sorry. It's just...the newspaper story a couple of months ago about some bad apples on the police force..." She trailed off, realizing that if she said more, she'd get much, much too close to the hijacking. She steered the conversation back to the current subject and told Officer Mayfield everything she could remember about the attack. He looked disappointed when she said she hadn't seen the assailant. "Only his baggy pants and a chain belt, with a sparkly crown thing dangling from the end of it. He had on leather shoes or boots. They were dark brown." When prodded, she repeated what the guy had said to her, over and over. Finally Officer Mayfield flipped his notebook closed and thanked her for her time.

Lannis saw through his courtesy and read his resignation at her inability to remember any definitive details. He left, and she dropped her head back on the pillow, equal measures of frustration and fatigue battling for her attention.

Fatigue won.

Orvis woke her when he brought flowers and a card from all the employees at Louisville Air. Then, in quick succession, an arrangement with balloons from the tower was delivered, followed by yet another from the radio stations. Lannis was dumbfounded at the visible support of people from whom she'd expected nothing. Betsy and Althea called between floral deliveries. Ben must have called them, or maybe Orvis.

"Will you come home to recuperate, Lannis?" Hope was evident in Millie's voice.

Lannis shook her head. "Thanks, Mom, but no. I need to stay here." She gestured at the flowers. "I'm afraid if I leave, I'll lose my momentum, my focus. Plus, I need to get back to work, even if it's just a ground job. How about if I come for a few days in a couple of weeks?"

Millie nodded, disappointed but resigned. "I could arrange for some vacation time, to stay, take care of you…"

Alarm shot through Lannis. Millie's hovering at the hospital was fine, but moving in with her, even for a limited time…not so much. She was grateful they'd reconnected, but that would be too much, too soon. "I know how strapped for staffing your unit is. Or at least, what it was like a few years ago." She shrugged, striving to convey a casual air. "I'll be okay."

"I'm concerned about how you're going to manage for the first week or so. You're going to need some help. Fortunately, you're not injured badly enough, so insurance won't cover home health aides." Millie delivered the last statement with a wry grimace.

"No offense, Mom, but I'd rather be alone." She hoped the sentiment didn't come across as rude as it sounded to her own ears.

"She's coming home with me, Mrs. Parker." Ben stood in the doorway. Showered, shaved, and rested, he looked considerably better than he had that morning. "I'll take care of her. If I have to go to work, my partner's wife can stay with her."

Lannis gaped at him. Gathering her wits, she scowled. "No, I'm not." She snapped her mouth closed over the imprecation. "Where do you get off—"

Ben interrupted her. "You *will* need help. Who else do you have?" He pinned her with a piercing look and stepped the rest of the way into the room. They both knew the answer to that question, and he waited for her to acknowledge it. He softened his voice and added, "You've accepted help from a lot of people in the last few months. This is just an extension of that—physical, instead of emotional. It doesn't mean you're weak, or needy." He leaned close and whispered, for her ears only, "You're not a prisoner."

Her mood morphed from mutinous to murderous, and she shot him a volcanic glare that her mother had to be blind to miss.

A shadow of pain flickered across his face. "This would never have happened if you didn't know me. Please, allow me to help. I'm sorry I didn't keep you safe from him."

Lannis adjusted her attitude from murderous to one of merely wishing to inflict severe bodily harm, and she muttered under her breath.

"What?" Ben asked, cocking his head to the side.

"I said *fine*." Her anger flared and she added a four-letter word. Shocked, she looked at Millie and said, "Oops. Sorry, Mom." Glaring at Ben, she said, "I hate it when you're right."

One corner of his mouth quirked up, and he said, "Glad to see you're feeling better, darlin'."

Chapter Thirty-Seven

MILLIE LEFT THE NEXT AFTERNOON, after extracting the promise of a daily phone call from Lannis. The following morning, Lannis was discharged from the hospital, and Ben took her home. To his house. In spite of her pique, once they arrived she peered about, curious to see his natural habitat. He turned down a wooded lane, the house set far enough back from the road to be invisible. The driveway crossed over a creek with deeply cut banks, and he stopped, punching a code into an automated ironwork gate on the bridge. The gate slid silently open, then closed after they passed through. Lannis recognized the simplicity and effectiveness of the security, at least in terms of vehicles.

Driving up a slight slope, the house came into view, a ranch-style brick home, built long enough ago to look intrinsic to the landscape. Huge trees, now naked, would provide ample shade come summer. Small gardens with low-maintenance perennials and patches of ivy decorated the yard nearest the house. She spied a covered bench swing out back, along with a wooden picnic table, both worn and comfortable from use. The nearest homes were a good quarter of a mile away through the woods, far enough to be invisible once trees leafed out in the spring.

The automatic garage door lifted to reveal a well-used workshop, which took up most of the second stall. Tools hung on a pegboard, and something mechanical—she had no idea what it was—lay strewn in pieces on the countertop. A shop light hung from a hook above, and the extension cord that powered it snaked across the wall, suspended on hooks, and dropped down to the outlet below.

Lannis maneuvered herself out of the car before Ben got all the way around to help her. Seeing that she'd stood on her own, he popped the trunk and grabbed her duffel instead. She slowly followed him up two stairs into the house, gripping his outstretched hand, as there was no railing. A fine sheen of perspiration formed on her brow from exertion and discomfort, and she caught her lower lip with her teeth. She halted for a recuperative breath, and examined her temporary home.

The living room was…lived in. Magazines lay scattered on the coffee table; a half-empty coffee cup sat atop an abandoned newspaper. Furniture and walls were in earthy, strong colors. A couple of throws were tossed over the back of the couch, which was the repository for a number of well-worn and mismatched decorative pillows. A bookcase took up one whole wall, a wide variety of titles evident at a glance. A couple of plants—as low maintenance as the landscaping outside—perched on a plant stand next to the picture window, along with an old-fashioned watering can. There seemed to be no particular attention paid to coordination of colors or patterns, but the overall effect was one of warmth and energy, rather than chaos.

"Here you go, Lannis." Ben dropped her duffel in the middle of the floor, led her to the couch, helped her sit down, then took pains to arrange cushions behind her back, beneath her arms, under her feet. Her eyebrows rose and she smothered a smile. He was fussing around her like a mother hen, an image that was very much at odds with everything she knew about him.

"Ben. It's okay. Thank you. Now stop," she said. "Or you're going to make me laugh, and then you'll really have to pay…just not today."

He straightened from covering her feet with one of the throws, sent her an exaggerated look of mock umbrage, then grinned and pulled a chair over. "Yeah, I guess I'm overdoing it a little, huh?" He sat, and said, "I haven't had a houseguest for quite a while, much less one right out of the hospital, so I'm trying to do it right. Why don't you just holler if you need anything? Otherwise I'll go about my business as if you weren't here."

Lannis relaxed her shoulders. "Yeah, that'll work. Actually, I'm really tired right now. The drive took more out of me than I expected." She carefully reclined and adjusted the pillow under her head. "I think I'll lie down and rest for a while, if you don't mind."

Ben snagged an afghan, covered her, tucked in the edges, and touched her forehead with the backs of his fingers, lingering there for a heartbeat. He switched the lamps off, then went to the window and started to pull the drapes.

"Please don't. I like being able to see out, see the trees, the sky," she said. He dropped his hand and walked to the stereo, turned it on. Soft strains of classical music floated through the room. He watched her for a minute, then quietly went through a door off the living room. She heard the clicking of computer keys and drifted into a doze, comforted by a barely articulated sense of safety.

By evening they established a routine of sorts. Lannis took ibuprofen about half an hour before moving much. Ben helped her walk, as she was still a bit unsteady. She lost track of the number of naps she took, and began losing track of the time. Had the drapes been closed, she would have been thoroughly disoriented. Now that the acupuncture treatments were over, pain was constant, draining her of energy she thought she'd stored up in the hospital. Ben alternately bullied and cajoled her into sipping Seven-Up or soup every time she woke up, and kept a supply of crackers at her fingertips. He made a sandwich for himself, and watched the evening news with the volume so low Lannis couldn't figure out how he was getting anything out of it. He settled next to her, and she leaned on him.

It wasn't late, but darkness had fallen, and Lannis suddenly couldn't keep her eyes open. "I'm going to bed, Ben. Where am I going to sleep?"

He glanced at her, and answered her question with a different one. "Would you like a shower or a bath first?"

She shot him a sideways look and said, "That would be heaven, but I can't get the dressing wet."

"I'll help you, and we'll keep it dry."

She looked at him sharply. "I'm not undressing in front of you." Between the mountains and her drinking binge, not to mention the hospital stay, he'd seen almost everything she had to look at. Almost. She'd hang on to the remnants with both hands, though.

"Use a towel to cover up, and I'll step out so you can wash what you're able to by yourself." He brought his hand up and massaged the nape of her neck. His breath feathered her hair. "I'm not pushing, Lannis, just offering. If you don't want to, it's okay." He brushed a kiss across her hair, squeezed her shoulder, and stood. "At the very least, let's get you into the bathroom for a spit bath. You'll feel better, and sleep better, too."

A few minutes later, Lannis struggled with the washcloth, near tears with pain and frustration. A bath or a shower would feel so good. He certainly wouldn't see any more than he already had. *I can trust Ben. It's my pride that hurts worse.* Defeated, she lifted her voice. "Ben..." The door swung open before she could get any further.

His gaze flicked over her, noting her trembling arms as she clutched an oversized towel close round her body. He was at her side in one step, one arm on her elbow and the other wrapped around her waist. Carefully he lowered her to the toilet seat.

"Are you still up for a bath, darlin'?" he asked.

She nodded, eyes downcast.

He started the water, adjusted the temperature, then gathered her up and helped her in, towel and all. He grabbed the showerhead, which was attached to a long, flexible hose.

"Tip your head back," he said.

She did, and warm water cascaded over her head, drenching the towel. She gave herself over to his strong fingers as they massaged her scalp. He moved the towel just enough to wash her shoulders and upper back, then gave gentle, matter-of-fact attention to her limbs. He handed the cloth to her and stepped out of the bathroom.

As soon as she was done she called him in and he returned, tipping her head for the rinse cycle. Less than five minutes after starting, he lifted her out, wrapped a dry towel around her body with the murmured instruction to drop the wet one in the tub. Two minutes later she was dry. He gently bundled her into one of his thick, colorful T-shirts, and handed her the robe Millie had bought for her from the hospital gift shop.

And he accomplished all of it without exposing any more of her skin than Lannis felt comfortable with.

She felt better than she had since the beating. She glanced in the mirror and made a small squeak of distress. The swelling around her eye had receded, but the bruises on her face bloomed in colorful glory. Lannis dismissed those; she had no control over them, and they'd eventually go away, but her hair stood up on end, and poked out at odd angles. She lifted a hand to the worst of it and tried to pat it into submission.

Alarmed by her squeak, Ben stopped wringing out the wet towel, and turned to see what had disturbed her. When he saw the source of her dismay, he grinned and pointed at a comb on the vanity. She tamed the spiky mess, then ran her fingers through it to fluff it. Peering at her reflection, she leaned back, satisfied, then caught Ben's amused expression and glowered at him.

"Feel better?" he asked laconically.

She poked her nose skyward and crossed her arms. Then winced, because the incision pulled.

He threw his head back and laughed. "Let's get you to bed." A hand on her elbow, he guided her down the hallway. He turned her into the master bedroom and had her nearly to the king-sized bed before she balked.

"Hold it, cowboy. We're sleeping in the same bed? No, no, let me rephrase that. We're *not* sleeping in the same bed." Turning, she looked up at him. "Don't you have a guest room?"

"Room, yes. Bed, no. I turned it into an office. I need to hear you if you need something in the middle of the night, and I won't if I'm on the couch." She stiffened, but he gently and inexorably moved her to the bed, reaching around her to pull the covers down. "I'll sleep on top of the sheet, like we did in Pigeon Forge." Her knees buckled and he lowered her to the sheets, helped her work her arms free of the robe, and pulled the covers over her. Leaning over, he kissed her cheek, then said, "I'm going to grab a quick shower. I'll be back shortly."

Lannis closed her eyes and took short, shallow breaths, willing the pain to subside. Gradually she slipped into a fitful doze, too weak to battle Ben, too.

Chapter Thirty-Eight

Someone set at butchering her, *slicing her belly open with a knife. In desperation, she tried to twist away, but pain and paralysis stilled her muscles. She screamed, over and over, a forlorn, futile, feeble effort that echoed throughout an abandoned airplane hangar. Tears streamed down her face, and raised the level of the Ohio River, turning it into a muddy, angry tsunami. She gasped for breath, tried to escape the water, but instead sank beneath the surface, the knife still stuck in her gut. Cold. So cold. Her hair, long, much longer than she'd ever worn it, swirled in silky ribbons in the murky depths. Despair paralyzed her thoughts, her will, and agony claimed her body.*

Heat, blessed heat, pressed against her back. Lannis welcomed it, tried to sink into it, but froze in position when pain stabbed at her belly again. Lucky for her, the warmth remained, and seeped bit by bit into her skin. Desperately, she thought, *If I can get warm enough, maybe I'll survive.*

A familiar voice called her out of the darkness. *Ben?* Nothing made sense, unless... *A dream. No, a nightmare...* She stopped fighting, stopped battling the water, the pain, the cold, and magically, they all receded.

"Come on, Lannis, wake up, darlin', and we'll get you something for the pain."

Lannis finally broke through the fog of sleep, realized that the warmth was Ben, and remembered she was at his house, in his bed. "Okay," she croaked, lying very still. The bed dipped slightly as he got up, pausing to place another blanket over her. Panting lightly, she waited, and became aware of just how dependent she was on him. *Mom was right.* She couldn't even get out of bed without help. *I'm glad it's Ben taking care of me.*

Shocked at the thought, she forgot to breathe for a heartbeat, and at that moment, Ben reappeared with water, pills, and a warm washcloth. He saw to her needs, then disappeared down the hall to the kitchen. By the time he returned, the medicine was kicking in.

Gingerly, she changed position, and watched him enter the room. He'd slept in a pair of athletic shorts and nothing more. The light from the hallway briefly highlighted his muscles, defined and rippling, with a couple of scars visible, even in the low light. The scar on his upper left arm looked new. It was still pink and puckered, ragged looking.

"What happened to your arm?" she asked without thinking. "It looks like it's still sore."

He glanced down at it, then at her, and one side of his mouth crooked up in a wry smile. "That's from the bullet I took before I hijacked your plane."

"Bullet?" Shock at his answer brought her fully awake. "But you weren't hurt," she blurted. "I never saw blood or anything, even in the motel in Pigeon Forge."

He turned off the light. "Yes, I was. I went to great lengths to keep you from finding out. You would've used it to create an opportunity to escape, and I couldn't risk that." He sat on the bed and stroked her arm. "You made it hard. I was a lot weaker than you thought. My acting skills—pretty much limited to one form of intimidation or another—were stretched to the max."

Bemused, she remembered snippets of the experience…like early on, when she'd banked the plane hard right, and threw him into the door, or when he'd tackled her. Both times his grunt sounded like he was in pain. Thinking hard, Lannis realized he'd never let her have unrestrained access to his left side, even—maybe especially—in sleep.

He rubbed her back, and it felt wonderful. "Let me help you keep the nightmares at bay," he said as his hand continued its lazy trek along her spine.

She relaxed into his touch, her eyelids growing heavy. He climbed into bed again and turned out the light. Gratitude quietly crept into her heart, along with trust—a concept she didn't want to examine too closely, even if she could stay awake.

She woke, Ben asleep next to her. Sometime during the night he'd ended up holding her, and the sheet had slid to hip level between them. Not only that, she'd turned to him the same way she had the first night in the forest, with one arm draped across his chest, her belly supported by his torso, one thigh across his hips. Her head rested over his heart, and its steady rhythm soothed with hypnotic dependability. His arm, the one that held her close, offered a sense of security. His other arm was outflung in self-assured confidence even as he slept.

His face was unlined, relaxed and open. It reminded her of the other time she'd seen him asleep. Mentally, she winced at the outcome of that particular situation, then pushed the memory aside. Even so, she stiffened with anxiety at his proximity, at the unintended repetition of that intimacy.

He woke, his one-armed embrace tightening protectively, and murmured in a sleep-roughened voice, "You hurting? I'll go get your meds."

Lannis cleared her throat. "Um, actually, Ben, I don't need any right now." Her voice faded. She remained rigid and still, except for one finger, which she allowed to trace small circles on his chest, deluding herself into believing that it was of its own volition. Mesmerized, drawn like a moth to the flame's danger, she flattened her palm over his nipple. His breath quickened, along with his pulse. His morning erection stirred beneath her thigh.

Ben captured her roving fingers with his free hand and disentangled himself, carefully rolling her away. "Your mom said to get the meds to you before you start hurting, that it works better to keep the pain down—" He got out of bed, stretched, and ran his hand through his hair, apparently in total disregard for his body's response to her touch. "—rather than having to put out a bigger fire, so to speak." He yawned and padded down the hall.

A bigger fire, indeed. Although he was referring to an entirely different subject than she was. *Why did I do that? Nobody touches me while I sleep, not even Rudy when we were married.* The thought made her muscles even more tense. She'd never actually *slept* with a man. After sex, she'd always retreated to her own side of the bed, provided she'd even stayed. None of the men she'd been with seemed inclined to want her next to them for sleep, and that suited her fine, because in reality, she hadn't wanted to be with them at all.

Betsy had helped Lannis recognize the seeds of her compulsion to control everything about sex after the rape, including her warped idea that sleeping around somehow proved she was in charge. The concept made her cringe with embarrassment now.

She'd had no choice, in April, about Ben's nighttime touch. Last night, she'd had a choice. She allowed his touch. What was more, she liked it, in spite of the anxiety it engendered. Being held all night was new. And strangely, more intimate than the physical union of intercourse.

Was she attracted to Ben? That way? He was definitely easy on the eyes. If she was honest with herself—and she had to be—she'd felt twinges of attraction when they were in the woods and at the gym. But she'd never considered him as a lover.

Their relationship was too complicated to capture with a label. Sometimes he was arrogant and demanding, and sometimes she hated him for it, but she couldn't deny his friendship, his constancy. Especially since—and in spite of—her drinking binge. Rather than abandoning her, he took care of her. Not that she could pull anything over on him. Not at all, because he held her accountable and expected her best effort, no matter the task at hand. But more important, Ben made her laugh—and made her laugh at herself.

In a flash of insight, she realized she'd toyed with him moments ago in a misguided attempt to neutralize the intimacy of his touch, to reduce their relationship to something she could control.

Sex.

Plain and simple.

Although with Ben, nothing was ever plain and simple. Discomfited by the revelation, she squirmed.

By the time Ben returned, she'd gotten herself up, and sat on the edge of the bed hoping he'd hurry. She felt weak and wobbly. She quickly downed the pills, and he helped her shuffle slowly to the bathroom.

Pain began to drive the episode from her mind, though Lannis was well aware of her skill at burying unexamined concepts deep in her psyche. *It'll come back to bite me.* Or...maybe she could face the demon head-on.

Yes, she could. Sweat began to bead around her hairline from pain. She would. Face the demon. Head-on. Just not this minute.

After her initial difficulty getting around, Lannis was able to get where she wanted most of the time, albeit at a turtle's pace. They ate breakfast in the kitchen, a welcome change that made her feel much less the invalid. Ben made scrambled eggs with cheese, but wouldn't give her any of the salsa he put on his. She speared a forkful off his plate anyway, humming in pleasure at the burst of flavor. He was worried it was too spicy for her, but it tasted wonderful. However, she limited herself to one pirated bite, in case he was right. She really didn't want to throw up. That would hurt. Nor did she want to endure a bout of nausea.

The morning passed in quiet companionship, although she couldn't bring herself to broach a conversation about sex, about crossing a line that she shouldn't have, about her less-than-flattering self-revelation. The resultant tension left her antsy. Lannis read the newspaper and worked on the crossword puzzle, a rare treat, which helped dispel her sense of fretfulness.

Ben did some work around the house, tapped away on the computer, and disappeared into the garage for a while. After lunch, he said, "I need to go in to work for a couple hours. Maggie Ross, Mike's wife—remember, my partner from the flight to Knoxville, in

July?—she's going to come over while I'm gone. If you need anything, call my cell phone."

As if conjured, the doorbell rang. Ben let Maggie in and introduced her. A couple of inches shorter than Lannis, Maggie sported a curvy figure and a riot of carrot-red hair. She regarded Lannis with sharp, bright blue eyes and unguarded curiosity.

"Hi, Lannis," Maggie said. "I've heard a lot about you. Ben talks about you all the time."

Lannis arched an eyebrow at Ben, shooting a silent question his direction.

He shrugged, and color brightened his cheekbones. "Gotta go. I'll be back by five." He grabbed a light jacket, and beat what sure looked like a hasty retreat.

Lannis looked at Maggie, and lifted her chin. "So, what does he say about me?" Expecting a litany of her failures and problems, she steeled herself.

"He thinks a lot of you. He told us life has thrown you some bean balls, but you're strong and smart, and you work hard. He says you've got a great, dry sense of humor, and you're an excellent pilot. We stayed with him while you were in surgery. I've never seen him so…distraught." Maggie paused for a moment. "He hasn't talked about someone this much for years, since Deb left him."

Lannis gaped at Maggie and tried to process all the information she'd just been handed. "Deb?" She felt an irrational spurt of jealousy. "Who's Deb?"

"Oh, I'm sorry. He must not have mentioned her." Maggie looked uncomfortable. "She's his ex-wife, and I suppose you should ask him."

"Um, sorry, no, he didn't tell me about her. Some about his family, and his brother who died, but not an ex-wife." Lannis felt like she'd blundered into Ben's private space. Even so, she couldn't contain her curiosity entirely, and asked, "Have they been divorced long?"

Maggie relaxed. "Oh, yeah, probably around six or seven years."

"You've known him for a long time, then."

"Yes. Mike and Ben have been together since they were in the Army. Ben was Mike's best man, and we've been married eight years." Maggie looked at Lannis with perceptive eyes. "You can trust him, you know. He's a good man. We both think the world of him. We named our son after him. Martin. Marty, for short."

Lannis ducked her head briefly and changed the subject, not wanting to linger here. They talked for an hour. Maggie treated

Lannis to glowing dissertations on her two children, who sounded like holy terrors. After bracing her belly so she could laugh for the umpteenth time, she pleaded fatigue and laid down on the couch for a nap.

When she woke, Maggie was gone, and Ben hummed along with the radio in the kitchen. The smell of roasting chicken drifted into the living room and stirred her appetite. She sat up, feeling off-kilter from the disruption in her normal routine. She was exhausted, even though she'd slept during the day, but she also felt wired. The pain no longer overwhelmed her, and unfocused energy set her teeth on edge.

She stood and made her way into the kitchen, knowing movement would, at the very least, provide a physical outlet for her emotions. She sat at the table while Ben pulled food out of the oven.

"So, did you like Maggie?" he asked.

"Yeah, I did." Surprised, she realized she truly liked the outspoken redhead. "She said you'd divorced several years ago." The words slipped out, and for a moment she didn't believe that she'd actually said them aloud. Apparently, surgery loosened either her tongue or disabled her normal thought-speech filters, since this had happened three times already today. Horrified, she said, "I'm sorry, Ben. It's none of my business. Forget I said anything."

He looked at her, and smiled slightly. "Turnabout is fair play. It was a long time ago, and the marriage was a mistake. I was too involved in my job, my career, to pay enough attention to her, and she was too insecure and clingy to deal with being a cop's wife." He paused to set the food on the table, sat, and dished portions of chicken and rice onto their plates. "No kids. Amicable, but still painful. She's remarried, happily, to a guy who has an office job and comes home every night. They've got a couple of kids now." A fleeting look of longing crossed his face when he mentioned kids, quickly replaced with a grin. "Jealous?" he asked, waggling his eyebrows at her.

Lannis flushed, because she *was* jealous, but she didn't want to admit to it. Flustered, she pushed away from the table.

He stopped her with a hand on her wrist, and said, "Sorry. I was just teasing." He released her. She got up, a bit more slowly than she would have a minute before, and looked down at him.

"What are we doing, Ben? Where is this going? Us, I mean. I'm in your house, in your bed. We're cooking and eating and cleaning up, and sitting in the living room like a married couple. But we're not, and I don't quite understand how this all happened."

He took her hand and tugged, a wordless invitation to sit back down. She hesitated, then sank into the chair.

"It's only going where you want it to go. I know what I want, but that doesn't mean I get it. For the moment, I'm your friend. I hope you consider that friendship a two-way street. Someday I'd like it to be more, but only if you want it, too." He squeezed her hand.

More? Her mouth went dry, and her tongue darted out to lick her lips. "Ben…" Sadness washed over her. "I…I'm too messed up for you. You deserve someone a whole lot…more stable than me." Lannis looked at the floor. *Honesty.* That didn't make it any easier to say.

She felt her face heat as she spoke. "This morning, in bed…it felt so intimate, I got scared. I needed to change it into sex, so I could handle it." She forced the words out, and then they nearly ran together once she got started. "You see, sex keeps me from actually getting close to anyone since the rape. I know it's totally irrational, not to mention really, really warped, but if I can control anything about sex, then I feel like I'm controlling the guy who raped me, like somehow I'm winning."

She huffed out a breath. "It's a bad trade-off, I know, but it made crazy sense at the time, and I just fell back into it this morning, mostly because I'd never let anyone get that close since I quit drinking."

Her voice dropped. "If I let you get close…I'm afraid you'll hate me once you really know me. I don't know what I can offer you in the way of friendship, anyway, much less anything beyond that." She pulled her hand from his, twisted hers together.

Ben took one of her hands, disengaged it from its mate, and put a finger under her chin, gently pushing past her resistance and tipping her head up until her eyes met his. She couldn't hide her misery or her unshed tears from him.

"I don't know where you get the impression you don't have anything to offer as a friend. You've already given far more than most people are ever asked to, as friends. The Bible says there's no greater love than to lay down one's life for a friend. You saved my life once, whether you intended to or not, and protected me in the face of great pain and at tremendous risk a few days ago. You give me pleasure and companionship, and you challenge me. As for your not being good enough in one way or another, well, you're a work in progress, *as we all are.*" He searched her eyes for a moment.

"In case you still subscribe to the notion that you're 'damaged goods' because you were raped, that's a load of bullshit. No more so than being the victim of any crime makes you *damaged goods*." A wicked twinkle flickered in his eyes. "Like having been hijacked and kidnapped." Squeezing her hand again, he stood abruptly. "Let's go sit in the living room. I'll get the dishes later."

Lannis woke the next morning cuddled up against Ben in a rerun of yesterday's intimacy. Alarm burbled through her veins, and anxiety skimmed across her skin. She clenched her hand to avert another foray into inappropriate sexualization of the simple comfort he offered. *Can I just let the moment be?* Betsy told her to let uncomfortable feelings come, to acknowledge them, and that they'd pass. *Feeling emotions won't kill you, but burying them will.* Lannis concentrated on slowing and deepening her breathing.

God, I hate being in my own skin when it's like this. The thought wasn't really a prayer and definitely wasn't a curse; it was more like a statement to him, and she didn't expect an answer. Yet, a sense of calm, unanticipated and unfamiliar, hovered, then settled over her with the gentleness of a gossamer coverlet. Whether it was the product of the breathing exercise or the almost-prayer, she couldn't say, but it granted her the patience to wait for the anxiety to pass. After several minutes the jittery, almost tingly, sensation in her limbs, fingers, and gut began to subside.

Surprised, she thought, *God, if that was you, thank you.*

No matter what had provided the moment of calm, Lannis decided to allow herself the fleeting pleasure of Ben's touch.

It would end soon enough. She couldn't see their relationship progressing to what he seemed to think was possible.

Sorrow flowed through her. She pushed it away, determined to take what she had, to stay in the present, even if heartache waited around the corner.

Chapter Thirty-Nine

"KEEP THE PHONE with you. Not nearby, or even in the same room. *With* you." Ben leveled a laser glare at her. "Call me if you need anything." He relented a little and pointed at the list of numbers on the counter. "Or Maggie."

Lannis held up the handset, waggled it at him, then deposited it in the pocket of her robe. "Got it. I'll be fine. Now go to work."

He kissed her nose, then fired up his Mustang and rumbled down the driveway. After he left, she prowled. There was no other polite word for it. The silence of his house was disconcerting after a week of constant contact, and she felt restless. Not quite trapped, but definitely at loose ends. She looked at the books, pulled some off the shelf, and returned them. Nothing caught her eye, and daytime TV sounded about as inviting as a root canal.

Then she noticed a couple of photo albums on the bottom shelf. Well, those could be interesting to look at, and wouldn't be an invasion of Ben's privacy. She pulled them out and laboriously moved them to the couch, one at a time, holding them close to her body. She wasn't supposed to lift much, but they weren't heavy, and since she used her legs to do the up and down parts, it seemed to work okay. After a moment's consideration, she went to the kitchen and brewed a cup of tea—he'd bought a variety pack just for her— then brought the steaming, fragrant infusion to the living room. She settled on the couch, adjusted the cushions, and took a sip before opening the album with the earliest date on the cover.

There were lots of little kid pictures, one of them obviously Ben. He was cute as a toddler, and some pictures included a boy so like him it had to be his older brother, and another child, a sister, perhaps, smaller than Ben. She couldn't remember him mentioning anyone other than his brother who'd died. Ben in grade school, Ben in Halloween costumes, Ben opening Christmas presents. Ben growing up, gangly and awkward in middle school, shy and eager with a prom date in high school. Confident, cocky even, in a track uniform. *That* expression was familiar. His high school graduation picture. Lots of family at the party afterward, an outdoor barbeque.

The second album had some pictures of military bases, and lots of young men in a variety of uniforms, followed by pictures of college-age kids, partying, and generally appearing cheerful and carefree. One young woman began appearing more and more often, and as Lannis turned the pages, she hazarded a guess that the girl was Deb. She was attractive, petite, and…pert.

Lannis's jealousy faded, and she felt sadness for the young woman whose hopes and dreams had come at too high a price. Vaguely, she recalled reading that people in law enforcement tended to have a higher than average divorce rate, and she could understand why. It would require a special sort of person to be able to send off their spouse every morning, knowing the potential for encountering violence was high, and that he might not come home. She felt a wave of compassion for Deb, and for Ben, too, that their marriage hadn't worked. She was a sucker for happy endings, although she'd lost faith in her own.

She came across a few pages that had blank spots, rectangular discolorations where pictures had been removed. Probably wedding pictures. She didn't have any pictures of Rudy, or their wedding, not that it had been much. He'd taken the few that existed when he packed and moved out, and she never asked for copies. When Ben's pictures started up again, they were of Mike and Maggie, and some other people she didn't know. With a jolt of recognition, she saw the guy they'd met in Pigeon Forge, the one who took her to the airport in Knoxville. Then Mike and Maggie and their children at various ages, laughing, playing, eating at Ben's picnic table. The rest of the album was empty.

Softly she closed the book, and sat thinking, sipping at her now-cool tea. While she still didn't know a lot about him, she'd discovered facets of him that were new to her, or helped explain how he came to be the person he was now. In any case, he was more human to her, more real. More vulnerable.

She'd expended a lot of energy trying to avoid seeing him as a human being. Initially, of course, that was pretty appropriate, and critical to her survival, at least from her point of view. Since then, acknowledgment of his humanity required a response from her that she hadn't been ready to give. That she was reflecting on said humanity implied she was moving toward acceptance. Wryly, she brought her cup to her mouth and took a final sip.

What was it he'd said the other morning? He was talking about her pain level, and putting out a fire before it got out of control.

Lannis realized the sentiment could also stand as a metaphor for their relationship.

Apparently her fire had flared into a blaze without her awareness.

After a nap, Lannis went to the kitchen and prepared supper in brief spurts, not that there was much to do. Salad from a premixed bag of greens. Measure rice and water. Chop a few veggies to garnish the rice. Rinse and pat chicken pieces dry. She found some marinade, put the chicken in it, and placed it in the fridge. Satisfaction bloomed at her contribution toward dinner.

She called Ben, and asked him to bring her stack of AA materials from her house. She had time—lots of it—and she might as well work on some of the steps she'd been stuck on. Plus, Betsy had suggested she write letters. To herself. To the rapist. Obviously they wouldn't be mailed, but might give her a voice that hadn't been allowed, or available, and enable her to look at events from another perspective.

The next morning after Ben left, she got a cup of tea and a notebook. She sat in a chair near the big window in the living room, and started.

Dear Rudy,

I caused you much pain with our marriage and divorce, and I'm sorry. My selfishness and immaturity, and especially my drinking, contributed to the failure of our relationship. Although it's not an excuse, it is important for me to tell you that I was also trying to deal with the aftermath of an event that had nothing to do with you, yet it overshadowed everything that we did, or were.

I especially apologize for hitting you, and putting you in the situation of hitting me. It's not something I think you would've done outside of that situation.

I sincerely hope you've been able to move on to greener pastures and a happier life.

Lannis

She got an envelope out of Ben's desk and addressed it to Rudy's lawyer, as she didn't know where Rudy lived, and hadn't, since the day he moved out. Then she started on the next one, which was a bit more difficult.

Dear Mom,

I know I apologized last weekend for cutting off contact with you and Lynette. I want to say it again. I'm sorry. Someday, maybe I can talk to you about why, but not quite yet. Meanwhile, I love you, and I'm thankful that you came to see me in the hospital, and I'm thankful that I've been able to talk to you every day since. You fill my life with blessings.

I'm sorry I caused you pain.

Love,

Lannis

She got an envelope for that one, too.

Dear Lynette,

By now, I'm sure that Mom has told you that we've re-established communication. I'm sorry I cut off our relationship. I've caused you a great deal of pain, I know, especially since I've never seen little Carly. I'm sorry I haven't been a support to you, or rejoiced with you, or been a good auntie to Carly. Please forgive me.

I hope we can rebuild our sisterhood.

I love you,

Lannis

Tears made little circular wrinkles on that envelope as she placed the stamp on it. She had to take a break and cry. She pulled a pillow from the corner of the couch and crushed it to her belly. Crying hurt more than laughing, and she curled up in a near-fetal position while she sobbed. Some time later, emotionally spent, she gathered up the wadded tissues and padded into the kitchen. She washed her face, brewed another cup of tea. With determination girded around her like a suit of armor, she headed in to write the hardest one.

Dea... She stopped, and angrily slashed through the word. There was no way she could use it. Hand trembling, she started over.

To Robert Davis:

You assaulted me. You brutalized me. You RAPED me. What you did very nearly ruined me. There's not one area of my life that has escaped impact because of what you chose to do.

I've isolated myself from family and friends because of a misguided sense of shame.

I've tried to cope by developing an addiction that's nearly cost me my job and my pilot's license—my livelihood, my passion, my joy.

You had NO RIGHT to do what you did. NO RIGHT.

I want you to say you're sorry, to acknowledge that you harmed me, and make reparations.

What I really want is to undo what happened.

Since none of that's likely, and the last is impossible, I hope the next woman you attack presses charges, and you go to prison for a long, long time—long enough that you're not able to do this to anyone else.

I'll be honest, and tell you I've fantasized about gruesome and painful tortures that you'd be forced to endure. I suppose that doesn't say much good about me, but I don't care. You forced me to endure gruesome and painful torture—and you nearly destroyed my soul.

But you didn't win.

I'm getting my soul back.

YOU DIDN'T WIN.

Lannis

She put the letter in a folder, to review later with Betsy. Feeling like she'd been through the agitation cycle of a washing machine, she decided to break for lunch. On the way to the kitchen, she changed the radio from the classical music to an alternative rock station in an effort to boost her spirits.

Lunch ended up being chocolate chip cookies. Homemade, fresh and hot, comfort food at its best. She licked the bowl, and put everything in the sink to soak while she waited for the first batch to come out of the oven. The mouth-watering aroma filled the house, and the reality was as wonderful as the anticipation. She took a plate of warm cookies into the living room, and went back to work. She had two letters left.

Dear... She paused, and added *est.*

Dearest Lannis,

What happened to you was NOT YOUR FAULT. You did NOT deserve what happened, even if you willingly walked into the room, or didn't scream or fight. You said "no" in verbal and nonverbal ways, and he didn't honor that. You did what you had to do—to survive. And you succeeded.

He was a predator. You were the prey. If it hadn't been you, it would have been another woman.

Cut yourself some slack. If it happened to your sister, or your friend, how would you react? Would you berate her? Shun her? Blame her? No. You'd hug her, wouldn't you? You'd support and nurture and care for her.

Give those gifts to yourself. Let other people help you.

You are lovable—and loved.

Signed,

Me

She put that letter in the folder, too. She took a deep breath, and dove into the last one.

Dear Ben,

Thank you for being my friend.

She paused and chewed on the end of the pen for a while, then resumed writing.

I don't know what else to say. Maybe we'll have to talk, instead.
Lannis

It was the first letter she'd gotten stuck on. She shrugged. *Oh, well.* She folded it, put it on the kitchen table for Ben to find, then washed the baking utensils. Longingly, she glanced out the window. She needed a break from the house, especially after today.

She grabbed the phone and dialed Ben's cell phone. "Can we go out for supper tonight? I've had a rough day."

"Are you all right?" Alarm and concern filled his voice. "Did you call Maggie for help?"

"Oh! I'm fine, Ben," she answered, flustered. "I just need a change of scenery."

"Ah. Cabin fever, huh?" He chuckled. "I'll be home in about forty-five minutes. Think about where you want to go while you're waiting."

Chapter Forty

BEN OPENED his front door and caught a whiff of cookies. He changed course and homed in on the kitchen with the accuracy of a guided missile. A plate was piled high with chocolate chip cookies. He snagged three, took a bite of one, and noticed a folded piece of writing paper on the table. He picked it up with his free hand and shook it open. *Dear Ben,* he read. He slowed and bobbled the cookies in his other hand. *Thank you for being my friend.* His heart paused, then squeezed. *Maybe we'll have to talk...* He smiled, folded the paper one-handed, and tucked it into his shirt pocket. Sounded good to him. Real good. Made the sweet torture of coaxing her out of her prickly shell worth it.

"Lannis," he called. She came down the hallway, dressed in the gray athletic sweats he'd brought from her house yesterday. She stopped to pick up three envelopes from the coffee table. Her shoes dangled from her other hand, and she held them up to Ben, looking chagrined.

She shrugged, trying for nonchalant and failing. "I can't quite manage these. Would you mind?"

"No problem." He stuffed another cookie in his mouth, bent and worked her feet into her shoes, and briskly tied them. He stood, kissed her on the forehead, and said, "Great cookies. Where do you want to go eat?"

"I don't care. I just want to get out of the house."

"Do you think you'd feel up to coming in to the station tomorrow for a voice lineup?" he asked.

"A what?"

"A voice lineup. See if you can identify the guy's voice, the one who did this to you. Evidence for court, since you can't identify him visually."

Surprise was clear in her expression. "Uh, sure." Trepidation and fear flitted across her face, but he saw the moment she decided to face the prospect, no matter how difficult. She squared her shoulders and looked him in the eye with a determination that didn't waver. "Yes."

Lannis perked up once they got in the car, peering at houses in his neighborhood as they drove, commenting on one with naturalized landscaping. He took her to a nearby retro diner, not sure if she was up to a longer sit-down meal. Luckily the lines were short, and he sent her to a table to wait while he ordered. He brought the tray with their food, and slid into the booth next to her. She scooted over and asked him about his day.

"Paperwork. Legwork on a meth investigation." He popped a fry into his mouth. "I found the letter you wrote me. Anytime you want to talk, I'm here."

Lannis shot a sideways look at him, eyes widening with surprise. She shifted her gaze, flushing slightly. "Um, yeah. Okay." She swirled one of her fries in the little cup of ketchup he'd brought, then glanced up. "I'm not so good at that lately. Not that I ever was. Don't expect great philosophical debates."

Ben grinned. He pulled her close, caught her chin, and turned her toward him. Kissed her soundly. She tasted of ketchup, and salt, and herself—and she responded, her mouth molding to his. When he released her, she flushed deeply and glanced around the restaurant. No one paid them the least bit of attention. Amused, Ben watched as she studiously attacked the rest of her fries and tried to ignore him.

~

Lannis asked Ben to drive by the post office and she mailed her letters on the way home. She'd expected the outing would leave her fatigued, but she felt strong. Apparently she'd recovered enough that the more she did, the better she felt. To a degree, anyway. A twinge of discomfiture tugged at her when she thought ahead to the evening routine. "I'll do my bath alone tonight, Ben."

He took in her open, direct gaze, and nodded. "I'll be right outside, to help you get out of the tub when you're done." He pinned her with a stern look. "Don't you dare try that on your own."

"All right." Some things weren't worth fighting about, especially with Ben. Once home, she left the bathroom door slightly ajar so he could hear if she called out. She sighed, climbed in the warm water, and picked up the soap. The memory of his kiss tingled on her lips, and she brought her fingers up, touched them. Ben was clear about wanting to be more than a friend, or mentor, and if she'd had any doubts, the kiss banished them. He'd come right out and said that he wanted *more*, and while his touch all week had been businesslike, albeit gentle, there was a subtle possessive quality as well.

A lover's touch.

At a subliminal, primal level Lannis had recognized it, allowed it, and begun to crave it. Especially at night. Her ablutions slowed as she considered what *lover* would mean to Ben. He'd expect honesty, commitment, integrity—and he'd refuse to let her define and restrict their relationship to the physical.

He would demand her all. Her attention. Her focus. Her honesty. He wouldn't allow her to hold back, or run away— physically or emotionally. He sure hadn't yet. In the woods, or here.

At the same time, she realized he wouldn't ask her to change who she fundamentally was, in any way. In fact, he'd already encouraged her to become the best person she could be. Without pushing, he'd made it clear that his faith was central to who he was, and that he held a deep desire for her to make peace with God. She shied from that thought, but not as quickly as she usually did.

Intimacy. He'd already breached her walls on that front, and she hadn't even seen it happening. She wasn't entirely sure that she could have resisted him effectively even if she had. She'd certainly tried to resist him at different times, all attempts futile. Yet she knew, bone deep, Ben would honor her decision if she said no to a relationship with him. She dropped her hand into the water, which was beginning to cool.

The next step would be trust, some measure of which she'd begun to develop already. She'd known back in April that she could trust Ben to do what he said he would. And she trusted him enough now to let him care for her. It seemed trust wasn't as tall a hurdle as she'd thought.

"Oh, Ben, why do you want *me*?" she whispered. Was his guilt over Danny's death driving his side of the relationship? Or did he see promise in her that she'd only recently begun to recognize?

Lannis curbed her propensity for overanalyzing other people's motivations. But did she dare believe in herself as much as he claimed to?

It was a heady thought, one fraught with snares. What if she let him down? Worse, what if she let herself down?

Still, she allowed the notion to linger. Hope or fantasy? Her lips softened into a slight smile. Either way, she liked the image of herself as a success.

Tugging a towel around her body, she called, "Ben, I'm ready."

He was there in an instant. As he helped her out of the tub, Lannis pondered the levels of meaning of her words.

I'm ready. Ready for exactly what?

Chapter Forty-One

"Do YOU WANT to put this off, Lannis?" Ben watched her twist her hands in her lap and couldn't miss her withdrawn silence. "You don't have to do it today. In fact, it's up to you whether you do it at all." The sun glinted off the hood of his Mustang, which vibrated with the barely restrained energy of its three hundred twenty horses. He reached across the console and snagged one of her hands. "I can't come into the room with you, because I'm involved in this case, too. My presence could taint your response. I know it's hard, but sometimes the anticipation is worse than the actual event." He slanted a look at her, squeezed her hand, and said, "You'll be fine."

She swallowed and nodded once, her lips tight, set with a mixture of determination and trepidation. Then she squared her shoulders and got out of the car.

Ben watched from behind a two-way mirror as she listened to the tape recording of six male voices saying, "Listen up. Tell Mr. Ben Jackson he can expect a bullet real soon." The detective had told her the script before he ran the tape, and explained that she needed to listen to all six before making an identification. Nonetheless, when the fourth voice came on, her face drained of color and she flinched. She sat rigidly through the next two voices, head inclined in concentration. Ben's gut clenched, and he wanted to comfort her—as well as praise her courage.

"Number four," she said, clearly and with absolute certainty.

Ben's lips curled into a humorless smile. *She's nailed LeMasters.* Terrance had attempted to disguise his voice with inflection that was radically different from his usual speech pattern. *Oh, yeah. We've got a strong case.* Ben's tape, with LeMasters using a name for Ben that he'd only used undercover, and only on that particular sting. Lannis's identification in the voice lineup. The crown, reigning over the evidence room in silent, tacky glory. Ben doubted the case would even go to trial. LeMasters would prostitute himself trying to get the best deal he could from the DA's office, but Ben knew the prosecutor better than LeMasters did. The guy had no patience for broken plea deals. *He'll do hard time—with his crooked cop buddies.*

Lannis opened the door and scanned the room, her gaze zeroing in on Ben. A few quick steps brought her within arm's reach, and she pulled him close with an urgency that shouldn't have surprised him, but did. She burrowed her face into his shirt, slid her hands around his waist, and bunched his shirt in her fists. He cradled her in his arms, stroking her back.

"God, I want a drink right now." She groaned. "I'm tired of feeling this way."

He barely controlled a small jerk of shock at her words. A sliver of frustration insinuated its way into his gut. Sometimes he got tired of it, too. "Are you going to give in to it?" It took every bit of discipline he possessed to dredge up a neutral voice, and his heart plummeted in anticipation of her answer.

Lannis rubbed her face back and forth on his chest, then pushed herself away so she could look into his eyes. "I want to—it's scary how strong the *wanting* is—but I can get past it if you stay with me. Does this mean I'm just substituting one crutch for another?" Her eyes held a wounded expression, and her lower lip trembled slightly.

His heart's freefall ceased as suddenly as it had begun. "No, you're not, darlin'. You're reaching out to another human being instead of isolating yourself with alcohol. There's a big difference." He took her face between his hands and dropped his forehead to hers. "You're doing okay. Let's go for a drive on the way home. A diversion. A little change of scenery."

~

Lannis's spirits lifted as Ben drove through Cherokee Park, then parked near a small waterfall. Lannis got out and sat on a stone overlooking the stream, and turned her face to the warmth of the Indian summer sun. Relief left her feeling weak and strong at the same time. Giddy.

She was glad the voice lineup was over. Ben had been right. The anticipation was awful, worse than actually hearing the guy's voice. Hearing it had brought the memory of the attack back in full force. But it was over. The attack *and* the voice lineup.

She took a deep breath and turned to Ben. She smiled, and it stretched into a grin. "I did it, Ben! I did it!" One hand bracing her belly, she leaned toward him...and kissed him, giving life to exuberance she couldn't contain. She felt his surprise, but he got over it quickly and gathered her in his arms. He returned as much as she gave him, and exhilaration made her dizzy. With a groan, he ended the kiss and pulled away. Gravely, he gazed at her for a moment, then broke the spell by smiling and tapping the tip of her nose with his forefinger.

"You ready to head home?" he asked.

She nodded and laboriously worked her way to her feet. She glanced at him, and suddenly realized how open she'd let herself get with Ben, how close he'd gotten. How she'd let go of her death grip on control. Control of her environment, her circumstances. Her emotions.

He'd bridged the gap of her emotional detachment that, taken to an extreme, had been her salvation. The ability to "not be there" during parts of the rape had kept her sane and ensured her psychological survival—despite the wounds that remained. However, detachment created a pervasive damping of emotion, which did a great job of blunting pain…and deprived her of joy, as well.

Another thought prodded at the edge of her awareness. Her craving for a drink had dissipated, like a ghostly wisp of morning fog burned away by the sun. Distracted by her musings about Ben, she'd forgotten about the voice lineup and the resulting turmoil. With a spurt of mingled wry humor and disgust, Lannis thought, *Well, that's one way to cope.* He was pretty good at redirecting her thoughts. She scowled. In fact, that was a trademark of his—that and his ability to read her mind. She got in the car, pointedly avoiding his eyes.

Whistling cheerfully, he closed her door.

They drove home in silence, and in very different moods.

Chapter Forty-Two

LANNIS'S FOOTSTEPS SOUNDED, coming down the hall for the fifth time in the past hour. Ben frowned and tapped his pen against the legal pad he'd been using. She slipped past the door to his office, a quiet wraith prowling like a caged tiger.

He leaned back in his chair and stretched. "Wanna go for a walk around my property?" A break sounded good to him, and he didn't think either of them could stomach another card game. He'd also discovered Lannis wasn't a television or movie junkie, although she'd tolerate the Comedy Channel if he turned it on. Trouble was, there wasn't anything worth watching at the moment.

She appeared in the doorway. "You think it's okay?" The surgeon had removed her staples a few days ago, and for some reason she seemed fearful that the wound would reopen.

"Don't see why not. Your restriction is on lifting, not walking." Ben stood. "You're wearing a hole in my carpet. Might as well do your pacing outside."

Her face lit up and she headed for the coat closet, her steps eager and already lighter.

He led her around the inner path first, in case she had less stamina than either of them expected. The waves of her cabin fever began to dissipate as soon as the house disappeared behind the trees. He stole frequent glances to make sure she could handle the exertion, but rather than going pale, her color pinked up.

"This reminds me of April." She shot him a crooked smile.

With a pang, he realized she was right. "Minus the drama." He grinned. "Gotta say I appreciate hot showers and the bed."

"Yeah." The light in her eyes dimmed, and she looked away.

Ben stopped and tugged her around to face him. "Darlin', don't beat yourself up because you had another nightmare last night. They'll fade in time."

She gave a half shrug. "I know." She shoved her hands into the pockets of her jeans. "I wish there was something I could do to speed up the process."

"I don't know much about how the subconscious works, but I'm pretty sure you can't rush it." He started walking again. "Did you talk to your mom today?"

"Yes."

The relief in her voice told him he'd done the right thing in changing the subject, although truth be told, he'd done it more for his benefit than hers. He didn't mind comforting her when the dreams got the best of her, but every time she woke with a scream on her lips, it underscored his helplessness. It would be a good day for both of them when she could look back on a stretch of months without a demon dream.

"I'm going home to visit this weekend."

Ben frowned. "Bus?"

Lannis nodded, and seemed content with the idea. He wasn't. It would be a difficult trip for her. The bus would take longer. A lot longer. Nor would it be nearly as comfortable or accommodating as a car.

"You sure you won't let me drive you?"

Lannis shook her head. Her hair glinted in the dappled sunlight.

Ben sighed. He wished she wouldn't be so stubborn about accepting help. She'd kept her distance from him since the kiss in the park, and sent a bevy of *don't touch me* signals. Anyone with a brain could see the intimacy had rattled her. They'd crossed a line he hadn't anticipated—at least not yet—but somehow she'd decided it meant more than he thought it did.

Leaves crunched underfoot as they ventured deeper into the woods and toward the creek. He held a hand out to steady her as she descended the well-worn path. She took it, and his mind short-circuited at the touch. He gripped her a little too hard, then forced himself to relax his hold. Guilt still gnawed at his conscience over the attack she'd suffered on his account. Rather than dwell on it, he dragged his mind to another subject. "What's Orvis got to say these days?"

"He has an archiving job I can do, half days, starting next week." She grimaced. "At least it's only for a few weeks."

He stopped in a clearing. "Bet you can hardly wait to get back in the air."

"True." She smiled and it transformed her face. "Plus, he's changed the staffing so at least one other person will always be there." Her smile wobbled. "He felt responsible for this." She made a vague motion toward her midsection. "I told him it was LeMasters's fault. Not his." She looked up at him. "It wasn't your fault, either, Ben."

He couldn't stop the muscles in his jaw from tightening. He shifted his gaze and cleared his throat. Swallowed. Took the coward's way out. "So, do you want to go to church with me in the morning?" When he dared look back at her, she was focused on the ground.

She nodded, and drew a circle with the toe of her shoe. "If you're okay with the fact that it's mostly because I'm going stir crazy…" She slanted a glance at him.

"No problem." Ben took a chance and draped an arm over her shoulders, and was heartened when she didn't pull away. "Ready to head back to the house?"

"Yes." She breathed out a soft sigh. "Your land is beautiful and I love being out, but I'm tired."

He took a direct path to the house, secretly glad for the reprise from her knack for cutting to what he'd thought were his hidden vulnerabilities. Apparently she could see his flaws—and with uncomfortably direct vision.

~

Lannis looked through Ben's closet, searching the section he'd cleared for her clothing. Maybe she should renege on his invitation to church. "Ben? All I have is my work pants and shirt."

He stuck his head inside. "If you're asking me if that's okay to wear, it's fine." He had donned a button-down shirt sans tie, and slacks.

She chewed her lower lip for a moment. The decision made itself. She couldn't stand the thought of being home alone again, even for an hour. The outfit would do, and if she ended up being underdressed, she wouldn't let it bother her.

Twenty minutes later, Ben guided her in the side door of a stone church that rose out of the earth as if it had sprouted like a tree. As she'd suspected from their time in the wilderness, he was Catholic. He toed a kneeler out of its upright, out-of-the way position and flipped it down with a practiced motion of his foot, stopping it just short of the floor so it landed silently. He knelt, crossed himself, and bowed his head.

Once the service started, she followed Ben's lead for when to stand and when to sit—she skipped the kneeling parts—and concentrated on the words. The readings seemed to be written specifically to her, focused primarily on faith during adversity. How could that be? She shook her head slightly in wonder. She'd tried reading the Bible a few times after the rape, but the words either confused or seemed to condemn her. Today, though, they brought comfort, and she wasn't going to argue with that.

A profound sense of recognition—*I've come home*—shimmered through her heart. She'd been missing a measure of serenity, even with AA, because she still struggled with the concept of a higher power worthy of her trust. Peace crept in to fill the cracks of her glued-together spirit, and she relaxed, determined to accept without analyzing. Maybe that was the key. Mystery was mysterious precisely because it couldn't be explained.

Her ruminations were interrupted when the priest said, "Let us share a sign of peace." Immediately Ben turned to her, clasped her hands in his, and leaned down, brushing her cheek with his lips. Stunned, Lannis's thoughts went straight back to the park and his other kiss. The one that she'd been thinking about for days, and the thoughts of which were totally inappropriate in church. Her face flamed.

"Peace be with you," he murmured into her ear.

Fearing that her voice would give away the detour her imagination had taken, she whispered, "Uh, yeah. Peace." She'd deliberately kept her distance from him since that day. Intrigued by the kiss, drawn like a mindless moth to a flame, she wanted more and it scared her. She'd never wanted more, unless she was drunk, and didn't know what to do with the urge when she was sober.

He released her, his body language already moving toward other people, but his gaze lit on her and he halted. A knowing smile lifted the corners of his lips. Heat flared in his eyes.

Her face grew hotter, though she hadn't believed it possible. She sent him an annoyed scowl, and he grinned.

If anyone could get through her defenses in that arena, it was Ben. Lannis turned and shook hands with everyone within reach, murmuring, "Peace," while the conundrum of Ben and sexuality distracted her.

In her experience, most men believed an erection unrelieved by intercourse with the nearest available female was a terminal condition. Ben had…well, exhibited was the wrong word, because he hadn't drawn one iota of attention to his, but he'd refrained from acting on them. Even when it was clearly a sacrifice on his part.

Her mind flew to the one instance when his control had slipped. In his sleep—and who could exercise discipline while unconscious? He'd grabbed her hip and ground himself against her through the "chastity sheets," as she'd begun to refer to them privately. She'd gasped her surprise, although, oddly, she hadn't been frightened.

He'd awakened at the noise, tightened his grip for a moment, then gently pushed himself away and disappeared into the bathroom. Sounds of the shower's running water had lulled her back to sleep. When he returned to bed, he'd touched her arm with icy fingertips, as though he needed reassurance of her presence, but kept a careful distance the rest of the night.

Another facet of his personality fell into place like a tumbler in an old-fashioned lock. Ben lived his beliefs with unbending loyalty, but expressed them via a mile-wide streak of pragmatism.

Maintaining a distance from Ben wasn't going to work. Maybe she didn't need the distance. Her stomach clenched at the prospect of letting her walls down.

The thoughts lingered with her through the rest of the service, and for the next few days as her improving physical condition created an illusion of ability to do more than she should.

Finally the day came when Ben dropped her off to see Betsy while he volunteered at the children's hospital. Betsy gently pushed her to talk about the attack, the voice lineup, and how those events resurrected her emotions connected with the rape.

"I'm giving you a homework assignment." Betsy's low, melodic voice contradicted what Lannis knew would be a challenging prospect. She'd learned that as unassuming as her therapist sounded, she always pierced the core of whatever issue Lannis was wrestling with at the time. It was *never* easy.

Betsy smiled. "Make a list comparing your responses after the rape to your response after this attack."

Lannis saw the obvious immediately. After the rape she'd isolated herself, blamed herself, hadn't sought help of any kind. After LeMasters's assault, she'd gotten help, and allowed herself to be supported. She hadn't blamed herself, or Ben, for that matter. While the beating threatened her physical survival, the rape had threatened her psychological survival. She hadn't seen that so clearly until today.

Deep in thought, she went outside to wait for Ben, opened her journal, and began to write.

Forty-five minutes later, she surfaced from her writing, glanced around, and looked at her watch. He was late, by thirty minutes. *This is not like Ben.* Brow wrinkling, she went inside and asked if he'd called to leave a message. The answer was no, so she walked back out and peered up and down the street, as if that would magically make him appear. When it didn't, she shrugged and went back to the planter she'd been sitting on, and pulled out her notebook again. Something must have happened. She certainly wouldn't have missed the rumbling of his dual exhaust system. *He'll be here. At least I think he will be.* A spurt of anxiety gripped her, and she pushed it aside, irritated. *He* will *be here. Something happened.*

Chapter Forty-Three

LANNIS HEARD HIM, or rather, his car, before he came around the corner some twenty minutes later. She snapped her notebook closed, having accomplished very little the second time. He pulled up to the curb and she got in. "What happened, Ben?" She didn't try to keep the concern out of her voice, but attempted to dampen the anxiety. She glanced at him as she was fastening her seat belt, and froze. His eyes were red and swollen, and he looked…old. "What's wrong?"

He scrubbed a hand over his face, then looked at her and said, "Sorry I'm late."

"I knew you'd come, so something important came up." She heard the sharp edge in her voice, and softened her tone. "Don't apologize for something out of your control." She touched his arm.

A wave of sorrow rippled across his features. "Jason, the little guy I've been seeing, died this afternoon." A muscle in his jaw worked, then he crumpled. He dug the heels of his hands into his eye sockets, and huffed his breath out. It ended in a harsh sob, and Lannis winced at the raw grief of it.

"Oh, Ben." She dropped the seat belt and lifted her fingers to his face, softly tracing the tears. "I'm so sorry." He blindly reached across the console, wrapped his arms around her, and crushed her in his embrace. Her incision hurt, but she shifted slightly and the discomfort eased. He buried his face in her shoulder, and dry, harsh sobs convulsed him. "It's okay, honey, go ahead and cry. I'm here," she murmured. After a few moments, he let out a shuddering breath and quieted. His grip relaxed, and he rested his head in the crook of her neck.

He spoke into the space below her chin, his breath feathering across her chest. "He had an adverse reaction to one of his meds. They tried everything they could, but…" His voice trembled, and he sounded stunned at the turn of events. "He died before I got there, so I stayed with his parents."

"Do you need to go back?" Lannis asked. She considered his thought process and added, "I'm okay, if you're worried about that."

He shook his head. "No. They've gone to the Ronald McDonald house for tonight." His voice hitched. "There's nothing to go back for." He inhaled, let the breath out in a giant sigh, then lifted his head and looked at her with a watery glint in his eyes. "'Honey,' huh?" His lips curved up in a weak approximation of a smile.

A slow blush crept up her neck, and Lannis cleared her throat. Changed the subject. "Um, do you want to go through a drive-through, or order in for supper tonight?"

His smile strengthened, then grew into a grin. "You don't get off that easily. I heard it. 'Honey.'"

Her face heated even more, enough that she wished she had a fan, one of those old-fashioned woven palm things, like Southerners used in churches before air conditioning. She mumbled, "Yeah, in a moment of weakness. Don't get too cocky about it, or I'll take it back." She pushed at his chest, but his steely arms didn't budge.

He lifted his face to hers and kissed her. Lannis's mind stuttered to a halt, and she went still. All the reasons she should pull away, should stop this, hovered at the edges of her awareness. She knew they were there, but she couldn't articulate even one. Her eyes fluttered closed and she surrendered. The world faded as she welcomed his strength, his warmth, his comfort, as she lost herself to the pleasure of his touch.

~

Heat exploded between them, like a match to dry tinder. Ben, stunned at how quickly it spiraled out of control—for him, anyway—clutched her shirt to keep his hands from diving under it. *Not the time or place for this.* Never mind that she was barely two weeks out of major surgery. With granite control, he forced himself to break the contact of their mouths. She followed him, though, like his lips were a magnet, and she, iron filings.

Jerking his face away from hers, he muttered, "Time out." Breathing heavily, and surprised to note a fine sheen of sweat on his forehead, he set her gently away from him. Her eyelids parted, revealing huge black pupils. She looked at him, uncomprehending for a moment, then realized where they were, and what they'd done.

"Oh, God!" she breathed, scuttling back to her side of the car. After a quick, mortified glance at people walking by, she studiously attended to her seat belt and gathered up her notebook and pen, averting her gaze the entire time.

He ran his hand through his hair, and shook his head to clear it. Suppressing a groan, he turned to start the car. *Supper will have to wait. I need a cold shower first. So does she!* He ground his teeth at what that image did to him, and forced himself to think about taxes. Long, boring meetings. Going to the dentist. *Not working,* he thought with some desperation. The Arctic, and blizzards.

Jason. That did it. The pressure in his groin subsided. Focus recovered, he cleared his throat. "Jason's funeral is most likely going to be on Friday, in a little town southwest of Lexington. I could drive you to your mom's, by way of the funeral. It'll be a lot more comfortable for you than the bus. I can hang around for the weekend and bring you home, if you want." He didn't dare glance at her yet.

"Okay." The word was muffled, like she was talking to the window. Ben heard a rustle, and she sounded clear again. Direct. "I'd like to go to the funeral, if you think it'd be appropriate. I don't know his family, but I'd like to be there for you, and to honor Jason. How old was he?"

"Six." Renewed emotion made Ben's voice gruff. He shot a glance at Lannis in time to see her grimace, tears pool in her eyes. He said softly, "His parents were so thankful to both be with him at the end. As hard as it was to lose him, they consider it a blessing that his dad got here in time to say good-bye."

Lannis's tears spilled over. She grabbed a napkin from his glove box, wiped her eyes, and looked at him. "I'd really like to go to the funeral," she said.

Ben nodded, his throat constricted.

~

On Friday Lannis stood with Ben, gripping his hand, both giving and deriving support. Wind whipped her jacket and hair into a frenzy, and sent puffy clouds on a mad race across the sky. Bright sun alternated with moments of solemn shadows as they joined Jason's family at the pitifully small grave. The weather punctuated the mood of Jason's parents, saying their good-byes with tremendous dignity and celebrating his short life with soggy smiles. Lannis was humbled by their strength. Their faith. Faith in a loving, approachable God in spite of their grief.

She shot a glance at the young mother, seated at the graveside, distractedly holding her squirming toddler. *She's no older than I am.* Shaken, Lannis realized that terrible things of all varieties happened to a lot of people. She didn't hold any kind of monopoly on bad stuff. *If I had to choose between being raped versus losing a child...*

It was no contest. Somberly, she chose the hand she'd been dealt over the burden Jason's parents now carried.

Chapter Forty-Four

"Lannis!" A softer, shorter, shapelier version of Lannis stood silhouetted in the doorway. Looking back over her shoulder into the house, Lynette shouted, "Mom, she's here!" Then a bit more softly, "Come here, Carly. Let's go meet Auntie Lanny." Scooping up the toddler, she started toward the curb.

Ben raised an eyebrow and looked at Lannis. "Auntie Lanny?" he said, incredulous.

Blushing, Lannis muttered, "Yeah, we used to be Lanny and Lynnie when we were kids." She shot a dagger look at him. "Don't you dare say *anything* to anybody back in Louisville."

He gave her an evil smile and tousled her hair. "I've got the goods on you now. You'd better behave when we get back."

She scowled at him, then her lip quirked up. "I'll have to come up with some way to keep your mouth shut," she whispered, then flashed an equally wicked grin back at him. Turning, she opened the door and got out to meet her niece.

Millie overruled Ben's intention of going to a motel and sent Rich, Lynette's husband, back out to the car with him to help bring in their bags.

"Hey, man, thanks," Ben said. "Nice to meet you."

Rich didn't make eye contact, and his lips pressed together in a slash across his features. He leaned in the car, grumbled something, and snatched Lannis's duffel with an abrupt motion, yanking it out of the trunk with more energy than necessary.

"What was that?" It wasn't difficult to pick up on the other man's antagonism.

"Nothing." Rich bit the word out.

"Well, you said something, and you seem a bit torqued off." Ben stood up next to the car. "You want to clear the air before we go back inside? I'd hate to upset Millie."

Rich stared at Ben, resentment clear in his expression. "Lannis hurt Lynette pretty badly, especially since Carly was born. I don't want to see her hurt anymore. Lynette has cried her heart out because her big sister doesn't care about her baby." He absently pushed his glasses up the bridge of his nose with one finger. "Then Lannis comes home like the prodigal daughter or something, and Millie and Lynnie are all gaga, but I don't trust her. Millie says she's been going to AA, which means she's an alcoholic. A lush." The words dripped with derision. "I don't want my daughter exposed to a drunk. I don't know how much you know, or where you stand in all this, but since you're with Lannis, I have to assume you're on her side." Stiffly, Rich faced off with Ben.

Ben moved subtly in case Rich decided to throw a punch. The younger man was two or three inches taller than Ben, lanky, and had adopted a laughably ineffective stance. He was also very concerned about his wife and daughter, ready to step into a role for which he was ill suited, in order to take care of them. Which might give him an edge Ben shouldn't discount.

Ben looked directly at Rich, and held his gaze. "*Recovering* alcoholic." His voice was quiet, but underlaid with steel. He waited a beat. "That's very different than being a drunk or a lush." A flicker in Rich's eyes indicated he'd made his point. He softened a bit. "Lannis can't undo what's done, but wants to fix what she can. We might do our women a big favor by letting them work through this themselves. *I* plan to stay in the background, anyway."

Rich gave Ben a long, uncertain look, then warily nodded his head. "Okay, but if she hurts Lynette again, or shows up here drunk—*ever*—she'll answer to me, and she can kiss off any relationship with Lynette or Carly."

Ben didn't figure it was Rich's place to make that decision for his wife, but he could understand the guy's protective impulse. For the moment, it wasn't worth pointing out. "Fair enough." He picked up his suitcase, and motioned for Rich to precede him up the walk. Truce attained, Rich hefted Lannis's duffel and strode to the house. Ben followed, whistling tunelessly. *Gonna be a real fun weekend.*

In spite of the tense beginning, the rest of the evening went well, with lots of talk, laughter, and good-natured kidding tossed around. Carly soaked up the attention lavished on her, obviously considering it her due. When she got cranky, Lynette took her upstairs for a bath.

Lannis, looking exhausted, excused herself and went upstairs to her old room, which had been converted into a sewing room with a twin bed.

Ben took the opportunity to pull his gun from under his shirt at the small of his back and eject the magazine. He glanced up and met two sets of wide, startled eyes. *Oops.* He wore his weapon as easily as his shirt and sometimes forgot other folks weren't used to guns. He cleared his throat. "I don't want to run any risk of Carly getting into it, but can't leave it in the car, in case of theft." He slid the chamber open and tipped the extra round out, showed Rich and Millie the empty weapon, and handed the ammo to Rich. "If you'll put those in a safe place, Rich, I'll keep the gun under wraps." He looked at Millie quizzically. "Unless you have a gun safe here?"

She shook her head.

"Okay, this'll do in the meantime. Are you all right with that, Rich?"

Rich nodded solemnly, and pocketed the ammunition. "Yeah. Thanks. I didn't realize you had a gun."

"I don't go anywhere without it. I've an enemy or two in my line of work, so I try to keep the scales even." Standing, he replaced the gun with practiced ease, and said, "I'm going to say good night to Lannis."

He took the stairs quickly and tapped on Lannis's door, waited for her quiet invitation, then stuck his head in. "You okay?" he asked.

She nodded. Her face was pinched and pale.

He stepped in, closed the door, and said, "You know better than to lie to me, darlin'."

She made a face at him, then smiled. It held more sadness than joy. "I'm more tired than I thought. It's been a long day."

That's an understatement. She looked drained. He crossed the small room and gently pressed her down onto the bed. "Roll over. I'll rub your back for a while."

She complied, and sighed in relief at his touch. "I'm going to miss having you close," she mumbled into the pillow.

He squeezed her shoulder. "Me, too. I'm in the living room, if you need anything." He massaged her muscles for several more minutes in silence, the kinks softening as he did. When he saw she'd drifted off, he kissed her temple, covered her, and turned the light out as he left.

~

The scream was muffled, but Ben was out of his bed on the pull-out couch, gun in hand out of habit and instinct, before the echo faded. He stubbed his toe on a coffee table in the dark, bit back a curse, then pushed the pain aside and took the stairs two at a time. He reached her door at the same time Millie did, and just before Rich, both pulling on robes. Carly, startled awake, cried out in another room, and Lynette, looking torn, returned to the makeshift nursery to calm her. Soft whimpers came from Lannis's room. Millie looked at Ben with questions and alarm in her eyes.

Ben belatedly remembered the gun was unloaded, and dropped it to his side, trying to make it less conspicuous in the folds of his athletic shorts. "She has nightmares, Mrs. Parker. She'd probably respond best to me. I'll let you know if she needs you." He'd used his cop voice without conscious thought, and didn't wait for a response from either Millie or Rich. They both stood stock-still and silent.

He rapped on the door more in warning than permission, then opened it. He let his voice turn warm. "Lannis, I'm here. You're okay." He closed the door on her family and deposited the gun on top of the sewing table. Moonlight kissed her as she huddled in the corner, back pressed to the wall, arms wrapped around her knees. Tears glinted on her face.

"Ben?" she asked tremulously. Relief gave strength to her voice. "Ben!" She let go of her legs and reached for him.

Released from the need for caution, he strode to the bed and scooped her up, then sat and settled her on his lap. He stroked her hair, pressed her to his chest, not that she needed much urging. She buried her face in his T-shirt and snaked her arms around his torso.

"I freaked everybody out. I woke Carly up—"

"Hush. Don't worry about it. Hush." After a moment he felt her sag into him. "It's been a rough day."

She sniffed, then released her hold on him to rub her face with one hand. In a low voice she said, "I need you tonight, Ben. I don't want to upset Mom, but I need you next to me." She sounded miserable. "I've been doing so well…" She made a disgusted noise and tried to push away from him, but he tightened his grip. She abandoned the effort after a moment, then sighed. "Three steps forward, two steps back," she muttered.

"Stop being your harshest critic." He sat up and eased her off his lap. "Go wash your face and reassure your mom."

Gingerly she stood, pulling her sleep shirt straight. Squaring her shoulders, she went to the door and opened it. Light from the hallway poured over her.

"Mom." Surprise flared in her voice at seeing her brother-in-law. "Hi, Rich. I'm sorry I woke you, and I'm really sorry I woke Carly," she said. Pint-sized sniffles and hiccups drifted from the other room, along with a lilting lullaby. "Lynette has such a pretty voice," she said, sounding wistful.

She brought her attention back to her mom and Rich. "I've been having nightmares since the attack, but they're getting better."

She paused a moment. "Well, sort of. It doesn't take quite so long to get over them now." She looked her mom in the eye, and said, "Ben's going to stay with me the rest of the night. Is that a problem for you?"

Ben blinked in surprise, then stepped up and draped his arm around her shoulders. The tension in her back diminished marginally at his touch, and he gave her a light hug. He watched Millie take in her daughter's words and his not-so-subtle body language.

She curved her lips into a smile that didn't vanquish the concern in her eyes. "Of course not. Feel free to do what you need to do."

Rich cleared his throat and took the opportunity to slip away, murmuring that he needed to help Lynette. Lannis padded down the hall to the bathroom.

Millie's eyes were anguished. "Take good care of her, Ben." She briefly touched his hand.

"Don't worry, Mrs. Parker. I have, and I will."

Lannis and Millie were subdued the next morning, but Carly's exuberance more than made up for it. By midday the house rang with the laughter of all three women. True to their word, Ben and Rich stayed on the fringes, guarded but civil. In the afternoon, while Lannis and Carly napped, Millie and Lynette began supper preparations, their conversation muted in the kitchen. Ben glanced at Rich, who had a vaguely trapped expression on his face. Spontaneously, he said, "You wanna go pick up a six-pack and watch the football game?"

Rich's face registered surprise, then relief quickly followed by caution. "Yeah, I would. That sounds good. But what about Lannis?"

Mystified, Ben raised his eyebrows. "Uh, she's taking a nap. She usually has the nightmares at night, so I think she'll be okay if we run to the store."

"Well, I meant…" Rich stopped. Drew a breath. "Should we drink around her? Will that, like, set her off or anything?"

Ben's confusion cleared. "She's going to have to deal with it eventually. I don't drink much, and I won't rub her face in it, but I'm not going to quit. We could go on a beer run and hold off having any until we check with her, though."

Rich nodded, serious. "I think that would be best." Frustrated, he added, "I like visiting Millie, but it's not home, and I need to get out of the house."

Ben grinned, and snagged his jacket and car keys.

Chapter Forty-Five

LANNIS WAS IN the kitchen making a salad when Ben and Rich walked in. She waggled her fingers at them. Ben deposited a kiss on the top of her head and reached around her to put a six-pack of beer in the fridge.

"Do you mind if Rich and I have a beer while we watch the football game?" he asked.

"What football game? No, of course not." She snitched a piece of celery out of the salad bowl, and looked at Ben quizzically. "Why would—?"

Understanding dawned.

"Oh." She felt vaguely embarrassed. "Don't change what you do on my account. We talk about that in AA all the time. My problem is my problem, not yours." Then she grinned, a little devil raising its head and prodding her to add, "I hate beer, anyway. I'd drink rubbing alcohol first, and I haven't sank that far yet."

Ben slanted her a look, saw she was joking, and winked. He pulled two longnecks out of the carton, and she shooed him out of the kitchen. "Go on. Have a blast."

Millie took advantage of the opening to bring up AA. After their initial conversation in the hospital, her mom had avoided the subject. Reminding herself of her new commitment to honesty, Lannis explained the program and shared her struggles with some of the twelve steps. Millie listened with close attention.

"I'm having trouble with the concept of God's role in bad things happening to people—especially when they don't deserve them—and free will, and sin, and forgiveness." She paused for a moment, considering, and Millie snorted.

"Well, that just about covers most of the difficult concepts of religion! Theologians have been discussing those things for centuries, for heaven's sake." Millie's eyes twinkled. "I don't know why you haven't gotten it all figured out already!" She hugged Lannis. "Some things are easier to just accept and act on, rather than overanalyze." She gently poked Lannis in the chest with a manicured forefinger. "If anyone overanalyzes, that would be you."

Lannis laughed, then turned serious. "Why would a loving God let something like—" She stopped abruptly, and dropped her gaze to the floor. Pressed her lips closed against the words she'd almost blurted out. Scrambled for an ending that made sense, something she felt safe in disclosing to her Mom. "Like the guy who beat me up and did this to me." She gestured at her side.

Millie looked at her. "I don't think God abandoned you. Maybe in your pain you've turned your back on him…or her, or it. Maybe if you think of God as spirit, as pervasive and as close to you as the air you breathe, rather than a person. Think outside the box on this one. God is limitless, so don't put limits on your concept of him."

Lannis nearly gaped. Her parents had made sure she and Lynette attended Sunday school and warmed the pews at the nearest Lutheran church, had provided them with a basic didactic understanding of Christianity. Any more than that, like sharing individual responses to anything more superficial than occasional comments about music, or the sermon? Nope. Never happened. While Millie's take wasn't personal or profound, it nonetheless offered perspective she hadn't considered.

"Fair enough," she said. "I'll think about it." Then, tucking tail and skulking from a discussion that had strayed way too close to her secrets, Lannis changed the subject.

~

The remainder of the weekend went smoothly, and Ben stood back as Lannis shared tearful, affectionate good-byes with the female contingent of her family. Rich thawed a bit, giving Lannis a stiff, one-armed hug, and surprised Ben with a handshake. When they finally got on the road, Lannis leaned her head back on the headrest and let loose a huge sigh. Her bangs fluttered with her breath, then settled back on her forehead in disorderly wisps. She looked like an inner tube that had sprung a leak. Deflated and suddenly insubstantial. He snagged her hand and squeezed it. She kissed his knuckles, then closed her eyes.

"I'm glad you…*encouraged* me to do that." She rubbed her face. "And I'm glad you came with me. It wouldn't have gone as well without you." Her lips curved into a sad smile. "Between the nightmare and Rich's hostility, it could've turned nasty."

Ben raised his eyebrows. "I didn't think you picked up on that."

"Oh, yeah. I don't blame him. I talked to Lynette about it. She felt like she was being forced to choose between husband and sister. I told her Rich was trying to protect her and Carly because he loved them, and I apologized to both of them for not being around for Carly's first year."

He returned his attention to the road. He'd never had a relationship like this one, dancing around a minefield of issues, taking it so slow. It felt like walking on thin ice, and he suddenly realized why.

Lannis wasn't the only one who had a past to work through.

Ben huffed out a breath and glanced at Lannis, who had already fallen asleep. He hoped she didn't bail, like Deb had. His heart squeezed. Or Danny.

Then he snorted. She hadn't even committed to a deeper relationship, in spite of the complex mix of attraction and need that forged an intimate bond. He'd have to guard against holding on too tight.

Never mind that that was his default method of dealing with life.

Chapter Forty-Six

LANNIS SNEEZED and grabbed her midsection, biting back a moan. Dust motes swirled in the oversized closet that served as a temporary storeroom for old records at Louisville Air. Unfortunately, temporary had turned into permanent, and Orvis had jumped at the prospect of Lannis putting it in order. She hated filing, hated paperwork, but was grateful he'd come up with the task. She'd get paid, and he was thrilled *he* didn't have to do the work. The corner of her mouth quirked up.

She glanced at her watch. Almost noon. She'd promised Ben she would walk home for lunch, and not try to weasel more time at work. *For now,* she thought to herself. She had no doubt that he'd enlisted Orvis as a backup, so she picked up some unused folders and marked her place for tomorrow's start.

She surveyed the piles and boxes with a somewhat dismayed eye. She would have made a lot more progress today, except... Except every person she knew who worked on the field had stopped by, poking their heads in the door of her tiny workroom. Coworkers first. Pilots, flight instructors, front desk clerks. Then mechanics and line guys. Tower personnel, some she'd never met but recognized immediately by their voices. The security guy who'd radioed for help gave her a gentle bear hug, as though she were made of delicate crystal.

Lannis had attributed the flowers in the hospital to duty, or something that was done because it was socially correct. It was obvious she couldn't have been more mistaken. She marveled at the heartfelt expressions of...*love*...she'd received since she walked in the door, and sighed. It was a relief to be back, to have the structure she craved, but the dynamics of her work environment had changed. She'd have to adapt, adjust...and remain vigilant to the pitfalls of stress. Change, even in a positive direction, carried unique tensions. She rolled her shoulders to dispel the bit that remained from the morning, and closed the door on the storeroom.

Dutifully, she checked out with Orvis and headed down the street toward home. Ben had dropped her off at the airport this morning, and would pick her up from her house when he got done this afternoon. She'd have the opportunity to both get outside and spend some time at her place.

Fifteen minutes later, invigorated and only slightly tired from the three-quarter-mile walk, she let herself into her house for the first time in weeks. It smelled musty, although it was clean, just as she'd left it. After Ben's house, and the boisterous weekend in Columbus, her house felt sterile. Lonely. *So quiet.*

"Quiet" she could fix. She went to her room and turned on the stereo system she'd bought with part of the money Ben had arranged for her in April. Classical sounded good. She dialed in the public radio station. Luckily they were playing Vivaldi. She couldn't have stood Brahms or Debussy. There wasn't much housework that needed doing. Just a fine layer of dust on the surfaces.

She glanced at the phone. The message light was flashing, so she sat down to listen. She doubted anything would require a reply, and she had all afternoon anyway, so she didn't grab a pen and paper. Pushing the button, she settled back and waited for the machine to play the messages.

"Lannis, this is Althea. I just want to welcome you home. Call me when you have time."

"Hey, Lannis, this is Mark from work. I'm sorry you got hurt. Hang in there. See ya around the patch."

"Lannis. Ramon. Cherie says you're a very lucky person, and I guess she'd know, being a nurse. I, for one, am glad you're lucky. Heck, *I'm* lucky you're lucky. I'm looking forward to you getting back in the air. Take care of yourself, kiddo."

Stunned, Lannis listened to nearly a dozen more messages with the same thread of caring woven throughout. Tears rose in her eyes. She blinked them away, took a deep breath, and wrapped her arms around herself.

Finally, the last one. "Hi, Lannis, this is Maggie. Mike said you'll be coming home for half days this week. If you need anything, call me."

Not alone. *I'm not alone anymore. Maybe I never was, but I didn't know that.* She got a tablet of stationery and a packet of envelopes, went to the living room, and sat on the futon couch she'd purchased with more of Ben's "April money." Crossing her legs, she bent to the heart-expanding task of writing thank-you notes to everyone who'd called.

She'd get to the sweeping and dusting tomorrow.

~

By midweek, her feelings had evolved and solidified, and Lannis knew she needed to talk to Ben. He wasn't going to be happy with her decision, but she knew in her heart it was necessary. She'd already put off the conversation for a day, but her anxiety was ratcheting upward, and it wouldn't be long before it transmuted into a craving for alcohol.

"Ben." She finished cleaning the sink and hung the dishrag on the faucet. They'd had steak for dinner, and the rich scent of barbequed meat lingered in the air.

He glanced up from the paperwork he'd brought to the table after dinner.

She'd rehearsed a rational, well-organized speech. She took a deep breath, opened her mouth, and blurted, "I need to move back home." Her pulse kicked up and her mouth went dry, in exact opposition to her hands, which went damp.

A black look flickered across his face, replaced almost immediately with a carefully neutral expression. Fascinated, she watched as a muscle in his jaw began to tick. She took a short step backward before she realized she'd done it.

He rocked back in his chair, put his pen down, and said, "Talk to me, darlin'. What's going on in that head of yours?"

She discovered she'd been holding her breath, let it go, and plunged in. "I need to prove to myself that I'm okay in my own skin, in my own house, before…" She glanced at him, and a blush heated her face.

"Before you're willing to become my girlfriend?" he guessed hopefully.

She looked at the floor and mumbled.

"What?"

Annoyed, she said, "Yeah." She ducked her head, face flaming, and muttered, "That is, if you want to."

He threw his head back and roared with laughter. Stretching to reach her, he snagged her hand and sobered enough to look her in the eye. "Yes. I do. I don't like it, but I understand. Are you sure?" He tipped his head. "You ready to tackle the nightmares on your own?"

Lannis nodded. "I've had them off and on since the rape, so they're not really new. It's just that the beating stirred everything up, and the pain from the surgery made it physically hard to deal with them. I think I can handle them now. The pain's manageable."

"Heck, I like to think that's in part because of me. You know—your knight in shining armor, protecting you?" He produced a lopsided grin. "Will you be okay on the alcohol issue?"

"That's the point, Ben. I need to know, to the bottom of my soul, that I can be all right on my own two feet, especially now. I'm not trying to isolate myself. If I need help, I'll ask for it. If I ignore the question and let you keep taking care of me, I won't be strong enough when it does come up—which it will, sooner or later. Even if we were living together there'd be times when you have to be gone."

Solemnly, he wrapped his arms around her waist and laid his head on her chest. "Promise you'll call?"

Ruffling his hair with her fingers, she nodded. Tears surprised her and choked off her voice. She managed something that sounded reasonably close to "mm-hmm."

His voice was gruff. "Okay. We'll stop by your place in the morning and drop your things off before work." His biceps bunched as he hugged her tightly for a long moment, then took a deep breath and released her.

She picked up the dish towel and began drying the barbeque utensils, but couldn't help noticing that Ben stared at the papers, unmoving, for a long time before he picked up his pen.

That night Ben slept on the couch. When he kissed her good night, he held her so closely she had to abandon the fear that he was angry at her decision. That made it easier to go to bed alone.

Maybe he didn't trust himself. Or maybe he didn't trust her. She wanted to cling to him, to hear his heartbeat, slow and steady, as his chest rose and fell like comforting waves. She wanted his heat. She wanted the security she felt when he looped a possessive arm around her and pulled her close in his sleep. She wanted his touch, and she wanted to touch him.

He was right to not trust her.

Lannis rolled over, grabbed a pillow as a poor substitute for Ben, and considered changing her mind. But she thought about her reasons again, and steeled herself to see it through.

Chapter Forty-Seven

Ben LOADED HER DUFFEL in the car, and glanced at Lannis. The skin beneath her eyes looked bruised, but she seemed to be at peace. They didn't speak until he stopped in Louisville Air's parking lot.

He pulled her close for a kiss. Lannis wound her arms around his neck and returned it. With interest. He allowed himself another few seconds, then reluctantly, gently, pushed her away. Her slow, serene smile bordered on sensuous before she left a kiss on the tip of his nose.

He tweaked hers. "Time to go. Call me."

~

She didn't call.

Ben kept himself busy, but checked his voice mail frequently and kept his cell phone within reach. He missed talking to her, missed her companionship. He still felt guilt that he hadn't protected her from LeMasters. Maybe she had a point, in making sure they were each okay as individuals before becoming a couple. Ben knew she had issues to work on. His mind slipped to his own. Over the years, he'd reconciled Danny's choices and their consequences, but the history remained—and affected his relationship with Lannis. As did Deb's abandonment of their marriage, and Roger Grantree's double-cross.

He had his own devil to wrestle. Could he trust her enough to let go? Their relationship, though he'd tried his hardest to keep the power base on an even keel, still had an element of his manipulation of whatever circumstances he could—a human and reasonably normal response, he supposed, one that could be labeled as proactive, even laudable. Was he controlling Lannis by subtle methods, trying to protect himself from her potential abandonment?

Which led him to an unsettling notion. Did he trust God enough to let him take care of Lannis? *Let go, let God.* Ben was all for the AA slogan, quoted it frequently. Then he realized he quoted it for Lannis's benefit. Not his own. Ben shifted with discomfort. He knew full well the mere existence of the question meant he needed to take a step of faith, one that would result in growth. Which meant it was an uncomfortable step. He grappled with his own resistance to submission to God, embarrassed that it was an issue, and consequently was in a foul mood when the phone rang Sunday afternoon.

He dropped the wrench he was using on his car, and swiped at his forehead with a greasy wrist. "Martin," he snapped, not glancing at the caller ID.

"Ben?" It was Lannis, sounding taken aback at his curtness. "Is this a bad time? Should I call back later?"

"Aw, Lannis," he answered, his voice gentling. "Sorry. No, this is a fine time. I was just, uh, distracted."

"Um, okay." She still sounded a little hesitant. "Would you like to come over for supper? I got a couple of steaks…"

"Yes. I'd like that. Can I bring anything?" His voice was firm and warm.

"If you want beer, bring your own. I'm not up to testing myself in a liquor store yet," she said with a smile in her voice.

A grin split his face. "I'll be there in about an hour."

~

It was the first time she'd invited him to her house. He noted the differences from the first time he'd been there. More than just clean and serviceable, it fairly sparkled. She'd washed the windows, inside and out, and the cupboards gleamed. The hardwood floors shone, and the linoleum in the kitchen and bathroom had been replaced with attractive low-end ceramic tile. New curtains decorated the smaller windows, and it looked like she'd had the drapes professionally cleaned. Small potted plants adorned the kitchen window. Their pungent scents livened up the kitchen, and he deduced they must be herbs. A red and white gingham tablecloth dressed the garage-sale vintage Formica table. Fresh-cut mums in a quart-sized mason jar graced a coffee table.

"Nice couch. It's new, isn't it? I noticed it when I stopped by to pick up the stuff you needed while you were staying at my house," he said. "You didn't have it the first time I was here." He set the one beer he'd brought next to the mums and patted the cushion of the futon.

"Yeah, it is. I bought it with the money you gave me, or rather, arranged for me last April. I got the stereo right away, but didn't get the futon until after I started with Betsy." A delicate flush of pride colored her face, and her eyes lit with affection at Betsy's name.

"Actually, it was an assignment from her. I was supposed to see what one thing I could do to make my house more of a home, more welcoming. Since I didn't have any furniture, it was a no-brainer, but it was hard for me to accept I was worth spending the money on. Once I got past that, it turned into a fun project. Betsy made me wait until the style and color I wanted were available, instead of just taking what the store had, which was hard for me to do, too. I got it on sale, to boot."

Gesturing to the rest of the house, she said, "Then it snowballed. I traded rent for materials to do the floors. I did the kitchen in the fall, before the attack, and finished up the bathroom this week, in the afternoons." Her smile expanded until a slight dimple appeared. "You're here to help me celebrate."

He gathered her into his arms. "Your house looks great. I'm proud of you." He kissed her forehead. "It mirrors your life. You *know* I'm proud of all your hard work there."

Wrapping her arms around him, she snuggled against him. "Yeah, I am, too. Thanks."

He enjoyed the embrace for a moment, then gently disengaged himself before he enjoyed it too much. "How about those steaks?" he asked. She accepted the diversion happily, and went into the kitchen.

~

After dinner they sat on her back steps, thighs and shoulders touching, taking advantage of the last vestiges of the Indian summer. A cold snap was predicted in the next day or so, ending the unseasonably warm weather. Lannis sipped hot tea with lemon and honey, then cleared her throat. "I've been thinking a lot."

Ben cringed inwardly, but steeled himself and said, "Uh-oh. You know that leads to brain strain. A rapidly fatal disorder."

She poked him in the ribs. "You are such a tease!" She looked at her tea. "No, I just wanted to talk to you about something. It's…well, it's about us, and sex, and how I feel about it."

Blushing, she cleared her throat again and plowed on, refusing to meet his eyes. "I've never been this careful about it. I mean, I wasn't promiscuous before the rape, but I wasn't a virgin, either. There was only one guy before—" Her color deepened. "I didn't really make a decision the first time. It just sort of happened, and I didn't do anything to stop it, because I didn't want to stop it. But I didn't want to take full responsibility for making the choice to go ahead, either."

Ben put his hand on the nape of her neck and rubbed gently. As difficult as this was for him to hear, it had to be harder for her to say.

She sighed and swirled her tea. "This sounds really awful, like I was a slut or something. I wasn't. In any case, I've never talked to a guy about it at all, and especially not before the fact."

Ben made a noncommittal noise meant to keep her talking, mostly so he didn't have to respond.

Slanting a glance at him, she continued. "Anyway, after the rape I was punishing myself. At the same time, I was trying to redeem myself in a really warped way, trying to control everything I could about sex. Trying to prove I was lovable. Mostly, though, I was going to bed with guys because I didn't think I deserved to be allowed to say no. At that point, I *was* a slut. Thank God Rudy and I got married, or I would have slept with most of Louisville by now. You know the rest."

He shifted, uncomfortable with her revelations. He'd guessed as much, but never expected her to bring it up.

She paused to sip her tea. "Now there's you. You've made it clear that you want more. I'm not sure what 'more' means to you, though. You're the first guy who hasn't pressured me for or expected sex. You've also made it clear that whatever happens between us is my decision. I'm faced with actually taking responsibility for my actions for the first time."

Her voice dropped. "I'm scared."

Ben continued to massage her neck, although the conversation had veered into totally unfamiliar territory.

"I feel totally vulnerable. I've always been able to keep enough of an emotional distance from guys that I didn't feel that way. I know you'll demand commitment, at least for as long as we're together. That scares me, too. I have to admit it excites me, and makes me feel secure, all at the same time."

She fingered her mug. Finally she looked at Ben. "I guess that's it." She gave him a tremulous smile.

He laced his fingers through hers and took a deep breath. If she was brave enough to broach the subject, he'd do his best to give her honesty in return. "I'd be lying if I said I'm not attracted to you. I have been since we met." He felt her small jolt of surprise. "I'm glad you're thinking seriously about it, because I am, too. You're not the only one with issues that need attention. Going slow is good for both of us.

"I've been taking care of you since the surgery partly out of guilt at not keeping you safe from LeMasters, but also out of…something I wasn't sure how to define. I…uh…I've come to understand that it's—" He swallowed, then, feeling naked, said, "Love." Lightheadedness washed through him, and his palms dampened. He had to finish this.

"I respect you, and what we have together, too much to cheapen it by looking for short-term pleasure." He blew his breath out. "Yes, you're right about the commitment. I want the 'as long as we're together' part to last for a long, long time. A lifetime. As in marriage."

Lannis leaned back to look at him, her eyes wide and unguarded.

He tightened his grip. "But there won't be any lovemaking until we're married."

She jolted, and her shock wave echoed through Ben. He hadn't anticipated this conversation, hadn't rehearsed any declaration of love or even thought through his intentions. Maybe it was best she'd caught him by surprise. His response was honest and spontaneous and genuine. He shook his head, searching for words. "I feel like I stepped out of an airplane and don't know if I even *have* a parachute."

Lannis was silent for several moments, then raised her head and looked at Ben. "I hadn't thought that far. Honestly, my expectation was that the next step would be sex, and somehow that's easier to contemplate than marriage. My feelings for you are stronger and more complicated than they've been for anyone. Either way, I'm not quite ready to commit to anything beyond friendship."

Ben squeezed her hand again. "Then let's leave it as is. We'll have to knock off the kissing, though, because you push me to the edge of control within seconds." He slanted a glance at her. She'd gone very still except for her lips, which were trembling. "Hey, what's wrong?"

Her breath caught. "I'm trying to tell myself you're not rejecting me. Your words don't say that, but—"

He cupped her face with his hands and turned her to face him. "No." His voice was firm. "I'm not. I'm saying you are too precious to be used for recreation or simple physical gratification, and I think that's your only frame of reference."

"You'd never use me, Ben."

He was gratified at the confidence in her voice. "No. However, you need to know beyond any doubt that *you*—Lannis the whole person, not your sexual parts—*you* are the basis for my attraction, our relationship."

She stared at him for a moment, eyes luminous. He could almost see her struggling to accept what he'd said at face value.

"Besides, I am committed to the church's teachings, including abstinence outside of marriage."

Her eyes widened, then narrowed. "You haven't had sex since you divorced Deb?"

"Nope." His face heated. He felt defensive, and a little irritated that he had to explain himself. "Develops character, and all that."

She regarded him for a long moment, her expression inscrutable. He knew her well enough to know she'd have to mull over *his* revelation and examine it with wary caution before she accepted it. An image of a bomb squad preparing to detonate a suspicious package took shape in his mind. A smile tugged at his lips.

Lannis finally nodded, although it wasn't clear to Ben whether it indicated understanding or simple acknowledgment.

He broke his self-imposed rule. His kiss was tender and he pulled away before it flamed out of control. "I'd better go home. Call if you need me. Otherwise, I'll pick you up Thursday afternoon, now that you've been cleared to volunteer again." Tousling her hair, he went around the house to his car.

Chapter Forty-Eight

LANNIS FLATTENED the wrinkles out of a lone piece of paper that fluttered loose from folders she'd just picked up. A monthly fuel report sandwiched between tax returns for two nonconsecutive years. She sighed and shook her head. *Orvis, Orvis…* He was way worse than she was.

She knew exactly where the sheet belonged, thanks to her efforts over the past few weeks. She opened the correct drawer, double-checked the date, and slid the report into place. A quiet glow of satisfaction warmed her as she surveyed the small room. File cabinets with systematic cataloging had replaced boxes of loose paper and disorganized folders. She'd waged a war against hapless dust bunnies and desiccated bug remains. New shelving lined the walls, tripling usable storage space.

She'd be thoroughly grateful when she was freed from the archiving chore, though. Occasional relief from the tedium of filing had come in the form of quick tasks for the front desk personnel or ground school sessions with students.

She could hardly wait to get back in the air.

Next week.

Meanwhile, she let her mind wander as she filed. She took an internal inventory even as her hands sorted, sifted, and settled documents into proper order.

Nightmares. She'd had a couple. Bought a night-light and used it, even though she felt silly. Put the dreams to paper, which took the sting out of them, then burned the pages. Called Ben in the middle of the night once. His voice calmed and anchored her, and the memory warmed her now.

Alcohol. Surprised, she realized she hadn't needed to call Althea, just saw her at the meetings. Hadn't had a craving for weeks. She said *one day at a time* to herself real quick, in case complacency tempted her.

Betsy…had graduated her. A bittersweet moment. As she'd found with Alisha, it was harder than she'd expected to say good-bye, but she'd accomplished her goals, and it was time to move on.

Ben. Her fingers slowed. Ben. She saw him two or three times a week, and thoughts of him crept into her mind often. She pondered—again—his remarkable and unfathomable stance regarding sex. At first she'd felt insecure, and floundered at what his boundaries meant. The blend of potent desire in his eyes and the iron discipline he exhibited reassured her, though. Her simple admiration of Ben's fidelity to his beliefs had undergone a metamorphosis. Because of his faithfulness to something bigger than himself, she'd developed a deeper sense of her own worth.

Yet he never made her feel dirty for the choices she'd made. He left her past squarely in the past, and she struggled to do the same. Lannis finally understood what Althea had talked about months ago—her need to forgive herself, though that was easier said than done.

She knew one thing for sure. Their abstinence was as hard on her as it was on him. *Well, maybe it's "harder" on him.* She grinned at the pun, then sobered at his…devotion…to her.

~

"Lannis, would you pour the wine, please?" Maggie's face was flushed from heat and the rush of final preparations of a Thanksgiving feast. She pushed a lock of hair away from her face, then turned her attention back to the oven. Mike stood by to help her unload the turkey. "Megan! No, you may not taste the macaroni and cheese! Dinner's almost ready. Go with Lannis." She shooed the preschooler out of the kitchen.

Lannis held her hand out for Megan, who looked longingly at the counter packed with side dishes ready to be taken to the table. She gave the exaggerated sigh that only young children could execute with credibility, then skipped to Lannis's side, her face aglow.

"Come here, Megan. Let's go see what Ben and Marty are doing." *Watching football, of course.* Lannis smiled. Actually, Ben was ostensibly watching Marty, but called a running commentary on the plays for Mike's benefit in the kitchen.

She only had one day off for Thanksgiving, and had been pleased at Ben's invitation to spend it with Mike and Maggie. The cheerful chaos was a perfect antidote to solitary holidays she'd endured in past years. She was well enough to play with the kids this time, and play, she did. They'd all giggled themselves silly.

Lannis burst out laughing when she saw Ben. He'd snagged Marty's coveralls with a finger and let him have free reign of the coffee table while Ben's eyes stayed on the large-screen TV. Marty, drooling and babbling his version of the game, slapped happily at the table as he cruised up and down its length. "Here, Ben." She sent Megan his direction with a gentle touch and winked at him when his attention splintered, dismay crossing his features.

"Hey!" he said, but there was no heat in his protest.

"Run them to the bathroom and wash their hands. I'll come help in a minute."

He shot a look of longing at the screen that looked so much like Megan's for the macaroni and cheese that Lannis laughed again. He gathered up the kids and trundled down the hallway with a sigh that wasn't nearly as convincing as Megan's.

Lannis picked up the bottle of wine, and her smile faded. This was the first time she'd handled alcohol since July. Maggie was distracted, or she'd never have asked Lannis to do this. The bottle was smooth and cool and familiar in her hand. Mike had uncorked it earlier, and the rich, almost-sweet, fruity aroma floated to her nose.

Just a sip, just this once... The desire surprised her. But it was a twinge, not a craving, and Lannis set the bottle down. Removed her glass from the place setting before she could justify its presence. Then picked the bottle up again and poured for the other adults. *Sniffing isn't the same as drinking,* she thought, but acknowledged it could easily lead down the proverbial slippery slope, or at least to its edge.

She'd been holding a secret hope, a covert attitude of superiority to the rest of the AA members, even Althea. She saw it for the first time with painful clarity. Her face heated. A fairy tale, that she'd someday be able to drink again socially, that *she*, among all of them, would succeed and be immune to the siren song of alcohol.

No.

Sadness flowed through her as surely as the wine flowed out of the bottle. Drinking, social or otherwise, would never be part of her life. Ever. It was a small price to pay for freedom from cravings and binges. She firmed her spine and recalled the heavy cost alcohol had already levied on her life. *I'm making the choice. Now. Today. That's as far as I have to think. Just for today.* When she'd first heard the AA slogan, she had thought it corny and trite. It was a workhorse today, though, carrying a load too heavy for Lannis to bear.

She sighed, soft and light. Set the wine bottle down, gently and with finality. Turned her back on it and her regret. Went into the kitchen to join the celebration of blessings.

Of life.

Chapter Forty-Nine

LANNIS STOMPED SNOW off her feet as the bitter wind blew her into the line shack. She yanked the door closed behind her, and the wind helped, slamming it. Two guys huddled over a space heater, and Tim—at least she thought it was Tim under layers of hat, scarves, coat, and gloves—moaned.

"Don't tell me—" he said.

"Sorry." She was. But the battery on her plane was dead and she needed a jump. She'd already spent fifteen minutes in the wind defrosting the wings and preheating the engine. At least she could warm her hands along with the plane's parts. These guys got to endure wind chills of who-knew-how-low, albeit for a brief time, when they jumped the planes. Johnny, the more accommodating of the two, slapped his hat on and grabbed the auxiliary power unit. All three of them plodded through small snowdrifts made by the plow earlier that morning, the auxiliary power unit squeaking its protests across the ice behind them.

Lannis had removed the access panel for them and hopped in the cockpit, displaying the ignition key to them through the windshield as a safety precaution. Once hooked up, Johnny took up the most miserable post—just inches behind the propeller—and gave her a thumbs-up. She shouted, "Clear prop," and cranked the starter. It fired immediately, a blessing for her but a curse for Johnny. She marveled, even as the prop wash blew his hat off and whipped around his now-exposed face, that she'd never heard a word of complaint from him. She kept the RPMs as low as she could while he set himself to replacing the access panel, then stepped back, his face bitten red with cold. He grinned, waved her off, and loped across the ramp to retrieve his hat.

She taxied out, most of her mind on work and half an ear to the radio transmissions, keeping track of air traffic. Orvis was sending the plane to Lexington for some radio work and she'd have plenty of time to think once she got there. A sliver of her mind mulled over Christmas presents, and she tabled those thoughts until she was airborne.

Takeoff to the east sent her over Oxmoor Mall, and she spared a moment to remember Christmas shopping with Ben last evening. It had been fun—a first for Lannis. She didn't like to shop and detested crowds, so had never much enjoyed the shopping aspect of the season. She loved snow and cold temperatures and crisp air and Christmas carols. Airplanes performed better in the cold, and fairly leapt from the runway, and she got a rush from that, too. But shopping? Nope. She'd rather take Johnny's spot behind the prop.

Yet Lannis wanted to give gifts this year. Her budget was tight, though, and she'd been challenged to come up with ideas that would convey her sentiments.

She'd settled on homemade cookies and cards for Althea, Betsy, and Orvis, and a handmade book of coupons to be redeemed for free babysitting for Mike and Maggie. A cute book of "Mom" pictures for her mother, plus a decorative candle. A CD of relaxing music for Lynnie and Rich, along with another handmade coupon for child care so they could have a weekend alone. Lannis wasn't at all sure Rich would allow her the privilege, but she had given a mental shrug and sent it anyway. It was a gift. They could choose to accept it or not. Carly got a doll with a built-in rattle.

That left Ben. Lannis was stumped. The engine droned as she mulled over ideas. She couldn't figure out anything he needed or wanted. A few evenings ago she'd stopped in a gift store and found a plaque with a quote about friendship on it. It expressed her feelings for him on one level, but didn't do justice to their depth or intensity. Shocked, she'd realized all the plaques that *did* capture her sentiments were for married couples. She'd wheeled and fled the display as if burned.

She huffed her breath out. The "friendship" plaque would strike the right tone, keep him at a less-than-intimate distance. She snorted. Tightening her grip on the yoke, she buried the temptation to contemplate why the "married" ones felt more right. She had no trouble understanding why they felt more terrifying.

Luckily, she'd arrived in Lexington's airspace and couldn't spare any more thoughts for Christmas shopping. She keyed her mike and called Lexington Approach.

~

Lannis lay in bed and watched the shadows of tree branches waving rhythmically on her wall. Another cold front was moving through with snow forecast by midmorning. There would be very little flying tomorrow. Only two students were on her schedule, fairly standard for the holidays, and she mentally planned ground school for them.

Almost reluctantly, her thoughts drifted to Ben. It was time. Time to make a decision. Find the courage to move forward in a relationship, or be fair to both of them and cut him loose. The honesty she'd been practicing through AA compelled her to admit she was avoiding the choice. Hiding in the comfort of their friendship.

They'd spent Christmas with their respective families, and had a belated Christmas together last night. He'd slipped when she gave him his Christmas present, and kissed her. His hands slid around her, up her back, coaxed, commanded…and elicited the responses they both craved. It had been frighteningly easy. He'd fisted his hands and drawn back, face flushed with the effort of restraint.

Lannis had wrapped her own unruly hands around her waist. If he hadn't stopped…

He lowered his forehead to hers for a few moments.

Shaken, Lannis had said, "I guess I'd better go home." She made no attempt to move away from him, though. "This is really hard for me, too, Ben." She felt muscles in his jaw working.

"I know, darlin', I know." His lips had quirked up in a crooked grin, and he kissed her forehead, then stood and got their coats.

She punched her pillow and rolled over on her stomach. Groaned. Ben's unwavering condition of marriage before sex scared the living daylights out of her. Sex without commitment—her personal fast track to self-destruction—avoiding that was a no-brainer. But marriage? Did he really expect her to make that *big* of a commitment? Yup. He did. That was the one quality about Ben that never, ever changed. *What you see is what you get.*

She frowned. How did he hide that part of his personality when he went undercover? She supposed his basic objective stayed constant, so he probably just did what he had to in order to attain it. No difference, really. Lannis dragged her mind back to the issue at hand.

Ben's adherence to his values in the face of temptation and frustration, his decision to say no, and his ability to follow through on it were remarkable. In doing so, he'd created time and space that allowed Lannis to finally understand and finally reclaim *her* right to say no—a concept key to her healing, a key she wouldn't have unearthed and examined and polished without his stance.

She was grateful to him for that.

Married or not, the prospect of sex was laden with its own baggage—her fears of flashbacks, emotional intimacy, and oddly, at this stage in her life, an emergence of shyness and modesty she'd never before experienced. The thought of disrobing before Ben made her mouth go dry and her palms damp—and not only from arousal. The mere idea made her feel far more vulnerable than any other sexual encounter ever had. Including the rape.

During the assault, she'd endured physical vulnerability of the most intimate spaces of her body, along with terror for her life, but there'd been no emotional connection. In fact, that emotional disconnect had ensured her psychological survival. Intimacy with Ben was far more daunting, because he would allow no barriers. And she knew it.

Yet she desired him with a passion that shook her to her core.

Still, doubt kept her from embracing the idea of marriage. Even though he said by his actions and his words that it wasn't so in his eyes, she still felt somehow tainted. Dirty. Stained. Irredeemable.

God, he deserves better than me. The thought sprang forth spontaneously, and Lannis felt a moment of silliness for thinking God might be actually listening, but she remembered another night, a night at Ben's house. A night when a response of sorts had followed a…prayer…like this. She hesitated. Was it a prayer? Maybe.

Whatever it was, she got an answer in the next heartbeat. Words flowed across her heart as clearly as if they'd been spoken aloud. Quiet words. Not her words. *I forgive. I choose you.* Then, *I am.*

Stunned, she sucked in a breath and widened her eyes. In a flash of understanding, Lannis realized she'd been holding her failings as being bigger than God. How futile was that? With a rush of humility, she struggled to recall her favorite words of the Mass. She didn't think she had them quite right, but in a moment of perfect clarity knew it didn't matter. She whispered, "Lord, only say the word and I shall be healed."

Peace flowed into her heart and expanded, filling every crevice, every fiber of her body. Her soul. She put her hands to her face and discovered tears trickling down her cheeks. After a moment the intensity receded, leaving a deep, unshakable sense of serenity.

That's all she'd ever needed to do. Trust. Reach out. She wanted to pray, but couldn't think of any words other than *thank you.* It seemed to be enough, and she sank into a deep, sweet sleep, understanding for the first time the verse Ben whispered to her as a nightly benediction.

In peace I shall both lie down and sleep, for you alone, Lord, make me secure.

~

Lannis woke slowly, stretching in the pearly morning light, and rolled over. Peace, pervasive and comforting, still occupied every cell of her being. It had been real, her conversation with God last night, and she smiled. "Good morning," she whispered, and reached for the phone.

"Hey, Ben," she said when he picked up. "You awake?"

"Mm." His voice was a sleepy rumble. "Am now."

A laugh bubbled up and she said, "Well, it'll be worth it. I want you to be the first to know." Suddenly shy, she looked at the floor, then continued, her voice both serious and vibrant with excitement. "I get it now, Ben. God and I, uh, had a talk last night. I don't have all the answers to my questions, but…I finally understand he didn't abandon me during the rape. Since he didn't answer my prayer the way I wanted, I stopped reaching out to him. I've got a lot of things to work out, but I think the most important part just happened."

Ben cleared his throat. His voice was thick with emotion when he answered. "You're right, darlin'. This is the best wake-up call I've ever gotten."

She could hear the smile in his voice, and answered it with her own. "Ben? I'm ready to say yes to marriage. But I want to do it right this time."

There was dead silence on the phone. She had a sneaky suspicion he'd been flummoxed. In a good way. She stretched, waiting for his response, her lips curling upward in amused confidence.

Ben whooped, and she held the phone away from her ear. She could almost see him pump his fist in the air.

"So," she said dryly, "you won't be needing your morning coffee today, huh?"

Chapter Fifty

LANNIS SCRIBBLED a notation on the billing sheet as she walked into the lobby, and glanced up to make sure she wasn't walking into someone's path. Nope. All clear. A lone customer stood at the counter, head bent in concentration. His pen tapped down a column of numbers on an invoice while Nancy waited for him to sign it. Lannis returned her attention to her figures, made one additional note, then flipped her student's folder shut and leaned across the counter to put it in the wire basket destined for the accounting department.

"Here, Nance. My last one for today." She smiled at the receptionist, then expanded her cordial manner to include the customer, as well. He raised his head at her voice and looked at her.

Those eyes...

She froze.

It was *him*.

The man who'd raped her.

Every cell in her body jangled in recognition. *Run. Fight. Hide.* Her muscles quivered in disorganized response. Her breath and her heart met in her throat and choked her. Her vision narrowed, went red around the edges, then flickered. A wave of dizziness slammed into her.

Nancy's lips moved, and Robert Davis looked at Nancy and his lips moved. A loud, rushing sound filled Lannis's ears, and everything suddenly went surreal, each movement excruciatingly sluggish, every detail shimmering in gut-wrenching clarity.

The short sandy-colored hairs of his head limned by the overhead fluorescent light.

The faint promise of a five o'clock shadow on his cheek, the sharp angles of his jaw that hinted at cruelty.

Hands, long-fingered and strong, their promise of violence camouflaged beneath civilized, clean, clipped nails and an elegant ring.

Ridiculously long eyelashes for a rapist.

I can't faint. Please, God...

An ugly image, the memory she'd almost succeeded in burying, bullied its way into her mind. Davis's other short sandy hairs against her skin. Davis, gloating as he dominated her. His cold eyes alight with approval at her shrieks of pain. His arousal at her screams of terror and despair. His disgust when they faded to whimpers.

She stiffened in revulsion, and it was enough to keep her upright. Time and space and sound snapped back in a jarring rush and she heard Davis's smooth voice as he asked Nancy about the courtesy car.

Bile roiled in her gut and her stomach clenched. Lannis slapped one hand over her mouth as if that would stop the acid's upward path. Her feet finally made sense of her brain's commands and moved. One step back, then another, and she wheeled and fled to the restroom. She staggered against the door and it slammed open, the loud crack echoing like a gunshot in the small tiled room. She lurched to the toilet and grabbed the rim.

Her stomach emptied with a violence that would have frightened her—had it not been for the larger threat of the man in the other room.

~

Orvis walked out of his office to give a stack of invoices to Nancy. A cursory glance took in a customer, Lannis, and a student at the counter. But...

Something about Lannis seemed odd. He sharpened his gaze. She was still. *Too still.* Her eyes were huge and dark, her face pale. Her expression radiated stark fear. Suddenly she spun and fled as if from the devil himself.

Alarmed, he dropped his papers on the counter and went after her, moving faster than he had in years. He heard a door slam open and identified it as the women's bathroom down the hall. He heard her throw up, the uncontrolled gagging audible in the lobby. Thrusting propriety aside, he rushed in. He put his hand on her shoulder. "Are you—?"

She erupted. Her elbow stuck his shoulder in a blow that would have bloodied his nose had it connected with his face. She spun to face him. The lid to the toilet tank rattled. She curled her hands into fists and raised them. A noise, almost a growl, rose from deep in her throat.

Orvis caught his balance and retreated a step. Her eyes were blank and full of terror, and her chest rose and fell rapidly as she fought for breath. Her distress was contagious, and his heart skipped a beat. "Lannis, what's wrong? Are you sick?"

Slowly her eyes registered awareness. "Orvis?" Her voice shook. "Ben. Please. I need Ben."

"I'll call him." Orvis regarded her with bewilderment—and kept his distance. "Will you be all right until he gets here?"

She nodded. Misery was written on her features and she seemed oblivious to the tears now tracking down her cheeks.

Orvis backed out of the room, and bumped into Nancy and Lannis's student, both peering around him in unabashed curiosity. He pushed them out of the way, sharply ordered Nancy to stay with Lannis, and shooed the student out the front door.

The customer at the counter looked at him as he rushed past on his way to his office. "Anything I can do to help?" the man asked. "What's going on?"

Orvis dismissed him with a brief wave. "Nothing that concerns you. Thanks anyway." Reaching his desk, he grabbed the sheet of paper with contact numbers that Lannis had given him in July. In his haste, he tore the page and cursed as he lined up her precise, careful handwriting, then grabbed the phone and punched in Ben's cell phone number.

~

"Lannis." Ben shouldered past Orvis into the tiny restroom. "I'm here."

She stood with her back against the wall, rigid and silent, arms wrapped around her torso as if physically holding her body together. Her face was white, and smudged where she'd swiped at her tears.

He blocked her view of the hall and the few employees gathered in concern and curiosity.

"What's wrong, darlin'?" He kept his voice gentle and carefully extended his hand, leaving it up to her to make contact.

She gave a keening cry and reached for him. Her entire arm trembled, and she grasped his sleeve. The fabric tightened at the shoulder seam from the strength of her grip. Tears shimmered as they slid down her face again. Ben gathered her into his arms and rocked her.

She took a long, shuddering breath and rubbed her face on his shirt, then dropped her head to his chest as if her neck could no longer support its weight. Exhaustion made her voice almost too soft to hear and Ben leaned in.

"It's the guy…the guy who raped me. He's here. In the lobby. Oh God, Ben! *He's here!*"

Her voice rose on the last phrase, and he could tell that she was teetering on the edge of hysteria again.

Still.

Then the meaning of the words sank in. Fury darkened Ben's sight, and he gripped her tighter. Took a breath, and another, and willed his rage to abate. He needed to focus.

"Orvis." His voice was sharp. Was the bastard still here, or had he left? Orvis would know. It had taken Ben nearly twenty heart-in-his-throat minutes to get to the airport from downtown in heavy rush hour traffic, so the guy could be long gone, and probably was, either in his plane or a car.

But if he was still in the building, Lannis needed to be protected from further trauma. Ben wasn't sure how much more she could take, but he was quite certain that coming face-to-face with her rapist again wasn't anywhere on *that* list.

Ben beckoned Orvis close and spoke in a low voice meant to carry no farther than her boss's ears. "Orvis, there was some guy in the lobby when this all started. He's a pilot, but not local. Is he still around?" Ben cradled Lannis's head to his chest, and traced lazy circles on her back, in direct opposition to the steel in his voice.

"Uh, no, he's not. He took the courtesy car about fifteen minutes ago." Orvis looked at Ben in confusion. "What does he have to do with this? With Lannis?"

Ben murmured into her hair, "Can I tell Orvis what's going on?"

She nodded.

Ben squeezed her shoulder in encouragement and looked at Orvis. "He raped her several years ago. Seeing him in person, without warning, blindsided her."

Orvis's mouth opened in a silent *O*. The man looked like he'd just gotten bad cancer news. Ben paused to allow him the opportunity to regroup. "Since he's gone, I'll take Lannis home. It'd be best if you could do some crowd control here"—he nodded at the people in the hallway—"let her save face, a little, at least. Give her some time to decide what she's comfortable saying to them."

Orvis nodded, a sheen of moisture in his eyes. He lifted one hand, then turned into a statue of uncertainty, his hand hovering near Lannis's shoulder.

"I think Orvis wants to give you a hug. Is that okay, darlin'?"

She nodded and mumbled into Ben's shirt, her breath warming his chest. "Orvis, I'm sorry I hit at you. I thought it was *him*, and I was s-scared."

Orvis cleared his throat, found his voice. "Don't worry about it. I'm so sorry, Lannis. So sorry." He gave her a brief one-armed hug, then turned and gruffly ordered everyone to leave. This time they dispersed, a soft hum of speculation filling the spaces between them.

~

Ben took Lannis to her house and bundled her into the shower. While she was in there, using up the entire hot water supply, if the steam seeping out from under the door was any indication, he got on the phone.

Lannis had never told Ben her rapist's name, but since there was only one transient pilot parked at Louisville Air tonight, it wasn't hard to obtain his identity. Orvis was more than glad to provide it, along with the license, make, and model of the courtesy car. Hearing the cold anger in Orvis's voice, Ben cautioned him to not do anything rash. Or illegal. He hadn't worked all the details out because he needed to talk to Lannis first, but he reassured Orvis that Robert Davis wasn't going to walk away, or in this case, fly away unscathed.

It was ridiculously easy to find out where the guy had gone. Clearly he figured he had nothing to hide, nothing to fear. His arrogance grated at Ben, and he focused his temper where it would do the most good. Justice. At Lannis's hand, if Ben had anything to say about it.

He made one more phone call, and hung up at the same moment the shower stopped running. He stood and filled the teapot, put it on the stove, turned the burner on high, and pulled out her favorite mug. When the teapot whistled, he set the tea to steep, and sat.

Lannis finally emerged from the bathroom, and Ben caught a glimpse of her face before she turned away. Her skin was pink and wrinkled, eyes still puffy and bloodshot. She padded silently to her room, and came out dressed in cargo pants, T-shirt, and an oversized, well-worn, nubby-knit sweater she wore when she was distressed. He wasn't surprised to see it, but swallowed his flare of anger that she'd been given a reason to need her version of a security blanket.

Ben added a generous teaspoon of honey to the tea and set it on the table, then pushed it toward her. She sank into a chair, took a sip, and made eye contact with him at last. Her eyes widened and she froze with the cup halfway back to the table.

He supposed he looked as grim as he felt. "We know where he's staying. He's in a bar near his motel. At the very least, if you want the opportunity to tell him what he's done to you, how he's damaged your life, it's yours. We'll make sure you have it."

He leaned forward and engulfed her still-cold hand in his. The aftereffects of shock hadn't been totally erased by her shower, and he willed the heat from his hands to warm hers. "Kentucky doesn't have a statute of limitations for felonies, and darlin', what he did to you was a felony. If you choose to file charges, we can set you up with a wire, see if you can get him to say enough, anything that substantiates your story, and bring him to justice."

That was his choice for her, but it wasn't his call. The muscles in his face tightened, and the pressure of clenching his jaw made his teeth hurt. He forced himself to keep talking, and to stay neutral. "Or you can do nothing. You can let it go and walk away from him. I'll support you no matter what you choose to do or not do. If you choose to confront him, I'll be right there with you."

She stared at him, set her tea down, and finally responded, incongruously, "We?"

A slight smile slipped out. "Mike's tailing him." He hesitated, then said, "I took the liberty of calling a detective from Sex Crimes. He should be here any minute, but he won't come in if you don't want to pursue it."

"Pursue it?" The pink flush from her extended shower paled a shade.

"You have to tell the detective what happened if you want a wire that will hold up in court."

"Oh." She sat motionless, her other hand clasped around the steaming mug, and looked at him blankly. "I never thought I'd see him again. I never wanted to. In fact, I would've avoided the city he lived in, if I knew what it was." Her voice was thin and she took another sip of tea, then cleared her throat. "I don't want to do this…but if I run away from confronting him and he goes on to rape another woman—more women—I…"

Lannis faltered, but her eyes focused and darkened, and when she spoke again, her voice trembled. "Ben, I wouldn't be able to live with myself. I'm not responsible for his crime, but I have firsthand knowledge of what he's capable of and willing to do. He's gotten away with it, which makes him think he can continue to get away with it."

She shifted, and sat up straight. "I'm in a unique position, aren't I? Do you think he will say enough for charges to stick?"

Ben shrugged. "You never know when you go in with a wire. But you're the only person he might slip up with, especially if he thinks he's rubbing your face in it because you're helpless. He'd probably really get off on that."

He saw the moment she made her decision. Her lips thinned with determination and her eyes cleared. Raw pain still lurked in their depths, but resolve accompanied it. She nodded her head once briskly and said, her voice stronger, "You'll be there. Close by, right? You'll tell me what I need to get from him?" She looked at him for confirmation.

Ben nodded. "Dutch Bennett—he's the detective—will. He'll send me out while he takes your statement, but he'll let you know what you need on the wire."

"Okay. Let him in when he gets here." She left her tea and went to get her shoes, her movements purposeful. And angry.

Chapter Fifty-One

LANNIS RODE IN SILENCE, pretending the familiar rumble of Ben's car was imparting courage along with horsepower. She caught herself biting a fingernail and shoved her hands onto her lap, but couldn't help that she then wrung her hands together. She couldn't hide a flinch when Ben's cell phone rang, and watched from the corner of her eye while he listened, grunted a response, then snapped the phone shut.

He slanted a glance at her. "He's trolling for women, already hit on one, and they're having a drink."

Fear and memories flooded her, constricting her throat and making her lungs feel tight. *That's exactly what happened to me. He's going to rape her.* Panic tried to unfurl in her belly, and she noticed with detached, clinical accuracy that her hands no longer twisted with each other. They were fists, and her knuckles were little white points along the tops of her hands.

Lannis took a choppy breath and called on every tool she'd learned over the past months to force herself to stay here, in the present. Now. *Now.* Not four and a half years ago. This wasn't necessarily a replay of what had happened to her—no matter what it felt like. This was one moment she needed to listen to her head as well as her heart and her gut.

It didn't help that she'd just had to verbalize, in excruciating detail, every moment of Davis's precise and calculated attack, every blow, every vile way he'd used her body and messed with her mind. She'd never told anyone, not even Betsy. Not the details. Just the prospect of doing it now, today, had made her vision waver, but she hadn't let her resolve waver with it.

Dutch had eased her into making the statement with his straightforward, professional demeanor...although he'd used anatomically correct terms the same way she used terms like lift and drag, which gave her a moment's pause.

However, he made it possible for her to utter the words she'd held deep inside her. It didn't hurt that he was a small man, and that he hadn't offered his hand when Ben introduced him. He'd asked Lannis where she wanted to conduct the interview, where she wanted him to sit. He had respected and stayed outside her boundaries at the same time he prodded her to speak the unspeakable.

Afterward, he'd cautioned her to stay focused, calm, neutral. "Set your emotions to the side," he'd said. "It's a job. Do your best; we'll see where we can go with the results." He left, tapping numbers into his cell phone on the way to his car.

Which brought her full circle. This woman might actually want to be with Robert Davis. Lannis couldn't make any assumptions about what was going to happen between them. However, she could make clear what he had done to *her*, and if that influenced this woman to not go to his room, then maybe, just maybe, she'd save one other woman from the hell she'd experienced at the man's hands.

~

Lannis took a deep breath and pushed the door to the bar open. *God…* She remembered the night a few months ago when she'd recognized God's presence, and she leaned on that memory for a moment. He was here and would be with her, no matter what. She had to admit, though, it helped that Ben was already inside, and Mike, too. And Dutch. The wire was invisible under her T-shirt, but poked and tugged just enough to reassure her it was there, that *they* were there. The guys had earphones, and Mike was recording. She was supposed to steer the conversation to the rape, and let Davis think she was emotionally vulnerable. *Like that's a stretch.* She doubted Davis would flat-out confess, but when she'd expressed her misgivings to Ben, he'd shrugged, and said stranger things had happened.

Her eyes adjusted to the dim light and she scanned the room. She found Ben and forced her gaze to pass over him without pausing. Her hands began to tremble and she shoved them into the pockets of her cargo pants.

There. Robert Davis, sitting in a booth with a young blonde woman. Seeing him wasn't nearly as bad as this afternoon had been, but her breath hitched and her pulse kicked up all the same. She had the fleeting thought, *I can't do this*, but her feet carried her to the booth in spite of the sentiment.

She stopped three feet away and looked at him, at a loss for words now that she was within touching distance.

Davis glanced up and his eyes widened for just a moment. He sat back and looked at her. Surprise, calculation, and caution crossed his features. He ended the barely perceptible pause by baring his teeth in a smile. His eyes narrowed, then turned cagey and observant. "Hey, how ya doin'? What a surprise to see you again! Are you feeling better? It looked like you were coming down with something this afternoon."

His words dripped with sincerity. Surprise rippled through Lannis, but it was replaced almost as quickly by fury. She grabbed on to the anger, using it to provide focus, to move her into conversation.

"I'd like to speak to you." She glanced at the woman. "In private."

Davis draped his arm over the woman's shoulders and pulled her close. "Don't think so, doll. Nothing to talk about, anyway."

An involuntary shudder shook her. "Suit yourself. But we do have something to talk about." She hunched her shoulders and looked at the floor, then straightened and looked him in the eye. "Remember—"

He interrupted. "Yeah, we went on a date. A long time ago." The woman in his embrace glanced up at him, questions in her eyes. A muscle ticked in his jaw. "I think you'd better leave."

"No." It came out sharper than she'd meant. She turned to the woman and said, "He's right. It's best that you hear this."

Davis jolted. "I don't know what you think you're doing, but that's enough. Buzz off." He withdrew his arm from his companion and straightened.

"You don't even remember my name, do you?" Lannis flashed cold, then hot. "You remember our 'date,' though. Why else would you bother to tell me to buzz off?"

The woman grabbed her purse and picked up her drink. "I have better things to do than listen to a jilted lover spiel." She scooted out of the booth and stood. "Or maybe she's going to tell you about the baby you fathered and left her with." She shoved past Lannis and sashayed back to the bar.

A bubble of nervous laughter made its way to Lannis's lips, but died as she looked at Davis. "There's no baby, but you already know that, don't you." She slid into the booth opposite him before she could think much about it.

He leaned toward her and pointed his finger at her, stopping inches from her nose. His voice was tight, his words clipped. "You're nuts. Crazy. Wacko. You ought to be locked up. Pretty obnoxious, aren't you, coming to a public place and making unfounded accusations. Thanks for ruining my evening, bitch."

"What accusations, Robert? Tell me. I haven't accused you of anything." Lannis lifted her chin in a silent dare. "It's just you and me. As public as it's going to get."

He was all but grinding his teeth, and a slow flush crept from his neck upward. "I remember you, all right. You were a real dud in the sack. A ho-hum lay. You needed some livening up." His flush receded and the calculating look returned to his eyes. "Of course, if you'd like to try to make it up to me...? Especially since you've put a damper on my good times tonight."

Lannis's hands went cold and bloodless. Terror and outrage roiled in her gut and threatened to paralyze her. He had a lot of gall to go on the offensive like that. She took a quick gulp of air. *Of course.* That's exactly why he'd done it, to throw her off-balance. She scrambled to gather her thoughts. He'd already verified they had sex. *All I have to do is get him to say something—anything—that shows it was against my will.* She dug her fingernails into her palms.

"What do you mean by 'I needed some livening up?' Is that why you beat me?" Lannis drew a circle on the table with a fingertip, trying to hide the trembling of her hand. "You can talk to me, Robert. I'm just trying to understand what happened between us, almost five years ago."

"Come to my room, and I'll show you." His lips curled in a malevolent smile.

"No." Lannis shuddered. "What makes you think I wouldn't be a dud again?"

His gaze sharpened at her involuntary quake. "Now you're turning me on." He smiled lazily at her. "You were a pretty good screamer. You did have that down pretty well. Although you disappointed me in the end."

"Really?" Lannis's tone was as dry as her lips. She raised an eyebrow and fought the urge to bolt. "How's that?"

"Doll, you didn't fight nearly as hard or as long as I figured you would."

Guilt sliced through her, and an involuntary moan sighed from her lips. He was right. But...she'd talked to Betsy a lot about her response that night, and had come to understand that shutting down in the face of certain and continued failure may have tipped the scales toward her survival. Davis thrived on her resistance, and when she stopped, he'd lost interest.

She swallowed hard. "So that's what made it good for you. That I didn't want to have sex. That I fought. That's what turns you on now, right? The chance to see if you can make me beg you for mercy?"

His eyes glittered, and he picked up his glass. Took a long sip. Set it down. "I wonder if you'd be better this time? I've never done it twice with the same one." He spoke absently, almost to himself, then leaned toward Lannis, his attention suddenly focused. "Would you fight harder, doll?" He flicked his tongue out and licked a drop of liquor off his upper lip.

She couldn't help it. She shrank away from him, and he laughed.

"It's just a game," he said, and called her an obscene name. "Everybody knows 'no' means 'yes.' You just want us to beg for it. All of you"—he used another derogatory name for women—"you're sluts and teases and deserve everything you get. What you want or don't want doesn't matter. All you're good for is to give me what *I* want."

Lannis froze. A small part of her brain said calmly and with great clarity, *Well, that should cover everything Dutch needs.* The rest of it churned with images and fragments of emotion from the night she'd blocked out of her conscious mind. Her heart hammered at her rib cage so hard it hurt.

"I'm up for another go-round." Davis looked at her with the eyes of a hunter who'd stalked his prey and was ready to pounce.

"*No.*" Lannis exploded up from the booth. "That's rape. That's what you did to me, and you're not going to do it again, to me or to anyone else."

She'd finally stood up to him. And the memories.

Her voice was low and vibrated with energy. "What you did nearly destroyed me. I've entertained vicious fantasies of revenge, and I know that doesn't say anything good about me. Your pain won't make mine go away. It's taken me years to learn, but I finally understand that won't help me heal. No matter what happens to you, my best revenge is a life well lived."

Her hands shook and her heart was galloping now, but suddenly Davis didn't seem as tall or as overwhelming as he had a moment ago. She saw a man before her, not a monster. A twisted man. A cruel, evil man. But just a man. A man who no longer had a hold on her soul.

She took a deep breath. "I'm letting go of my grudge against you, so it no longer holds me bound. It's the only way I'll ever be truly free from you."

Peace, deeper than she'd known in her life, deeper than the night she'd made her peace with God, flowed through Lannis. She felt lighter, buoyant, like a burden she'd carried for far too long had been lifted.

Davis snorted. "I don't need your forgiveness, if that's what you're talking about."

She looked at him with a sentiment oddly akin to compassion and her heart expanded. "You'll be held accountable for what you've done in this world, and God will judge both of us in the next. But now God's free to work in your heart, at least around the events that occurred between us. We've both been given a second chance."

She turned her back on him and strode out of the bar. There was a rustle behind her and Lannis sensed Ben's presence, then caught a whiff of the aftershave he used. She turned to him, and knew her face had to be radiant with joy. There was too much inside her to be contained.

Lannis didn't need to say the words, but it felt good, too good to pass up. So she said them anyway. "I'd like to report a rape." And threw herself into Ben's arms.

Epilogue

"CAMPING?" Lannis raised an eyebrow and looked at Ben. "You want to go camping?"

Rolling over lazily in the grass, he said, "Yeah. It'll be fun." Spring had come unusually early this year, and the daffodils had already flowered and faded. Tulips waved their brightly colored heads in the sunshine. Dogwoods and redbud trees were providing lacy color to woods and forests that hadn't fully leafed out yet.

"We already did that," she said dryly.

He glanced up at her and burst out laughing. "Yeah, I guess we did, didn't we." Pushing himself up on an elbow, he cajoled her. "Just think. We can remember old times. We have some old times to remember now," he added, his tone hopeful. He must have seen indecision on her face, because he said, "I just thought it would be fun to do something different, a little break after the Derby. Besides, you need to celebrate."

She was quitting Louisville Air after the Kentucky Derby. She'd promised Orvis she'd stay long enough to help him with the extra traffic and photography flights around the event. Her new job as a pilot for the regional children's hospital started after that, but she did have some free time in between.

Celebrate. Robert Davis languished in jail awaiting trial, which Lannis resolutely refused to dwell on. Meanwhile, his DNA had been collected and would be run through the national database of unsolved crimes if he was convicted.

Lannis's courage, tardy as it had been, would garner justice for any women who had reported. Statistics said up to nine women carried their secret in silence for the lone one who spoke out. She still felt sadness for those victims of Robert Davis who wouldn't see justice.

Yes. Celebration would be appropriate.

Lannis smiled, then tipped her head to the side. "Can we take, oh, for instance, sleeping bags, and a tent, and"—she held a finger up in the air, as though nobody had ever had this particular thought before—"*food?*" She slanted a mock glower at him.

Ben grabbed her around the waist and tumbled her down, pinning her and running his fingers through her hair. "Yeah," he murmured. "Anything my darlin' wants."

Lannis smiled slowly. "Okay, but only if we take *lots* of food."

Grinning, he leaned down and kissed her. She looped her arms around his neck and kissed him back, secure in his love for her—and her love for him.

Before she lost herself in his kiss, she thought about camping. She had loved camping, before… *No.* Not "before the rape," and not "after the rape." *That's not going to define my life any longer.* It had happened; it was history. She loved camping. Period.

Her last coherent thought was, *I don't believe I'm going to have any problem with flashbacks once we get married.* Then, as if to substantiate the notion, Ben drove awareness of anything except him from her mind.

As they watched the sun set, Lannis rested her head over Ben's heart, listening to its comforting rhythm. Her thoughts wandered to her future. Their future. She couldn't imagine it without Ben. It had been hard won, and all the more precious for that.

She hugged him, and breathed a silent prayer. *Thank you.*

A gentle breeze lifted her hair. *You're welcome,* drifted by, swirled in the light wind, and floated toward the stars.

Toward the future.

Acknowledgments

While writing is a solitary activity, no book reaches its finished state without help along the way. I'd like to thank the following people, though this list is in no way inclusive of all those who have contributed to my growth as a writer.

Thank you:
English teachers who laid the foundation. This book would not have been written without you!
Marj Barat, my cheerleader, who believed in me before I did.
Susan F. Isaacs, who unwittingly launched me on this incredible journey.
Critique partners Caroline Fyffe and Sandy Loyd, whose challenges and guidance have made me a better writer. I am indebted.
Editor Pam Berehulke, whose generous spirit made the process fun. You taught me much and made my work shine.

Finally, and most vital:
My family, whose unwavering love and confidence give me strength and courage.
My husband, who keeps me grounded while encouraging me to fly. I love you.

Made in the USA
Middletown, DE
23 January 2020